Invasions
of
Eden

W I L L   W H E T S E L L

DORRANCE
PUBLISHING CO
EST. 1920
PITTSBURGH, PENNSYLVANIA 15238

Dorrance Publishing Co
585 Alpha Drive
Suite 103
Pittsburgh, PA 15238
Visit our website at *www.dorrancebookstore.com*

ISBN: 978-1-6376-4074-6
ESIBN: 978-1-6376-4917-6

FOREWORD

Wansaw Island is an all-but-forgotten place in this world. A tiny sliver of land off the coast of South Carolina, it has probably existed as long as North America itself, but it has always been something of an outcast. As one of the barrier islands along the South Carolina/Georgia coast (called the sea islands by locals), Wansaw is smaller than its siblings, farther out in the ocean and precariously aligned for cruel lashings by Atlantic hurricanes when Mother Nature decides to discipline her lonely little step-child.

Six miles long and barely two miles wide, Wansaw lies lengthwise north-to-south parallel to the coastline 12 miles east of Charleston. Centuries of abuse by merciless weather notwith-standing, it still bears an aura of mystery and mystical beauty. Maritime forests of pine and palmettos rise behind heavily duned beaches. And beyond, swaths of marsh and grassy savannas stretch toward a dark interior populated by old-growth forests of pine, cypress and live oaks sheltering scattered swamp ponds. Long before the arrival of the white man, some of the larger sea islands were inhabited by robust tribes of Native Americans called the Edisto and the Cusabo. Though there is no evidence that Native Americans ever lived on Wansaw, perhaps because of its size and remote location, according to local lore there were eventually two periods of occupation.

The first occurred during the 17th and 18th centuries when it became a so-called pirate island. Conveniently distanced from the other islands and the mainland, it was well-suited for that role. The cove at its northwest corner covertly harbored small, fast-moving ships (pinnaces or single-masted sloops) used by marauding pirates who terrorized the shipping trade as well as coastal inhabitants for nearly 200 years. As the pirate era gradually dissipated, Wansaw receded back into oblivion. But that cove, known today as Stede's Cove, is alleged to have served as an occasional refuge for the infamous "gentleman" pirate, Stede Bonnet, who was pursued by colonial militia leader Col. William Rhett, captured at Cape Fear, North Carolina, and tried and hanged in Charleston in 1718.

It was not until near the end of the Civil War that the second occupation occurred when most of the landowners fled the sea islands leaving thousands of slaves behind. A small band of those people, believing they could build a peaceful life on that remote island, bravely transported themselves on wooden skiffs to uninhabited Wansaw. They were descendants of African people brought to the Low Country of South Carolina and Georgia from West Africa in the 16th, 17th and 18th centuries, people who came to be known as Gullah* people. Others gradually joined them until ultimately almost 300 were living there. They were amazingly stalwart and hearty enough to endure the primitive conditions on Wansaw, and somehow, by their own devices, grit and determination to survive, they were able to establish a virtually self-sufficient settlement at the edge of Stede's Cove.

Regional oral history asserts that life there was built entirely around the Gullah culture, a culture based on centuries of West African traditions, language and deeply held beliefs in powerful supernatural spirits and spectral beings, both beneficent and malevolent. Despite being ignored by the outside world, inhabitants on Wansaw existed peacefully for decades surviving intermittent droughts, stifling summer heat and humidity and more than their share of hurricanes. However, sometime mid-20th Century, the population began a mysterious decline. Though they accepted it as a fate ordained by vengeful spirits, no one has ever known why Wansaw slid slowly but inexorably back into oblivion, once more uninhabited and deserted.

---

* The word Gullah is believed by some to be derived from the word Angola. It has come to identify a large group of descendants of the Mende, Kisi, Malinke, Mbundu, Golas and Bantu people of Angola, Sierra Leone and Senegal who now live in the Low Country of South Carolina and Georgia. For historical information, refer to The Penn Center, St. Helena Island, South Carolina.

CHAPTER ONE

Richard Kanaby, kneeling in one of the long beds in his 2-acre perennial gardens, was deep into what he called his rite of Spring, coaxing his treasured perennials back to life. It was a ritual he had savored on weekend afternoons in March for the past 28 years: removing the detritus of winter, trimming dead stems and leaves, loosening soil, gently cultivating or separating and transplanting parts of his treasures. Lenten roses were already blooming, and burgeoning shoots of peonies, daisies, astilbe, yarrow, phlox and daylilies emerging from winter dormancy were reappearing like faithful old friends.

He'd been at it for almost four hours when, out of nowhere, he was struck by a wave of spinning, nauseating vertigo. He dropped his trowel and glanced up. He could feel his throat closing. He grabbed at the base of his neck, gasping wide-eyed. The bushes and trees around him morphed into distorted images laced with tiny starlike flashes. When he tried to pull up on his knees, he lost balance and lurched forward barely catching himself on his outstretched arms. He braced on all fours and closed his eyes as he took in big gulps of air. He didn't move for several seconds. His breathing slowed, and his throat began to relax. When he opened his eyes, the flickering images were gone, but everything around him still seemed blurred and distorted.

He sat back on his heels and pressed his folded arms hard against his chest trying to minimize his shaking. The spinning and nausea gradually subsided. In another few seconds, his vision cleared, and he began to come back to himself. He pulled off his gloves and rubbed his eyes. Nothing like this had ever happened to him. He could make nothing of it, but with twilight beginning to descend, he decided it was time to stop.

He gathered gloves, clippers, trowel and spade and moved toward the greenhouse. He was unsteady on his feet, and when he went through the door, he felt himself losing balance again. The gloves and tools fell away. He braced himself against the door-jamb struggling for breath. The distorted images were back, and the work table in front of him, the flats of seedlings on the bench, the floor, the glass walls were all moving in slow, wave-like patterns.

He staggered to the work table and grabbed the edge lowering himself to his knees. As he did, he saw what appeared to be a dark figure standing at the back of the greenhouse. He closed his eyes tight for a second then opened them again. The figure moved toward the bench and extended both arms across the flats of seedlings. He recognized the face. It was Mose. Mose Funchess, his long-dead gardening helper. When he called the name, the figure backed away and disappeared behind the bench as if being pulled down into the dirt floor. But the flats, the bench, the table, the floor, the walls, all continued moving in coordinated undulations. He eased himself down and lay back on the floor. He closed his eyes, and all went black.

After some minutes, he came to but lay still and stared vaguely upward until the slow rotation of the ceiling fan caught his eye. He raised up on his elbows and shook his head then reached for the edge of the work table and pulled himself onto the stool beside it. Now everything looked normal. Maybe it won't happen again, he thought. No need to tell Evelyn. He sat for a few more minutes, then stood, put away the tools and headed to the house.

*****

Richard Kanaby was a chemical engineer. After graduation from Cornell 40 years earlier, he took a job at Monsanto in St. Louis. During 10 years there, he established a solid reputation developing effective agricultural fertilizers and pesticides with low environmental toxicity. He loved the research, and his fascination with plants and "the chemistry of making things grow," as he put it, gradually segued into a passion for gardening. When he was offered a plum job with an agricultural engineering firm in Marietta, Georgia, he took it and moved to Atlanta with his wife Evelyn and their two children. That was 30 years ago. Within a year and a half of their arrival they bought the house he was now walking toward, a comfortable farm-house style set on three wooded acres in Dunwoody, a few miles north of the Atlanta City Limits and convenient to Marietta. It was a great place to raise a family. But the best part for him was that it was such a perfect place to create his gardens.

*****

Evelyn's voice greeted him as he came through kitchen door. "Almost time for supper," she glanced up from her preparations on the island counter. "Get everything done?"

"I guess so," he said, "but I'm not feeling so good." The thought of supper did not appeal. "Think I'll just have some soup, if you don't mind."

" 'Course not, but where do you suppose that came from?" She took notice because he was never sick. "What's wrong? Headache?"

"Just feel a little achy and kinda queasy," he said.

"Maybe I should call Dr. Holleran," she said.

"No, Evie. Not Sunday night. I'll be okay."

"If you say so," she said with a hint of impatience, "but you know you've been working too hard out there the last few weekends. Go get ready for bed. I'll bring you some soup and tea."

He walked into the hallway. "Vegetable or tomato?" she called after him.

"Tomato," he called back as he entered their bedroom.

An impressive four-poster bed stood against the far wall of the room. Along the wall to the right, three tall windows gave a wide view of the gardens during the day. Along the wall to the left were floor-to-ceiling shelves holding rows and stacks of books and family photograph: Richard and Evelyn on their wedding day, their two children, Allen and Martha Ann at different ages, five grandchildren along with group pictures of the family at Christmas, birthdays and other celebrations. There were also pictures of Evelyn and Richard in Red Square, the Kremlin in the background; the two of them in Nairobi; the two of them in the French wine country standing with a wiry little vintner wearing a black beret cocked to one side and holding a bottle of wine.

Two club chairs sat in the center of the room. Between them, a round pedestal table held a sturdy lamp and a few books. With the children grown and gone, this room had become a special retreat for Richard and Evelyn. It was a peaceful place where they often settled after dinner to chat or read. But now as he made his way to the bathroom, he was overcome by a sense of foreboding.

He washed his hands and splashed water on his face. The coolness felt good. He reached for the thermometer in the cabinet over the sink and stuck it under his tongue. It registered 99.6. He returned it to the cabinet and went back to the bedroom. He was changing into pajamas when Evelyn came in with a tray.

"Feeling better?" she asked studying his face. He said nothing.

"Come have some soup." She set the tray on the table. "Think you have a fever?" She reached toward his forehead.

"Prob'ly not," he said offhandedly and pulled away.

"Here. Sit," she said. She pulled a side-chair from the corner up to the table. He sat and sipped the tea and began to spoon the warm soup to his lips. But after only a few spoonfuls, he stood and moved to the bed.

"That all you want? That's hardly anything."

"It's enough," he said. "I need to lie down." He lifted the coverlet and slid between the sheets, pressing the pillow behind his head.

"Okay," she said. "I'll just clean up. Be right back."

She picked up the tray and returned to the kitchen. She put away the supper things, finished the remainder of the tomato soup, rinsed the pot, bowl and cups and went back to the bedroom. He was sleeping.

She changed into a nightgown and went into the bathroom then came back to the bedroom, switched off the lamps on the center table and the bedside table, and climbed in beside Richard.

*****

The alarm clock roused her promptly at 7:00 Monday morning, but Richard did not stir, which was unusual. She studied his face as she propped up on one elbow and shook him gently. "Good morning, honey."

He opened his eyes. "Good morning." He looked confused as he spoke.

"So? Feeling better?" She tried to sound upbeat.

"Not so good." He blinked and rubbed the side of his face.

She put her hand on his forehead. "I think you've got a fever. Let's check." She went to the bathroom, retrieved the thermometer and shook it as she came back. "Open." She slipped it under his tongue and stroked his forehead. "Looks like a beautiful day," she chirped as she waited. She extracted the thermometer. "Hmm. Hundred point four. I'm calling Dr. Holleran.

"Okay. And call my office too," he said as she left the room. "Tell'em I won't be in."

She made the calls in the kitchen and came back to the bedroom with a large glass of orange juice. He was sleeping again. She shook him awake again. "Dr. Holleran says stay in bed and take as much fluids as you can," she said holding the glass of juice toward him, "and Tylenol." She handed him two tablets. He gulped them down with the juice and promptly lay back and went to sleep. She woke him just before noon. When she asked what he might like for lunch, he said only, "Not hungry."

As instructed, she called Dr. Holleran again at 1:30 reporting no real change. He told her to keep up the same regimen and keep an eye on the temperature. She woke Richard twice more during the afternoon checking temperature and plying him with water and juice. At 7:00 she tried a cup of bouillon and tea. No interest. More water. Two more Tylenols. At about 7:45 the phone rang. Dr. Holleran. "Yes, Doctor.," said Evelyn. "Juice and water. And Tylenol, but he's not eating anything, and he's slept practically all day." She paused then, "Yes. I've checked twice. One-hundred point two both times."

Joe Holleran said he'd stop by on his way home to check Richard. It was an unusual offer because as a general policy he didn't make house calls. But Richard and Evelyn had been among his first patients some 15 years earlier, and they still ranked among his favorites. He closed the door to his office in the Medical Office Building, and with a small black doctor's bag in hand walked briskly to the garage. Twenty minutes later he pulled into the driveway. Evelyn opened the door looking quite agitated. "I haven't waked him up since you called," she said as she led the way to the bedroom. She stood at the bedside for a moment then stroked the sleeping Richard's shoulder. "Wake up, honey. Doctor Holleran's here."

Richard opened his eyes and raised his head. "Huh? Dr. Holleran?"

"Yes. He said he wanted to come by to check on you."

"I must be sicker'n I thought," he said, bracing up on both elbows. "What time is it?"

"Not so late," said Joe in a jovial tone as he came across the room. "I just wanted to see what's ailing you? How're you feeling now?"

"To tell you the truth, Doc, I feel like hell. Don't hurt anywhere. Just feel like hell."

"Okay. So let's see what we can find," Joe said. He put the doctor's bag on the foot of the bed, and took out a stethoscope hooking it around his neck. Then he took out a blood pressure cuff and its minicomputer. "Sit up for me, can you?" Richard complied as Joe wrapped the cuff around his upper arm, pressed the button and watched it register. "Looks good. Now let's gets this pajama shirt open," he said as he pulled off the cuff and began to unbutton the shirt. Richard sat motionless and silent. Joe warmed the stethoscope bell with his palm and placed it on Richard's chest moving it slowly, stopping as several points. "Okay. Now breathe in…and out. Again. Good. Now lean forward." He lifted the pajama shirt and placed the stethoscope bell on Richard's back. He began move it around slowly as he said, "Big breath and let it out slowly. That's it. Again. One more." He lifted the bell away and dangled the stethoscope from his neck. He pressed his left hand flat against Richard's back percussing lightly with his right index and middle fingers of his right hand.

Richard heard the dull thuds. "Anything in there, Doc?" He chuckled..

"A little congestion, but it's not bad. Is your throat sore?

Richard shook his head. Joe placed both hands at his neck pressing lightly. "Let's check that temperature again." He took a thermometer from the bag, wiped it with a cotton pledget and slipped it into Richard's mouth. After long enough he withdrew it.

"Ninety-nine eight," he said. "So it's coming down."

Richard leaned back against the pillow. Joe said, "I think you're okay for tonight, but I want you to come to the office tomorrow, and let me go over you completely, okay?"

"Okay," said Richard.

"If you need anything during the night, here's my cell number." Joe jotted on a small pad, tore off the page and handed it to Evelyn. "Call my office in the morning, and let them know when you can get there. And, Mr. Kanaby, you get some sleep," he directed.

"Okay," Richard whispered lying back on the pillow.

Tuesday morning he woke before Evelyn. He eased out of bed and began to move toward the bathroom when the nauseating vertigo gripped him again. He got through the door and leaned against the counter but felt himself sliding uncontrollably downward. He collapsed onto the floor and closed his eyes, his mind spinning as he faded to blackness.

CHAPTER TWO

On Friday, the day before the weekend at Richard and Evelyn's place, a man in Dallas named Blaine Purcell was gathering the fragments of his fractured life. After a bitter, gut-wrenching divorce, he was about to depart for what he hoped would be a new life in Atlanta. He knew it would be tough, but he was determined to stop by the house that used to be his home to say goodbye to his little girls. Lucy, his now ex-wife, had told him she thought it was a bad idea because it would be too hard for them, but she'd reluctantly agreed to one last visit.

He pulled into the driveway and got out slowly. His stomach churned as he moved along the brick walk and onto the front porch. He pressed the doorbell and stepped back a few feet feeling awkward standing there instead of turning the key and walking in as he had so many times. The door opened, and they bounded out: Beth, 6, Amy, 8, and Carrie, 11, all blondes with huge blue eyes, all appearing to be cut from the same pattern. He felt an incredible stab of pain in his mid-section, but he tried to hold a frozen smile as they ran to him, their voices bubbling, "Daddy, Daddy, Daddy."

He opened his arms as he knelt and hugged them all to him. He'd always felt such joy when he pulled them into an embrace like that. But now, he was overwhelmed by the realization that this was the last time this would be. It would never be the same again. Even if he might come back to Dallas eventually, they would be older, and he would have become something of a stranger, no longer part of their lives except sometimes and peripherally.

He couldn't speak. He tightened his arms around them, but there was no stopping them as they began to sob uncontrollably, begging him not to leave. For those agonizing moments he felt paralyzed while six little arms draped over his shoulders and clung to him as three wet faces brushed against his.

Lucy appeared at the door and stared impassively at the girls gathered in his arms. After a few moments she told them it was time to come in. She spoke quietly at first, then louder and more forcefully. Blaine released them and rose as they retreated. She guided them in with a brief glance back at him and closed the door. He stood looking at it for a few seconds, then turned and went back to the car. He got in looking toward the door again as if expecting them to come rushing back out. There was nothing, He closed his eyes as images of the girls running, squealing then sobbing so pitifully flooded his mind. He could hear their voices, feel their arms around him, their tears on his face. He leaned forward and rested his head on the steering wheel as his eyes moistened, and a muffled groan caught in his throat. Now he felt not only paralyzed but bereft and desolate. After a few long breaths, he leaned back against the seat and opened his eyes. He backed into the street and drove away toward his office.

There he collected a box of books and CDs, a portable file of personal papers and records, photographs of the girls and two boxes of clothes he'd stored there for the past month. Three other boxes of clothes and a few more items were to be shipped to him once he got settled in Atlanta. By 9:30, he was on the way to the freeway. He noted the time because he expected the trip to Atlanta would take at least 12 hours, and he'd lose an hour when he crossed into the Eastern Time Zone. Driving all day through the plains of East Texas, across Louisiana and Mississippi and into Alabama, the pain of those early morning moments seemed even more intense as they mingled with flashbacks to a life that had been truly beautiful at times until complexities of his problems spun out of control.

Seventeen years earlier, in the beginning of his second year of the internal medicine residency in North Carolina, another resident named Luke Manning and his wife Janie, introduced him to a girl named Lucy. She was a graduate student in art history at the University where Janie worked. He remembered so well the first moment he saw her. With her brilliant blue eyes, the smile, and the delicate face framed by lovely shoulder-length blond hair, she was an adult embodiment of the three little girls he'd just left behind. Until that time, he had proudly owned a reputation as the fun-loving, carefree, young bachelor doctor, but all that changed as he got to know Lucy. Her vivacity and charm, as well as her looks, were too much to resist. He was hopelessly smitten. Ten months later, they were married, and that was that.

It was good for a long time. Passionate. Full and complete. And when the girls came along it was even fuller, but eventually, so full it seemed that he and Lucy had little time for each other, and he was being pushed aside. He began to feel he was losing his manhood, and that he couldn't stand. It was late one afternoon shortly after his fortieth birthday when a young woman named Christina came into his office to deliver a batch of medical records he'd requested. As she approached his desk, her smile and the lingering glance that accompanied it stoked a flicker of excitement in the suppressed-but-not-extinguished embers of his bachelorhood, and she seemed eager and easy. The prospect was tantalizing, and she did not shy away as he made an advance. But he soon found other opportunities. Over a few months then a year, then two, it became a compulsion. A delicious exploration of discreetly orchestrated possibilities. He thought he covered this double life well, but inevitably his preoccupation and his distance became painfully obvious to Lucy. After almost two and a half years of deception, bitter confrontations, separations and miserable attempts at reconciliation, Lucy ended their marriage with the same resolve she'd begun it with. She was not a woman who changed her mind once it was made up. The divorce would happen, and that was that.

Now with wife, children and home all gone…all of his own making…he was beginning this lonely journey with only bare essentials of what was left in his life. He was scheduled to begin a six-month cardiology fellowship at the Brakefield Medical Center on Tuesday.

*****

The letter he had mailed three weeks earlier came as a jolting surprise to Luke Manning. Luke leaned back in his desk chair barely believing what he was reading:

C. Blaine Purcell, M.D.
InterMedical Cardiology Associates, P.C.
2403 Linebough Boulevard, Suite 331
Dallas, Texas 75243

Tel: (214) 289-5105
Fax: (214) 289-6352
Email: cbp@intermed.org

March 3

Dear Luke:

I hope a letter from me after such a long time won't be too big a shock. I've been thinking of you lately, and I wanted to write to give you some news. Part of it is not so good though, so I thought a letter might be better than a call.

First off, Lucy and I have decided to call it quits. It's been really hard going through this, especially for the kids, but so much has happened to our relationship, the decision is just irreversible. We've filed, and the divorce should be final in a couple of weeks. I wish I could give you more of an explanation, but not here. Maybe someday I can...in person.

The next part is that I am coming to Atlanta for a six-month fellowship in transesophageal ECHO cardiography. I've got a few things to finish up here, but I plan to leave Dallas as soon as possible after the divorce is final. I'll be working with Dr. Thomas Reed at the Brakefield Hospital. I've spoken to him several times, and he says he remembers you when you first came to Atlanta. He seems like a nice enough guy though I know he's got a reputation for being tough. I decided it might be best not to say anything about the divorce for the moment. I just told him I would be coming alone, and my family would be staying in Dallas. I'd like to find a small furnished apartment somewhere near the hospital. I've contacted a couple of real estate agencies, and I'm looking online as well.

Under the circumstances, I think this move is a pretty good solution for a lot of reasons. I need to get out of Dallas for a while. The fellowship will give me some space, and I've been wanting to get into transesophageal for some time. I must say I am leaving a good practice and some great partners. They've been very understanding, and we've worked out an arrangement where I can take a break for six months. After that of course I'll have to decide whether to come back here or move on somewhere else because I'll have to get back to a reliable income to be able to keep up with the financial part of all this.

Please don't think I'm expecting you and Janie to do anything special for me, but I'd love see you again. I'll be in touch with you when I get there and get settled in.

Blaine

He looked away for a moment then looked back at the letter. Recollections of those days so long ago began to come to him: Blaine, the smart, energetic, cocky, irrepressibly funny bachelor, the guy who had the world on a string with women always after him. He thought of the friendship they developed in the first weeks of their residency and how within a few months, he and Janie introduced Blaine to Lucy. They'd seemed to be so right for each other. He recalled how even after residency, when he and Janie moved to Atlanta and Blaine and Lucy moved to Dallas, the four had kept up their friendship and special bonds for a long time in spite of the distances separating them. But now, in this letter, Blaine seemed detached....almost blasé, as if he were ready, no eager, to move on. It made Luke sad. Very sad. For Blaine...and for Lucy and the kids. He'd tell Janie, of course, but it might be best to wait to hear from Blaine again as the letter said.

*****

By 10:30, passing the Anniston, Alabama, exit on Interstate 20, Blaine spotted the sign: Atlanta 92 miles. He could make it. He turned up the volume on Sirius radio and pressed the accelerator as the music soared. The sleek, aerodynamic body of the all-black Jag XKR coupe seemed to glide through the air launching him into the night as he gunned it. It made him feel strong and in control. Sailing. Flying. He loved it, Just what he needed after this terrible day. The speedometer registered 90 then 95 then 98. The rush was *so* delicious...until an unmistakable flashing blue light appeared in the rear-view mirror riveting him back to the moment. The siren on the approaching cop car wailed. He lifted his foot, but it was too late. Damn, he thought. This'll be good for at least a hundred. He coasted down to 90 then 85, 80, 75, and gradually braking, he guided the car to a stop on the shoulder. The siren ceased as the cop car pulled in behind him, but blue light was still flashing. He opened the window and watched in the side mirror as a big, barrel-chested man in uniform got out and sauntered forward. He shined a flashlight at the back of Blaine's car and approached the driver's side. "In a hurry, Buddy?" he drawled.

"I guess I was going a little faster than I meant to," Blaine replied.

"I reckon so, Mistah," said the cop. "I need you to step out please, and...I'll need to see your driver's license."

Blaine got out, reached for his wallet, took out the license and handed it to the policeman.

"You got the registration for this thing?"

"Yes," said Blaine. In the glove-box. I'll get it."

"Hold on a minute," said the cop. He studied the license in the flashlight beam. "This your license?"

"Yes," said Blaine.

"Says here you're five-'le'm. I'm six-foot, and I know I'm more'n a coupla inches taller'n you. You look more like five-se'm or eight."

Blaine winced. "That's a misprint." .

"I reckon so. A misprint or somethin'."

Blaine looked down remembering how long ago he registered his height as five-eleven on the license application because he hated being short. No one had ever noticed.

"Where you headed?"

"Atlanta," said Blaine.

"I see," said the cop looking at the license again then at Blaine. "Whatchew doin' in Atlanta?"

"I've got some business there."

"I see. So what kinda business you got ovah there?"

That question seemed a little out of line, but Blaine let it go.

"I'm a doctor."

"Oh, doctor, huh? Nice car, Doc. So you tryin' to get to a sick patient ovah in Atlanta?"

"No," Blaine bristled at the sarcasm. "Just wasn't paying attention to my speed. Guess I was deep in thought."

"Yeah, well you gonna be deep in the groun' if you keep this up," said the cop. His eyes narrowed, "I clocked you at better'n 95 miles an hour."

"95? Really?"

"More like 98," said the cop. "Jus' stand right here while get this ticket filled out. Then we'll settle up." He turned and walked to his car.

An 18-wheeleer growled past pushing a wall of exhaust-filled air over Blaine. The night fell silent except for the static and staccato voices of the police radio. Blaine's mind throbbed like the flashing blue light as the words "I'm six-foot and I know I'm more'n a coupla' inches taller'n you. You look more like five-se'm or eight. You look more like five-se'm or eight" came back like a mocking echo. He leaned against his car and closed his eyes. He could see the faces of his two older brothers, hear them laughing at him like they always did. "Hey, Runt!" brother Neal would taunt. "What about it, Fudd?" (for Elmer Fudd) brother Martin would chime in.

At 13, he began to harbor an indelible resentment at being diminished as the youngest and the smallest of the three. It was always made worse when some thoughtless adult in his small hometown in western Pennsylvania would quip something like, "When you gonna grow tall like your brothers?" He never did, and as his resentment grew into bitterness, he promised himself he would show them all what he could do.

His mother seemed to understand his frustration and pain, but just when that became so important to him, she was diagnosed with ovarian cancer. For the last two years of her life, her sympathy was diverted to her own pain and preoccupation with her impending death. He'd never felt close to his father, so after her death, he began to feel more and more estranged from father and brothers. Through it all, though, what he perceived as the knowledge and wisdom of the doctors who took care of his mother made a lasting impression on him. Inspired by those he had so admired, he gradually began to think of becoming a doctor. He saw it as a way to prevail, and it galvanized his ambition. Dogged determination and academic success through high school won him a full scholarship to the University of Pittsburgh and later, a prestigious foundation scholarship for medical school at the University of Pennsylvania. During his college years, he gradually, almost unconsciously, distanced himself from his father and brothers. During his third year of medical school, his father died. He went back home for the funeral but never again after that.

*****

The cop's door slammed. Blaine opened his eyes and straightened as the man came toward him shining the bright flashlight beam as he walked.

"This is your summons to court in Heflin on April twenty-third." He shined the light on the printed form. "If you cain't make to court, you c'n send a cashier's check to the clerk o' court. Says so on the ticket. I'm Officer Terry. My signature's right there. Just sign and you can be on yo' way."

"What's the fine?"

"Be a hundred sixty-five dollars."

"A hundred and sixty-five dollars?" Blaine blurted in amazement

"Now listen, Doc. You was goin' more'n 95 miles an hour. I usually take people in fo' goin' that fast. But you bein' a doctor and all and lookin' like a pretty nice fellah, I thought I'd just give you the ticket. If you're wantin' to argue, you can come on in town and we can talk."

Blaine took a breath. "Where do I sign again?"

The cop pointed, and Blaine signed without another word. He handed Blaine the license and a copy of the ticket.

"Awright now, Doc," he said, "I advise you to take it easy. Whatever's waitin' fo' you ovah there in Atlanta c'n sure wait a little bit longer." He turned and walked away.

Blaine opened door, lowered himself into the seat, clicked the seat belt and pushed his head back against the headrest watching the cop's car disappear. He sat for moment longer. In the night's stillness, the cop's words played in his head: "Whatever's waitin' for you over there in Atlanta can sure wait...." Only emptiness was waiting.

He switched on the ignition and flipped on the headlights. The powerful engine revved as the car sprang onto the highway. But he had to hold it down. Another cop tonight would *not* be good. After an hour and a half, he was approaching the outskirts of Atlanta. At every exit on both sides of the highway, motel and gas station signs glowed. Momentarily, he pulled off the highway and followed a sign to a Best Western. Within minutes, he was registered and parking in front of room 142. He got out, lifted a leather shoulder bag from behind the driver's seat, locked the car, and walked to the door. He pushed in the keycard and opened the door to a slightly stale-smelling, predictably furnished room lit only by light coming through the window from the parking lot. He flicked on the ceiling light and dropped the shoulder bag on a table in front of the window. Then he locked the door, closed the drapes and sat on the bed with a relieving heave.

Arching backward, he fell across the bed blocking the glare of the overhead light with his forearm. But he couldn't block the relentless intrusion of unwanted thoughts. Images of his little girls' tear-stained faces and the crushing loneliness he'd felt all day—

loneliness that had only grown with each mile until it had become the overwhelming desperation he felt now. He rolled onto his side, drew his knees up, wrapped his arms around them and pulled them hard against his chest as if the sheer force of that would squeeze the thoughts and feelings out of his mind and his body. He released his arms slightly then tightened even harder, grunting and gasping. But the thoughts, so firmly embedded in his mind, his heart, his gut, took no notice of his efforts, He buried his face in a pillow. His body began to shudder and finally gave way to wrenching sobs.

After several convulsive moments he exhaled heavily and wiped his eyes with two fingers. He rolled onto his back and stretched longways across the bed. He felt worn out and far too exhausted to face down the cavalcade of misery stomping through his mind. He would, he knew, eventually have to, but tonight was not the night. His mind flickered to a place to which he could wish never to return. But it was irresistible.

He had first visited this dark place during his first separation from Lucy. He was staying, actually retreating, to a hotel near downtown Dallas and drinking himself to sleep every night. Late one evening he went into the hotel bar, took a seat and ordered a Scotch/rocks. The place was empty except for the bartender and a man seated across the corner of the horse-shoe shaped bar. He looked to be in his early fifties, clean-cut, thick dark hair, neat blazer, crisp open-collar shirt. He greeted Blaine with a casual, Texas-friendly "Long day, huh?"

"Prob'ly wouldn't believe it if I told you," said Blaine as the bartender delivered a Scotch.

"Worst of it over?" asked the man, leaning over his drink on one elbow.

"Is now," Blaine said as he lifted his glass.

"Where you from?"

"Oh, I live here," said Blaine. "Just stayin' in town tonight for an early meeting tomorrow."

The man sipped his drink. "So what do you do round these parts, if you don't mind me askin'?"

"I'm a cardiologist."

"Oh. Cardiologist, huh?" the man said with obvious admiration in his voice.

"Yep. Been in practice here almost 12 years."

"Well, hello, Doc," the man said as he rose, picked up his drink and walked around the corner of the bar. "I'm Miguel."

"I'm Blaine. Nice to meet you," said Blaine as they shook.

Miguel took a seat two stools away. They ordered another round and chatted for a while. Miguel said he'd been divorced for three years. Two teenage kids. "They live in Houston with their mother. "You divorced?"

"No. Separated, but it's pretty rough right now," said Blaine.

"I know what you mean. Been there myself," said Miguel. "Y'know," he looked at Blaine with a sympathetic expression, "I think maybe I can help you." He lifted his glass and tipped it toward Blaine.

Blaine raised his eyebrows. "Oh? How's that?"

"Why don't we drink up and take a little walk. Get some air, and I'll explain."

Blaine looked down at his Scotch. Sounded a little strange, he thought, but why not? What did he have to lose? His only immediate plan was just to go back to his room after another drink. Anything seemed preferable to that. "Okay. Sure," he said and drained the glass.

"I'm buyin'," Miguel flipped a credit card out of his shirt pocket and handed it to the bartender.

"Oh, no. Let me get this," Blaine said, fumbling for his wallet.

"My pleasure, Doc." Miguel signed the bill and slid the card back into his shirt pocket. They went through a side door and out into a parking area where there were a few cars parked along the wall of the building. Miguel stopped behind a BMW650i. He took out a car key and pressed the clicker. The door locks snapped, and the interior lights and headlights switched on.

"Great car," said Blaine.

"Well, you know how it is. You need a nice car to get around, and it makes a good impression. That's important in my business. Like I said, a lot going on right now. My partner's from Mexico City, but he loves all the development up here. Lot of Mexican money wants to come up this way. Much safer. So we got a couple a good real estate deals goin' over in Richardson." He walked to the driver's side. "Wanta take a ride?"

"I thought we were gonna take a walk?"

"Aw, come on, Doc. Hop in. Let's take a ride,"

"I don't think so. Really I've gotta get up early. 6:30 meeting."

"Le'me just show you how sweet this baby runs," Miguel insisted. "Just a spin around the block." He pressed the clicker in his hand, opened the driver-side door as the interior lights came on and waited for a response.

"Okay. Quick spin."

Blaine opened the passenger-side door, slid onto the smooth leather seat. "Nice," he said as Miguel got in and shut the door.

With a quick, startling move, Miguel reached across to the right side of the dash and popped the glove-box open. Blaine arched back and watched as Miguel lifted out a square of glass, four inches or so, and set it on the console. The interior lights switched off automatically. Only the light from the glove-box illuminated the interior. Miguel reached into his shirt pocket and took out a small cellophane envelope. Blaine continued to watch through a relaxed

Scotch-induced haze as Miguel opened the envelope and shook a small amount of white powder onto the glass. Then he drew the credit card out of his pocket and began to push the powder into a thin line with the edge of the card. Blaine was silent, disbelieving but fascinated as Miguel proceeded.

"This is what I was talkin' about, Doc. Makes your troubles melt like lemon drops," His voice was changed, now a harsh more aggressive tone. He reached into the inside pocket of his blazer and drew out a short pencil-thin metal tube placing one end next to the powder. "It's easy. Just like this." He bent down and lowered his head so the upper end of the tube went just inside his right nostril. Then he pressed the left side of his nose with his left thumb and inhaled moving the tube along the thin white line as it disappeared. He lifted the tube away, held his head back and exhaled. "Ahh. That's good." He laughed a rough, visceral laugh. "Wanta try?

Tonight, lying on the bed in the Best Western, Blaine could hear that sinister laugh as if it had been a warning to stay away. But he had not stayed away. He tried it, and he liked it. It did seem to make his problems melt away, at least for a little while, and he felt energized.

"Anytime you need it, Doc, all you gotta do is call," Miguel had said. "It's grade A stuff. Cash only, you understand."

Blaine kept up the contact. Miguel obliged him with a private phone number and a little cellophane packet from time to time when he called. Each time, he carefully concealed the packet and the number in the side-pocket of his leather travel case. When he told Miguel he was moving to Atlanta, he got special instructions and another number: "Just ask for Mr. Alcon. A-L-C-O-N. Tell him Miguel from Dallas sent you."

*****

Lying motionless on the bed, staring at the ceiling, he drew a deep breath. Suddenly, without provocation, thoughts of his mother and the withering terror he had felt when he first learned she was dying and his helpless loneliness when she died came flooding back to him. The memories of unrelieved pain were so excruciating he had suppressed them, forced himself to turn them off whenever they surfaced. Forced himself to forget. As he lay so exhausted and drained, all the ungodly pain came back. He recalled waking from frightening dreams, crying out to her several times in the night when he was 14 and 15. How she would come to him, lie beside him and stroke his tear-stained face. Now, at this moment, he heard himself speaking in a broken, almost childlike voice, calling out to her. It was as if he could feel her hand on his forehead and her warmth against him. Memories ignored for so many years because he could not bear them. Tonight was no different. He could hear her saying his name trying to soothe him. Still unbearable, tonight was one of the worst of times.

He opened his eyes and stared again at the ceiling as an image of the little cellophane packet came to his mind and completely overpowered his resistance. He sat up, reached into the shoulder bag and took out the leather travel case. He tucked it under his arm and walked into the bathroom.

CHAPTER THREE

When Evelyn came into the bathroom Tuesday morning to find Richard lying unconscious on the floor, she shrieked. "Richard!!" The intensity of her voice was enough to wake him, but he didn't move. Just stared up toward her like a surprised infant opening its eyes to a loud noise.

"Richard," she said again, "*wake up*! What happened to you.?"

He replied weakly, "The floor.....got all purple and wavy."

"Okay. Here, let me help you get up."

She took him by the elbow as he struggled to get up. She guided him to the bed where he immediately curled into a fetal position. He stared sideways at her for a moment then he raised his head and grinned as he said, "I'm glad I got that basement cleaned out yesterday. It was a mess."

"What are you talking about, Richard?" Evelyn asked, perplexed.

"You know," he said as he lay back against the pillow and closed his eyes. Her face registered a flicker of despair. Until that moment, perhaps trying to deceive herself, she had tried to believe that he was coming down with the flu. Now she was shaken by the realization that whatever he had was not something to be cured by tea and hot soup and a few days off work.

"You just stay here and relax," she said. "I'm going to call Dr. Holleran."

She hurried to the kitchen and grabbed the telephone dialing nervously then waited for the receptionist to connect her. "Hello, Dr. Holleran. Evelyn Kanaby calling."

"Hello, Mrs. Kanaby. Things better this morning?"

"No. Worse. Much worse," she said, urgency in her voice.

"How do you mean?"

"About 10 minutes ago I found him passed out on the bathroom floor. I was able to wake him up and get him back to bed, but when I did he started talking funny, saying weird things. Not himself at all. Told me he was glad he'd cleaned out the basement yesterday, but Dr. Holleran," her voice broke, "we don't even *have* a basement."

"All right. Just a minute, now," Joe said trying to calm her. "Try to relax and listen to me. Where is he now?"

"He's in bed. Sleeping. Just dozed off right after he said that."

"I think I'd better see him."

"Yes, I think so. Something is seriously wrong. I can see it in his eyes," she said, her voice rising with emotion. "Doctor, this is *not* Richard. Should I call an ambulance?"

"Hold on a minute. Did he complain of any pain? Like a headache or if he might have hit his head in the bathroom when he fell?"

"No. When I got him up, we walked back to the bed. He got in and just sort of curled up. That's when he said that about the basement."

"And he's breathing all right now?"

"Yes."

"Okay. So do you think you could bring him in to the office?"

"I....think so. It'll take a little while to get him ready. But yes, I think I can."

"I see patients here 'til noon and again at 2:00, but if he's okay and you can get here around 1:00, I can see him before my afternoon appointments."

"Okay. I think we can get there by then."

"In the meantime, if he seems to be getting worse, call me again, and we'll see about getting him transported. I'll tell the receptionist to be looking for you. She'll get you right into my office."

"Thank you, Doctor. I don't know what we'd do without you."

She checked and double-checked on Richard during the morning. He didn't stir until she woke him up at 11:00. He opened his eyes again, staring blankly at her. An expression of recognition appeared on his face, and he smiled.

"Was I asleep?" he asked. He glanced around the room. "What time is it? I've got to get up." He propped himself up slightly and looked toward the large windows then back at her.

"This is a strange place, you know. Those windows. They have such a funny-looking face."

Evelyn's attempt at a reassuring smile immediately gave way to a look of dismay. "The windows?" she said glancing at the windows, half expecting to see something bizarre.

"You know," He smiled emptily and glanced toward the floor. "Twisted. And a big mouth. You see it?" he said as he closed his eyes and slid down onto the pillow.

Evelyn was frightened. She shook him gently and coaxed him out of bed. "Dr. Holleran wants to see you at 1:00," she said. He didn't protest as she led him back into the bathroom. "Let's get you shaved, and comb your hair." He rather automatically reached for the razor on the shelf where he kept it. But then to her astonishment, before she could stop him, he began to smear toothpaste on his face. "Wait, Richard, honey. You're not paying attention. You're putting toothpaste on your face."

"Huh?" Richard stared at her then at his fingers. "Toothpaste?"

She wiped the toothpaste off of his face and hand and put the razor away as he stood motionless, arms hanging limp. "Where's your electric razor?"

"Electric razor?" he said.

Why had she even asked, she thought. "Here it is," she said as she opened a drawer in the cabinet, took out the razor and plugged it in. Richard sat on the vanity seat, slumped in complete submission, eyes closed. She passed the buzzing razor over his cheeks and chin. "There. That's better." He opened his eyes. "Now you're more presentable," she said. "Let's comb your hair."

"Okay. Comb hair," he parroted.

She drew a comb through the thin gray hair. Her hand was beginning to shake as she sensed panic welling up inside of her. She put the comb down. "Okay, now let's get you dressed." Her voice was more commanding. Richard rose and followed her into the bedroom standing stiffly beside the bed as she hurried into the closet.

She came back with pants, a shirt, socks, underwear and a pair of loafers in her arms. She laid them on the bed as he stood fidgeting with the buttons but slowly unbuttoning the pajama shirt. It slid away from his shoulders as he stared at the floor.

"Come on, Richard, honey, wake up," she pleaded, pulling the shirt from his arms. "Here's your underwear. Can you put on your shorts?" He ignored her as she pulled the drawstring for the pajamas pants. They fell to the floor leaving him standing naked and motionless in the middle. He made no move to step out of the crumpled material pooled around his feet. She took his hand and led him forward. She knelt in front of him and held the waist-band of the shorts open. He looked down at her then at the shorts as though he had no idea what she was doing. She pulled his left hand onto her shoulder to try to steady him, then guided first his left foot then his right into the shorts and lifted them into place around his waist. She stood and pulled the undershirt over his head, and gently guiding each arm through the arm holes. He offered no resistance. She coaxed him to the side of the bed where he sat as she knelt and slipped on a pair of wool socks. Fighting back tears, she pulled him back to standing and got him into a flannel shirt and loose-fitting slacks. He sat on the bed again. She set loafers on the floor in front of him. He looked down and without her coaching, slid his feet into them. "See, Honey," she said, relieved. "See how easy that was. I knew you could do that."

"Yeah. Easy, right?" he said with a childlike inflection.

"Come now. Let's have a little lunch before we go to see Dr. Holleran."

"Yeah. Lunch."

"We have to be there at 1:00."

He followed her to the kitchen and went automatically to his usual chair at the table. He picked up the newspaper lying there. She watched him as she began to prepare sandwiches.

"Anything interesting in the news?" she said.

"Let's see," he said appearing to scan up and down the page.

"Let's see."

"Let's see what, Richard? What does it say?" she said, slight exasperation in her voice.

He looked up startled by her abrupt tone. "Olympics. Coming to Atlanta." He smiled.

Her hands shook as she continued with the sandwiches.

"Honey, the Olympics were here a long time ago."

"Oh, okay," he said flatly.

She moved toward the table to see what he was reading. He looked up again and smiled again. Her eyes widened as she realized he was holding the paper upside-down. She took the paper from him gently and turned it right-way up.

"Read me what it says, Richard," she said.

He focused on the upper corner of the front page. "Today the weather in Atlanta....will be balmy early...in the day. Turning to clouds in... the afternoon. Late evening....20% chance...of showers." Even though he read haltingly, she was relieved that he read verbatim.

She finished making sandwiches and set them on the table. "Here you are. Turkey, lettuce and tomato, just like you like," she said in a loud voice hoping to jolt him back.

*****

"Central Medical Associates. May I help you?" came a southern-accented woman's voice through Blaine's cell phone.

"Yes, hello. This is Dr. Purcell calling Dr. Manning. Is he available?"

"Just a moment, Doctor. Do I need to pull up a record?"

"No. It's personal."

"Yes, sir."

There was a click then then Luke's voice: "Hey, you ol' son-of-a-gun. Where are you?"

"Standing at the front entrance of Brakefield Hospital," said Blaine emphatically. "Got here late Friday night. Actually Saturday morning about 2:00."

"You should've called us," said Luke.

"At 2:00 in the morning? I don't think so," said Blaine.

"Well, we didn't know when you'd be getting here, so we were just waiting to hear."

"Sure. That's fine," said Blaine. "I didn't call sooner 'cause I had to recover a little Saturday morning. Slept 'til noon then drove around some in the afternoon and again on Sunday. You know, just to get my bearings. Yesterday I was able to find a little furnished apartment in Dunwoody. Place called Quail Creek Apartments. No luxury, but at least it's convenient to the hospital, and I was able to move right in. 'Course, I didn't have much to move." He laughed and continued, "So I guess you could say I'm settled." He laughed again.

"So when do you start with Dr. Reed?" said Luke.

"Meeting with him at 2:00 today. After that I've got to, you know, do the usual paper work then have some kind of orientation. I start full-time tomorrow."

"So when are we gonna see you?"

"Whenever is good for you. I have no plans."

"How about tonight? Come for dinner," said Luke.

"Aw, you don't have to go to that trouble. Let me take you two out."

"No, no. It's no trouble," said Luke insistently. "One or both of us stay home with the kids on school nights anyway. And besides, it'll be a lot more relaxed at home. I'll check with Janie and call you back. We want you to come over and catch up. Better sooner than later. Judging from your letter, I guess things've been pretty rough lately."

"Yeah, things have been rough," said Blaine. "I'll fill you in."

"Okay. I'll get back to you." said Luke.

"I'll be waitin'. This is my cell number."

CHAPTER FOUR

Evelyn and Richard arrived in the parking garage at the Brakefield Medical Center at 12:50. "Come on," she said, anxiously tugging at his hand as they hurried along the walkway to the medical office building. They moved through the lobby and along a hallway toward double doors marked **Brakefield Internal Medicine.** As they came through the doors to the waiting area and over to the reception desk, the receptionist greeted them. "We were expecting you, Mr. Kanaby. Mrs. Kanaby. Doctor Holleran wants you to wait in his office." With that, she led them into a hallway behind the reception desk and on to an office door marked **Joseph P. Holleran, M.D.** As she held it open she said, "Please have a seat. The doctor will be here shortly."

She closed the door, and they sat in the two leather armchairs set side by side facing the front of the large desk in the middle of the room. Richard glanced around seeming not to focus on any particular thing. Evelyn watched him silently. Being in that room at that moment was at once frightening and comforting to her. She had gotten Richard here safely. Now she had to trust that this kind and gentle doctor would know what to do.

All of a sudden, Richard bolted upright and stared across the desk at the group of framed photographs on the credenza. His movement startled Evelyn, but she didn't move or speak. "That looks like Doctor Holleran's wife," he said as he stood and walked around the desk. He picked up the framed 8X10 photograph of Nancy Holleran, her blond fashion-model looks radiating from it. "Boy, she's sure a pretty lady," he said as he put the frame down. Evelyn watched him standing slightly stooped, staring emptily down at the picture frames.

Her feelings of panic were gone. Now she felt deep sadness. He looked so old and beaten down.

"You see the picture of Dr. Holleran there?" she asked quietly.

"Picture of Doctor Holleran? Where's Dr. Holleran?" he said glancing around the room with a vague, questioning look on his face. "Is this his office, Evie?"

"Yes. We're here to see him. In just a few minutes," she said struggling to keep her composure.

Richard looked back at the credenza. "Oh, yeah. There he is… .with his kids." He picked up another framed photo, one of Joe at the helm of a sailboat: rugged good-looks, strong, happy smile, dark hair tousled, two wind-blown children beside him.

There was a knock at the door. It swung open, and Joe Holleran strode in. "Good afternoon to two of my favorite people," he said. He put his hand on Evelyn's shoulder and squeezed slightly. She felt embarrassed that Richard was standing behind the desk holding the picture. "So you're checking us out, are you, Mr. Kanaby?" He gave a gentle laugh as he walked around the desk and put his arm over Richard's shoulder.

"Hi, Doctor Holleran. Nice picture," said Richard. He held the frame out to Joe.

"Thank you." Joe took the frame and set it down. "Glad you like it. Now, come back around and have a seat. Let's talk." He guided Richard back to the chair beside Evelyn and stood in front of the desk, looking down at both of them. From her perspective his long white coat made him look especially tall and strong, while his calm expression and quiet, confident voice were reassuring. He looked at Richard. "So I finally got you to come in to see me."

Richard looked up again with the same vague look. Joe could readily see the change in his eyes that Evelyn had described on the phone. "So how're you feeling so far today?" he said, watching Richard's face. "Anything bothering you?"

Richard's gaze shifted to Evelyn as if he expected her to answer for him. She glanced away as a tear welled in the corner of her eye. She brushed it away and turned back. "Richard, answer Doctor Holleran. He wants to know how you're feeling," Evelyn said forcefully.

"Oh, yes, Doctor. I'm just fine." He looked up. "I woke up this morning, and I wasn't exactly sure where I was. But then I got okay, you know. And I'm just fine now."

"Good. I know what it's like to wake up sometimes and wonder where you are. But then when you get completely awake it's okay. So tell me how you felt this morning. Did anything hurt? Your throat or your chest?"

"No. Not as I remember. Just seemed like the window looked funny. I can't exactly tell you. Just seemed kind of twisted and yellow. You know what I mean?"

"No. Not exactly. Tell me more about it."

"Well it was just twisted, that's all. Except the floor was tilting for a while too. Moving up and down."

"You mean like a boat?" Joe asked.

"Yeah," said Richard, grinning, "like a boat."

"So can you tell me anything else?" said Joe.

"Well, sometimes the window looked yellow. Sometimes purple, but not all the time. The colors kept changing back and forth sometimes," Richard continued, but his words became more jumbled and incoherent. "You know. Moving around. And a big face. In the middle. You know. Smiling." He spoke faster. "The lights are very bright tonight. I noticed that when we came in here. Very bright." He squinted. "You probably see that, too, don't you?"

Evelyn's alarm was obvious as she shifted uneasily in the chair beside Richard.

"Okay," said Joe, "so I want to examine you. You know, check you out. You come with me, and Mrs. Kanaby, can you just wait here for a few minutes?"

"Sure, Doc. Anything you say," Richard giggled as he spoke, now suddenly jaunty and jovial. "She'll be fine right here in this nice place. Where we goin'?"

"Right through here." Joe opened the door in the side wall of the office and turned to Evelyn. "I'll get him settled then I'll be back. I have a few questions for you."

"All right," she said watching Richard now staring at Joe with a blank expression.

Joe guided Richard into the examining room where a rather portly woman in a nurse's uniform was waiting.

"I want you to meet Mrs. Jernigan," said Joe.

"Hello, Mr. Kanaby," said the woman. "If you'll have a seat right here, we'll get started. I need to check your blood pressure and your pulse…and your temperature and….get your shirt off for the doctor." Richard sat obediently and folded his hands in his lap, staring vaguely at her.

"I'll be back in a few minutes," said Joe then he turned, went back into his office and closed the door. Evelyn looked up nervously.

"So," he began as he sat on the edge of the desk in front of her, "can you think of anything unusual about his behavior recently? I mean before yesterday or today?"

"No. Nothing. He's been his usual self. Spent Sunday afternoon in the garden. When he came in he said he didn't feel well. But he didn't want me to call you Sunday night. He had a little supper and went to bed. Seemed to sleep okay."

"Did he seem confused yesterday?"

"No, just sorta groggy. Kept saying he didn't feel well. Slept a lot. That's very unusual."

"Well, what's puzzling and frankly quite concerning to me now is that he seems much more confused than when I saw him last night. There are not many things that could cause such a sudden onset of confusion. Some medicines and of course alcohol, but he doesn't drink, right?" Evelyn nodded as Joe continued. "Some types of stroke can do that, but other things go along with that. Things I don't see at this point. I have been thinking about exposure to something toxic. A toxic chemical of some kind."

"You mean like something poison?" she asked.

"Well, something that would have the effect of a poison, yes," said Joe. "Specifically, I am thinking of chemical compounds like pesticides. Certain pesticides can cause confusion and dis-orientation...even hallucinations. Since he works with that kind of thing in his business, that made me think of the possibility. And I suspect he uses things like that with his gardening too,"

"I know he uses some kind of chemical things in the gardens and the greenhouse," she said, "but goodness knows what. He has what he calls secret formulas. He won't tell anybody what they are, but whatever they are, they seem to do the trick. Everything thrives, spring to fall."

"Is he taking any medications right now?"

"Just the Tylenol you said to give him."

"All right. So I'm going to examine him now," Joe said. "I'll do some testing, then we'll both come back and talk a little more."

Joe returned to the examining room and closed the door. Evelyn sat in the silence of the office fighting back tears, her mind flooded with thoughts of the worst possibilities. She felt helpless and desolate. She stared at the desk phone. Maybe she should call the children. No. Wait until Dr. Holleran comes back, she told herself. She looked across the desk at the photographs on the credenza, then up at the large framed document on the wall above it. She walked around the desk to read it: **THE OATH OF HIPPOCRATES**, its words formed in elegant calligraphy. She looked down at the photographs again, focusing on the one of Joe and his children. She picked it up. How she wished he could step out of the frame, put his arm around her shoulders and say everything was going to be all right. She touched the glass just over his face with a trembling finger. Her eyes welled with tears as she murmured, "Please."

✶✶✶✶✶

In the next room, Mrs. Jernigan had exited, and Joe was proceeding with his examination: stethoscope to chest, abdomen, back, neck; palpation of neck, abdomen, groin, axilla; check of reflexes. All normal. Next, the nose, throat, ears: normal. Finally, eyes.

Richard sat slightly slumped on the examining table.

"Now I want you to watch my finger," Joe instructed holding up his right finger. "Just follow it around." Richard closed one eye. "No. Open both eyes and watch my finger as I move it around." Richard closed both eyes and grimaced. "Okay. Just relax." Joe picked up the small ophthalmoscope from the metal cabinet beside the examining table and switched on the light.

"Let's try this. Keep both eyes open and look at the clock up there on the wall behind me. I'm going to shine this little light into your right eye." He brought the beam up along the right side of Richard's face to the eye. Richard jumped back abruptly.

"That's bright," he said in a loud voice. "Too bright! Flashing!"

"Did that hurt your eye?" asked Joe.

"No. Just bright. Flashing. "

"Okay. Let me try the other side," said Joe as he brought the light toward the left eye. Richard jumped away again.

"Oh!" Richard howled in a childlike tone. "Too BRIGHT!"

"All right, Mr. Kanaby." Joe put the ophthalmoscope back on the table. "Let me ask you a few questions. I'm going to check to see how your brain is working today. You understand?"

"Yeah. Sure. How your brain is working today," Richard mimicked

"Who's the president, Mr. Kanaby?" Joe spoke deliberately.

"Who's the president? Oh, Yeah. The President? Reagan."

"Do you know what month this is?" said Joe.

"Ah'm….October."

"No," Joe said gently. It's March. The month of March."

"Okay. March. Month of March."

"Right. Very good. Now remember that. I'm going to ask you again in a few minutes." Joe paused then said, "What year were you born?"

"Nineteen hundred, right?" said Richard.

"No, nineteen forty-five," said Joe.

"Okay, Doc. I remember. Nineteen forty-two."

"Correct. Now look at this. What am I holding in my hand?" Joe reached into his pocket and took out two keys on a key-ring.

"What is this?"

Richard's gaze shifted to Joe's hand. "Lock. That's lock."

"Okay. What is this?" Joe held up his fountain pen.

"Ah'm…stick. A stick," said Richard.

"Okay. What is this?" Joe held a quarter between his thumb and index finger so that it was clearly in Richard's view.

"Money," said Richard.

"Right," said Joe. "Can you tell me how much money?"

"Ah'm….not much money," said Richard.

"Okay. One more thing. What is this?" Joe held up his left wrist pointing to his watch.

"Time. That's time," said Richard.

"Is this a key?" said Joe.

"No," said Richard.

"Is this a pen?

"No," said Richard.

"Is this a watch or a clock?"

"Watch clock doc," Richard giggled.

"Okay, Mr. Kanaby. Do you remember what month this is?

"Friday."

"What year were you born?"

"Nineteen hundred and nineteen hundred."

Joe could see that any further exam now was futile. Something far more complex than he could diagnose in his office was going on.

"Okay," he said, "I think we're about through for now. Just one more question. Can you tell me how you make your special secret formulas for your flowers?"

"Oh, sure. You know, lots o' stuff." His eyes brightened as he said the words. "Magic. Just like magic."

"So tell me how you make magic for your flowers?" said Joe.

"Oh. Lots o' stuff. You know." Richard released a short loud cackle. "Just throw it all in and mix it up!" He swirled a hand in front of him.

Joe patted Richard's shoulder. "So we'll get you dressed, now," he said pressing a button beside the door into the hall. "Then you'll come back to my office and we'll talk."

"Okay, doc. Sure." Richard looked down at the floor, both arms now dangling at his sides, slumped and shirtless on the edge of the examining table.

Mrs. Jernigan returned, and Joe went back into the office and closed the door.

"You doing okay?" he said to Evelyn.

"Yes," she said quietly but with an expression of desperate expectation on her face.

"I've been over him as thoroughly as I can in the office. I think he should be seen by a neurologist as soon as possible, hopefully this afternoon."

"Oh. A neurologist?"

"Yes. I'm going to call right now to see if our chief neurologist, Dr. David Dittrich, can see him," said Joe. "I don't think you should take him home, at least not until Dr. Dittrich or one of the other neurologists can see him."

At that moment, the examining room door opened and the nurse led Richard in. Evelyn stood and moved anxiously toward them.

"How do you feel, honey?" she said.

Richard looked surprised. "Hi, sweetheart. When did you come?"

His words were excruciating. She felt on the verge of hysteria, but she knew she had to hold up.

Joe guided Richard toward the leather chairs as the nurse exited. "You sit here," he said. "Mrs. Kanaby, you sit with him, and I'll be back in a few minutes. Just open the door and call if you need anything." He walked out and approached the reception desk. "I have to make a call. Is Dr. Elfing's office free for few minutes?"

"Yes," the receptionist said. "He's over in the hospital."

Joe walked into the office just across from his, picked up the phone and dialed. "Hi, this is Dr. Holleran. Is Dr. Dittrich available?" After a short pause, Dittrich's voice came on.

"Hi, Dave. I need a little help if you have a minute. I'm seeing a patient I've been following for almost 15 years. He's a 64 year-old man, always in excellent health. Had a kind of a flu thing over the weekend. Or at least what I thought was flu with a little congestion when I saw him last evening. Anyway, he woke up this morning confused and disoriented. He's in my office now. To me, he's

41

showing some signs of an acute-onset dementia. I think we need to admit him for observation. I believe something is evolving." A pause. "We can bring him over to you." Pause. "Okay. Thanks. I have to tell you, this man is a very special patient to me."

Evelyn and Richard sat motionless and silent as Joe came back into his office. "I just spoke to Dr. Dittrich," he said. "He's another doctor here, Mr. Kanaby. I want him check you out, too. If you don't mind waiting here, we'll take you over to his office in a little while."

"Okay, sure." said Richard, glancing up at Evelyn looking confused.

Joe left the room. Richard looked down at the floor, motionless and silent. Evelyn watched him from the side angle where she sat. She did not speak intentionally waiting to see if he might react to the silence. He did not. But after a few minutes, as if following some unseen object through the air, his gaze moved around the room coming to rest on Evelyn's face. She smiled, but he looked at her without a hint of recognition. His eyes wandered toward the framed Oath of Hippocrates. "See that face?"

Her attempt at a smile quickly disappeared. "What face, Richard?"

"On that big picture right there." He seemed frightened and pitiful pointing toward the framed Oath of Hippocrates.

"Yes, a face." she tried to soothe him reaching out and touching his knee. She knew there was no use trying to fathom what he was seeing. She was at once bewildered and terribly sad, but this time, sad not so much for Richard as for herself. It seemed that in just these few short hours she was losing a lifetime. He was in a world completely separated from her though she was only inches from him. She reached out again, this time taking his hand. It felt good to hold that hand she had held so many times. It had the same feel, but it was different. There was no response from him. No squeeze of unspoken understanding. She clenched her teeth and tightened her lips trying hard not to cry.

"Richard, honey," she said once she had choked down the lump in her throat. "Maybe we can go for a ride after that other doctor sees you."

He looked at her still with the same empty stare. In the next instant, his eyes closed and his head snapped sharply back. His body stiffened and began to jerk rhythmically as he slid to the floor. He rolled onto his side, heaving and gasping with breathy, gurgling noises as the rhythmic jerking intensified. Evelyn screamed his name as she stood and lunged to pull the door open. "Oh, God!" she screamed again. "Please! Help!" She went back and dropped to her knees beside Richard still crying out, "Help! Somebody! Pleeeeese!"

The receptionist was at the door immediately. Seeing Richard convulsing on the floor, she rushed to the examining room across the hall to get a nurse. They both came back across just as Joe appeared. He knelt beside Richard's thrashing body. He held the head back as the jerking and flailing continued and reached into the pocket his white coat for a tongue depressor. Not there. He pulled the pen from his shirt pocket, gripped it firmly and pushed it into Richard's mouth, forcing the clenched teeth apart. "Get me an airway! Quick! On the cart. GET ME AN AIRWAY!" he yelled into the hall. "Mrs. Jernigan! The cart!" The cart-wheels clattered in.

Evelyn stood back against the chair horrified as she realized Richard was having a seizure. The rhythmic movement of Richard's body gradually subsided as Joe continued to hold his head back. Mrs. Jernigan standing above Richard and Joe, handed him a plastic airway. He slid it between Richard's teeth and pushed it back into his throat.

"Should I call a code?" the other nurse asked.

Joe continued to kneel over Richard, checking for a pulse. "No. Just hand me some tape." The nurse handed him a strip of narrow white adhesive tape, then another and another. He wrapped the exposed end of the airway and pressed the ends of the strips onto Richard's jaw. Then, bending intensely over the flailing body, he ripped the front of Richard's shirt open and slid the left sleeve off. The nurse handed him a syringe and a cotton pledget.

"Phenobarb. One-thirty," she said, telegraphically.

Joe swiped the side of Richard's upper arm with the pledget, pushed the needle into the muscle and pressed the plunger. He handed the syringe back to Mrs. Jernigan and gripped Richard's wrist again for a pulse. Then, hunched back on his bent knees, he looked up at Evelyn. "I'm so sorry you had to see this," he said quietly then looked back at Richard as he drew his stethoscope from his coat pocket and positioned the ear-pieces. He pushed Richard's undershirt up and brought the bell onto his chest.

Evelyn stood frozen, gripping the back of the chair. Her face was wet with streaming tears. Her lips trembled, and she shook with inaudible sobs. The other nurse, now standing next to her, turned and embraced her. She buried her face against the nurse's shoulder. The room was silent except for Richard's deep, sonorous breathing.

Joe lifted the metal bell away from Richard's chest and pulled the ear-pieces away. "We've got to get him to the hospital," he said to the receptionist, "Call transport and tell them to get over here stat!"

He looked at Richard again who was breathing more easily but was still completely unconscious. Evelyn pulled away from the nurse, wiped her eyes and looked down. "Oh, Richard," she whispered fighting back tears. Joe, still kneeling over Richard, reached for her hand. She moved closer to the sleeping body. "What if he…has another…?" She broke off the sentence.

"He might, but we've got an airway in, and we broke the seizure. Right now we need to start an IV and move him to the hospital."

Evelyn took in a stuttering breath, and after a moment, asked, "Can I touch him?"

Joe nodded. She bent down far enough to stroke Richard's forehead with two fingers. Then she stood straight and, sounding suddenly resolute, said, "You know he always tells me 'Don't panic.' I was thinking about that right before he fell. I keep telling myself I'm not going to panic no matter what." She paused. "I think I better call my daughter."

"Yes," said Joe looking up at the nurse beside Evelyn. "Ms. Corey here can take you over to the office across the hall to use the phone."

The nurse led Evelyn toward the door.

Almost simultaneously, two attendants pushing a gurney approached from far end of the hall, stopped for a moment just outside Joe's office then went in quietly. Joe stepped back as they quickly spread a sheet on the floor beside Richard, slid his limp body onto it, and gently, expertly lifted the sides of sheet laying him on the gurney.

"Hold up now, guys," said Joe. "We've got to get an IV started before you take him." One attendant pushed a steel IV pole into a corner the head-end of the gurney. The other covered Richard with a sheet. Mrs. Jernigan inserted the needle for the IV line into his forearm and hung a small bag of clear fluid on a hook at the top of pole. Securing his torso with two black straps, the attendants slowly pushed the gurney through the door. "Thanks, guys," said Joe. "Mrs. Jernigan will go over with you. The neurology resident will meet you in Radiology."

*****

Joe went over to the office where Evelyn waited. "Did you reach your daughter?" he asked.

"Yes. She said she'll be here in about 20 minutes."

"Okay," said Joe. "They're taking him over to the hospital. The resident in neurology is waiting for him there, so he'll be in good hands."

"Thank you, Doctor," she said, "but shouldn't I go there too?"

"I think you should wait for your daughter. You told her to come here, right?"

"Yes. To your office."

"That's fine. You stay here 'til she comes. I'll be back to speak to her, then both of you can go over to the hospital," said as he exited.

Evelyn sat silently, eyes downcast.

"Can I get you anything?" said Ms. Corey.

"Oh, no thanks. You don't have to stay. I'll be fine."

Presently, the door opened again and Martha came into the room, a younger version of Evelyn in looks: slender, medium-length dark hair, pretty if not beautiful face now expressing stress. Evelyn rushed into her arms sobbing.

"Oh, Mom, Mom," Martha said sympathetically holding Evelyn close and stroking the back of her head. "Tell me what happened."

Evelyn drew in a quick breath. "Dr. Holleran had just been in to talk to us," she said. "He went out to call another doctor. We were just sitting there, and all of a sudden, Daddy just fell out of the chair." Her voice broke and she began to sob again, this time louder and deeper.

"Here. Sit down." Martha edged her back toward the chair.

Joe appeared at the door. "Hello," he said. "I'm Joe Holleran."

"I'm Martha Colby, their daughter," she said holding out her hand. He shook it gently.

"This has been quite a shock to all of us," he said touching Evelyn's shoulder with his other hand. "Your father had a major seizure in my office just after I had examined him. He's stable now and he's on the way to the hospital. The neurologist is waiting for him there."

"Is he conscious?" said Martha.

"He roused a little, but he's not really conscious. Usually after a seizure of that type, such an intense seizure, people don't regain consciousness for a while.

"What could it be, Doctor?" Martha asked, wide-eyed.

"Well, there are several possibilities, but we won't know anything definite until there's more testing."

"You think it could be a brain tumor...or a stroke?"

"Possibilities," said Joe pensively, "but there's no clear evidence right now of a stroke or a brain tumor. The suddenness of his confusion and disorientation is quite puzzling. We're admitting him to the Neurology Service. Dr. Dittrich, our chief neurologist, will be in charge."

"Can we go there, Doctor?" said Martha.

"Yes," he said, "but it will be a while before you see him because the neurologists will be with him. I suggest while you're waiting you go to the Admitting Office to give them the information they'll need. It's right off the lobby. I'll meet you there in about thirty minutes, and we can go up to the floor together."

By 5:30 the MRI was finished, and Richard, still unconscious, was taken to the third floor, room 306N. The MRI showed no evidence of stroke or hemorrhage, no evidence of a tumor and nothing to indicate infection. The brain appeared normal in all respects. Once he was in the room, David Dittrich and the Resident, Andreas Locarnos, began their examination. When Evelyn and Martha finished in Admitting, Joe met them and escorted them to the third floor conference room. He asked them to wait while he went to check Richard's status. Some ten minutes later, he returned followed by the two neurologists. He introduced them, and after they described the MRI findings and chatted a few minutes, Joe excused himself to make his rounds.

Dave Dittrich, sitting beside Andreas at the conference table, spoke. "He seems to be resting quietly, but he's quite sedated. His breathing and his heart rate and blood pressure are all normal, and he's receiving intravenous medication to prevent further seizures." He paused. "We've begun a series of lab tests and expect to have preliminary results shortly. He's now on continuous EEG monitoring, which will alert the nurses if there is any more seizure activity."

Martha said, "What does continuous EEG monitoring mean?"

"It's a way of recording the electrical activity in his brain. The brain waves. We have a recording device which is a sort of a cap or small helmet that fits over his head. The recordings are referred to as EEGs. Abbreviation for the word electro…encephalo...grams." He said the word slowly.

"Is that painful?" Evelyn asked anxiously.

"No," said Dr. Dittrich, "it fits comfortably, and it records continuously on a computer so we can detect any evidence of abnormal brain activity. If there should be any seizures, the machine will alert us instantly."

"When can we see him?" said Evelyn.

"Dr. Locanos can take you in now if you don't have any other questions" said Drittich. "He seems to be comfortable, but remember he is sleeping deeply."

"Thank you, Doctor," said Martha. Evelyn echoed her.

Dr. Dittrich excused himself. Andreas stood, "Shall we go now?"

When they reached door of 306N, he pushed it open and looked in.

"He's sleeping," he said. They filed in quietly.

The helmet-and-wires arrangement on Richard's head startled Evelyn but she remembered what the doctor had said.

"Can I touch him?" she said. Andreas nodded. She put her hand on the chest and leaned toward him. "Richard. It's Evie," she said weakly. No response.

"He's pretty sedated like Dr. Dittrich was saying," said Andreas.

"Oh, how I hate to leave him," Evelyn sighed. "We'll come back in the morning, but you'll call us if we should come back sooner."

"Of course," said Andreas. "We have your phone numbers. I hope you can get some rest." The women thanked him and walked to the elevator.

Andreas went back to the nurses' station to look for preliminary lab results on the AcuPanel computer. Everything in the first round okay: white count, hematacrit, glucose, electrolytes, enzymes all normal. He went back to 306N and proceeded with a lumbar puncture. The spinal fluid appeared normal; nothing to indicate bleeding or infection. He ordered a stat return on the analysis. He reviewed the overnight orders with the nursing staff then went into the monitor room behind the nurses' station and sat for several minutes watching the wave patterns cross the monitor screen. No sign of abnormal activity. He reviewed the night orders with the nurses, went back in to check on Richard once more and headed for the call room for the night. He would check AcuPanel from there for anything more.

CHAPTER FIVE

A little more than an hour after Richard Kanaby had been brought into room 306N at Brakefield Hospital, Blaine Purcell pulled into the driveway of a handsome two-story brick Georgian in an entirely different part of Atlanta. He killed the engine and started up the front walkway as Luke Manning stepped out onto the broad portico holding two half-filled highball glasses. "Hey, ol' man," yelled Blaine as he bounded up the steps.

"Hey, bud," Luke replied, almost as loud. Blaine wrapped an arm over Luke's shoulders as Luke pushed one of the glasses toward him. "Thought you might need one of these about now. Single malt."

"Oh, man, do I ever," Blaine responded as he took the glass and stepped back. "Look at you. You haven't changed a bit."

"Tryin' to hang on," said Luke holding up his glass motioning toward the door.

As they walked in, Janie came across the foyer. "Blaine," she exclaimed with full-voice enthusiasm, "it's so good to see you." She took his hand and leaned forward for a peck on his cheek.

"Same to you, pretty lady," he said grinning as she led Blaine into a large, handsomely furnished living room. Luke right behind them said, "Be right back with your wine, babe."

"Have a seat. Right here," she motioned to a large upholstered chair at one end of the sofa. He took the chair and she sat on the sofa.

Blaine glanced around the room as Luke came back with a glass of white wine. He handed it to Janie and sat on the matching chair at the other end of the sofa

"Some place you guys have got here," Blaine mirated.

"We like it," said Luke. "It's got some age on it, but it's a great family house.".

"It's beautiful," said Blaine. He took a sip of Scotch and forced a smile as the words great *family* house pricked him like a dart.

Luke sensed his discomfort and shifted. "So how'd it go with Reed?"

"It was fine," said Blaine wanting to project nonchalance. "I met with him at two, then got that paperwork I told you about done and had sort of a tour around the hospital. That was it. Rounds at eight tomorrow morning. I'll be set up in what he calls the fellows' office. And he says he's got a *lot* of *reading* for me to get through this week." He smiled and nodded acknowledging a heavy task.

"I'm sure he does," said Luke. "He's pretty intense."

"No kidding," said Blaine, nodding. "He's even scheduled to introduce me at the monthly staff meeting…tomorrow. Just so happens the monthly meeting is like the day after I get here. Says he doesn't want to wait 'til next month. Says he'll present my bio then he wants *me* to say a few words about myself." He raised his eyebrows in a resigned expression and shrugged slightly as he took another sip of scotch.

"Sounds like he's got you programmed."

"Yeah. But you know," said Blaine, "it's not all bad. Right now I could use a bit of a steady hand on my rudder."

"Well, it's great you're in Atlanta," said Luke, raising his glass trying to be upbeat.

"I'm glad to be here," said Blaine wistfully. "I mean it. Right here, right now." He looked away to stifle a little rise of emotion.

"Daddy." A child's voice surprised him. He turned to see a lovely little girl, ten or so, standing shyly in the doorway with one arm behind her back.

"Hey, Helen. You need something?" said Luke, "Come meet

Dr. Purcell."

Blaine was not prepared for the sharp pain he felt in his stomach as Helen walked toward him.

"Hi, Dr. Purcell," she said holding out a hand with precocious poise. "Nice to meetcha. I remember seeing you on some Christmas cards."

"Oh, yes," said Blaine. He stood as he shook her hand. It felt good to touch that little hand. It reminded him so much of Amy.

"Your daughters look very pretty," she said as he let the hand go.

"And so do you," he said forcing a smile. "I'm so glad to meet *you.*"

"Thank you. Daddy, you have to sign this permission slip for the field trip." She held a piece of paper toward Luke.

"Okay. Tomorrow before school," said Luke as he took the paper.

"You go back and finish your homework," said Janie, patting her daughter's shoulder. "We'll call you when we're ready for dessert."

"Okay," said Helen as she skipped away.

"How about a refill before dinner," said Luke.

"Sure," said Blaine.

"I'll go check on things in the kitchen," said Janie as she stood.

"Okay," said Luke, "and we'll go check out the bar." He stood and motioned to Blaine to follow him.

They crossed the foyer and entered a smaller room, wood-paneled and furnished with a comfortable looking seating area of two easy chairs and a sofa upholstered in a burnished leather around a square brass-and-glass cocktail table. They walked to the bar on the wall to the right. Luke poured two more drinks and motioned toward the chairs. They sat.

Blaine, beginning to feel more relaxed, took a big draft of the Scotch and said, "You know you're a really lucky guy. You've got it all, man. Janie, your kids, this place." He glanced around the room and raised his glass.

Luke smiled looking down at his drink and back up. "It's not all luck," he said. "I say we've had to work pretty hard to make it all happen. But look. I know that's not what you need to hear right now. I know you're havin' a rough time and trying not to show it. But what we want you to know is that we want to help you any way we can, you and Lucy."

"And you already have, Luke," said Blaine. "Just being here means a lot to me right now," he sipped again. "But I have to say it's damn hard to talk about it. 'Specially with Janie. I'd like to explain things, but I...I don't know where to begin. I made such a mess of everything that after a while there was just no turning back."

He swirled the drink slowly and looked up focusing intensely on Luke. "I can't tell you exactly what happened to me. I just lost control. Maybe I was never in control. I felt myself getting older and like I was, I don't know...missing out on things. Seemed like the kids took up all the oxygen." He paused a moment. "But I can't put it on them. God knows I adore them. It was my fault. I just *fucked up. Bad.* No other way to say it." That was enough, he thought. Anything more about his dissolute life would be more than he wanted to go into even with his trusted friend.

It was not hard to sense what Blaine would not put into words. Luke remembered well his early days, the sporting bachelor. This might have been predictable, he thought as he felt a wave of compassion.. "You don't have to explain anything," he said. "It's none of our business except to try to help you get through it. All of you."

"I knew I couldn't stay in Dallas," said Blaine. "Coming here for this fellowship with Reed gave me a reason to leave. I mean an acceptable, respectable reason. I think if I'd stayed in Dallas, under the circumstances, it would have been harder on the girls than me leaving."

"Sounds like it was the best thing," said Luke.

"Yeah, well I guess so. But coming here tonight, seeing how you and Janie have your life so together, makes me realize more than ever what a damn fool I've been."

"Okay, guys," Janie's voice floated into the room as she appeared. "Dinner's ready,"

"We're ready too," said Luke leading into the breakfast area off the kitchen.

The sight of the steaming pot-roast and vegetables on the table was the purest form of comfort for Blaine. Luke poured the wine, and they began dinner. The conversation never lagged. Mercifully, the talk was about Brakefield Hospital, about the fellowship, about Atlanta and what spring would be like and eventually about Helen and her three-years-older brother, Jamie. "He's at Scouts tonight," Luke had explained.

Twice Blaine threw out a casual reference to his girls to test whether that might bring hints from Janie for more explanation. Both times she steered gracefully clear. Whether she might be distancing herself in subtle condemnation or simply respecting his privacy, for now at least he was spared having to share any more details of his tattered life.

When they finished the main course, Janie went out to the foyer and called Helen for dessert. Presently she and Helen came from the kitchen carrying plates of pecan pie and ice cream. That sight topped off Blaine's comfort. It was depressing to feel the evening slipping away, but a few minutes after dessert was finished, with a glance at his watch he said, "I've got a big day tomorrow. My *introduction,*" he laughed. "So…guess I'd better get packin'." He laid his napkin on the table as he looked first at Janie then at Luke. "You don't know how good this is being here with you guys again."

"Okay, so we'll let you go," said Janie, "only if you promise you'll come back soon."

"That's easy," Blaine said as they all stood.

"Think you can find your way back out to Dunwoody?" Luke teased.

"I think so. Just follow the trail of bread crumbs I left." He laughed.

Helen said goodnight, and Janie and Luke walked toward the foyer with him. "Remember your promise," said Janie. She kissed him lightly on his cheek. "We'll be in touch."

"I'll go out with you," said Luke as he opened the door. They moved across the portico and on toward Blaine's car.

"Quite a machine you're driving," said Luke.

"Oh, yeah." Blaine flashed a delighted, almost adolescent smile. "I love it."

"Why am I not surprised?" said Luke.

"I guess some things never change." Blaine chuckled. "Thanks for rescuing me tonight."

"Just get yourself into the work." Luke put a hand on Blaine's shoulder. "The rest will take care of itself."

" 'Nite, buddy," said Blaine.

Shortly back at his apartment, as he unlocked the door, he realized that for the last few hours he'd felt better than he had in weeks. When he flicked on the ceiling light, though, the dreary sight of the living room jolted him: cheap Danish-modern sofa, two spindly- legged chairs, ugly blond-wood coffee table with scattered cigarette burns and a side table holding a green ceramic lamp with a sagging shade. It was a furnished apartment all right, but with all the starkness of a bad motel. He turned off the light and made his way upstairs. He flipped on the bedroom light and walked into the bathroom.

There sat the leather travel case on the counter. He closed his eyes and shook his head as he realized how his mind had seemed to steer him to it. He thought again how nice it was at Luke and Janie's. But he wasn't there anymore. He was here, alone and miserable in this sad little place. He reached for the case, but when he touched it, the thoughts… *Don't do that tonight… early morning tomorrow…* blasted him. He backed away, set the alarm on his phone for 5:30am, turned off the lights and fell across the bed fully clothed.

CHAPTER SIX

When Andreas woke at 6:15 Wednesday morning, he felt an urgency to get back up to the third floor. Once there, the overnight nurse reported that Richard had stirred only minimally at hourly checks. Vital signs were stable and there had been no more seizures, but he had been "completely unarousable." Andreas entered 306N to see Richard lying supine under a sheet with eyes closed, breathing deep regular breaths. He did not react when Andreas tried for a response with firm hand squeezes and pinches to cheeks and forearms. Andreas checked the pulses at wrist and neck, stethescoped the chest and went back to the monitor room.

Electrical activity showing on the monitor at that moment was normal so he wanted to do a quick review of the overnight records. Following his usual method looking at 4-to-5 minute runs at 30minute intervals would give him a survey. He saw nothing unusual until the five-minute tracing at 4:30 am. It was a pattern he'd never seen. He changed to ten-minute intervals. At 4:40 the same pattern came up again, then at 4:50 but at 5:00 and 5:10 it was gone. He jotted down the time-points.

Just before 8:00 Dave Dittrich and Joe Holleran appeared almost simultaneously.

"Good morning, Andreas," said Dr. Dittrich, "Have you looked in on him?"

"Yes. He's really out. The nurses weren't able to rouse him all night. I tried too. Nothing."

"How about EEGs?"

"I've just finished a check," said Andreas trying to hold back his excitement. "There *is* something."

"Not prion, is it?" said Joe.

"No," said Andreas, "this is different. Bilateral cortical bursts, recurrent 6-to-9 seconds, high-frequency, low voltage. Looks like it started around 4:30 this morning as far as I can tell."

"Still going on?" said Dittrich.

"No. Back to normal by 5:00. It seemed to be sustained for about 20 to 25 minutes, but there were no seizure alerts during the night."

"So what does that mean?" said Joe glancing at Dittrich.

"Beats me," said Dittrich raising his eyebrows. "Nothing I know of, though it does make me think more of toxin than infection."

"Possibly," said Joe, "but he doesn't have all the features of an acute toxic syndrome. Remember that old adage for the symptoms: red as a beet, hot as a firecracker, mad as a hatter and blind as a bat? He does have the mad-as-a-hatter part if acute dementia qualifies, but he has no skin changes, no fever and pupils were normal."

"Toxicology screen was ordered, right?" Dittrich addressed Andreas.

"Yes, but it'll take a few days," said Andreas. "For organophosphates and organochlorines, specimens have to be sent to a lab in Minnesota."

"That's important," said Dittrich. "Organochlorines certainly can produce hallucinations and seizures."

"Immunoglobulins?" said Joe.

"You have something specific in mind?" asked Dittrich.

"Nothing specific, but I'd like to see'em," said Joe. "Might suggest something we haven't thought of. Somethin' kickin' up antibodies. We need to get an Infectious Disease consult."

"Yes," said Dittrich. "So Andreas. Please put in a request for a stat I.D. consult, and check on the turnaround time for the tox screen."

"I've just had another thought," said Joe. "Since we don't know it's *not* something infectious, I think we have to consider starting Universal Precautions."

"Good idea," said Dittrich, "We can get that done right away. I'll inform the nurses. And I'm going to take a look at the EEGs."

"Okay," said Joe, "and I'll call John Lowndes as soon as I finish rounds. As Chief of Staff he should be informed. I'm going to look in on Mr. Kanaby right now." He waved slightly and walked away.

He entered the darkened room and stood beside the bed. Richard's eyes, now open, seemed to stare at the ceiling. Joe waved a hand in front of the eyes. No response. He lifted one limp hand and squeezed it, gently at first then more firmly. For an instant Richard grimaced and tried to pull away, but the stare remained fixed straight upward. "Mr. Kanaby," Joe said firmly. The head turned slightly, but the blank stare didn't change. "Richard. It's Doctor Holleran," he said louder, "Can you hear me?"

Richard seemed to try to speak, but made only guttural unintelligible noises: "Huh...huh...dah...dah," gasping between each utterance.

"That's it. Holl...e...ran, Doc...tor Holl...e...ran," Joe said slowly. "Try again." Richard's head turned away, eyes back to the ceiling as he took a loud open-mouth breath. Joe pulled the sheet a little higher over Richard's chest, and went back into the corridor.

By 9:15, Joe was in his office. He dialed the number for John Lowndes. "Good morning. This is Dr. Holleran. Is Dr. Lowndes available?"

"He's on another call, Doctor, but I think he's almost through. Can you wait, or shall I have him call you back?"

"I can wait a few minutes."

"Yes, sir."

The line went to hold, and momentarily a distinguished voice came on. "Good morning, Joe. What can I do for you?"

"Hi, John. We've got a problem I need to discuss with you."

"Hope nothing too serious," the voice replied with a short, rather patronizing laugh.

"Well, possibly. A patient we admitted last night to the neurology service. I've been following this man for a number of years. He's always been in excellent health, but yesterday morning he had what seemed to be a sudden-onset dementia. The wife called me, and I had her bring him to my office. Right after I examined him, while he was still in office, he had a full out *grand mal* seizure."

"Oh," said Lowndes.

"There was nothing that might have predicted it," said Joe. "No history of mental status changes and certainly no history of seizures. I brought Dave Dittrich in to consult right away. He's now taking care of the man, but I am following him too because of my personal interest."

"I see," said Lowndes.

"We've been trying to put things together while we're waiting on some more lab results," said Joe. "The man is a chemical engineer, 64 years old. He owns a chemical company in Marietta. Over the years, he's done quite a bit of work with pesticides and insecticides so we're thinking something toxic may be the cause. However, there's no history of any exposure. The wife tells me that in recent years, he hasn't worked directly with any chemicals."

"I guess you can't rule that out though, can you?" said Lowndes.

"No," replied Joe, "but without a better history, we'll have to rely on a tox screen, and that takes a few days. Anyway, brain MRI last night was normal. No evidence of hemorrhage or infarction and no tumor. All routine labs so far are normal. No evidence of infection. He's still out. Basically unresponsive now for more than twelve hours."

"Any more seizures?"

"No," said Joe, "but he's on I.V. anticonvulsants. He was on a continuous EEG monitor throughout the night. Dave's reviewing the records as we speak." Joe paused for a moment. "In the meantime, since we cannot rule out some kind of maybe unusual infection, we think it would be prudent to start universal precautions. That's why I'm calling. To let you know."

"I think that would be prudent. Have you talked to Infectious Disease?" said Lowndes.

"We're requesting a stat consult."

"Anyone in particular?" said Lowndes.

"I don't know. The neurology resident put in the request," said Joe.

"Well if I may suggest, I strongly recommend Dr. Garriman," said Lowndes. "Trained at Hopkins. World class and very sharp."

"Oh, yes. I know about Dr. Garriman," said Joe. "Good suggestion. I'll pass that along to Dave. But while we're waiting for the consult, we're going ahead with Universal Precautions."

"Let me know if you need me to pitch in here," said Lowndes.

"Okay. Sure. Thanks."

*****

After a quick call from Joe to inform him of Lowndes's suggestion, David Dittrich dialed the Division of Infectious Diseases. "Good morning. This is Dr. Dittrich in Neurology. Is Dr. Garriman available?"

"One moment, Doctor. I'll check. Is this regarding a patient?"

"Yes. A consultation on a patient on the Neurology Service."

"Yes, sir. Please hold."

Then "Good Morning, Dr. Dittrich. This is Dr.Garriman. What can I do for you?"

"Yes, good morning," replied Dittrich. "You're probably not aware yet, but my resident, Dr. Locanos, just put in a request for a stat I.D. consult on a new patient on Neurology. I don't believe he directed it to anyone in particular on your service, but Dr. Lowndes has recommended you highly. We would appreciate it if you could accommodate us."

"That was very kind of Dr. Lowndes. Can you tell me a bit about the case?"

With that Dittrich related the details of Richard's plight finishing with "Of course some of the lab work is still pending, but we think it's important to get your opinion as soon as possible. And by the way, you should know that under the circumstances, we've decided to initiate Universal Precautions."

"That's quite reasonable. If you'll give me the medical record number, I can review the information right away. If I need to see him, I'll go up to the floor in the next few hours and leave a note on the record."

*****

Blaine had arrived in the cardiology suite at 7:00 that morning. The secretary, Mrs. Sanders, opened the door to the Fellows' office and handed him the key. "Dr. Reed left all those papers for you last night," she said pointing. On left side of a small desk beside the window were three stacks, the journal articles and technical reports Reed had told him would be waiting. In the center was a laptop computer and a desk phone on the right side.

He thanked Mrs. Sanders and closed the door to discover a crisp white doctor's coat hanging on the back of the door. The words **Blaine M. Purcell, M.D**. were embroidered in dark blue block letters just left of the lapel and **Cardiology Service** just beneath the name.

He was impressed. He slipped off his blazer and pulled on the white coat. It fit perfectly. He hung the blazer on the door hook and sat at the desk, surprised to see a numbered list of the articles on top of each stack. Again, he was impressed.

It was 7:20 by then. Time to look at a few articles before he met Dr. Reed for rounds. But first he should make a few notes for what he was going to say at the Staff Meeting at noon. The idea of standing before a room full of doctors whom he'd never met but who would be sizing him up as he talked about himself made him uncomfortable. He shrugged as he pulled a pad from his briefcase and began to make some notes.

At exactly 8:00 the telephone rang. It was Mrs. Sanders. "Dr.Reed is ready for rounds now, Dr. Purcell." In another minute, he was standing beside her desk as Reed, a slightly stocky, medium height, balding, red-faced man wearing a long white doctor's coat came through his office door. With a brusque greeting he led the way out of the suite.

They finished rounds about 9:15. Blaine returned to his office and made a page of notes for his self-introduction. He wanted it to be short. After that he spent the rest of the morning perusing the stacks of articles and planning how he would get through them in a week. At exactly 11:50 there was a knock on his door. He heard Reed's voice. "Okay, Blaine. Let's go."

Blaine picked up the page of notes and opened the door. "All set," he said in a tone he hoped was confident enough to belie his uneasiness. The two walked quickly along the corridor, through the lobby and on to the hospital conference room. The medical staff doctors were beginning to assemble. A number of chairs, Blaine silently estimated at least sixty, were arranged in rows in the middle of the room. Reed directed that they both sit up front.

Dr. Lowndes called the meeting to order in a no-nonsense fashion, and the room quieted. He began to plod through what seemed a rather pedantic agenda, but Blaine paid little attention preoccupied as he was about what he had to say about himself. After 20 minutes, Lowndes called on Reed. He came forward energetically and announced Blaine's appointment as the new Cardiology Fellow. He gave a surprisingly detailed summation of Blaine's medical background and training, and described what Blaine would be doing at Brakefield for the next six months. Then he said, "Now Blaine, let's hear a few words from you."

Blaine rose and moved to the podium beside Dr. Reed. There was a light ripple of applause which gave him a moment to gather himself as the turned and looked at the audience. In a flash, he was struck by the sight of a stunningly beautiful woman in a white doctor's coat seated near the end of the fourth row. She was staring at him intensely. He looked down and tried to focus as he began to speak. He thanked Dr. Reed and launched into the short biographical recitation: where he grew up, where he went to college and medical school, why he had gone into practice in Dallas, that he was married with three daughters. He ended by saying he looked forward to his time at Brakefield and was "glad to have this opportunity." There was another bit of applause which he acknowledged with a quick nod feeling the heavy scrutiny he knew he was receiving. Only then did he allow himself to look back at the face in the fourth row. The eyes seemed fixed on him again. He glanced away. But the aura— the face, the eyes, the stare—-was penetrating.

The meeting concluded and the group dispersed, Reed directed Blaine over to meet Lowndes who greeted him with a firm handshake and a perfunctory glad-to-have-you-aboard. But as they stood chatting, Blaine watched the woman leave through the double doors.

A tall man in a white doctor's coat approached, greeting Lowndes and Reed. "Wanted to come over and say hello to our new fellow," he said, smiling at Blaine. "I'm Joe Holleran." They shook hands. "I'm in the Medicine Group here. I'm originally from Massachusetts, so I thought you might like to meet another refugee from the North." He laughed.

"Absolutely," said Blaine. "I guess we can both claim refugee status though I have to admit I haven't been back to Pennsylvania in years. By now I've claimed naturalized Southern citizenship." He also laughed.

"Well, we're glad to have you," said Joe.

"Thanks for coming over," Blaine replied. "Good to meet you." They shook hands again.

Blaine and Reed left the room together. Reed headed to the Cardiology Suite; Blaine, to the cafeteria for a quick lunch as the tension left his body. Meantime in another part of the hospital Joe Holleran hurried back to his office. He had to call Evelyn Kanaby.

CHAPTER SEVEN

"Has he waked up, Doctor?" Evelyn's voice pleaded through the phone. It was 1:30.

"No, but that's likely due to the seizure medication," said Joe. "He roused a little when I went in to see him around 9:00. I expect he'll begin to come around over the next 24 hours. Will you be coming in this afternoon?"

"Oh, yes," she said, "in about an hour."

"Very good. When you come in, I'd like you to come by my office before you go up to the room. There are a few things I need to discuss with you."

"Oh?" she said, "What kind of things, Doctor?"

"I want to explain some of the tests, and I have a few more questions about his work."

"All right. Anything you say. My daughter will be with me."

"That's fine. I'll tell the receptionist to expect you," said Joe.

They arrived promptly at 2:30. The receptionist escorted them into Joe's office. He greeted them and motioned toward the two leather chairs where Evelyn and Richard had sat less than 24 hours earlier.

"I was up to see him about 30 minutes ago," he said as he walked around the desk and sat in the desk chair. "He's still unresponsive, but he hasn't had any more seizures. So far nothing abnormal shows up in the lab tests. The EEG, that's the brain-wave test Dr. Dittrich told you about, indicates some damage to his brain. That could be caused by an infection or exposure to some sort of toxic substance. That's what I want to ask you about." He stopped for a moment pacing his words. Evelyn was silent. He continued, "I know he worked with various chemicals over the years. I thought you might know something about that, or maybe someone at the company who could tell us something."

"We don't know anything about that," said Martha, "but I could ask."

"Good," said Joe nodding. "Now, Mrs. Kanaby, yesterday you told me about his secret formulas. It reminded me that once when he came over to our house to give us some advice about our garden, he mentioned the special mixtures he used. He didn't say there was anything secret. Just said he'd learned about them from a man who helped him with his gardens."

"Yes," said Evelyn. "That was Mose. I think things Mose taught him was what he meant. I always thought it sounded like hocus pocus, but I never told Richard that."

"Can you tell me anything about Mose or could I talk to him?"

"Oh no. He died quite a while ago," she said. "Richard's the one who knew about him. All I know is he was from South Carolina. Came here sometime in the '30s "

"Do you know how he died." Joe asked.

"I think he had a stroke," she said, her voice stronger, "but he was sick for a long time."

"Did he have a family? Maybe someone we could talk to," said Joe.

"They lived up in Alpharetta," said Evelyn, "Mose, his wife Emma and two children. A son named Charles and a daughter, but I can't remember her name. Their last name was Funchess. She paused pensively for a moment then said, "You think they might know something about those mixtures Richard talked about? That couldn't have anything to do with what's wrong with Richard, could it?"

"Probably not, but it would be good to know whatever the mixtures were," said Joe. "Possibly something he was using even after Mose died. Is there somewhere out at your place he keeps fertilizer or chemicals or...."

"Yes." Martha cut in quickly. "The storage shed. Could be something in there."

"You know of anyone who could check that out? See what's there," said Joe.

"Maybe my brother, Allen," said Martha.

"That might be dangerous," said Joe. "It would be best if someone from the Health Department or an environmental agency could do that since we have no idea what we're dealing with. Or perhaps someone from Mr. Kanaby's company could help."

"I'm sure someone there could. Maybe Ray Elerby," said Martha glancing at Evelyn. "He's a chemical engineer. He's been working with Dad at the company a long time. I'm sure he'd be willing to help us. I'll try to get in touch with him."

"Okay," said Joe, "and it's important to get in touch with Mose's son or the daughter if you can find them."

"We can try," said Martha, "but it's doubtful. We haven't been in touch with them for years."

"Okay. But if you could see what you can find, it might be helpful," said Joe. "Now there's one more thing. Since we have not yet been able to determine if this is some kind of infection or something else that could be dangerous to people like the hospital staff or even you and your family, we've decided we should take certain precautions. An infection specifically involving the brain is a possibility even though there are several things that go against that. One, he has no fever. Two, the brain does not show evidence of swelling which we would expect if there were a significant infection. Three, the blood tests don't indicate any kind of inflammatory reaction. And last, the fact that this came on so quickly. This whole picture is very unusual for an infection. But in spite of that, we still have to consider it until we find out otherwise. In such situations, we use a standard procedure. It's called the Universal Precautions Protocol."

"And what does that mean?" said Martha with a puzzled frown.

"It's a very straight forward procedure we can set up so everyone is completely informed and protected. Nurses, doctors, technicians, the aids, housekeeping staff as well as the patient's family. When you go up to the room, you'll see a sign on the door that says Universal Precautions. There's a cart in the hall by the door with some gowns and hats and masks. The nurse will show you about all that." He took a breath. "I am sorry you have to go through this, but for now, we think it's the best thing to do."

"Whatever you say, Doctor," said Evelyn nodding slightly.

"I hope the next few hours will begin to give us some answers. In the meantime, he's stable, so we should be able to reduce the medication and decrease the sedation."

"But, Doctor," Martha looked up quickly, "if it *is* an infection, why can't you give him some kind of antibiotic?"

"Well, in order to give an antibiotic, we have to know what kind of infection we're treating. So far, we don't have enough information."

"What about uh'm, hepatitis?" Martha pressed. "My husband and I have a friend who had severe hepatitis. She got really mixed up, and she even had seizures."

"Good question, but hepatitis would not come on so suddenly without some preceding symptoms. The blood tests for liver function would be significantly abnormal. They're all normal for your dad." He paused. "Anything else?"

"No. I don't think so," said Martha. "Mom, you have any questions?"

"No," Evelyn sighed. "Can we go up now?"

"Yes," said Joe leaning forward in the chair. "I understand how distressing this is for you. I think you know how much I think of Mr. Kanaby, so it's painful for me, too. I wanted to take this time to explain these things because I want to be sure you understand the full significance of what might be going on. The precautions have already been started. If you can wait here, I'll be back in about 10 minutes, and I'll go up with you."

"Of course, Doctor. We know you have other people waiting to see you," said Martha.

"It's okay. I don't have any appointments until 3:30," he said. "I just have to take care of one thing." He left the room closing the door behind him.

Evelyn's eyes flooded as she looked at Martha. "It's all gone, Martha," she said. "All the wonderful years, all our time together. Gone." She began to sob.

Martha felt powerless. It seemed so bleak. "Mom, we've got to be strong," she said. "You know Daddy would want us to. We've got to try to find something." She felt a wave of emotion as she spoke. "Maybe it *is* something toxic. If we could find out about those chemicals or find Mose's son or the daughter." She glanced at her watch, "Allen said to call him as soon as we know anything. Now would be a good time." She reached into her purse and drew out a cell phone. She punched in a number as she said, "I have to tell Allen everything Dr. Holleran said. You mind hearing it all again?"

"It's okay," said Evelyn.

Martha spoke into the phone. "Hi, Mr. Kanaby please. This is his sister." She waited. "Hi, Allen. Mom and I are in Dr. Holleran's office. No. We haven't been up there yet." Pause. "No, they don't know. Dr. Holleran just spoke to us about it. He says it could be some kind of infection of the brain or it could be something toxic like a chemical." Pause. "No. He says it's nothing like that. That would have showed up in the tests." Pause. "Yes. All the tests so far are negative except the brain-wave test shows some damage to the brain." Pause. "Yes. She's here with me.

She's okay. You think you'll be here before long?" She looked at her watch again. "Okay. But listen. There's something we need to find out. You remember how Daddy always talked about those mixtures Mose taught him about…for the garden and the greenhouse. Dr. Holleran wants us to see if we can get someone to look around the greenhouse or the shed and see what might be there. Chemicals, fertilizers, insecticides… whatever. And he also thinks we should try to find someone in Mose's family who might know something about those mixtures. Mom says she thinks the son's name was Charles, up in Alpharetta."

Another pause. "Okay. As soon as you can. It's room 306 North." She turned off the phone just as Joe came back into the room.

"Ready to go up now?" he said in a quiet, reassuring voice.

*****

Evelyn and Martha stood side-by-side in front of the door for 306N. The sign posted there said **NO VISITORS** in bold letters.

Beneath that a smaller, more discreet sign read **UNIVERSAL PRECAUTIONS**. They watched as Joe pulled a green paper gown over his white coat then paper shoe covers, an expandable cap over his head, a cup-shaped mask over his nose and mouth and finally, thin rubber gloves. He pushed the door open and went in. The nurse standing with them lifted one of the folded gowns from the cart and shook out the folds. "You have to put this on backwards like Dr. Holleran did," she said holding it up as Martha slid her arms into the long sleeves. The nurse tied the gown at the back. "This is just a precaution. We do this whenever there's a possibility of infection. Here's the cap. Just pull it over your hair like a hairnet." She demonstrated. "Now, let's get these booties on." She lifted two paper shoe covers and held each for Martha to step into. "And the mask."

She lifted the mask up to Martha's face and pulled the elastic band over her head. "Over your nose and mouth like that."

Evelyn stood stiffly, overwhelmed by the thought, the realization, that she was about to be sheathed in a barrier that seemed to symbolize her separation from Richard. She held out her arms as the nurse began the same procedure. She felt trapped, enshrouded, wrapped in despair, cut off from all of her life that had preceded yesterday. She might never again feel Richard's vitality, his strength, his return of the profound love she felt for him. She felt totally immobilized standing stock still in the hospital corridor, staring at the ominous signs on the door. She was sad beyond comprehension. Tears began to trail down her cheeks. As the nurse put the cap over her head and placed the mask over her face. She pressed her upper teeth hard against her lower lip. Martha watched wordlessly. She wanted to pull Evelyn to her, embrace her as she had yesterday in the doctor's office, but she stood still too, feeling inevitability.

Joe came out of the room. "He's not conscious, but I don't think he's in any discomfort." Evelyn stared beyond him into the dim light of the room as he spoke.

"Now the gloves," said the nurse as she pulled several thin vinyl gloves from the box on the cart and handed them to each woman. "They're a bit oversized. One size fits all. Just slip them on...like gardening gloves."

Gardening gloves. The words tore at Evelyn with unimaginable cruelty. Dear God, what happened to Richard? It *could not be* the gardening. All he had loved so passionately.She swallowed hard and pulled the gloves on as they followed Joe into the room.

He went to the far side of the bed. Evelyn and Martha moved to the near side. They reached for each other's hand as they stood looking down at Richard lying motionless, breathing slowly, eyes closed, the EEG monitor cap still on his head. Joe lifted a limp wrist and laid it back down.

"Daddy," Martha spoke at first softly then louder. "Daddy." There was no response.

Evelyn leaned over the bedrail and spoke. "Richard. Honey. Richard." His eyelids flickered open and his head turned toward her. She repeated his name. "Richard." She spoke in stronger tones trying to force her words into his mind. "Richard. It's me. I'm right here." She wanted to reach out and shake him and say *Richard, wake up. Come back to me. Don't go. Don't leave me, Richard.* But instead, she stood quietly hoping for a response. The eyes closed, the head turned away and the even breaths continued.

After a few more silent moments, they left the room. They all removed the gowns, caps, masks, shoe-covers and gloves. The nurse showed them how to dispose of the garb. They spoke quietly to Joe for a few moments. Then the two women walked toward the elevator.

Joe went to the nurses' station. It was almost time for his afternoon appointments, but he wanted to see if there were any response from the Infectious Disease people yet. He pulled up Richard's records on one of the counter computers. There was a note, time: 1:35 pm, but it was only Dr. Garriman's acknowledgement of receipt of the consultation request. He headed back to his office.

At around 3:00, Martha was able to speak to Ray Elerby. He seemed quite disturbed by the news of Richard's illness but assured her he'd be glad to talk to Dr. Holleran and help any way he could. He'd be glad to take a look around the shed or the greenhouse. She called Joe's office with Elerby's number.

At little after 5:00, Joe had a call from Dittrich. "Looks like Garriman reviewed everything. There's a preliminary note. The recommendations are to get viral titers, confirm that bacterial and viral cultures are underway and order fungal cultures on blood and spinal fluid which, by the way, we've already done. PCR is recommended too. I'll follow up on that."

At 5:15, Joe dialed the number for Richard's company in hopes of catching Ray Elerby. He was still there. "Oh, yes, Doctor. I've known Richard for more than 25 years. I was real sorry to hear he's so sick. We worked together out here a long time. Lotta chemical work...with pesticides and herbicides."

"Did you ever work with either organochlorines or organophosphates?" asked Joe.

"Oh sure, back years ago," said Eberly. "We worked with organochlorines until they were banned in the Government. At that time, we got rid of all of'em. We still work with certain organo-phosphates in pesticides, but we're always aiming for low environmental toxicity."

"Any idea how long it's been since Mr. Kanaby worked with them?" Joe asked.

"He hasn't worked with *any* chemicals since he took over the company. Some years, now," said Eberly. "Leaves all that up to us." He laughed.

"I see," said Joe. "I hope you understand. I'm not prying into your business, but considering the circumstances of his illness, we're trying to explore every avenue."

"Of course. I understand. Just wish there was something I could tell you that would help."

"We have a toxicology screen underway," said Joe. "If we find anything that might suggest any kind of toxic chemical exposure, I'll get right back to you. In the meantime, if you can get out to the Kanaby's place perhaps tomorrow and look around in the shed or the greenhouse, that would be very helpful."

"Okay, Doctor. I'll call Martha right now and arrange it."

Richard remained unconscious throughout the evening, the night and on into Thursday. When he occasionally opened his eyes, there was no sign of recognition of anyone or anything around him. There were no more seizures so the EEG monitoring was changed from continuous to intermittent monitoring for 20 minutes every two hours, but the patterns gave no further clues. There was nothing new from further lab results on blood, spinal fluid or urine blood, except for a repeat immunoglobulin assay recommended by Dr. Garriman. That showed a mild elevation of IgG.

CHAPTER EIGHT

Blaine arrived at his office at 6:45 Thursday morning trying to get into his new routine: early morning reading until 8:00 rounds then full immersion in reading, pulling up more articles, cross-referencing, organizing and making notes until 5:00 rounds. Since yesterday, he had thought several times of the face, that beautiful face at the Staff Meeting. But he was on to other thing as the morning passed. He had a deadline.

Meanwhile, Allen Kanaby sitting in his office in Sandy Springs just after lunch, got his search underway to locate Mose Funchess's son or daughter. He began by dialing information through all the area codes in and around Atlanta and North Georgia. He found five listings for the name Funchess. None in Alpharetta, but one, the only Charles Funchess, was listed in Gainesville. He dialed the number. No answer. He tried three more times. Finally in the late afternoon, a woman answered. Allen introduced himself and said he was trying to reach Charles Funchess. At first the woman sounded suspicious, but when he explained who he was and why he needed to speak to Charles, she became cordial. She said Charles was away until late Friday night, "but if you can call back Saturday, I know he'll want to talk to you." Allen said he would call, and if possible, he'd like to come up Saturday.

*****

Blaine finished the afternoon rounds with Dr.Reed at about 6:00. The idea of another boring, lonely cafeteria dinner was not appealing, but since he had just been introduced at the staff meeting yesterday, he thought he might find some companionship there. Didn't happen. So after dinner, he returned to his office, shed the white coat and picked up the brief case and a bundle of reprints.

Driving out of the garage, it occurred to him that a good diversion might be to shop for a TV. The BestBuy in the mall near his apartment should be the ticket if it was still open, which luckily it was. He found a flat-screen he liked and managed to fit the carton into the passenger seat.

When he pulled into his parking spot in front of the apartment, he sat for a moment. He dreaded going in. He switched off the engine and ferried the carton through the front door and up to the bedroom then went back to the car for the briefcase and reprints. Mission accomplished. Now for a drink.

He reached for the bottle of scotch which he'd bought Monday morning after his first bit of grocery shopping. He pulled one of the disposable plastic cups from the stack on the counter beside the bottle. He poured generously. He liked it neat. The burn coursing down through his chest felt warm and reassuring. He took a deep breath and moved slowly up the stairs, scotch in one hand, cell phone in the other.

He set the phone and the cup on the bedside table and pulled open the carton eager to get the TV set up. He connected it quickly hoping to bring some life to the place and take his mind off of his isolation. No dice. The picture was fuzzy and distorted, but at least for now he could listen.

He put his keys and wallet on the bedside table. The bundle of reprints still on the kitchen counter crossed his mind. Too late for reading now he thought. He loosened his belt, slipped off his shoes, took a big slug of scotch and laid back on the bed. The news came on momentarily, a monotonous background of voices as his mind wandered. He thought of his girls. He glanced at his watch: 10:00; 9:00 in Dallas. They were probably already in bed. Too late tonight.

Maybe tomorrow. His cell phone jingled. It was Luke's number. He hit the button.

"Hi, Luke."

"Hey, Blaine. Not waking you up I hope."

"Oh, no. I just got in. Had to shop for a TV tonight." He laughed a self-deprecating little laugh. "So how's everyone at your house?"

"We're fine. Just calling to see how things are going."

"Everything's falling into place I guess," said Blaine. "Reed's been great. He's got me set up in the fellows' office. Looks out into a nice little courtyard." He paused. "I'm spending most of my time reading. He's given me a ton of stuff. Reprints plus a bunch of online references."

"Sounds like you're busy," said Luke.

"Oh yeah. He's made it pretty clear he expects me to get through it all by Monday when I start in the clinic and the lab. But it's actually pretty convenient reading in my office all day without any interruptions. Easy to concentrate. I've got a brand new PC with access to all the links I need and a laser printer right out by the reception desk. 'Course, I need to take a break this weekend to get this apartment a little more livable."

"What kind of schedule has he got you on?" said Luke.

"Oh, I'm the only fellow right now. Another one comes in July, but Reed's making it relatively easy on me 'til he gets here. I start taking call the middle of next week. Every third night and every third weekend. I alternate with a couple of medicine residents."

"That's great 'cause Janie and I want to get you back over again soon. We'll see what we can work out maybe for next weekend if you don't have plans."

"Sounds good," said Blaine. "I've got *nothing* booked." He laughed.

"Okay, man. We'll get back. Hang in there."

"Thanks," said Blaine. He switched off the phone feeling less alone and grateful for his friends. The news was over. A late-night talk show had just started, but the reception was so terrible he clicked it off, laid back again and dozed.

When he woke, he was startled to see it was 12:30. Early day tomorrow, he thought. He stood and began to undress as he walked into the bathroom. At the sight of the travel case on the counter, the same feeling from two nights ago flashed through his mind. But he told himself again, *not tonight*. He could, after all, control it. He brushed his teeth and went to bed.

He got to his office at 6:30 Friday morning. No one else was there. He put his briefcase and the reprints on the desk and hung his jacket on the door hook. He sat at the desk thumbing through his yesterday's notes then picked up a reprint and began reading. After 40 minutes, he took a break to get coffee from the corridor vending machine and came back to continue. A little before 8:00, he heard the receptionist outside. He pulled on his white coat and walked out.

"Morning, Mrs. Sanders," he said brightly. "Oh, good morning, Doctor," she chirped, "You're so quiet, I didn't know you were in there."

"Yep. Still trying to get through all those papers. Dr. Reed in yet?"

"He's in his office. I'll let him know you're here." She buzzed Reed's office.

Momentarily, Dr. Reed appeared at his office door. "Good morning, Blaine. Ready to go?"

"Yes. Sir."

They finished rounds at about 9:15. Blaine went back to his desk until 1:00 and after a short lunch, he sequestered himself again. At 4:30, he perused his notes on the last 33 papers, laid the notepad aside, pulled on the white coat and made his way to the cardiology floor in the hospital to check lab results before rounds. Punctual as usual, Dr. Reed appeared at 5:00. They finished a little after 6:00. But since it was Friday, he decided not to stay late. He bid good evening to Reed and headed back to his office.

As he walked along the connector between the medical office building and the hospital, the thought of the weekend ahead loomed in his mind. He tried to focus on the shopping he had to do making mental notes as he walked staring vaguely at the floor: Towels and sheets, some decent glasses and dishes; the ones that came with the place were disgusting. A good lamp for the bedside table, and a comfortable chair for the bedroom where he could sit and read would be nice. Then there were groceries. He should stock up on coffee and some frozen dinners.

The list slogged on in his mind until sharp, repetitive clicks at the far end abruptly broke his concentration. The clicking sound of high-heels on the terrazzo floor. He looked up to see a rather small woman, maybe 5-feet-4 or 5, coming toward him. She wore a white doctor's coat over a stylish high-neck blouse and skirt. She moved with quick, determined steps, right hand on the stethoscope tucked into the coat pocket, left arm swinging slightly at her side. The face was up-turned. A mane of light-auburn hair flowed behind. It was the woman he saw at the Wednesday staff meeting.

As she approached, he caught her eye and held her gaze for a few seconds. She formed a slight smile then looked away. As she passed, he could see a name embroidered on her coat in dark block letters. It was partly covered by the lapel, but he could read **Garriman, M.D**. She passed without interrupting rate or intensity of the heel-clicks. He pivoted slightly and watched until she reached the hospital lobby and disappeared. He continued on toward his office thinking how, for just those few seconds, the smile and the eyes eclipsed the professional *persona* with an aura of femininity so striking he could feel it.

He entered the deserted cardiology suite and stopped at the receptionist's desk picking up the medical center directory. He flipped it open to the G listings and quickly found Garriman. Only one was listed: Cassandra M. Garriman, M.D., Division of Infectious Disease, Department of Internal Medicine, Medical Office Building, Suite 342. Telephone, 758-3820; Fax 758-3893; email: CGarrison@BrakefieldMC.Org. He jotted the name and phone number on a notepad, tore off the page and slipped it into his shirt pocket, pleased with his sleuthing.

He closed up and started toward the garage again with the briefcase and a bundle of reprints to perhaps break the weekend monotony. He stopped by KFC for a chicken dinner to go and arrived at his apartment at 7:30 ready for a drink. He went into the kitchen, dropped the box of chicken, the briefcase and reprints on the counter and reached for the scotch. He poured into another plastic cup this time dropping in a couple of ice cubes from the somewhat abused plastic ice tray in the freezer and slowly climbed the stairs, cup in one hand, briefcase and reprints in the other.

It was 8:00, 7:00 in Dallas, he thought. Call now. The chicken can wait. He dropped the briefcase and reprints on the floor beside the dresser, sat on the bed and pressed the number into his cell phone as he sipped the scotch. A child's voice answered.

"Hi, Beth, honey. It's Daddy."

There was a short silence then, "Daddee!! Mommy, it' Daddy," came the excited, breathless words. "Where are you, Daddy?"

"I'm in Atlanta. I got here last weekend, but I've so been busy, this is the first chance I've had to call. I've got a new apartment, and I go to work every day just like…" he stopped himself. "It's really nice, but I sure do miss you guys."

"All of us, Daddy? Mommy, too?" The question hit hard.

"I miss all of you, Beth. I do." He could feel his voice give way slightly. "You know we talked about it though. You remember what Mommy and Daddy told you."

"I know, Daddy. Dr. Montgom'wy told us about that, too."

"Who's Dr. Montgomery?"

"She's this lady Mommy took us to…to talk about divorce and stuff." She tossed the words out so easily, it surprised him. "She says sometimes mommies and daddies don't love each other anymore and they just get divorced." It was painful to hear the way she said the words "they just get divorced" though he knew she didn't really understand what she was saying. "Dr. Montgom'wy said when that happens, it's better for the family instead of fussing all the time. But she says you and Mommy can still be fwiends, though." Her childish speech tugged at him. "Me and Amy and Carrie want you to be fwiends like Dr. Montgom'wy said, so you'll come see us soon."

"Well, sweetheart, of course I'd like for Mommy and me to be friends. And I want to come see you real soon. But right now, I have to stay here to work for a while. Maybe in a few weeks I can come."

"And you and Mommy can still be fwiends?"

"I hope so, honey."

"Okay, Daddy. Here's Amy. I love you, Daddy."

Amy's voice, more reserved, came on the phone. "Hello, Daddy. I hope you're doing okay." The words were measured.

"Hey, Amy. Yeah, I'm doing okay, but I sure do miss you all."

His words elicited no ploy from Amy to bring him back together with Lucy. "Okay, Daddy, well…..I'm glad you called. I love you. Here's Carrie." Her words were, to say the least, unenthusiastic, but her sudden abrupt end to that conversation was unexpected. Carrie came on the line and spoke briefly but made no mention of his coming to see them. She told him about her day at school and about her friend who was sick then turned the phone over to Lucy.

She spoke in cold, impersonal tones asking how he was, how he liked Atlanta and if he had a home phone number yet "in case we need to get in touch with you." He said he wouldn't be getting a land line, but he always had his cell phone with him. When he asked about Dr.

Montgomery, she said, in clipped words, "Under the circumstances, the girls needed some help understanding things. Dr. Montgomery is a clinical psychologist with the same pediatric group we've always gone to. She specializes in counselling for children. I chose her because I thought it would be best for the girls to talk to a woman. Anything else?"

No. He guessed not. He was just calling to say hello.

She responded only with, "Thanks for calling."

The line clicked off. He sat staring at his phone still in his hand, hearing the little voices in his head. He switched on the TV, sipped the scotch and laid back on the bed. The KFC dinner sat on the kitchen counter growing stale.

Restless dreams and the sounds of the TV woke him around 2:30. He reached for the remote and clicked it off. He lay for a few minutes still hearing the conversations with Lucy and the girls as they blasted finality into his head. He stood up and lifted the cup from the table. The scotch was watery and almost tasteless. He went down to the kitchen, dumped it and poured again, this time almost filling the cup. He took a big swallow and went back up.

He sat again on the edge of the bed staring at the cup, rolling it between his hands, slowly swirling the liquid as he thought: He *had* to pull himself together. Maybe put himself on an antidepressant. Watch his drinking. Control his urges. Forget about Miguel. He owed Reed a big debt for accepting him into the fellowship. No doubt, if he betrayed that confidence, his future would hang in the balance. He closed his eyes trying to dispel it all when, out of nowhere, his mind flashed to images of her face, her hair, her slight smile, the look in her eyes for those few seconds. He took a deep breath and more scotch then set the cup on the nightstand, lay back on the bed and drifted off again.

He woke about 7:30 Saturday morning. He went into the bathroom and splashed cold water on his face as he stared at himself in the mirror. "Get busy," he said in loud disdainful voice. In another 20 minutes, he showered, shaved and dressed and stood in the kitchen making coffee. No food here except the box of KFC. Breakfast would have to be somewhere else before the shopping.

CHAPTER NINE

By 10:00 that morning, Allen Kanaby passed the city limit sign as he drove into Gainesville. About 15 minutes later, thanks to his trusty GPS, he turned onto Loomis Street. It led through a neighborhood of modest, well-kept houses on narrow lots. He passed them slowly as he read house numbers. At 482, he pulled to a stop. To the right side of the house, a huge semi- truck rig sat in the driveway, one of those with the high cab and a pair of chrome exhaust pipes projecting upward on either side behind it. He got out and hurried up the short walkway and onto the narrow porch. He pressed the doorbell. Almost immediately the door opened, and a tall, handsome, smiling African American man, late 40s or so appeared.

"Allen Kanaby!!" the man exclaimed with a broad grin. "I cain't hardly b'lieve what I'm seein'. My wife told me you called."

He held out a big hand. "She said you might be comin' up here."

"Hello, Charles," said Allen as they shook. "After all this time it *is* hard to believe."

"Jus' le'me look at you," said Charles stepping back slightly. "I bet it's been more'n 30 years since I seen you. Come on in this house," Charles waved a welcoming arm toward the small living room. "Take a seat." He motioned to the two cushioned chairs and sofa furnishing the room. "Tha's my rig out there," he said proudly. "I'm independent, but I drive for a coupla long-distance haulers. One outa Atlanta and one up in Dalton. I was on a run up to Omaha is why I was gone when you called. I was sorry to hear about Mr. Kanaby."

"Thank you," said Allen, "and I know you're probably tired, so I won't take too much of your time, but as I told your wife, I wanted to talk to you because I think you might be able to help us."

"I'd be glad to if I can, but how you think that is?" said Charles in a sympathetic tone.

"It's kind of a long story. It has to do with when your dad used to work with my dad out at his place in Dunwoody."

Charles looked perplexed. "That was a long time ago."

"Yes, and I know your dad passed away some time back, but I'm hoping maybe you might have some memory of what I have to ask you about."

"Oh?"

"Let me give you a little background. Dad is 64. He's been in excellent health all his life, but this past Tuesday morning he woke up very confused. My mother took him to the doctor, and while he was in the doctor's office, he had a seizure. A big epileptic seizure. He never had any problem like that before, ever. But since then, he's been unconscious."

"Sounds bad," said Charles shaking his head.

"The doctors have done all kinds of tests, but they don't know what's caused it," said Allen. "First they thought he'd wake up after 24 hours, but he's been out for almost five days now. They say he has some serious damage to his brain. And one thing they're thinking is he might have been exposed to some kind of toxic chemical. Of course he's been working with chemicals all his life. You might remember he has a company in Marietta. A chemical company."

"Yeah. I do 'member that."

"They specialize in making pesticides. You know, like insecticides and different kinds of agricultural chemicals. When we told the doctors about all that, that's when they began to focus on toxic chemicals. And when we mentioned about Dad's garden and his greenhouse, they got real interested. They're thinking there could be something he was using with the plants. Maybe something toxic."

"But that wouldn't hardly be somethin' from way back when my daddy was workin' with him out there, you don't reckon?" asked Charles.

"I don't see how it could be," said Allen, "but I'm wondering if you ever heard your dad talk about any kind of chemicals or anything my dad might have used on his plants. Any special kind of, you know, mixtures or concoctions." Charles pursed his lips thoughtfully as Allen went on, "and did he ever have any kind of unusual sickness that you can remember?"

"Naw, he never did talk about no chemicals or nuthin' like that." Charles shook his head. "And he never had no kind o' sickness, least ways not 'til he had his first stroke."

"What was that like?"

Charles looked away for a moment then back. "It just come on him sudden like, a few months befo'e he died. Paralyzed his whole one side to where he couldn't move his arm and leg and couldn't talk neither. It was sad to see." He shook his head slowly. "Then, right befo'e he died, they said he had another stroke. He went unconscious and never woke up. They said that second one jus' killed his brain."

"And he never had any other kind of illness before that? Fainting, seizures, anything?"

"Naw, never did. He did have the high pressure. They said tha's what caused him to have strokes. But right up to when they found that, I mean the high pressure, he was always in good health."

Dead end, thought Allen. Go on to something else. "I remember Dad talking about how your dad knew so much about plants, raising seedlings, growing vegetables, all that. Did he ever talk about that?"

"Naw, not really. Never did talk about nuthin' like that. Oh, sometimes he'd talk 'bout things he learned from the ol' folks when he was growin' up over there on Wansaw. 'Bout how they use natch'l kind of stuff for fertilizin' and keepin' bugs off the corn and beans and things. Ol' African ways, they called it. He loved tellin' 'bout how it was back then. 'Bout his momma and daddy and his grandmomma, too. He always said she taught him a lot about the ol' natch'l ways." He smiled as his eyes brightened with nostalgia.

"Where did you say he grew up? "

"Over in South Carolina. A small little island close to Charleston. When he was 'round twenty o' so, he left and went to Charleston for work. Then later on, he came over here. But he'd go back ever' so often 'cause his momma and daddy was still livin' there. I went with him a coupla times myself when I was real young."

"When was that?"

"I can't 'member exactly," said Charles. "I think I was 'roun' 'bout eight the first time I went. His momma was still livin' then. Only other time I went there was when she passed. I guess I was 'bout eleven or twelve. I never went back again, but Daddy went back a few times after she passed. I think the last time was sometime in the late '70s o' early 80s."

"And you say it was an island where he grew up?" Allen said.

"Yeah. They called it Wansaw. W-A-N-S-A-W. Wansaw Island. Real small. Daddy always said it was one of them islands where there was a lotta black folks after the war. You know, the Civil War. After they was freed. Apparently a whole lot of'em was left on all them islands and lived out there. But the real small ones didn't have so many people. Daddy said Wansaw was like that. Said it was so little and so far out in the ocean, it wasn't no good for growin' no big crops. People just thought it was useless. He said wasn't nobody ever livin' on Wansaw befo'e his people went there. They set up like a little village. Once they was livin' out there, nobody bothered'em 'cause it was so far out and so small. He said he loved it out there, and he hated to leave. The reason why he did leave was 'cause there wasn't nuthin' there for young folks. He couldn't see no future in stayin'.

"When we was little," Charles continued, "my sister and me, we'd always be wantin' him to tell about how it was. He said the ol' folks claimed it was like Africa, an' they didn't never want it to change. Different ways of doin' things. Special ways of raisin' animals, growin' little crops, curin' sickness. He said the ol' folks passed it all down, one generation to next. Even the way they talked. Like they had their own language. Gullah is what they called it."

"Was he born there?" said Allen.

"Yeah. Accordin' to him, 'round 1908," said Charles. "I 'member because he claimed to be 87 in 1995. That was a year before he died. His grandaddy and grandmomma, they was reg'lar slaves. No more'n 10 or 12 years old when they was freed after the war. Tha's when they went to Wansaw.. But his daddy and momma they was born on Wansaw in the 1880s is what he said."

"So after your dad stopped going there, did he keep up with anybody there?"

"He never talked about anybody bein' there in his last years. A few times I 'member him sayin' the old folks was just dyin' out and the young folks was leavin'. He said life was so hard out there. No 'lectricity. Nowhere to get food except what they could grow right there. Or catch fish. Plenty o' fish from the ocean. Anything else they needed, they'd have to wait for the steamboat to come by to take'em to Charleston. It came by just a few times a month, accordin' to Daddy. Then there was the storms. You know, hurricanes. There was one real bad one. He said it was in the early '50s. Even drowned some people. Daddy went back to see 'bout his momma. He said after that, mo'e and mo'e people started leavin'. That was befo'e I was born, but I 'member later on, the times I went there with Daddy, there wasn't many people. That last time, when his momma passed. They had a little funeral jus' right up to the grave. Folks standin' around. Some singin'. Strange songs like I never heard. African songs I guess. Then they covered up the grave, and that was all to it."

"How did his mother die?"

"Oh, she was real old, too. Daddy said she lived to be 96. He said it was a stroke, but he said some people claimed it was the *hags* that took her. Daddy said that was just superstition, but 'course his momma, she believed in all that stuff. In fact, she used to wear a little bag o' herbs tied on a string around her neck to keep the hags off. Daddy called it ass—feddy (*asofoedita*)....or somethin' like that. I don't know exactly what it was, but I can tell you it smelled *awful*." He grimaced and shook his head as if he could smell it again. "It woulda kept anything off."

"What did he mean, the hags took her?" said Allen, his interest now piqued.

"Evil spirits."

"When did you say your dad left Wansaw?"

"Sometime 'round 1930," said Charles. "Like I said, he went to Charleston to work for a while then he came over here to Atlanta when he was 'bout 25. Worked in a warehouse for a good while. Saved up some money, and after a few years, he bought a little piece of land out from Alpharetta. About ten acres. Back then it was real hard for black folks to own any kinda land. But he managed to hold on to what he had. He kept on workin' the warehouse, and when he got enough money together, him and Momma they built a little house out there. We moved out there, and me and my sister, we went to school in Bayteel. Not much of a school. Jes' only black kids, but Momma said she was gonna make sure we got educated. We went to school ever' day on a bus."

As Charles began to ramble, Allen wanted to bring him back to the island conversation. "Anything else you remember about the island?"

"Nothin' really," said Charles, "but I was there only jes' two times."

"What about the place itself, how it looked?" Allen asked.

"Oh, jes' little cabins kinda grouped together. Like a little village. Daddy used to call it a settlement."

"What did he tell you about what you called African ways?"

"Jes' they had special ways of growing little crops. Raisin' animals," Charles went on, "an' special ways o' curin' sickness. But he did love tellin' about the ghosts and spirits folks claimed was there. He'd tell us some o' them stories and throw back his head and laugh 'cause it would scare us so." Charles burst into a deep bellow of a laugh, at that point entertaining himself, but stopping abruptly. "Now I do 'member him tellin' about somethin' real strange happenin' after a big hurricane. He said awhile afterward, some people took sick sudden-like and died in jes' a few days. He wasn't there, but he heard about it. He said what they told him was when people took sick, they couldn't talk. Didn't know nobody. Jes' fell out in fits and couldn' breathe. They said it was the hags ridin 'em an' suckin' the wind out of 'em. An' nobody could save 'em."

Allen was stunned as he processed what he was hearing: *Took sick sudden-like. Couldn't talk. Didn't know anybody. Fell out in fits. Couldn't breathe. Died in a few days.*

"That was back in the '50s, but Daddy said back around 1940 after another big hurricane, same thing happened. He said so many people died back then, they called it....the dyin' time."

"The dyin' time?" said Allen, incredulous at what he was hearing. "So if that really happened, maybe it had something to do with the hurricanes."

"Coulda been I guess," said Charles. "All Daddy said was nobody knew what caused it."

"You think there's anyone there now who might remember those times?"

"Nobody livin' there now," said Charles shaking his head.

Allen was frustrated. There seemed to be no more information to be gained from Charles. He glanced at his watch. "I should've been checking the time," he said. "It's past noon. I've taken to much of your time, and I've gotta get back to Atlanta." He stood. "Guess I'm just trying to find something that could give us a clue. Something about the gardens or the greenhouse. Doesn't seem very likely. But that sickness on the island…" His voice trailed off in an inquisitive inflection shaking his head. "I really appreciate you talking to me, Charles. If you think of anything else, please call me." He stood and handed Charles a business card.

"I will," said Charles. "I sure wish I could tell you somethin' to help."

As he moved toward the door, Allen said, "I'm glad we could meet," he said. "Makes me feel sorta reconnected to your family after so many years. Especially since Dad and your dad were such good friends."

"Tha's right,' said Charles, "they really was. Good friends. Always seemed like they enjoyed bein' together workin' out there all those years. Don't see that much anymore. Ever'body's too caught up in their own ways."

"Yeah. It's sad to say." Allen nodded.

Charles put a hand on Allen's shoulder. "Now you let me know how he gets on." He opened the door.

"I will. Thanks," said Allen.

*****

At 1:30, Allen turned into the driveway. He parked beside the garage and went through the back door. Ellen was busy making lunch. She greeted him with a quick kiss. "Martha called a little while ago. Says things are the same. She's with your mom now. They were at the hospital this morning, and they're going back at four. She wants you to call her." She set a plate of sandwiches on the table. "What'd you find out in Gainesville?"

"It's Mose's son, all right," he said.

"And?" she pressed.

"He had a lotta stories about Mose and where he grew up on this island in South Carolina near Charleston. And about how Mose eventually came to Atlanta. But he didn't know anything about Dad and Mose working together. I was hoping Mose might have passed something on to him, you know, about plants and growing things. Maybe something about those secret mixtures Dad used to talk about. But he said Mose never talked about any of that. Said Mose just called it African ways of doin' things." Allen pulled out a chair and sat beside the table. "Apparently Mose's grandmother taught him about African ways and what he called the old, natural ways." He paused. "And think about how far back that goes if Mose's grandmother died in the 1960s and she was 96. Apparently. Mose claimed his grandmother and grandfather went to that island when they were just youngsters. As freed slaves. Only 10 years old or so. Charles said he went there a couple of times himself with Mose. He was just a kid, but he seemed to remember some things about it." Allen stretched and yawned.

"You must be tired," said Ellen. "Let's have lunch. Then you take a nap."

"I'm okay." He looked up at her. "But there is one thing he told me that's really got me wondering. He said Mose used to talk about something that happened after a hurricane on the island. He said it was in the 1950s. I don't know if the grandmother was there then, but apparently lot of people on that island got sick. The way he described it, it sounded exactly like Dad. Said they couldn't talk, didn't recognize anyone. Couldn't breathe. They all had seizures. …he said fits….and they died….quickly."

"Darling, how could that possibly have anything to do with your dad now?" said Ellen.

"I know it sounds impossible, but I can't get it out of my mind. I mean, Mose growing up there in such an isolated place. A sickness there so similar to Dad's, and him working with Dad all that time. Just seems too strange to be a coincidence. I don't know how there could be a connection, but that's what I keep wondering about."

"You said he told you it was more than 50 years ago." She sounded exasperated, but trying to be sympathetic she said, "Where exactly is this island anyway?"

"I told you. South Carolina. Near Charleston."

"What name?" said Ellen.

"Wansaw. Wansaw Island. W-A-N-S-A-W."

"Anything like that ever happen there before?" she asked.

"Yes," said Allen. "Charles said Mose told him it happened after hurricane in the 1940s too."

"So if you seriously think there's some kind of a link," she said, "maybe you should tell Dr. Holleran. In fact, I definitely think you should."

"So what should I tell him...and he wouldn't think I'm nuts?"

"Tell him what you just told me."

"Yeah, well," he said vaguely, "it *is* pretty far-fetched. And that's all the information I have. Maybe I could find out more if I could find somebody over there to talk to."

"Allen, you don't even know where over *there* is," she said. "You have to find where the island is before you can find somebody ... over there, as you say."

"I just told you where it is," he said impatiently. "I'll find it."

"Okay. Then what?"

"See if I can find people who know something about what Charles told me. Or maybe some kind of records."

The children came into the kitchen and sat silently at the table as Allen continued. "I just keep thinking there could be some clue in what Charles told me. Something that might help before it's too late…if it's not already too late." He looked at the floor nodding dejectedly. Ellen set four glasses of iced tea on the table and sat.

After lunch, Allen tried to nap on the den sofa, but his mind churned, and he couldn't rest. A little before 3:00, he called Martha. He said he'd been to see Charles Funchess, and he'd fill her in later. She and Evelyn were waiting for him in the 3rd floor conference room at the hospital when he arrived. They chatted briefly, and he told them about Charles's description of the illness on Wansaw, cautiously speculating about a connection to Richard's illness.

Evelyn was silent. Martha said, "How would we ever know?"

They all proceeded quietly to Richard's room for the afternoon visit. Richard, lying motionless and unresponsive, struggled with deep, labored breaths. They stood by the bed for a full minute, each silently pondering the futility of what they were seeing. Then with no words, they walked back into the corridor.

CHAPTER TEN

Blaine's Saturday shopping had gone more smoothly than he'd expected. At a department store near BestBuy, he picked out a set of glasses, a set of sturdy dishes and matching bowls, four bath towels in a rich brown color, two sets of sheets, two blankets, a couple of down pillows and finally an okay-looking lamp for the bedside table. At a furniture store in the same shopping center, he found a comfortable upholstered chair for the bedroom and a floor lamp which the salesman suggested would be good beside the chair. They could deliver both by late afternoon, so a little after 2:00, he dropped into Burger King for a quick lunch then tackled the only thing left, the grocery shopping. That certainly lived up to his expectations as an onerous nuisance, but by 3:30, he was back at his apartment.

He put everything away in short order: Groceries, glasses and dishes in the kitchen and sheets, towels, blankets and table lamp up to the bedroom. The chair and floor lamp arrived a little after 5:00. The chair fit perfectly in the corner of the bedroom, and the salesman was right, the floor lamp was great beside it. He thanked the delivery guy and tipped him as he left.

He was glad to be done and ready to settle in. He glanced at his watch. 5:45. He began to feel relaxed as he sat in the new chair. But oh, the thought of how he would fill the next 36 empty hours. At least he had the reading to do. He picked up his briefcase, laid it on the bed and pulled out the thick bundle of reprints. There was more than enough to occupy at least half the time until Monday morning. He separated the papers into three piles then he went down to the kitchen and poured himself a generous scotch. As he poured, it occurred to him, he hadn't thought about it all day. Maybe he could find out something. Nursing the scotch, he went back upstairs, picked up his cell phone and punched in 411.

"Welcome to directory assistance. City and state please," came the computer voice.

"Atlanta, Georgia."

"Please hold for an operator." There was a pause then a live voice.

"What is your listing?

"Cassandra M..Garriman. G-A-R-R-I-M-A-N."

"A residence or business?"

"Residence."

"No listing for Cassandra M. Garriman in the Atlanta Metropolitan Area."

"How about Dr. Cassandra Garriman?"

"Would that be a business listing?"

"Yes."

"Here's your listing." Then the automatic voice again, "For the number and more information, please press one." He pressed. The voice said, "Area code 770-758-3820." That was a Brakefield number. No home phone listed. He clicked off. Maybe she liked her privacy. Or maybe if she were married, a home listing might be under a different name. But she didn't look married, he thought, as he sipped the Scotch again and picked up a reprint.

By 8:00, he had read 10 more papers making notes as he went. Time for a little dinner. Another one of those frozen things. He went down to the kitchen and took out the first package from the freezer stack. "Chicken Piccata" the box colorfully announced. He microwaved it, stirred it and poured another scotch. The chicken was bland, almost tasteless, but it was filling and the scotch made it bearable. He finished it mechanically and went back up for more reading. After another two hours, he dropped the paper he was reading on his lap and leaned against the back of the chair. Cassandra Garriman. Nice name, he thought. He mouthed the words in a whisper as the face flashed into his mind.

He glanced at his watch. 11:08. Still at least another 30 hours before this weekend was over. He could feel himself sliding back into the abyss of his loneliness. Oh, the sooner he could get out this apartment and back to that office, the sooner things would be better. But maybe right now, a little hit would help him through. Pick him up. Focus his concentration. And after that, he could sleep. So he really *wasn't* ready to forget about Miguel…or Mr. Alcon yet.

CHAPTER ELEVEN

Richard remained unconscious through the night and into Sunday morning. Allen, Martha and Evelyn came in at 11:00 for a short time after which Martha and Evelyn returned to the Kanaby house for lunch, and Allen went home for lunch with Ellen and the kids. At a little after 3:30, his cell phone rang. It was Martha. "Dr. Holleran just called. He says Dad's breathing is much worse. Mom wants to go back right away."

"Okay," replied Allen, "I'll meet you at the nurses' station."

When he stepped out of the elevator, he saw Martha and Evelyn standing against the wall talking to a young doctor, one he'd never seen. As he approached, Martha came toward him.

"What's happening?" he said.

"It's really bad," she said. "Dr. Holleran was here about 30 minutes ago. They want to put Daddy on a respirator," she said, "but he says it's our decision." Her voice weakened.

"It's a no-brainer," said Allen sharply. "They've *got* to do it. Let me talk to the doctor." He turned toward Evelyn and the doctor and walked forward holding out his hand. "Hi, I'm Allen Kanaby."

"Yes, Sir. I'm Dr. Shelton." They shook. "I'm the neurology resident. We're just discussing the…."

"I know. My sister told me. Yes! We want a respirator if that's what he needs to keep him alive. We don't know what the problem is yet, so why should we *not* keep him alive. We're not God!" Allen's words exploded from him. The two women backed away, wide-eyed. Allen didn't let up. "Call whoever you need to call. Tell'em we want that *godamn respirator* right away."

"Okay, Mr. Kanaby. Certainly. Excuse me for a moment," said Dr. Shelton turning toward the nurses' station.

Allen looked at Martha and Evelyn standing stunned and silent. "Have you seen Dr. Holleran?" he said.

"No," said Martha, "but that young doctor says he'll be coming back by shortly. When he called me, he said the breathing is really unusual. They think it's related to the brain damage rather than the lungs. He says there's no pneumonia. They did another chest x-ray a little while ago. He says he's never seen anything like this. And the neurologists say the same. They think the respirator will be necessary until...."

"Until what, Martha?" Allen snapped as his frustration broke through again. "Until they can think about it some more? Is *that* what they want? The man is dying. They don't know why and furthermore, they don't know what to do about it."

"Hold on, Allen." Martha's voice became stronger.

"Will you two please stop. I can't stand it." Evelyn's voice wavered as she tried to end the confrontation.

"I know, Mom. Let's go in here." Martha put her arm around Evelyn's shoulder and guided her into the conference room. "Allen, you're not helping. We've got to do what Dr. Holleran says." She pulled out a chair for Evelyn.

Allen followed them. "I'm sorry, Mom," he said. "We're all on edge. I guess all we can do now is get that respirator going and wait." He looked at Martha. "Have you been in to see him yet?"

"Yes. Just before you got here."

"Okay. I want to go in for a few minutes," he said. "You mind waiting here?"

"No. We'll wait," said Martha.

He went back into the corridor. Stopping at the cart beside the door to 306N, he gowned, masked and gloved and entered the room. Richard's sheet-covered body lay motionless, eyes closed, breaths irregular and sputtering. Allen thought of Charles's description of people on that island. He wondered if they looked like this when they were dying.

The silence was broken by the clatter of cart wheels in the corridor. It stopped just outside the room where two scrub-clad men quickly garbed, pushed the door open and rolled in a large stainless-steel box with its array of dials and gauges and tubes. Allen lifted Richard's hand and held it for a moment then laid it on the sheet and walked out into the corridor. He removed the cap, mask and gown, the shoe covers and last, the gloves, tossed them into the hamper and returned to the conference room.

The women stood as he entered. He took Martha's right hand into his left and put his right arm around Evelyn's shoulders looking down at her fragile, exhausted face. "It looks pretty bad, Mom." She leaned toward him. His arm tightened around her. She looked up and nodded.

"I think we should go home now, Mom," said Martha. "They'll call us if there's any change."

"I'm going to stay a while longer," said Allen, "in case Dr. Holleran comes back."

"Okay." Martha leaned up and pecked him on the cheek.

He bent slightly and kissed Evelyn's forehead. As the women left, he walked to the window and stared out across the hospital lawn. He began to pace slowly toward the door, back to the window, back toward the door, his anxiety building. He walked out to the nurses' station and spoke to the woman seated there. "You know if Dr. Holleran is coming back?"

"Oh, yes sir," she responded "He was just here. He's in Mr. Kanaby's room."

"Thank you." Allen turned and walked away quickly. The door to 306N was closed, but he could hear a rhythmic whooshing sound inside as the respirator relentlessly pressed breath into Richard's lifeless body.

The door opened and Joe came out. He looked surprised. "Oh hello, Allen. I didn't expect to see you."

"We came back when you called my sister. That young doctor, Shelton I think he said. He was here. He explained about the respirator. After they brought it in, Mom and Martha left. But he said you'd be back so I waited. I wanted to talk to you a bit." He fumbled the words while Joe removed the disposable garb.

"He seems a little more relaxed," said Joe. "Not struggling as much, and his color is better now."

"That's good to hear," said Allen. "He was definitely struggling."

"Let's go to the conference room," said Joe. "I'll explain what I think is going on." He led the way. "I just spoke with the neurologist. They repeated the chest x-ray about noon." They sat at the table as he continued. "There is still almost no sign of congestion and no evidence of any other abnormality. The problem seems to be in the part of the brain that controls his breathing. That's why the respirator should give him the support he needs."

"But how long can that go on?" said Allen.

"We don't know. It could be quite some time, but it's important to keep his lungs clear and be sure he's being well-oxygenated."

"So we just sit by and wait?" Allen said with a hint of impatience.

Joe picked up on Allen's tone. "Yes. And try to prevent any more seizures or any infection while we're searching for a cause."

"I understand," said Allen. "We know you're doing all you can. But what I wanted to talk to you about is something I've just learned that might shed some light."

"Oh?" Joe's curiosity was piqued.

"My sister said you wanted us to try to locate the family of the man who used to work with Dad in the gardens. His name was Mose

Funchess. I was able to locate his son Charles. He lives in Gainesville. I drove up there yesterday to talk to him. Tried to find out if he knew anything about any chemicals or such that they may have used in the gardens back when his father was working with Dad."

"Did he?" said Joe.

"He didn't know anything about chemicals, but what he told me got my attention. It seems so strange though, I feel a bit reluctant to tell you about it, but my wife insisted I should."

"Please don't hesitate. I'm ready to hear anything that might give us some answers."

"Well I don't know what to make of it. It's certainly not what I was expecting. Charles told me that Mose used to talk about an illness...he called it a sickness...on an island off the coast of South Carolina where he grew up. It sounded exactly like Dad's illness."

"How so?"

"According to Mose, shortly after a hurricane on the island in the early 1950s several people—-he didn't know how many—suddenly got sick and died. He said they were confused, couldn't speak, couldn't breathe...and had seizures and died very quickly."

"Do you think that could be related to your dad's illness?" Joe sounded skeptical, but he wanted to be empathetic.

"I don't know, but it sounded so much like...the same thing," said Allen. "It was a shock to hear the description and that it happened where Mose grew up. Thinking about Mose and Dad working together for so long, I couldn't help but wonder if there might be some kind of connection. Something here and something there, but I have no idea what."

"You say this happened in the 1950s?" said Joe.

"Yes, according to Charles," said Allen.

"Seems to be a sad coincidence, but I think any kind of connection would be extremely unlikely," said Joe. "If what Charles told you is true, that was more 50 years ago. I can't see how there could be any relationship to your dad's illness."

"Okay, well, so as I said, I was reluctant to tell you about it," said Allen," but I wanted to see what you might think. I guess you just told me.

"I'm not saying there absolutely could not be a link," Joe replied, "but I'm saying it seems a very remote possibility. Did he know if anything like that has happened since?"

"No, but he did say Mose told him it happened earlier, like sometime in the 1940s."

Sensing Allen's frustration and despair Joe said, "Unfortunately we don't have much time to check into all that, but I can try to make some contacts tomorrow. See if there are any records of what that might have been. What's the name of this island?"

"Wansaw Island," said Allen. "W-A-N-S-A-W. In South Carolina…near Charleston."

Joe jotted the word on his pocket pad. "Got it," he said. "Maybe the health department in Charleston would be a place to start."

CHAPTER TWELVE

It was a palpable relief for Blaine when the alarm sounded at 6:00 Monday morning: to get up, get dressed, get out of his miserable apartment and back to his office. Richard had remained unconscious throughout the night. But in spite of respirator support, his heart rate had become more irregular, pulse thready, blood pressure unstable. At about 9:45, he slipped away. The resident who pronounced his death notified Joe Holleran as well as Dave Dittrich and Andreas Locanos. Joe interrupted his morning appointments and went up to the floor. He quickly gowned, gloved and masked and entered the room.

Richard's body lay completely covered by a sheet. Joe pulled it away from the head and chest and studied the pale, gaunt face then lifted a wrist and automatically felt for a pulse. He laid it back on the bed, slowly pulled the sheet up again and returned to the nurses' station. Andreas was standing at the desk.

"I'll contact the son," said Joe. "I think it's best for him to tell Mrs. Kanaby rather than my calling her. I want to be sure he understands how important it is to have an autopsy, and most important, to examine the brain. I've discussed it with Dr. McCants in Pathology. He spoke to the neuropathologist out at the Hefner Cantrell Institute, Dr. Lang. He's willing to do the autopsy and all the neuropath studies. McCants said to let him know and he'd make the arrangements with Lang. Getting the brain is imperative."

"We want to look at the lungs, too, Dr. Holleran," said Andreas. "That's been a real puzzle. Lungs were still clear as late as last evening on plain film even though he couldn't breathe on his own."

"Of course," said Joe. "I've discussed that with Dr. McCants. It can be a limited autopsy, but we definitely need to get heart and lungs as well as brain."

*****

Allen Kanaby had just returned to his office from a 9:00 meeting when the secretary put the call through. "Hello, Mr. Kanaby. Dr. Holleran."

"Hello, Doctor."

"I'm calling to tell you…your dad passed away about 9:45." Joe spoke slowly wanting to be gentle. "I'm calling you first because I thought it might be better for you to notify your mom and your sister than for me to call them."

There was a momentary silence then Allen spoke, "Thank you, Doctor. We were expecting it," his voice broke slightly. He took a breath. "I can let…them know…right away." He paused again then said, "Please tell me…was the end…easy for him? I mean… peaceful? "

"Yes, very peaceful," said Joe.

"Did he have any more seizures?"

"No."

"We all knew he couldn't last much longer," Allen continued, "but it's still hard to deal with when it begins to sink in that..…he's gone."

"Of course," said Joe, "I understand. And it'll be especially hard for your mom."

"Yes."

"Please explain why I didn't call them directly," said Joe. "And please be sure they understand how important it is to have an autopsy. I know it's a delicate issue especially for your mom. You have to be gentle but firm about it. It is so important."

"Yes.," said Allen, "we've talked to Mom about it. She does resist."

"I would like for all of you to come back to the hospital as soon as possible today so we can make the arrangements. I'll explain everything when you get here. If you think a phone call to her would help after you've told her, I'll be glad to…"

"I think we can deal with it. When do you want us to come?"

"I would say early afternoon if possible," said Joe. "Just call my office and tell them what time would be good for you."

"I will," Allen replied.

He hung up and sat quietly for a moment then dialed Martha. "Hey. Where's Mom?"

"She's getting dressed to come back to the hospital."

"Listen. Dr. Holleran just called me. Dad passed away at 9:45."

"Oh. You mean just," her voice waivered.

"Yes. Can you tell Mom or do you want to wait till I get there?" He heard rapid footsteps in the background then Evelyn's voice.

"Who is it, Martha? Is that Allen?" Her words were intense and anxious.

Martha continued speaking into the phone but now trying to give Allen a coded answer to his question. "Yes, okay, Allen, I understand. Please check on Dad. We'll be here a while longer."

Allen understood. She wanted to wait until he arrived to tell Evelyn.

With a quick explanation to the secretary, he hurried to his car. Within 5 minutes, he was on the expressway. In another 15, he was pulling into the driveway. Joe Holleran's words filled his mind: "I'm calling to tell you…your dad passed away about 9:45…your dad passed away…"

He parked at the back of the house and got out, standing for a moment and gazing around in a broad sweep. Signs of his father were everywhere. The tool shed, the upturned wheel-barrow, the garden cart, the greenhouse and stacks of empty plastic pots and trays beside the entrance, the mulch pile and beyond, on all sides, the neatly laid flowerbeds and brilliant azalea hedges. He closed his eyes and pressed a finger over his tight-lipped mouth trying to quell a sudden wave of emotion. Then taking a deep breath, he turned and walked to the house.

When he came through the kitchen door, he found Martha and Evelyn sitting at the breakfast table each holding a steaming cup of tea. Martha stood. Evelyn did not move, silently studying Allen's face and anticipating what he would say.

"Hi, Mom." He walked toward the table. "How're you doin'?"

"He's dead isn't he, Allen?" She spoke in a calm, slightly bitter tone, her eyes fixed on his.

He put his hand on her shoulder and said, "Yes. He is Mom. Just a little while ago."

She reached for his hand and squeezed it. "I knew it," she said. "I had a feeling when we left yesterday." Martha came close and bent down with a gentle embrace as Evelyn bowed her head and began to sob with weak, muffled sounds.

"Dr. Holleran called me at the office about 10:30," said Allen. "He said he thought it would be better for me to tell you than for him to call you. He wants us to come back to the hospital so we can make some arrangements as soon as possible this afternoon."

She looked up suddenly. "Arrangements? What kind of arrangements? Can't the funeral home do that?"

"No. It's not that simple, Mom." Allen braced. "There are some papers to sign."

"Papers? You mean about that autopsy thing don't you?" Evelyn's voice strengthened.

"Yes, Mom. It has to be done. I know it's a hard, but I don't think we have a choice." He was trying to be sensitive, but he had to convince her. "It's the only way they can find out what was wrong and if it's something that might be dangerous to us or somebody else. That's why it's so important."

"Oh, Allen, no. No, I can't bear it. He was so sick. Why can't we just let him be at peace, Allen?" Evelyn leaned over and buried her face in her arms folded on the table. Martha put a hand on her shoulder.

Allen was silent letting the intensity of the moment pass. "Mom," he said, "I know how you feel. It's hard to face. You've got to realize he *is* at peace now, but we still have to know why he died. Dr. Holleran says the only way is to do some studies on his brain to see if they can determine what happened to him."

"On his *brain*. Oh, Dear God!"

"He wants to explain it to us," Allen said quietly. "He wants us to meet him in his office."

Evelyn drew a stuttering breath. "Oh, Allen. Not his *brain*. Oh, my precious Richard." Her voice pitched up in a child-like wail and broke. "What will they do to you?"

"Mom," said Martha, "just take a breath." She pulled a chair up beside Evelyn and sat stroking her shoulder and holding her hand. "It's a painful thought, but like Allen said, he's at peace now. No more suffering. And you know he would want us to know what caused this. I'm sure Dr. Holleran will explain exactly what has to be done...so you'll understand how important it is, Mom."

"I know, but it's so hard, Martha. It's so hard." Her hand trembled as Martha held it.

"I'll call Dr. Holleran and tell him we can be there in about an hour," said Allen. "Can we do that?"

Evelyn nodded as he crossed the room to the kitchen wall phone. Drawing a slip of paper from his pocket, he dialed and waited in silence. "Hello, this is Allen Kanaby. I'm calling for Dr. Holleran. He's expecting my call. Thank you." He paused. "Hello, Dr. Holleran, Allen Kanaby. I'm here with Mom and my sister." Pause. "Yes, about 1:00?" He glanced at Evelyn. She nodded. "Okay. That's fine. Your office."

At 12:45, they drove into the Brakefield garage. When they arrived at the reception area for Joe's office, the receptionist directed them to a small conference room midway down the hall. "Dr. Holleran is just finishing up," she said. "If you'll have a seat, he'll be with you in just a few minutes. Can I get you anything? Water? Cokes?"

"No thanks," said Allen. "We're fine."

She exited and closed the door. After few more minutes, the door opened and Joe entered. He looked at them with a sympathetic expression as he walked to Evelyn and took her hand.

"We did all we could, Mrs. Kanaby," he said. "He was very sick." He stood for a moment more then let her hand go and sat at the end of the table. "This has been a very difficult time for all of us... ..including me. As I said earlier, I hope you know how much I thought of him. And I think you know how concerned and puzzled we, I mean all the doctors, have been in spite of all we did to try to find out what it was." He looked first at Evelyn, then Allen, then Martha. "We know it was not cancer. Not a stroke. Nothing abnormal about biochemical substances in his blood and all the other lab studies. I think you recall we talked about that when you brought him to my office. All the tests for...."

Evelyn tuned out. She had heard all this before. Last Monday, exactly a week ago, the same words about lab studies and cancer and a stroke and brain waves and that electro- something and on and on. Why was he going over it all again? She forced herself back to what he was saying.

"You know we've talked about the possibility of some kind of infection, even a very rare infection, but there is no evidence of that. And we've talked about exposure to some sort of toxic substance. But so far there's no evidence of that either."

His words seemed to Evelyn to be leading nowhere.

"He didn't respond to any of the medicines except the seizure medication. And even though the records show he had only the one seizure, we know he developed severe brain damage very quickly. And it was irreversible." Evelyn listened stoically until she heard, "The only way we can find out what the brain damage was. or what caused it. is to carry out an examination of the brain." She cringed.

She knew she had to be strong and rational, but she could not hold back. She had to speak. She had to know why this was so important? Why should they do this to her beloved Richard? Why? She spoke with a strong tone, "What do you think you can find if you do this… this examination you want to do to poor Richard's brain?"

"I know this is very difficult for you, Mrs. Kanaby," said Joe, "but I want you to understand that if we can see exactly what and where the damage is in the brain, we may be able to determine what the cause was."

"So what difference does it make now…..if you do what you're talking about?" said Evelyn, suddenly aggressive and almost belligerent.

Allen and Martha Ann looked at each other surprised.

"Well," said Joe trying to be gentle, "we do know that some of the parts of his brain were severely damaged, but we still don't know what kind of damage. If we can determine exactly where and to what extent, we should be able to find out a lot more about the cause." He paused. "And if it might be something that could affect other people, knowing more about could help save lives"

Allen spoke up. "Dr. Holleran, we've discussed it. We know how important it is and we know it has to be done. So we want you to go ahead with whatever arrangements you have to make."

Joe looked at Evelyn who was now silent and stoic once more.

"Okay," said Joe, "I appreciate your willingness to let this go forward." She stared straight ahead as he continued. "We've talked to the Hefner-Cantrell Institute. Have you heard of it?" He said glancing quickly at each of them.

"Yes, but I don't know anything about it."

"It's out on the Old Buford Highway," Joe continued. "It's a private research institute. An absolutely state-of-the-art kind of place. They have two doctors there who work exclusively in the area of brain diseases. They are called neuropathologists." The words didn't impress Evelyn, but she continued to listen. "They do a lot of research in the area of diseases that cause dementia and degeneration of the brain. Dr. Dittrich spoke to one of them about Mr. Kanaby last Thursday. Dr. Stephen Lang. He agreed that the symptoms and the course were extremely unusual and did not fit the pattern of any neurological disease he could clearly identify. But it seemed closest to either a very unusual infection or some toxic exposure." He paused. "I spoke to him just a little while ago. He's willing to come here later this afternoon to do the necessary procedures for the examination." Evelyn closed her eyes and tightened her lips as he continued. "I told him I would contact him when we finished our discussion here to let him know whether he should plan to come this evening. Can you all agree to that?"

"Okay. Yes." Evelyn spoke, now with a tone of resignation.

"We agree. You have some papers to sign?"

"Yes," said Joe. "I can get those in a few minutes. I just wanted to be sure you all understand. You have any questions?"

"Yes, Dr. Holleran, we do," Martha Ann spoke. "What about the funeral plans? I mean, do we have to wait for some reason?"

"What plans do you have?"

"He always said he wanted to be cremated," said Martha Ann.

"That's right," Evelyn nodded.

"I think that would be the best way," said Joe. "And there is no delay once the procedure is finished. I'll get the permission form for you to sign. Excuse me for a moment." He left the room. As he had requested, the pathology department had faxed the form to the receptionist. She'd left it on his desk. He picked it up and returned to the conference room. "I'd like for all of you to read over these few paragraphs then you can sign where I've marked, Mrs. Kanaby." He pointed. "I'll fill in the details at the top. Date of birth, age, medical record number, all that."

In only a few minutes, it was done. They all stood. Joe put a hand on Evelyn's shoulder. "He was a wonderful man," he said gently. "Nancy and I were very fond of him. Please let me know your plans for a service. We'd like to be there."

Evelyn reached an arm around his big frame and looked up at him. "Thank you, Doctor," she whispered and pulled her arm away.

The three of them walked out silently as Joe stood back watching.

CHAPTER THIRTEEN

At 4:30, Dr. Stephen Lang, a lanky silver-haired man with a serious expression and an autocratic air, pushed the double doors open and strode into the autopsy room at Brakefield Hospital. It was a large square space with a gray stain-resistant floor, stark white walls and painfully bright overhead fluorescent lights. Four bonneted spotlights hung above two long, stainless steel autopsy tables parallel to each other in the center of the room. Above one end of either table a metal scale and scale pan were suspended, and a curved-neck faucet with retractable water-spray nozzle rose from each table beneath the scale pan. Above the center of either table hung a small microphone.

Just to the right of the double doors there was a metal desk holding a computer screen and keyboard and a telephone. Standing against the right wall, a stainless steel refrigerator and two upright freezers hummed quietly. On the wall to the left, there was a metal counter, cabinets above and below, two deep wall-hung steel sinks and a large floor-mounted porcelain basin with attached flushing apparatus. The back wall held an imposing plaque about six feet long and a foot wide mounted at eye level. Against its black surface, bold gold letters proclaimed in Latin:

HIC EST UBI MORTUI VIVO VIRTAM DOCENT
(This is the place where the dead teach the living about life)

As Lang entered, two gowned, gloved and masked autopsy assistants were transferring the sheet-covered body of Richard Kanaby from a gurney onto one of the autopsy tables. "Good evening, gentlemen. I'll be right with you," said Lang in a somewhat authoritative tone as he disappeared into the locker room. One assistant pulled the sheet away to reveal the torso loosely draped with a white hospital gown. He then pulled the gown away and dropped it and the sheet into a nearby orange plastic tub marked BIOHAZARD while the other man rolled the Gurney away and pushed an instrument cart up to the head-end of the table.

Lang re-entered the room wearing a white paper jumpsuit. At the bank of shelves to the right of the door, he took out a pair of paper shoe covers and a plastic apron and put them on, then picked up a paper cap, a face mask and two pairs of rubber gloves and moved to the desk. He laid the gloves and face mask on the desk, put the cap on and picked up the medical chart. "Let's double check the toe-tag," he said to the assistants as he opened the chart. The man held the tag up as Lang walked to the table.

"Okay. Thanks." He went back to the desk and sat, beginning to examine the chart. Momentarily, Joe Holleran came through the entrance. He introduced himself to Lang, and after a short conversation pointing out a few details in the records, he went into the locker room to change into the green scrubs and a jumpsuit. Lang pulled up his chair squarely in front of the computer screen on the desk and reached for the mouse. Having clearance and a standing password to the Brakefield Medical Records network because of his willingness to consult and participate in cases at Brakefield, he logged in, navigated to the patient records section and quickly pulled up the pages for Richard Kanaby's entire hospital course. He scanned through making a few notes, and clicked back to the homepage. He stood and slipped on a pair of the gloves as he spoke to the two assistants again. "Looks like we're about ready." He put on the second pair of gloves as he approached the table. "You guys should double-glove, too. I'll need twelve snap-top conical freezer tubes, medium size, and six Petri dishes."

"Yes, sir."

"And three 20 cc. syringes with 18 gauge needles for the cardiac blood and two 10 cc. with 18 gauge needles for CSF." He continued. "You've got formalin in the brain bucket?" The man nodded. "How about dry ice? "

"Yes, sir," said an assistant. "In the storeroom."

"Put a couple of slabs in the carrier 'til I'm ready."

The assistant left the room as Andreas Locanos walked in. "Dr. Lang?" he said.

Lang turned toward him. "Yes. Hello," he responded.

"Hi, I'm Andreas Locanos" he said. Neurology resident."

"Oh, yes. I saw your notes."

"I was wondering if I can come in for the procedure?"

"Sure. Fine. It'll take a while, but you're welcome," said Lang. "You'll have to change, though. Dr. Holleran's in the locker room right now getting suited up. It's right over there." He pointed. "Oh, and we'll need the path resident for the chest."

"Yes, sir. I can page him." Andreas started toward the locker room as the door opened and Joe came through in a white paper jumpsuit.

"Hi, Andreas," said Joe.

Lang, measuring the length of the body, looked up when he heard Joe. He addressed both men. "I'd favor a complete autopsy if we had a better idea what we're dealing with, but since we don't, I'm restricting to head and chest. I don't think we need the abdomen," He retracted the tape-measure with a snap and laid it on the cart.

"Sure," said Joe. "Your call."

"Dr.Dittrich has kept me pretty much informed since Thursday," Lang continued. "Said you and he have been consulting with the infectious disease doc, Garriman. I saw her note, and I agree infection has to be a consideration here, but there's not much evidence for that so far. The labs say virtually nothing. The IgG elevation's not so impressive in my opinion, and the cultures are all still negative. Anything new from the electrophoresis?"

"Some still pending I think," Joe replied.

"Yes," Andreas spoke up. "I ordered a repeat IgG and IgA and IgM on Friday. The IgG was still elevated; IgA and IgM, still normal, but I thought it might be helpful to check IgD and IgE, since it's such a strange case. That had to be sent out though, so nothing's back yet."

"Okay, so in any event, we're using the precautions ," said Lang. "Standard infection protocol."

"I'll call the path resident," Andreas said as he headed into the locker room.

Lang continued, "Judging from Garriman's notes, she concurs with the consideration of something toxic."

"Yes," said Joe, "but we don't have anything back on the tox screen yet, so it's speculation at this point. By the way, I paged her a little while ago to let her know about the autopsy. She wants to come in to see the brain, so I expect she'll be stopping by. Do you know her?"

"Only by reputation," said Lang. "Never met her. How long's she been here?"

"Five or six years," said Joe. "Came from Hopkins. She's *quite* a woman." He smiled slightly.

"So I've heard," said Lang looking at Joe with an expression both inquisitive and speculative. "I guess I need to get started." He turned toward the table. He pulled the elastic band of the face mask over his head, "We'll take cardiac blood for cultures and chemistries, and we can also re-check the immunoglobulins." He adjusted the mask over his nose and mouth. "There're aprons and masks…and shoe-covers and gloves, everything is over there," he said to Joe as he pointed. "You and the resident have to stay over in the clean area by the desk until we make some progress. Once we get the brain out, you can come up to the table."

He turned back to the autopsy table. "Okay, gentlemen," he said, "let's do the cardiac stick first." The assistant took a gauze sponge from the cart and placed it into a steel scissor-clamp, dipped it into the small flask of orange-colored solution on the cart and began to swab the bare chest with vigorous circular motions. Then he took one of the large syringes from the cart, uncapped the needle and plunged it into the left side of the chest, mid-level. Dark blood appeared in the barrel as he pulled the plunger back. When it was filled, he lifted away the syringe, re-capped the needle, placed in a steel pan on the cart and repeated the same procedure two more times.

When the assistant finished, Lang pressed the foot pedal at the base of the table and dictated a description of the body into the microphone. Then he took his foot away from the pedal and instructed the assistant to position the head for the skin incision.

Andreas emerged from the locker room dressed like the others. He went to the desk area and stood with Joe as they watched the procedure. Lang moved to the upper end of the table and took a scalpel from the cart. And reaching forward with his left hand to steady the head, as he guided the scalpel blade to a point just behind the right ear, pushed it into the skin and drew it firmly through a deep semicircular incision around the back of the head to a point just behind the left ear. He lifted the skin at the edge of the incision and began to pull the scalp upward skillfully snipping at the white sheet of connective tissue on the underside of the thick scalp to release it as he gently lifted it over the crown of the head to expose the back and top of the skull.

He repositioned the head slightly with both hands and reached for the small electric saw on the cart beside the table. He flipped its switch initiating a shrill mechanical squeal. One of the assistants reached from the side of the table where he stood and held the head in place. Lang brought the rapidly vibrating blade down on the right side of the skull to make the initial cut through the bone. The shrill sound became a harsh buzz as he guided the blade, slowly encircling the exposed dome of the skull. When the bone incision was complete, he lifted the saw away and turned it off. Then using a stainless steel chisel, he carefully pried a cap-shaped piece of bone away from the top of the head exposing the thick fibrous membrane covering the brain.

He laid the boney cap on the table, picked up the scalpel again, and began to slowly incise the membrane all the way around the edge of the circular opening in the skull. Then, with large forceps and several releasing cuts with the scalpel, he lifted the membrane away exposing the glistening surface of the brain. "Ten cc syringe for CSF," he said. The assistant handed him a syringe. He pulled the cap off and pushed the needle deep into the right side of the brain. As he pulled the plunger back, a stream of clear fluid flowed into the syringe. He lifted it away and handed it to the assistant. "One more," he said. He inserted the second needle into the brain, withdrew more clear fluid and held the second syringe up in the light. "That's enough." He handed it to the assistant and picked up the scalpel again.

Bending closer to the table, he began to separate the brain from the inside of the skull. In less than a minute and with skillful strokes of the scalpel to release the optic and olfactory nerves and the brainstem, he lifted the brain out of the skull and moved to the other end of the table to place it in the metal scale pan. He moved slightly back to the side of the table, pressed the foot-pedal again and began to dictate into the hanging microphone details of the procedure he had just completed. He described the appearance of the outside of the skull, the membrane covering the brain, the inside of the skull and finally the brain itself, noting at the end the weight of the brain, 1,237 grams. He removed the pan from the scale, set it on the table, lifted out the brain and laid it on the stainless steel surface of the table. Then he pulled the spray nozzle from its socket and released a gentle flow of water over it. As the water rinsed away red-tinged fluid, the surfaces of the brain glistened in the light. He put it back into the pan and turned to Joe and Andreas. "You can come over now," he said.

They approached the table and stared down at the pinkish-tan mound covered with a delicate network of tiny blood vessels. Joe was suddenly consumed with reflection and paradox. This was not like what he remembered from the cadaver in medical school. This was entirely different, he thought, realizing what he was now seeing. Within this lifeless, barely three pounds of flesh had existed his patient and friend, Richard Kanaby. Exactly here was where he had thought and felt, loved, rejoiced and despaired. All he had learned and remembered, created, dreamed of and hoped for had flourished here until something malevolent, something monstrous, violated it and destroyed his capacity to function as husband, father, friend, scientist, creator.

Lang's voice interrupted Joe's thoughts as he directed the assistants to close. The two men went about their task at the head end of the table. Within minutes, the cap-shaped piece of bone was fitted back into place enclosing the empty skull, and the scalp was pulled back over the bone and carefully stitched into place so that from the front and either side of the head, there was no sign of the brief intrusion.

At the other end of the table, Lang was now holding the brain, turning it over in his hands as if he were examining a rare artifact or a precious gem. "Nothing abnormal over the convexities," he was saying. "No inflammation. No bleeding. Vessels look good. In fact damn good for a 64-year-old. Clean living, I guess." He continued to inspect as his fingers slid over the surfaces of the brain. "No atrophy. Hemispheres are symmetrical. Firm. No softening. No swelling." He glanced up at Joe. "I have to say at this point, it's pretty unremarkable." He laid the brain back in the pan, stepped on the foot pedal again and described what he had just observed. When he finished, he looked up at Joe. "I'll take what we need for the PCR and the other molecular studies," he said, "and for transmission in case we decide we need that. Maybe your Dr. Garriman will have some suggestions. You think she's coming in?"

"Shall I page her?" said Joe.

"Not yet. I've got a few more things to do here, and the path resident has to do his thing," said Lang as he lifted the pan and took it to the other autopsy table. He set it next to a collection of plastic Petri dishes and small plastic tubes containing fixative solutions neatly laid out on the surface. Lang began to label the tops of the Petri dishes: right superior frontal gyrus; left superior frontal gyrus; right hippocampus; left hippocampus; left cerebellum; right cerebellum; midpons. He stopped. He repeated the same labeling of the plastic tubes.

"You can bring the dry ice over now," he said to the assistant. "Put a piece on the cutting board," he directed, lifting the brain from the pan. He turned it over again and set it on a plastic tray. With tubes and dishes arranged in the order he liked, the steaming slab of dry ice sending up thin white vapors beside the tray, he began his meticulous dissection. Wordlessly, he cut away small portions of the brain in the ritualized fashion of someone who had done this many times and slipped them into the respective tubes or dishes. Those in the Petri dishes were fast-frozen by placing each dish on the flat slab of dry ice. Other portions were gently dropped into the tubes of fixative.

Joe and Andreas stood by silently. Momentarily, the double doors swung open and a slight young man, mid-twenties, dressed in green scrubs, entered.

"Hi, Paul," said Andreas. "Dr. Lang, this is Dr. Tillotson, the path resident."

Lang looked up. "Hello, young man. We need you for the chest," he said in a strongly authoritative tone. "This is a *precautions* case. Either an unusual infection or something toxic, but the bottom line is we don't know. Definite brain involvement.

Possibly some lung involvement. Lung could be the source. If you want to take a look at the chart, it's over there on the desk."

"Oh, yes sir, I reviewed the records online. I'll be right back." He disappeared into the locker room.

Lang went back to his dissections. The double doors opened again. This time it was Cassandra Garriman in a long white coat, blue eyes flashing, hair pulled back in a tie. She stood for a moment as all five men stared at her at once. "Hello, Joe, Dr. Locanos," she said crisply, nodding toward the two of them.

"Hi, Cassie," said Joe. "You know Dr. Lang?"

She glanced beyond Joe toward Lang. "Hello, Dr. Lang. I'm Cassandra Garriman. Infectious Disease." Her voice was all business. "Don't believe I've had the pleasure."

"Hello, Dr. Garriman," Lang replied but without looking up. "Be with you shortly. Hands full right now."

"Of course." Her tone softened.

Lang looked up. "Dr. Holleran says you want to have a look at the brain."

"Yes. I do indeed," she said.

"You'll have to get into one of these suits."

"Oh sure," she said. "Where can I do that?"

"Across the hall," Joe spoke up. "Ladies' locker room. Should be scrubs and jumpsuits in there. Everything else is here." He pointed to the shelves.

"Okay. I'll be back shortly." She exited, heels clicking sharply against the concrete floor.

Lang looked at Joe with a raised eyebrow. "I see what you mean." Joe did not react.

Paul Tillotson came back in now in a white jump-suit. He went to the supply shelves quickly donning apron, shoe covers, cap, mask and gloves. "All set, Dr. Lang."

"Fine," said Lang. "You understand, we only want the heart-lung block. We're not getting into the abdomen on this one. I've taken cardiac blood, so you can go ahead with your incision."

Paul approached the table. "Yes, sir."

"And be sure to get bronchial and alveolar cultures," said Lang as he lifted the scale pan and brought it to the head end of the table.

"Yes, sir." Paul took the scalpel from the assistant and proceeded with the chest incision.

Cassandra Garrison re-entered, now also in a white jumpsuit. She walked to the shelves. Joe pointed "Shoe covers are on the second shelf. Masks and hats, up to the left. Gloves, middle shelf." "Thanks," she said as she picked out the items he named and walked to the desk. She sat and pulled on the shoe covers.

"And you'll need one of those plastic aprons, too," said Joe. "Third shelf on the left."

Without a reply, she went back to the shelves, took out an apron, tied it on then put on the hat, the mask and the gloves.

"Okay, Doctor," said Lang, "Looks like you're ready." She approached the table. "Come around this way." he said. "You can see better." He lifted the brain from the pan and held it out in both hands to catch the best lighting. "Hemispheres are symmetrical. No swelling. No softening. See." He held it out to her. She reached forward and gently touched the surface. "Go ahead. Feel it. It's real firm all over. Nothing to suggest infarction or anoxia. 'Course there was nothing in the scans to suggest that either. And see, the surface vessels are clean. No congestion."

He held the brain out a bit closer to her. She stepped back.

"It's okay. Won't bite." He chuckled and continued. "No meningeal involvement. No inflammation." He turned it over slowly in his hands. "Cerebellum and brainstem look fine. See?" She leaned forward again and stared at it intensely.

"I took a few thin sections right there. Midbrain, pons and medulla." He pointed. "I believe you know he had significant respiratory problems, but there was very little indication of lung involvement." She nodded. "Certainly suggests primary brainstem involvement," he said and glanced at the assistant. "I think we're ready for the brain bucket."

The assistant lifted a covered plastic bucket from the floor and set it on the table beside the scale pan. When he opened the lid, the acrid odor and nostril-searing sensation produced by formaldehyde jolted Cassie. She moved away from the table as Lang placed the brain in the bucket and closed the lid.

"So…that's it," he said. "As soon as the young doctor here finishes, we can call it a day …or night."

"Yes, sir," said Paul. "I'm about to close. Lungs look okay. Heart's fine. Thorax is clean. Don't see anything abnormal grossly. You wanta take a look?"

"And you got the cultures?" said Lang peering into the gaping chest cavity.

"Cultures and touch preps. All lobes. Looked okay. A little congestion but no consolidation. No hemorrhage. Nothing purulent. Everything's in formalin."

"Great job, Doctor. Thanks for coming in," said Lang dismissing Paul and turning to Joe. "Okay, Dr. Holleran, anything else we need to do?"

"I don't think so," Joe replied. "We thank you for coming in so late."

"Interesting case," said Lang. "I'm taking the brain and these tubes and frozen specimens back to the Institute tonight. The brain has to fix for at least 10 days before we examine it. Meanwhile, we'll have some results from the frozen material and maybe something from cultures."

Lang walked to the plastic BIOHAZARD tub, stripped off the outer pair of gloves and dropped them into it. "Put all your aprons and suits and stuff in here." He pulled off the face-mask and cap and dropped them into the tub. "Thank you for coming in, Dr. Holleran. Dr. Locanos. And you, too, Dr. Garriman. Hope you'll find it helpful. You can leave your jump suit in this same kind of tub in the Ladies' locker room. And gentlemen," he turned to the assistants, "you can release the body."

"Thank you, Doctor Lang," said Cassandra crisply. "I'm eager to know what you find." With a quick glance and nod toward Joe and Andreas she said, "Good evening," and walked out. To Andreas, it seemed she was simply being professional, but Joe knew different.

CHAPTER FOURTEEN

It happened two years earlier. Joe Holleran was in New York for a meeting of the American College of Internal Medicine at the New York Hilton, late February. Nancy stayed behind in Atlanta. As the Thursday afternoon sessions were ending, Joe left the ballroom and wandered across the mezzanine toward the elevators. Walking and flipping through the program booklet as he moved, he heard a woman's voice call his name. He turned to see Cassandra Garriman. He had met her when she first arrived at Brakefield. He'd seen her subsequently at grand rounds and staff meetings, and he'd consulted with her on several of his patients. His impression had always been that she was bright, self-assured, very professional and quite beautiful....but always a bit aloof. So when she approached him with an animated smile and "Hi, Joe. I didn't know you were here," it was a surprise. She held out her hand.

"Hello, Cassandra." He shook her hand gently. "I didn't know you were here either. Did you come up yesterday?"

"Yes. Last night. Delta. Last flight to New York. And please, it's Cassie."

"Oh, Okay. It's nice to see you," he said somewhat awkwardly as her handshake lingered.

"Your wife with you?"

The question struck him as a bit odd so early in the exchange, but he dismissed it. "I'm afraid not. Hard for her to get away with all the kids' activities. She waits for meetings in exotic places."

"Oh, that's too bad." She smiled slightly. "Out in big old New York all by yourself are you?"

Again, a little odd he thought. "For just a couple of days," he said. Gotta get back tomorrow night, but I wanted to catch this part of the meeting. A few of the g.i. sessions I need. How 'bout you?"

"I leave Saturday. Going down to Baltimore to meet some friends for the weekend. That used to be home for me."

"Oh, yes. You came from Hopkins."

"Right. Six years there." They began to move toward the elevators. "I was ready for a change. Atlanta's nice, and I'm adjusting even though the southern lady thing is a little hard for me." There was a tinge of sarcasm in her voice as she looked directly at him with the same slight smile again. He fidgeted. "You going up?" She motioned toward the elevators.

"Yeah."

They started walking again.

"I'm trying to decide what to do this evening," she said as they reached the bank of elevator doors. "Thought I might try the Philharmonic. They're doing the Mahler Fifth Symphony. I love it."

"Oh?" He pressed the up button.

"You'd be welcome to join me if you don't have plans."

"I don't know," he said. "I really hadn't thought much past a quick dinner here at the hotel then maybe just reading the abstracts for tomorrow."

An elevator door opened.

"Well, I'm going to check with the concierge about tickets when I get to my room," she said. "I can let you know in case you're interested." Several people behind them pushed past into the elevator and the door closed.

"Mmm." He looked at his watch. "It's almost 6:00 now. Concert would be at 8:00, right? Not much time for dinner."

"Oh. I was just going for a drink before and then maybe a light supper somewhere in the neighborhood after. Probably wouldn't be much past 10:30. That too late for you?"

"No, not really," he said.

"You like Mahler?"

"Yes. Matter of fact, I do. I'd hate to miss it if that's what they're doing this evening, the Fifth, I mean." He brushed his chin thoughtfully. "Let me know what you find."

"Sure." She glanced up at the floor indicator lights over the elevator doors. One to the left opened. They hurried to it and stepped in. Three people already in the elevator were talking quietly. They both stood silently watching the floor indicator above the door for a few seconds as it ascended, then in a quiet voice she said, "I'm sure the ticket prices'lll be premium if we get'em here, but it'll be worth it."

"Umm." He nodded.

The car stopped at the ninth floor. Two people got off. The door closed. She looked up at the floor lights again then back at him. His face was expressionless. The numbers flashed: 11, 12, 14, and the car stopped at 15. The door opened "Talk to you shortly," she said as she stepped out.

He nodded. The door closed. What's she all about, he thought? The comment about being all alone in big old New York and the southern lady thing? And the half smiles? The elevator door opened on 17. He got out and walked toward his room assessing the last few interesting minutes. He slipped the key card into the door and entered, shedding his suit jacket and loosening his tie. He'd wait for her call before he got comfortable. He flicked on the TV to catch the news. The phone rang.

"Hi," a modulated voice spoke. Not Hello. Not Hi, Joe. Just hi, then a pause. "We can get you a ticket if you're game. It is the Mahler Fifth. We can pay the concierge and pick up the tickets at the box office. Just have to be there by 7:30. That okay?"

"Sure. I can make it."

"Shall we meet at the concierge desk in say twenty minutes?"

"Yes. Fine."

"If we grab a cab and go for the tickets, we'll have time for a quick drink somewhere."

"Sounds good. See you in at the concierge desk. Twenty minutes."

He hung up. He was impressed. She had it all worked out. He looked at his watch again. Almost 6:25. He had to call Nancy. He went into the bathroom washed his hands and face. He dried and checked himself in the mirror. No need to change. His suit would be fine for the symphony. He straightened his tie and combed his hair then splashed on a little aftershave, came back into the bedroom and dialed the number.

"Hello." Nancy answered.

"Hi, sweetheart. Just calling to check in. Everything okay?"

"Everything's fine," she said. "Just picked up Stephanie from swim team. Dinner in a few minutes. Then homework, homework.

How's the meeting?" Her voice lilted upward slightly.

"Oh, it's fine. Some parts interesting, some, you know, not so. But I need the credits." He laughed. "I've seen a bunch of people. Several asking about you. Remember Wesley Weeks, Cleveland Clinic? You met him and his wife at the meeting in Rome. She's here, too. And Henry Council from Duke and his wife? Remember?"

"Gosh, I guess," she said. "So what are you doing tonight?"

"Oh, some of us are gonna try to get tickets to the symphony."

"Oh. Lincoln Center?"

"Yeah."

"That sounds like fun," she said.

"Got to go in a few minutes to see what's available?"

"Okay, Baby," she said. "Have a good time. Tell everybody hello. I love you."

"Love you, too. Oh. I'm in room 1707."

"I know. You told me last night, remember?"

"Yep. Hi to the kids. Talk to you tomorrow." He hung up. He was late. He pulled on the suit jacket again as he moved to the door. He checked his pocket for the key card, stepped into the hallway and hurried toward the elevators.

She was waiting at the concierge desk. She wore a smart black suit with a low-cut neckline, an elegant pearl necklace and hair pulled back in a chignon. She carried a small evening purse and a black wool coat draped over her arm. He was unexpectedly dazzled. "You certainly made a quick change. You look lovely. Maybe I should've changed, too."

"Oh, you're fine." The soft voice again. "I just had to get out of those daytime things. Felt like something a little more evening." She turned toward the concierge then back. "Let's get confirmations then we'd better go."

"Sure." He reached into his inside jacket-pocket for his wallet. "How do we pay?"

"Oh, they'll just put it on your room. I'm doing that."

"Let me treat you," he said.

"Oh, no. Thanks. You're nice, but I think I started this," she said. "I'm glad to have someone to go with. You're room 1701, right?"

He nodded and stood silently, fascinated watching her as she negotiated the ticket sale. The concierge handed her the a piece of paper, and she turned back to Joe. "Now, a taxi," she said leading the way across the lobby. In her "more evening" outfit, as she had put it, she seemed to take on a different persona, less reserved, less strictly professional but still confident. And her feminine vibes definitely came through.

"May I help you with your coat?" he said.

"Thanks." She handed him the coat and turned as he held it for her. "What about you?"

"I'm fine. I love this cold weather," he said. "Just the kind of weather I grew up in."

She smiled at him over her shoulder as they exited. The doorman held the taxi door for them. She slid in. He tipped the doorman and slid in beside her as she said, "Lincoln Center, please." The cab headed up 6th Avenue then onto 59th Street, past Columbus Circle and up Broadway. As they approached 62nd Street, Cassie interrupted their conversation with, "Driver, let us out on the right at 63rd, the near corner please." She turned to Joe. "No need to get into that traffic trying to get over to the steps." She pointed across the busy intersection in front of the Lincoln Center plaza. The fountain in the center blasted its brilliantly-lighted white plumes upward. The line of cars in front of the steps was long, and the whole area bordered by the monumental stone-and-glass buildings was full of people. The taxi stopped at the curb.

He handed the driver a five and got out and held the door for her. "We made better time than I expected," she said as they moved toward the crosswalk. "Come on. We can make the light if we hurry." She grabbed his hand automatically and led him across the street to the corner of the small triangular park of trees and benches set among the busy streets. "Let's get the tickets then we can come back over here for a drink." She let go of his hand and pointed to a restaurant on their left as they moved. At the next corner, they crossed over to the steps and moved up onto the crowded plaza. "I love this. All the people, the traffic, the lights. I'm so glad we're doing this. I adore this city," she said excitedly, looking up at him.

He registered how easy it all seemed for her. He felt her hand slip behind his left arm and into the crook of his elbow. They stopped for a moment, halted by the spectacular sight of the façade of the Metropolitan Opera House, then she nudged him on, her arm still hooked onto his. "Let's go around this way." They entered the lobby of Philharmonic Hall and walked toward the box-office. When they reached the short reservation line, she said, "We made it. Look. It's only ten after. We've got plenty of time to go for that drink." This time the smile was a mischievous little one-sided one. "If we get back here by ten till, that'll be just right." He marveled to himself at her energy and surprising spontaneity. "I hope you really do like the Mahler. It's not for everybody, but I..."

"I really do," he interrupted. "I hadn't even thought about looking into the symphony tonight. Glad you suggested it."

"I'm delighted I suggested it." She stepped up to the window. "Garriman. C, first initial. Two orchestra seats," she said handing the clerk the confirmation from the hotel. He handed her a small envelope and she check quickly. "Yep. P32 and 34. Thanks," she said and turned to Joe. "Shall we?"

They exited and walked quickly back across, down the steps and across the corner to the restaurant. The maitre'd approached as they entered. "Two for dinner?"

"Two for drinks, please," said Joe.

The man showed them to a small table near the bar bowing slightly as he pulled out a chair.

"Thank you." She sat.

Joe sat opposite and signaled the waiter. Two vodka martinis up with olives. Her suggestion. Not usual for Thursday evening, he thought, but *this* was not a usual Thursday evening.

"See," she said checking her watch. "This worked out perfectly. We've got almost 30 minutes." She seemed pleased with herself. The waiter brought the drinks. "Even the service is working out perfectly." She delicately lifted her glass by its stem. "Here's to Mahler." She smiled and brought it to her lips.

"Here's to Mahler and New York," he said as he lifted his glass and sipped.

They re-entered the lobby at exactly 7:50. She handed the tickets to the attendant, and they approached the entrance to the hall. Joe took two programs from the usher. They moved down the aisle and got to their seats just as the concert master started the tune-up. The lights lowered, the audience quieted, the door to the left of the stage opened and the conductor strode out through the players. Applause rose as he stepped onto the podium. He made an elegant bow, then turned, lifted his baton with a forceful motion, and the trumpet fanfare sliced through the hall like a cold steel saber.

They sat motionless as the music proceeded. With an occasional side glance he could see that she was completely absorbed in the music. His mind wandered as he began to think of what he had heard about her before now: very professional, excellent training, solid research background, *expert* in infectious diseases. That was the general consensus. Each time he'd seen her at Brakefield, she was always well-dressed but conservatively and always with the long white clinical coat. But now it was apparent that beneath the reserved professional demeanor, she was a vivacious and strikingly attractive woman.

The turbulent music powered through the first three movements of the symphony until the softer strings in the fourth offered some relief. Joe turned to see that her eyes were closed and her head was tilted back in a transformed posture. As he watched, he wondered how she carried on her daily life in the restrained manner she projected at the hospital when the person he saw now was so the opposite. Which one was the real Cassandra Garrison?

The final movement ended to great applause. They exited for intermission, the lobby full of excited voices. "How about a little champagne?" he said.

"I'd love some." They moved toward the bar.

"You seemed to be really impressed with this piece," he said, exploring. "You know you never moved through the whole thing."

"Oh. I guess maybe I didn't." She tilted her head slightly as he handed her a flute of bubbling liquid. "I love that music. Especially the strings. The fourth movement is so…sublime. It absolutely transforms me." She drew out the words for emphasis. "My mom was a violinist. Still is actually. She played this piece with the Cincinnati Symphony back before I was born. She says she was once told it was one of Leonard Bernstein's favorites." She took a sip of champagne. "Uhmm…Good." She nodded and took another sip. "She graduated from the Cincinnati Conservatory and stayed on for a while with the Symphony. Shortly after she and my dad married, they moved to Detroit where he was from. Oh, you don't want to hear all this. Let's just say I was brought up on this kind of stuff."

"No," he said. "Tell me more. I'd like to hear. It's obvious you know a lot about classical music. Did your mom play with the Detroit Symphony?"

She continued as they drifted away from the bar, "That was her hope, to play full-time there, but it didn't work out. I came along about a year after their move, and I'm sure I complicated their life quite a bit. For a while, she played with a string quartet, and they did a pretty good business. It was mainly weddings, receptions, bar mitzvahs and occasional concerts, but only occasional. My sister came along two years after me. By then, Mom and Dad were starting to have problems, I mean with their relationship. That's about enough history, don't you think?"

"No. Please go on. We have time."

"So when I was about six, she and Dad split. He was a musician, too, a pianist, but he was never able to make much of a career of it. And he wasn't much of a father either. I think he resented any success Mom had. He became more and more verbally abusive to her. That's what I remember most about him. I hated him for it. It was a relief when he left."

"I'm sure," said Joe trying to think of how to lighten this suddenly darkened conversation. "You were saying you were brought up on this kind of music?"

"Let's just say I've been to my share of symphony concerts. Even right here. Many times."

"So that's why you know your way around so well," he said.

"I used to come up from Baltimore a lot," she said, "but it's a bit harder to get here from Atlanta. Not really harder, maybe, but you just have to plan better."

"I know," he said. "I grew up in New England. I remember how relatively easy it was to get to New York without a lot of advanced planning."

"So where'd you grow up?" she said.

"Newton, Massachusetts. Just outside of Boston."

"Would you believe I went to medical school at Tufts?"

"Oh, my gosh." He smiled broadly. "Small-world thing, huh?"

The conversation was comfortable and easy. He told her a bit about his family, his back-ground, medical school, residency. How he got to Atlanta. How he met Nancy. About their children. At one point he realized, with a flash of guilt, that he'd not even thought about them all evening….until now.

The lobby lights lowered and brightened two times. "Better drink up," she said finishing the last of her Champagne and setting the glass on a nearby ledge. He did the same. As they started back to their seats, she very gently slipped her hand into the bend of his left elbow again. Trying not to notice or seem surprised, he stared straight ahead until they reached their row and moved to their seats.

Just before the lights went down, Joe leaned toward her. "Any thoughts about supper?"

"Several places nearby are open late," she whispered.

"I've got a thought too," he whispered back, "but it's not all that close."

"Where?"

"It's a cab ride but not all that far either."

"Sounds interesting," she said.

"Good." He smiled back with a wink.

The lights went down and the conductor returned to the podium. The music started again. The last half of the program was lighter, fluid and romantic, and as the program finished, Joe was feeling pleased he'd decided to join her. He was thoroughly enjoying himself and definitely looked forward to a late-night supper. He hadn't been to the restaurant in more than two years, but as he remembered it, it should be just right.

The ovations and the bows ended, and the audience began its exodus. As they moved up the aisle, through the exit and onto the plaza she said, "Okay. So. Thoughts about where to go?"

"You go first," he said.

She shrugged and laughed. "Okay. I'll play this game. There's O'Neal's almost directly across on 63rd." She waved vaguely in that direction. "The Tavern on the Green's over a few blocks on Central Park West. And my favorite, Café Des Artistes, is on 67th at Central Park West. I know they're open late. So what's your idea?"

"Okay, but it's not in this neighborhood."

"So where, Brooklyn?" She looked at him with a wide-eyed expression feigning innocence.

"No, but what if I said Paris, would you believe me?"

"Paris…as in France?" She laughed delightedly.

"Well, just like Paris as in France but in Soho."

"Soho!" she exclaimed. "Are you serious? You know Soho? I didn't think you were into New York like that."

"Maybe not as much as you. But I know a few things."

"So tell me more."

They had almost reached the steps down to the street. "You up for that?" he said.

"I trust you, Doctor. If you say Soho's the place, I'm up for it."

The martinis and champagne or perhaps the impact of the place, the crowds and the music seemed to have lowered their threshold of reserve. As they crossed the street, he signalled for a taxi, and in spite of the crowds leaving the plaza, an empty one stopped almost immediately. Joe opened the door. Cassie got in. He followed leaning toward the driver. "West Broadway and Duane Street," he said.

"Yes sir. Okay." Joe got in, and they headed south. The traffic moved well and the driver managed to get the green lights all the way to 27th Street. Stopping there for the red-light, the driver turned and spoke through the plexiglass partition in a heavy Eastern European accent. "Yes, sir. I know West Broadway, but I do not know the other you say."

"Duane Street," said Joe. "Du – wayne." She snickered as he emphasized the syllables.

"Yes," said the driver, "I try to find."

"When you get to Houston, turn right and go over to West Broadway."

"Yes, sir. Okay."

"I'm impressed. How do you know Duane Street? All of a sudden you're this fount of New York information."

"Forget Duane Street. When you walk in, you'll think you're in Paris." he grinned.

Shortly the cab turned onto Houston then onto West Broadway. Joe instructed the driver. "Next street left. Where those limos are."

"Yes sir."

"Seriously. What is this?" she said.

"I told you. Paris. Paris in Soho." The car stopped. Joe paid, got out and reached a hand toward her. She took it and pulled herself out. They moved toward an elegant, double-doored entrance lighted on either side by large brass lanterns. On a discreet brass plaque to the right of the doors were bold black letters reading **Mon Petit Chou.**

Joe pointed to the plaque. "They say that's a French term of endearment," he said. He opened one of the doors, and with a deferential head-bow he smiled and said, "Mad'moiselle."

They walked into the dimly lit foyer. Through an archway beyond the reception stand was a moderate-sized room with creamy yellow walls and soft lighting.

"This looks wonderful. Really," she said. " How'd you know about it?"

"Tell you in a minute," he said as a stylish young woman with a short haircut and heavy eye make-up wearing a long-sleeve white blouse and a black miniskirt approached.

She spoke with a distinctly French accent: "Good evening and welcome to Mon Petit Chou, Monsieur," she nodded slightly to Joe. "Madame." She nodded to Cassie. "For two, supper?"

"Yes." Joe replied.

"Please. This way. I show you to your table." She led them through the arch. There were twenty or so small tables comfortably placed in the room, all with white table cloths and a single sparkling votive in the center of each. Most of the tables were occupied, and there was a quiet din of voices and tinkling glasses. Against the two side walls were banquettes upholstered in dark fabric. The tables in front of the banquettes were spaced far enough apart to allow diners quiet conversation. In the center was a marble pedestal urn holding an exuberant arrangement of fresh flowers seeming to explode from the top of it. Against the back wall, a wooden bar stood in front of mirror-backed wooden shelves filled with an assortment of bottles and glasses. On either side of the shelves was a door leading into the kitchen beyond. Waiters in white shirts, black pants and long white aprons passed intermittently through the doors or moved among the tables occupied by the chic clientele.

The young woman directed them to a banquette table and stood aside as a waiter stepped up and pulled the table out motioning to Cassie. She sat. He pushed the table back and pulled out a chair opposite for Joe. The woman smiled. "Monsieur, please, " she said as she handed Joe two menu cards and a bi-fold wine-list.

"This is amazing," said Cassie as she glanced around the room. "All this time I've been coming to New York, I've never even heard of this place. How long's it been here?"

"Years. Decades, maybe. Some friends brought me here almost three years ago when I came up for a meeting. Then I came back maybe two years ago. I was never here this late, but I knew they stay open for night owls." He smiled. "Good way to finish the evening, don't you think?"

"I do," she said as she brought her eyes to meet his.

A waiter approached. "Good evening." He smiled. "You like something from the bar mehbee? Cocktail? Wine?" Again a French accent.

"I think wine," Joe spoke. "Let us look a minute." He studied the wine list.

"Certainly, sir. This is wine list and there," he pointed to the cards they were holding," is menu for after eleven. A few more minutes perhaps?"

"Thanks." Joe nodded and looked at Cassie. "Wine okay?"

"Sure. Why not?" she said. "Just hope I'll be able to stay awake all day tomorrow." She laughed.

"Red or white?"

"You choose," she said.

The waiter returned with two glasses and a small pitcher of water. He poured the water as he said, "Wine, Monsieur?"

"Let's have the Pouilly. Number 38."

"I bring it right away."

Joe leaned back and looked around the room then at her. "This is nice," he said.

She glanced down at the table and rubbed a finger against the water glass as it refracted the light from the votive. "Yes," she said looking up at him again, "It is. Very nice."

The waiter came again, now with the wine and two glasses. He opened the bottle then poured ceremoniously for Joe to taste. "Fine." The clear pale-gold liquid splashed into the glasses.

"And for supper, monsieur? You wish a minute more?"

"Yes, please."

"I be right back."

"You looked yet?" said Joe. "I haven't gotten beyond the wine list." He glanced at his card.

"You've been here before, so…any suggestions?" she said looking at her card.

"I remember the sweetbreads were good, but that'd be too heavy this late I think."

"I think so," she said. "How about the veal? No. Poached chicken in white wine sounds good. Herbs and vegetables."

"Veal sounds good to me. With the tarragon sauce."

The waiter returned, and they ordered. "Oh, and could you bring some bread, now, please?"

"Oui, monsieur."

Joe sipped the wine and brought his left hand under his chin resting the elbow on the table as he fixed his gaze on her.

"I must say…this is not exactly the evening I was expecting at 5:45 this afternoon," he said as he set the wine glass down.

Her hand caressed her wine glass. She looked away wistfully. "Tomorrow we go back to what we expect," she said, "but it's nice to be here like this right now." She closed her eyes. He shifted slightly in his chair as he watched her. A few seconds passed. She opened her eyes, and her expression changed. "You go back tomorrow?"

"Yes," he said. "Late afternoon. I'll get to the morning sessions, but I still have to do some shopping before I leave. You know, for the kids."

She nodded. "Oh, I'm sure." She tried to sound casual. "How many?"

"Two girls and a boy," he said. The mood was broken. "They keep us busy with all their activities. The oldest is just now getting to be teenager, and the second one's not far behind."

"I can't imagine. Sounds a little overwhelming," she said her eyes fixed on him as she spoke.

"Sometimes it is, but they give us so much joy," he said.

"Must be a very satisfying part of your life," she said. Her enigmatic expression from earlier was gone. Now it seemed poignantly vulnerable. She looked down and swirled the wine in her glass. He wanted to get past the moment.

"So how about your friends in Baltimore?" he said casually trying to shift direction. "Known them a long time?"

She looked up again. "We were residents together. Four of us." She sipped the wine. "When we finished, we all stayed in Baltimore for a while. Then one went to Chicago. I came to Atlanta. The other two are still at Hopkins. We try to get together at least once a year. Having the meeting this year in New York made it really convenient for us to get together this weekend."

The food arrived at just the right time, he thought. The glances and wordless communication were beginning to probe too deeply. The conversation shifted to vague talk of France and French wines and then, more specifically, of meetings in Paris and vacations in Normandy and Provence.

Presently, the waiter came back to ask about dessert. They

waivered, but neither wanted to end the evening. "How about we split one with coffee and the rest of the wine," Joe suggested. The waiter poured more wine and took the order. Very shortly, the coffee and a small plate of molten chocolate cake with two spoons arrived. They tried to fill the last moments with inconsequential conversation about the flowers in the middle of the room, the service, the coffee, the second half of the concert.

"What time do you suppose it is?" She squinted at her watch.

"Oh, my gosh, Joe, it's 12:30. I had no idea."

Joe looked at his watch lifting his shoulders back in a stretch. He seemed unconcerned. "Guess we better head uptown." He signaled the waiter.

He came forward. "Monsieur?"

"Check please."

*****

The taxi moved quickly uptown. In less than 20 minutes, they were entering the hotel lobby. As he watched her move slightly ahead of him toward the elevators, he realized how much he was enjoying the spell she and the evening had cast on him. He caught up with her as she pressed the elevator button. The doors of one opened immediately There was no one else waiting. They entered, and she pressed 15. "You're 17, right?" she said. He nodded. She pressed 17. The door closed.

Leaning against the side wall, she opened her purse and took out a key-card. She looked up at him. Her expression was unsmiling at first, then one corner of her mouth curled up slightly, and her eyelids lowered. She moved closer to him. Her right hand holding the key-card came to rest on his chest. He did not move. The lights flashed. 14. 15. The car stopped, and the door opened onto the deserted hallway. She looked up at him and started to speak, but stopped herself as the hand with the key-card tugged at his tie. She stepped sideways across the threshold blocking the electronic sensor. She looked away for a second then back. The smile was gone. He felt himself moving toward her as she stepped out into the hall. The door closed behind them. His head rushed. Too much wine, he thought. Her hand was still on his tie, and now he felt the length of her body close to him. She turned her face up toward him again. Her eyes were intense. Still no words, no smile. She pulled at his tie again, this time more firmly. They began to walk to the right.

"Cassie, I…"

They stopped. Her hand moved to his lips, and she pressed one finger across them as she stared up at him. There was no quizzical look, no innocently raised brow or head tilting. This time it was a straight, firm stare that bore through his eyes and into his brain so strongly he could feel it in the back of his head. He grasped the hand and held it a moment, eye-lock unbroken. She released the key card into his hand. "What number?" he whispered.

"1518." Her arm slipped around his back as they began to walk again. He felt as if he were floating, being propelled without moving. They reached the door and stopped. He slid the card into the slot and pushed the door open. She stepped in and flipped foyer light on. He followed and closed the door. She turned and faced him, bodies again touching. Her arms were at her sides, then one hand went back to his tie. She turned her face and pulled on the tie. He felt his body obey as he bent toward her. Slowly, tenuously, their lips met. He pulled away and looked into her unsmiling eyes. His arms moved around her shoulders, and their mouths came together in a long, deep kiss. He could feel her breath as she uttered tiny sounds that caught in her throat.

With eyes closed and all the world around them shut out, he

savored the sweetness of it, the delicate scent of her, the slight tremble of her shoulders. Their mouths separated, and he held her face against his neck. The side of his face grazed her fragrant hair. His embrace intensified, and they stood locked and motionless for another long moment before her head lifted away and she breathed a quiet "Ohhh." He gently guided her head to the curve between his neck and shoulder and held it there, stroking the back of her neck. At that moment, he wanted to stay there, not move, only stand in the penumbra of the intimacy they were feeling. He wanted it not to end, certain it would when he broke his embrace. He knew he had to go. She knew he would go. But she made no attempt to pull away. There was this moment, not planned, not intended, just happening after an unexpectedly romantic few hours. Just that simple. Just that spontaneous. Or was it?

She stared at the wall, her head still on his shoulder. When she felt his arms relax, she pulled away and faced him. His arms came down, and he took both her hands in his. The key-card was still in his right hand. She stood motionless as he backed toward the door. When he felt the door against his shoulders, he slid the key-card into her hand and reached awkwardly behind for the door knob. She looked up, now with a soft expression that said *don't say anything.* He twisted the knob and opened the door a few inches. With his left hand still holding hers he squeezed gently then let go, opened the door wider, slipped through and pulled it shut behind him.

The next day at the meeting, he looked for her, but she was not in evidence. He returned to Atlanta in the evening feeling some relief that he had not had to face her but also realizing he was disappointed.

During the weekend and the next week, he could hardly keep her out of his thoughts, but he made no attempt to communicate. Part of him was hoping he would not encounter her unexpectedly in the hospital any time soon. He tried to suppress the whole episode, but another part of him was desperate to see her again. On Thursday evening, as he was about to leave his office, the telephone rang.

"Dr. Holleran," he answered with a crisp, professional voice.

"Joe, it's Cassie."

Surprise silenced him for a few seconds, but he managed, "Cassie...uh'm, how was the weekend in Baltimore?"

"It was good," she said then with a firm voice, "I want to see you, Joe."

"Cassie...I can't."

"Please. Just listen." Her voice softened. "I just want to see you. Just talk a few minutes. I've gotta work through this. Get it out of my system. I've got..."

"Cassie, I think it's best if we just consider it..."

"I can't ignore it, Joe." Her tone was serious. Enough to make him uneasy.

"Where are you?" he said as he took a deep breath.

"In my office. I *need* to talk to you. Can I come there now?"

"I really have to leave, Cassie. Besides, what good would it do?"

"Probably none, but I have to see you and talk to you...in person."

"You know where my office is?" he said.

"Of course."

Why "of course" he thought. Maybe he should hear what she had to say. What was going on in her head?

"Can you come right away?" he said.

"Yes."

"Okay. The door from the corridor into our suite'll be unlocked. Be sure it locks when you come through. I'll be in my office." He hung up and walked out to the hallway checking to see that no one else was around, then went to the suite entrance, unlocked the door and returned to his office to wait.

He sat absently flipped through one of the journals on his desk. But too distracted, he put it down and leaned back in his chair. The call had answered the question almost constantly in his mind for the past week: If she encountered him again, would she pretend it never happened or would she acknowledge it somehow? The image and the feeling of the two of them standing just inside the hotel room 8 nights ago came to him. No question. It was exciting. He heard the door at the end of the hall open and close then the unmistakable sound of heel-clicks. He sat up as she appeared moving across the threshold and closing the door.

"Hello, Cassie." He stepped around the desk.

"Hello," she said, barely inaudibly.

Their eyes fixed on each other before as he moved toward her wordlessly, opened his arms on an uncontrollable impulse and wrapped her in a heaving embrace. Her head turned sideways, her fragrant hair brushed against his nose and cheek, and again, just as in New York, the sensations closed out the world. Whatever he might have meant to say receded. As she tilted her head back and looked up at him, he crushed his mouth onto hers. He could not resist. Did not want to. Did not try.

When their lips separated, they stood, eyes fixed again.

"I'm so sorry," she whispered. "I..."

His hand covered her lips. "Don't," he said as he took the hand away and pressed her into another long, hungry kiss. When finally he pulled away and looked at her, he said, "I...want you." His arms tightened around her again.

Their thoughts thrashed. Of course they knew it was forbidden. But it had smoldered in both of them all week. Now, confronting it, each felt the burst of intensity that made resistance turn to desire. For a long time, they were silent, embracing, holding, breathing, each trying to think of something sensible, something mature, to say; each failing.

Then he said, "This is insane, but.....what are you doing next week?"

"What am I doing next..."

"I mean any chance you could get away toward the end of the week?"

She looked at him in speechless surprise. Then with a little laugh she said, "You don't mean Paris again?"

"No, Colorado."

"Colorado?" she said, even more surprised.

"Yes," he said quietly. "I said…it's insane." She was silent, waiting for whatever was next. He continued. "A wild thought, but… I have the Winter G.I. Conference in Vail next week. It ends Thursday, and I was planning to stay an extra day to ski. I was thinking," he paced his words, "maybe you could come out. To Aspen…or Snowmass might be better." He paused looking for her reaction. "I could drive over. We could get away somewhere for the day."

"So you want me to fly all the way to Aspen…for a day?" She was incredulous.

"I know. I said it's a wild thought." He pulled his arms away and stood back slightly. "God you're beautiful."

She glanced away. "I wasn't expecting this."

*****

At 9:35 the following Thursday evening, she landed at the Pitkin County Airport a few miles outside of Aspen and made her way to Snowmass on the hotel shuttle. She claimed her reservation and got into a room on the 6th floor a little after 10:00. She unpacked, got comfortable in a gown and robe, took off her makeup and washed her face. Then, with the drapes pulled back and the room lights off, she sat on the edge of the bed watching the spectacular panoramic view of the moonlit mountains. At 10:50, her cell phone jingled.

"You made it," came Joe's voice.

"Just got in."

"I just got out," he said with a quick laugh. "I thought the evening session would never end." He paused. His tone changed as his voice intensified. "I can't wait to see you. I wish I'd planned to get there tonight."

"So do I," she said almost whispering.

"It won't be long." His voice relaxed. "You tired?"

"Yes. I am," she said. "It's a long trip."

"I'll make it worth your time," he said. "I'm gonna leave by 5:30. If traffic's not too heavy I'll be there by 7:30. 8:00 at the latest."

"Okay," she said.

He made the drive easily. One of those crisp, clear, mid-March-in-Colorado mornings, and the traffic wasn't bad. At 7:40 he made the turn toward Snowmass, and in another 15 minutes, he pulled into the parking lot beside the mall. He pressed her number into his phone.

"I'm here," he breathed into the phone .

"I'm waiting. Room 623."

He zipped up his jacket, grabbed the leather duffle and hurried up the steps and into the hotel lobby. A few early skiers scrambled out of one of the elevators, boots clonking. He entered and hit the button. When he stepped out on the sixth floor, more eager skiers pushed boisterously past him and into the elevator. The door closed and the hall went quiet. He made his way quickly to 623. He could see the door was slightly ajar. He pushed, and it opened easily.

The window drapes were drawn. The only light in the room came from a small lamp on the desk in the far corner. But in the dim light, he could see her standing motionless and silent a few feet from the bed. She was wearing a light-colored ski suit. Maybe yellow.

Maybe pink. He couldn't tell in the dim light. Her hair, held back from her face by a narrow headband, flowed loosely over her shoulders. Her eyes fixed on him as he came in and pushed the door shut. She was silent. He dropped the duffle and moved toward her, shedding his jacket, stepping out of his shoes. "Are we going skiing?" he said in a low voice. Was he teasing? She made no reply. He placed two fingers under her chin, lifted her face and brought his lips to hers. She raised her hand and stroked his cheek. His arms slid around her shoulders, and the gentle kiss ignited into intense, breath-consuming combustion. They stood locked in the embrace for a several seconds. Then still locked together, he backed her to the edge of the bed and toppled them both sideways onto it. She pulled off the head band and tossed it away.

His fingers ran through her hair and onto her neck. He found the zipper-pull on her ski suit, and as she lay back and closed her eyes, he slowly drew it down. The soft quilted material parted and fell away from her bare breasts. His hand spread over them, down onto her stomach and around her waist. He pulled her on top of him. She raised herself to let her arms slip out of the sleeves. She slid her hands under his sweater raking her nails across his bare chest. Then with a frenzied, two-handed push, she forced the sweater over his head and arms and fell back onto him.

His hands and arms moved around her shoulders. He coaxed the soft quilted material of the ski suit down her back, over her thighs and legs and onto the floor. As the suit fell away, she raised herself and straddled his chest, her knees pressing into his armpits. He pulled her forward into another kiss wrapping his arms around her shoulders. Then letting go long enough to loosen his belt and trousers, he pushed them down over his legs and off. Still facing him, she stretched length-wise on top of him. She felt him hard against her. His arms wrapped her shoulders again, and he rolled her over onto her back. As she uttered short, passionate, open-mouth sounds, he fell onto her to begin the first of three unrelenting ascents to exhilarating heights over the next hours, each time so climactic, they fell away in gasping exhaustion.

*****

Driving back to Vail late Friday afternoon, flying back to Atlanta late Friday night and for the rest of the weekend for him those hours were like a dream that never happened. He left for his office early on Monday morning. After a weekend of self-flagellating guilt mixed with rushes of remembered passion he could never have imagined, now as he drove, the unavoidable realities came into focus: The reality of what had just happened mixed in mind with the reality of everything else in his life bore down on him.

Just happened? Yes, at first, it had just happened. In New York, what began casually but intensified in a late-evening-early-morning haze could have been considered spontaneous. But after that, clearly it was planned…and executed. By her when she called and came to his office the week after New York. By him when he suggested Colorado. And by both of them when they went through with their tryst in Snowmass. That did *not* just happen.

He was at his desk before anyone else arrived, the same thoughts still churning. He slowly swiveled around and faced the photographs, so familiar, on the credenza, snapshots of his life in its indescribably satisfying continuum. Cassie and New York and Colorado were altogether aberrant side trips, he thought to himself, trying to rationalize and compartmentalize. He knew it could not go on. Her words, "I've gotta work through this. Get it out of my system," reverberated in his head. Yes, get it out. Purge it. End it.

Now.

He turned back to the desk and took out a piece of paper from a drawer. He began to compose something in his mind. He lifted a pen and began to write: "Cassie, this has to stop. It's too disruptive to both our lives. Joe." That said it, but it was too much. He scratched through "Cassie." He scratched through "Joe." Now it said: "This has to stop. It's too disruptive to both our lives." Still too much. He scratched through "This has to stop." Now only "It's too disruptive to both our lives" remained. Cryptic, yes, but it didn't seem final enough. He stared at the words. Maybe a phone call would make more sense. Safer but too awkward, too open-ended. He had to come straight to the point, make it clear and *final*...and send it. He scratched through all the words and wrote again. "No. Too disruptive for everyone." Nonspecific. Not incriminating. But it did make the point.

He took out another piece of paper and printed the words carefully. He folded the page, sealed it in an interoffice envelope and addressed it: <u>Cassandra Garriman, M.D., Department of Medicine, Division of Infectious Disease.</u> He went out to the receptionist's desk and turned the revolving rubber-stamp holder till he found the "Personal and Confidential" stamp. He inked it, pressed it across the sealed flap of the envelope and walked quickly to the mail room just off the corridor to the hospital. He dropped the envelope into the slot marked **Interoffice Mail**.

He had no response from her nor did he see her for several weeks after that. But that was not surprising since they functioned in different parts of the Brakefield world. When he did eventually chance to see her across the hospital lobby, and she saw him, it was not acknowledged. From then on, in any encounter in the hospital corridors or at staff meetings, she maintained the detached, professional demeanor he had always seen before New York, just the same as when she stood beside the autopsy table watching Dr. Lang. In fact, that encounter in the autopsy room was the first time they had spoken to each other since Colorado, two years before. She'd never shown anything but total discretion. He was always relieved.

*****

What she told Joe about why and how much she hated her father was true. Her feelings had intensified over the years seeing her single mother struggle to make ends meet with no help from her father. Furthermore, it had led to a deep-seated, almost subconscious mistrust of men. And in no small way, the inevitable challenges she had experienced in a predominantly male professional world during earlier periods of her career had magnified the feelings. The challenge to dominate and win where men were concerned made her bold. Indeed, it was a challenge she enjoyed.

What Joe had not realized was the satisfaction she'd derived from seducing him. From the chance afternoon encounter at the New York Hilton to the torrid day in the hotel in Snowmass, she had cast her subtle hook, reeled him in then let him go in true "catch and release" fashion. He did not get that. Nor did he realize that he was not the first. Nor that he would not be the last because such scenarios reassured her that she could use her feminine wiles as well as her intellect to manipulate men….and prevail. Joe's cryptic note, a clear signal of his discomfort, had added to her pleasure because it confirmed that he would stay in his place never to make an issue of their incidental assignations. That's the way she liked it.

CHAPTER FIFTEEN

By late Monday afternoon and early evening, as Lang was finishing up in the autopsy room, Blaine was lingering in his office in the cardiology suite finishing up the reading Reed had thrust upon him. It was just in time since Reed had him scheduled to go into the cardiology lab after 8:00 rounds Tuesday morning to meet the staff and get started. And just as planned, at 9:15 Reed escorted him to the lab.

They entered the double doors and walked past a reception desk and into the patient area where there were two patient rooms, one on either side of a nurse/technician's station. Each room had a large plate-glass observation window clearly visible from the central station. A woman in blue scrubs sat at the counter facing four computer monitors. Jagged peaks of electrocardiograms were marching across three of the screens; the fourth was blank.

The woman looked up. "Good morning, Dr. Reed," she said.

"Good morning, Naomi," said Reed. This is our new fellow, Dr. Purcell. He'll be with us for six months."

She stood and held out her hand. "Hi, Dr. Purcell. Naomi Fowler. Pleased to have you join us." They shook hands.

"He just arrived from Dallas," said Reed, "He's been out there in cardiology for how long, Blaine? Fourteen years?"

"Yes. Fourteen."

"He said he wanted to come over here for a little refresher. See if we could teach him something new." Reed laughed good-naturedly.

"That's right. Just need to upgrade," said Blaine.

"Is Dr. Kersey around?" Reed asked.

"Yes. He's in room two with Mr. Blankenship. I'll let him know you're here." She walked around the desk and off to the right. "Kersey is the medicine resident rotating in the lab for two months," said Reed. "You'll be working with him the next several weeks. Let's go around here to the reading area while we wait for him." Reed led the way to a narrow walled-off space behind the station where there were two computers, two monitors and a printer on a short counter.

"Have a seat," he said as he pulled a chair back from the counter and sat. "Kersey will show you around the lab this morning, and tomorrow I'll take you to the clinic and get you introduced. There are two residents in the clinic. They'll familiarize you with the computer system and the protocols like scheduling procedures, labs, appointments, all that. And after lunch tomorrow, you'll go in as the attending. For the time being, I've got you lined up in the lab on Tuesdays and Thursdays and in the clinic on Wednesdays and Fridays. That'll give you Mondays to concentrate on your reading and get a good start on your week." He flashed a patronizing smile.

"Sounds good. I'm looking forward to it all, especially getting into the transesophageal techniques."

"You've come to the right place for that. Kersey can get you started with that, too. He's very good. He'll come on as our fellow next year."

At that point, a young man in blue scrubs entered. "Hi, Dr. Reed," he said. "Sorry to hold you up."

"Hi, Dwayne. No problem," said Reed. "Wanted you to meet Doctor Purcell. He's just in from Dallas for six months. He's our new fellow."

"Hello," said Blaine as he stood. "Nice to meet you." They shook hands.

"I'll leave you two to get acquainted," Reed interrupted. "See you this afternoon, Blaine."

*****

The rest of the day in the lab with Kersey was instructive. They finished an hour before five o'clock rounds with Reed. But the next day, Wednesday, was a much more intense day for Blaine. After 8 o'clock rounds, Reed took him to the cardiology clinic. There, after a short time becoming acquainted with residents and the nurses, he spent the rest of the morning, with the computers and the coding system. Following lunch, he went back to the clinic to start his routine there as the attending doctor: reviewing patients' records and moving from room to room as one or another of the residents presented patients to him.

He knew he was expected to provide erudite, insightful responses to *any* questions or make observations and recommendations for diagnosis or treatment. That would be his role as the fellow, and he could be sure that as he commented and interacted, he was being sized up by the residents. Opinions were being immediately formed about his demeanor, his level of competence and his medical acumen. These first impressions of the "new doc on the block", how he conducted himself with them and the patients and how he articulated his thoughts would influence how the residents would interact with him from then on. Furthermore, the opinions they would pass on to other residents would quickly establish his reputation among them regardless of where he had trained or how many years he had been in practice. His first afternoon in the clinic brought all that back into perspective for him; he became keenly aware of that subtle vetting as he moved from room to room. However, by the end of the afternoon, he felt a comfortable rapport, and he thought he'd passed the test.

The clinic ended just before 5:00. He hurried to meet Reed for rounds. They finished about 6:30, and he returned to his office for a few minutes of welcome down time. He slipped off his white coat and sat in his desk chair reflecting on the day. Busy but satisfying, in fact very satisfying he concluded silently. At about7:00, he decided it was time for dinner. He put the coat on again and made his way to the cafeteria.

Most of the tables in the main dining room were occupied, but the large alcove beyond the overhead sign reading **Doctors' Dining Area** was less crowded. He moved to the stainless steel food counter and pushed a tray along the rail rather indifferently making his selections. At the drink dispenser, he filled a glass with ice and water and carried the tray to the designated doctors' area. A few tables near the front were occupied. At one, a young man in a short white coat was seated across from a woman in street clothes stroking the head of a baby in a carrier perched on the table. At another, two older men in long white coats were sitting face-to-face engrossed in conversation. At a third, by a young man in a white coat was sitting alone. As Blaine passed, the man looked up smiling and spoke. "You're the new fellow with Dr. Reed, right?"

Blaine stopped short. "Yes. Right," he said. It was a welcome greeting.

"Hi, I'm Andreas Locanos. Neurology. Join me if you like." He stood and motioned toward the table.

"Oh, thanks." Blaine set the tray on the table and held out his hand. "Blaine Purcell." They shook. "How'd you know about me?"

"I was at the staff meeting last week," said Andreas. "Glad to have a chance to meet you. I've gotta get back up to the floor shortly, but I thought we might chat a few minutes."

"Sure. Of course," said Blaine as they sat.

"Seems you've had some interesting training and experience," said Andreas.

"Oh, well. Dr. Reed wanted to talk about all that at the staff meeting. I thought I would just sort of slide in without much notice 'til I got adjusted, but he insisted on that introduction right off the bat. The day after I started."

"Well, I must say, it sounded pretty impressive," Andreas nodded as he spoke. "And you've been practicing in Dallas for how many years?"

"Fourteen. Just wanted to take a little break. Refresh a little. Pick up some new techniques. I heard about this fellowship, so I contacted Dr. Reed, and the rest is history, as they say."

"Nice," said Andreas.

"Got here last weekend, actually," said Blaine as he picked up the knife and fork. "Reed had a lot of reading for me to catch up on the first few days, so I've just gotten started this week in the lab and the clinic."

"How long you here for?"

"Six months. Another fellow comes the end of September, but Dr. Reed had this opening now, and I wanted to take advantage of the opportunity." He looked down at his plate, probing the baked chicken with the fork.

"Family?" Andreas asked.

The question took him by surprise, but he was in no mood to go into any details of his family situation just now. "They're back in Dallas," he said. "Six months is too short a time to move'em, 'Specially three kids near the end of the school year. But it gives me time to focus on the work, and I guess that's a good thing because Reed's got me started at a pretty good clip." He cut off a piece of the chicken.

"So have you ever been here before? Atlanta, I mean."

Just at that moment, as Andreas spoke, a sudden, unexpected sight appeared in front of Blaine. A slender, white-coat clad woman passed just two tables away carrying a tray. It was unmistakably Cassandra Garriman. The face, the hair, the determined steps. His eyes followed her magnetically, but he caught himself and blinked coming back to the conversation. "Oh…uh'm I've only driven through a few times but never spent any time here."

Cassandra Garriman disappeared behind him at the back of the room and out of his line of sight.

"I think you'll like it," said Andreas. "I don't know much about Dallas, but I'd guess it's something like Atlanta maybe?

"Guess I'll be finding out." He smiled as he took a bite of the chicken. "So tell me about you? Where you're from and all that?" He wished he could turn to see where she went, but he kept up the small talk.

"Came here from St. Louis," said Andreas. "Did a couple of years of medicine at Wash U. then here for neurology. Actually I'm just finishing a fellowship. Planning to go back to St. Louis in July. My wife's family is there, and she'd like to be near them. You want coffee?"

"Oh, no thanks. I'll get some when I finish."

"Okay. Well," Andreas glanced at his watch, "Guess I should be getting back upstairs. I'll grab a cup on my way out." Andreas stood and lifted his tray. "It's good to meet you."

"Nice to meet you, Andreas. Thanks for flagging me down," said Blaine reaching across to shake with Andreas. He could hardly wait for Andreas to leave so he could look around the room.

He took another bite of chicken and turned for a sweeping gaze over the tables of diners behind him. There she was, seated alone at a table near the back wall. She appeared to be reading something as she ate. He watched for a few seconds and turned back to his tray. Who would have guessed it? The perfect chance to introduce himself. He could say he saw her at the staff meeting and that Andreas had just mentioned her name when she passed their table. He could say he thought he remembered her name from some publications on infections and heart disease. Maybe just a shot in the dark, but it would be worth the try. Test her reaction. Couldn't hurt to be friendly. But it had to be casual and credible.

He twittled the fork in the lima beans then took another bite of chicken as he considered a strategy. He looked toward her again.

She seemed oblivious to everyone around her apparently fixed on her reading. He had no more interest in dinner. He got up and ferried his tray to the return window and still watching her, sauntered over to the coffee urns against the side wall. He filled a mug and began to navigate between tables moving nonchalantly in her direction.

As he approached, she glanced up at him. He thought he could read the slightest bit of recognition in her face before she looked back at what she was reading. He kept walking, the coffee mug in his right hand. He stopped a few feet from where she sat and addressed her quietly.

"Dr. Garriman?"

She looked up again, but this time the expression was one of complete indifference. "Yes?" she said. The face and eyes said *Can't you see I'm busy.* He had seen that kind of reaction before. This could be fun.

"Pardon me for interrupting. I just wanted to introduce myself."

"Yes?" she said in a somewhat irritated tone.

"I was having dinner over there with Dr. Locanos when you came in." He glanced in the direction of his table. "When you passed, he pointed you out as the expert in infectious disease here."

"Oh?" she said, this time like *so what.*

"I told him I thought I knew your name from the literature. Some papers on infectious cardiomyopathy. I'm Blaine Purcell, the new fellow in cardiology."

"Yes. I remember seeing you at the staff meeting. But I'm afraid I haven't published on infectious cardiomyopathy. You must be thinking of someone else." She glanced dismissively down at her reading.

He persisted. "Maybe I'm thinking of a review you published a few years back, on antiphospholipid antibodies and infectious endocarditis?" He winged it. He had, in fact, just read such a paper.

It was not by her, but he thought it sounded good.

She looked up again, this time with a slightly pleased expression. She laid the paper she was reading beside her tray. "I have written on the antiphospholipid syndrome," she said, "but that was several years ago. Journal of Investigative Cardiology. It wasn't a review though. It was peer-reviewed article."

Bingo! He had piqued her interest?

"Maybe that was it." He smiled. "I'd have to check my references."

"I can give you the exact reference if you'll call my office." She followed right along, now speaking with unsuspecting, and unexpected, amicability. "Are you working in that area?"

"No. I'm just reviewing some relevant literature with Dr. Reed at the moment." He paused locking his gaze onto hers. "I'd like to have that reference."

She did not look away. Instead she stared back with the same intensity as at the staff meeting. He felt a palpable flash of tension between them in those few seconds before she said, "You can call the Infectious Disease office. Ask for me." Both the voice and the stare softened. "I'll leave the reference with the secretary in case I'm not in. Sorry. I'm afraid I didn't quite get your name."

"Purcell. Blaine Purcell. P-u-r-c-e-l-l," he said.

"Right. Okay. I remember now. From the staff meeting," she said smiling slightly.

"I'd better let you get back to your…"

"Oh. This is nothing urgent. Join me if you like. Have your coffee." She motioned to the chair opposite. The gesture relieved the moment, but there was no denying there had been that flash moment. "It's Cassandra." She held her hand across the table.

"Nice to meet you." He reached forward and shook gently then set his coffee mug on the table and pulled out the chair opposite. "Sure I'm not interrupting?" He motioned toward the paper beside her tray.

"Oh, no. That's just a little dinner entertainment. Article on a new Rickettsial classification. Real exciting stuff." She laughed slightly sarcastically. "It can wait." Her expression was warmer. The tension was gone.

He sat.

"So you've just arrived?" she said.

"Yes. Last weekend." He looked at her intent on holding eye contact. He could tell he'd broken through her armor.

"From Dallas I believe I remember," she said.

"Yes. I've been in practice there 14 years."

"So what brings you here after all that time?"

"Oh, it's just a little break. Like a mini-sabbatical I guess you'd say. Needed to refresh a bit, and Dr. Reed offered the opportunity."

She looked down as she took a small bite of salad then back at him. "Good for you. Everyone here says he's the best." She touched her napkin to her lips. "How long are you here for?"

"Six months."

"Then what? Back to Dallas?"

"Not sure yet. I'm keeping my options open. Actually, I've…," he hesitated for a moment, "just been through a divorce. Didn't need to bring that into my introduction last week, but to tell the truth, things are a bit up in the air for me right now."

"Oh," she said with a slightly sympathetic expression. "Sorry to hear that."

"Yeah, well," he diverted, "so how long have you been here?"

"Four years," she said. "Actually almost four and a half. It's been very good. Came here from Hopkins. I've had a good interaction with the university here, and I'm still collaborating with the group in Baltimore, so it's worked out well."

"You're from Baltimore?"

"No. Just residency and fellowship at Hopkins."

"You have family here?" That seemed to be an innocent enough question.

"Oh, no. Just me." She laughed. "You know anyone in Atlanta?"

"Well, as a matter of fact one of my best friends is a cardiologist here. Luke Manning. He's in a private group on North Highland."

"I see," she replied vaguely as her interest seemed to lag.

He tried moving in a different direction. "So what do people do for entertainment around here?"

"Oh the same as a lot of places. Some great restaurants. Good symphony. Very good symphony, in fact." She sounded knowledgeable. "Of course, there's the usual helping of golf courses. And then there's the Braves. And the Falcons. Some beautiful lakes not far away. And the mountains of North Georgia and North Carolina are pretty accessible."

"Oh, yes. When I was a resident in North Carolina, we drove over to the mountains a few times." He glanced at his watch. Maybe it was time to leave. "Guess I'd better let you get back to your classification," he said.

"I'm in no hurry. Just finishing my day." She seemed to be saying she didn't want to end the conversation.

"So how about some coffee? I could use another cup."

"Sure, if you're going back," she said.

"How do you take it?" he said.

"Black."

"Okay." He stood. "Be right back. Don't go away." He flashed a quick, teasing smile.

"I'll be here," she said lifting the paper on Rickettsia.

He walked toward the coffee urns thinking now he should play it lighter. He'd gotten past the divorce and future plans. Now something more social. Maybe she'd go for a dinner at one of those restaurants. Or maybe an night at the symphony. He glanced back at her as he stood filling two mugs. She was reading again, but as he came back toward her, she put down the paper and looked up smiling, now a comfortable, feminine smile. "That didn't take long," she said.

"Easy when you don't have to add extras." He put the coffee mugs on the table and sat.

"I must say, the coffee here is pretty good," he said as he lifted his mug and sipped.

She lifted hers and blew the steam across the top. "Uhmm, pretty good for a hospital cafeteria, but there are better places."

"Tell me about some of those restaurants you were mentioned."

"I don't do restaurants here all that often, but I know a few. One I like is Soto Soto. Italian. And the Float Away Café is fun." She smiled. "Or the Blue Ridge Grill…or Rathbun's …"

He interrupted. "I have an idea. If you don't think I'm being too ah'm…forward, how about we try one of the ones you mentioned some evening before long? I don't like exploring restaurants by myself. I definitely need some guidance."

"You really do move quickly, don't you?" she said setting the coffee mug on the table.

"You think so?"

"I think so." Her intense stare came back.

There was silence and another eye-lock. Then, eyes still locked, with the hint of a smile he said, "May I call you?'

"Sure." She picked up the coffee mug again as if to deflect his intensity.

"How would I do that?" he said.

She sipped the coffee. "You have a pen?"

"Yeah. And a little black book," he said holding the smile.

"I bet you do," she said.

He drew a pen and the black notebook from his coat pocket.

"Okay," he said flipping the notebook open.

"This is my cell number," she said. He jotted it down as she glanced at her watch.

"Oh," she said, "it's almost 8:45. Gotta go shut down my computer and get out of here."

He wasn't cutting off yet. "When's the best time to call?"

"When would you like to call?"

He stood bending forward slightly and said, "Immediately." His smile broadened as he reached for her tray. "May I take this," he said expecting her to refuse.

"Thank you." She nodded slightly and stood.

He set the two empty mugs on the tray. Starting toward the exit, he deposited the tray on the tray-return, and they walked out into the hospital corridor.

"Enjoyed our conversation, Cassandra," he said, now more casually. "I'll check with you."

"Glad you stopped by." She held out a hand. "And by the way, my friends call me Cassie."

He took the hand, held it lightly for a few seconds and said,

"Good night...Cassie."

CHAPTER SIXTEEN

Evelyn Kanaby, bewildered and bereft, was trying hard to absorb the reality of Richard's death, but Martha and Allen had to handle all the necessary details. The cremation was carried out the day after the autopsy. During that morning, Martha and Allen composed a dignified obituary and worked out arrangements for a memorial service which was to be held three days later, on Friday. Through it all, Allen continued to dwell quietly on his belief that something toxic had caused his father's death. Dr. Holleran had explained that although the preliminary toxicology reports were negative, some tests were still pending. Allen held out hope that those would give the answer. But the lack of anything conclusive kept him fitfully wondering. He'd had no time to investigate since he'd talked to Charles Funchess, but now he was even more driven to try to find out something about Wansaw.

Thursday morning, confirming that all was set for the Friday service for Richard, Allen returned to his office to search for information he might find online. He opened Google on his desktop and typed in the word Wansaw. To his surprise, the words **Wansaw Island South Carolina** appeared. He brought up the information page: "Wansaw Island is a barrier island off the coast of South Carolina. It is part of the Charleston-North Charleston Metropolitan Statistical Area. According to the U.S Geological Survey, Wansaw Island has a total surface area of 14.62 square miles comprising 9.78 square miles of land and 4.84 square miles of water including wetlands. Demographics: As of the 2000 census, Wansaw Island is uninhabited."

He printed the page then went to MapQuest and typed in **Wansaw Island South Carolina**. The response: "We did not find a match for your request." What next? South Carolina State Government maybe? He Googled. There were many choices on the website, but with a list so daunting, a phone call might be easier. He dialed the general information number.

"Can you connect me to a department for census information?" he said to the operator.

"One moment please."

Then: "Demographics and Census, John speaking."

"Yes, hello," said Allen, quickly composing his thoughts. "I need current census information for some of the smaller islands along the coast of South Carolina."

"Yes, sir," replied John. "We should be able to help you. Which ones do you need?"

"For starters, how about one called Wansaw? W-A-N-S-A-W. Could you check that one?"

"That's one I don't recall," said John, "but give me a minute, and I'll see what I can pull up." Allen could hear computer keyboard clicks. "Yes, I found it. One of the really small ones. My information says it's in Charleston County. Unincorporated. The last population figure for the year 2000 was zero. Going back to 1990, it was 45. But in 1980, population was 115. Dropped off completely from 1980 to 2000. That's all the information I have."

"Can you tell me anything about the location?" said Allen.

"My information says Access: Anson Point, South Carolina. That's the closest point of access by a registered highway. That means a highway designated and numbered as either state or national."

"Can you tell me where Anson Point is?"

"Yes. It's on James Island. Southwest of Charleston," said John. "You need the population figures?"

"No. That's fine."

"Any others you want me to check?"

"Ah'm...not right now. I'll get a few other names together and get back to you."

"Yes, sir. Call back whenever you're ready."

Allen went back to MapQuest: Anson Point, South Carolina. There it was. He clicked on Street Maps. It looked like one long street running parallel to a large body of water labelled Stono Inlet and four short side streets. He printed it and went back to Google which declared: "Anson Point is a coastal village in Charleston County, South Carolina, founded in 1846. It is located on James Island as part of the Charleston-North Charleston Metropolitan Statistical Area. The population at the 2000 census was 245." There were short statements on geography and demographics; industry was described as "Commercial Fishing." He printed it out, slid the two pages into his briefcase, turned off the computer and left the office.

It was almost noon. He'd promised Martha and Evelyn he would meet them at 1:30, but he had to make one stop, specifically to find a map of South Carolina. At the 7-Eleven four blocks away, he found one titled Southeastern United States on the map rack. He hurried back to his car and on home to study it before he headed to Evelyn's house.

Ellen was out and the kids were in school. He parked in the garage, went in through the kitchen door, and spread the map on the counter. He felt excitement as he focused on the South Carolina coastline. The words **Charleston** and **Savannah** stood out in bold letters. His finger went to Charleston and traced along the smaller print names just beneath: Folly Island, James Island, John's Island, Kiawah Island. Anson Point was not shown, but it was on MapQuest. That reassured him.

He heard Ellen's car pull into the garage. He folded the map and tucked it into his brief-case. When she came through the kitchen door, her face registered surprise. "I thought you were at your mom's," she said. "Are you okay?"

He put his arms around her. "Yeah. Just need a little time to get my head together."

"I know, sweetheart," she said. "Why don't you take a little rest. I'll make a quick lunch. What's going on with your mom?"

"Martha's with her," he said. "I'm sure there are plenty of folks there now, you know, bringing food ....or flowers. I had to check some things at the office, so I said I'd be there by 1:30."

"I've got to bring in the groceries. Go take a little nap." She started back toward the door.

"I'll help you." He followed her and opened the car door. Then timing himself as he lifted out two large bags of groceries, he casually said, "By the way, I found that island."

She looked up as she reached for the two smaller bags. "What island?"

"Wansaw Island. In South Carolina. Where Mose was from," he said as he pushed the car door shut. He followed her back into the kitchen and put the bags on the counter.

She set her bags down. "What do you mean, you found it?"

"I went on the internet and found it."

"And?"

"And...it does exist," he said, "but it's so small it's not shown on the map. I called the state government offices in South Carolina, and the guy in the census department told me where it is and even how to get there."

"How to get there?" she said looking dumbfounded. "You don't mean you're thinking of going there?

"Maybe."

"Oh, Allen," she said, "you're telling me you're going to try to go to some godforsaken island you only heard about because

Charles Funchess told you he remembered hearing about something that happened 50 years ago?" She tried to soften her tone, "Can't we at least wait to talk about this until after your dad's service?"

"Yes, of course, but I know I'm not gonna be satisfied 'til I go there to find out more. Maybe somebody there can tell me what happened," he said. "Why all those people died."

"Seriously, Allen, you don't know for sure that ever really did happen. You think going there because of what Charles said will tell you why your dad died?"

"Possibly," he said. "What Charles told me sounded exactly the same. Maybe I can find somebody to talk to."

"So who do you think you can talk to, the mayor?" Her tone hinted mild exasperation.

He just looked at her. "Okay," she said, "so I know you're planning something."

"We'll talk about it later."

"That makes more sense," she spoke more gently. "We're all stressed right now, but..," she paused thoughtfully, "tell me again how you found it." He obviously had gotten her attention.

"Googled it," he said. "I can show you on the map." He took the map from his briefcase and unfolded it on the counter again. "Here's Charleston." He pointed. "There's Kiawah Island and one called Folly Island. There's James Island." His finger moved slowly over the paper. "And right there is where I think Wansaw is." The finger stopped.

"Where you *think* it is? I thought you said you know."

"That's where it is. It just doesn't show on this map."

"Oh, Allen, honestly. I can't believe you're actually thinking of going there." She shook her head frowning. "How would you even get to it? "

"I don't know, but I'm going to find out. What I *do* know is I want to find out more. Seems the only way I can do that is to go there myself." He folded the map and walked into the den.

CHAPTER SEVENTEEN

The end of the week was less intense for Blaine as he got into the routine in the cardiology lab on Thursday and in the clinic with the residents on Friday. He stayed later than usual after rounds on Friday because he wanted to read up on the ECHO techniques they had demonstrated in the lab. That was exciting, and in fact, he became so absorbed in the reading, he forgot about dinner.

It was almost 9:30 when he left his office. By this time, it was easier to pick up something on the way home. A stop at Captain D's for takeout was a good choice. When he pulled into the parking place in front of his apartment, the dash clock said 10:08. He switched off the engine and lights and stared at the black windows of his apartment. His thoughts wandered idly back to nights alone in Dallas when he occasionally ventured out to one or another late- night bar. But as those vague memories slogged through his mind, the moments two nights ago in the cafeteria with Cassandra Garrison took over, images of her face and eyes still vivid. But more vivid were the last few minutes when she held out a hand and said, "My friends call me Cassie." He dwelled there for a minute then reached for the briefcase and the box from Captain D's and got out of the car.

Entering the apartment, he flipped on the overhead light trying to ignore the ugly furniture and the stark room. He went into the kitchen, turned on the overhead light, opened the Captain D's box and picked up the bottle of Scotch. He poured it neat and took a long draught then sat on the stool by the counter savoring the warmth and flavor of the scotch and the aroma of warm fried shrimp. This would be a good night after all, he thought. He loosened his tie and began to pluck out crisp morsels from the box one by one. In a few minutes, he finished the full dozen along with a good portion of French fries with intermittent sips of scotch. His hunger satiated, he poured more scotch and made his way up to the bedroom, glass in hand.

He turned on the bedroom light, set the glass on the dresser and reached into his pocket for the black notebook. He opened the book to her number. If he read the vibes right, he thought, she sent a pretty clear message. And if he hadn't, it wouldn't matter anyway. He glanced at his watch. 10:35. If he called now and she were out somewhere or asleep, she wouldn't answer. But what if she was home alone? He pressed the number into his phone.

Four rings then, "Hello," came a smoky voice.

"Cassie?"

"Yes."

"Hi. It's Blaine. Blaine Purcell." He waited.

"Oh. Blaine." She sounded surprised. "What are you...?"

"Sorry to call so late," he said. "Had a long day. Just came in. Not very sleepy so....thought I'd see if you were still up. You said I could call."

She could have said something like "Yes, but...it's pretty late. Can you call me tomorrow?" or "I wasn't expecting to hear from you this late" or "I was just about to go to bed."

But she didn't. Instead she said, "I'm still up." She paused noticeably long then breathed the words quietly into the phone, "I'm a late night person." Her tone was receptive, not resistive or annoyed.

"So it seems," he said trying for casual. "How late is late?"

"Oh, usually around this time," she said, "depending on my day...and my mood."

"So if the mood is right, you're up late?"

"Something like that." Another pause. "You're a late nighter too?" Her voice was playful.

"Oh, yeah. Always have been," he said. "Usually up 'til midnight."

"Same for me." she said, "In fact I think it's kind of nice."

"You mean coming home late?" Test-question.

"Well, not necessarily coming home late," her voice softened. "Just being home. Having late-night hours to relax and... let go." The last words floated on a suggestive sigh.

Was she teasing him? He wanted to see where this was going.

"But sometimes it's nice to be with someone late at night," he said.

"Yes, sometimes." Her voice changed to a flat, almost disinterested tone.

Back off, he thought, *but don't give up.* "A night like tonight," he said. "End of the week. Late and relaxed." Silence. "You still there?"

"I'm here." Again, the flat tone.

He pushed on. "Are you relaxed?"

"Yes. I am."

"So am I." *Don't stop,* he thought. *Go for it.* "I'd like to come over and...relax with you. Right now."

"You're kidding, right?" The playful tone was back. Maybe she was enjoying this.

"No. I'm not," he said.

"Where are you?"

That sounded promising. "I'm in Dunwoody," he said throwing off the words nonchalantly.

"You have any idea where I am?

"No. But I bet you could tell me," he said sure he was about to score.

"I'm at least 30 minutes away," she said, the tone changing again to a matter-of-fact one.

"No problem for me," he said. "Thought you said you're a late night person."

"Yes, but it's too late tonight," she said, now firmly. "Why don't you call me tomorrow?

Dong!! End of the round. Time to stop pushing. Best to end casually. At least she was leaving the door open.

"Okay. Sure," he said.

"We can talk."

He liked that. "Yeah, okay. I'll call you around noon. Maybe we can go for a quick dinner tomorrow night if you're not busy."

"We'll see. Call me." Her phone clicked off.

He slid his phone onto the bedside table and laid back on the bed thinking again of sitting across from her at the table in the cafeteria. When she'd looked at him in that flash of a moment and held out her hand, he knew he had broken through the cool distant aura she seemed to like to project. Now she was playing with him. Leading him on then cutting him off. "Damn what a *bitch*," he said out loud as he closed his eyes and drifted off.

Just before 1:30, his cell ringtone woke him. He sat up quickly, trying to gain his bearings. He looked at his watch and reached for the phone. He hoped there was nothing wrong in Dallas.

"Hello," he said with a loud almost cell-yell.

"Hello," came a quiet reply. It was the same smoky voice.

"Oh...hell—o," He tried not to sound surprised.

"You still up?"

"Yes. Just about to turn in," he said wondering what this was all about.

"Too bad."

"Why too bad?" he said.

"I don't seem to be able to get to sleep," she said, the voice even smokier. "So maybe it's not too late after all."

"Oh, really?" He was back on track.

"If you're up for a little early morning drive."

"I could probably manage," he said.

"Good," she said almost in a whisper.

"How do I get there."

"285 West to I-75 South toward Macon."

"Hold on a minute. Let me grab a pen."

"Okay."

He got up quickly and grabbed a pen from the dresser. "Okay. I'm back."

"Take 285 west to I-75 south," she said slowly. "I-75 to the Moore's Mill Road exit…254 I think. Left at the end of the ramp, two blocks to Coleman Avenue," Pause. "Left on Coleman, 6th house on the left. Number 4327." She stopped, then said, "You get all that?"

"Yep."

"Park in the driveway, and come in through the carport."

CHAPTER EIGHTEEN

Monday morning she pressed the number into her office phone.

"Neuropathology. May I help you?" a voice answered.

"Good morning. This is Dr. Garriman at Brakefield Hospital. Is Dr. Lang available?"

"One moment please." The line went to hold.

Then "Dr. Lang," came a stern voice.

"Hello, Dr. Lang. This is Cassandra Garriman at Brakefield Hospital. We met last Monday when you came in to do the brain autopsy."

"Oh, yes," the tone mellowed. "You're in infectious disease, right?"

"That's right," she replied. "If you have time , I'd like to discuss a few things about the case with you."

"Sure, but you understand we don't have any results yet," he said. "Nothing 'til at least the end of the week."

"I understand," she said, "but in the meantime, I've been studying the records, particularly the lab reports, and I've come across something interesting. The bacterial cultures on blood and spinal fluid are negative so far, and we don't have any results yet on viral and fungal cultures. Gram stains and rapid viral testing on the spinal fluid are negative as well. The routine immunoglobulins showed a slight elevation in IgG, but the IgA and IgM were okay. I mean, not elevated. But," she paused, "I just discovered that three days before this man died, the neurology resident ordered additional immunoglobulins. IgD and IgE. Not sure what prompted him to do that, but I guess it was a good thing."

"Oh?" said Lang.

"The results were delayed coming back because the specimens had to be sent out to a reference lab," she continued. "The report didn't show up 'til the day after the autopsy, but it indicates that IgE was significantly elevated. If that's accurate, it may be important, though I think the test should be repeated to make sure it's not lab error. I'm wondering if you might still have some serum you collected at the autopsy that we could send out for re-testing."

"Yes we do have some. Frozen in aliquots" said Lang. "How much do you need?"

"Five or ten milliliters if possible?"

"That's possible," he said. "We can ship directly from here if you'll fax me the shipping address to send it to with your requisition and how it's to be billed."

"Of course. I can, right now," she said. "Our pathology department has a standing account with that lab."

"So what do you make of an elevated IgE?" said Lang.

"Well, if it's not an error and IgG and IgE are the only ones elevated, that's a puzzle because an elevated IgE is quite unusual. Mainly associated with a hypersensitive reaction of some kind. How that fits here is a mystery. That's why I want to repeat it, in fact repeat all of the immunoglobulins."

"Okay. We can get that out today."

"That would be great," she said excitedly. "Now, just two more things if you don't mind."

"Of course," Lang responded.

"I've been focused on something infectious," she said, "but since all the studies for conventional infections are negative, I'm also considering some unconventional infections. The EEG pattern seems to rule out prion disease, but there are some other possibilities to consider though I don't think any of them would be likely to present symptoms or a clinical course like this. But switching horses a bit,

Dr. Holleran in particular, has been concerned about some toxic chemical exposure. This man was an industrial chemist."

"Yes. I saw in the record that he was a chemical engineer," said Lang.

"Right," said Cassie. "He owned a company which produces various kinds of pesticides."

"That I didn't know," said Lang sounding surprised. "I haven't heard anything about pesticides."

"According to his family, he hasn't worked directly with any chemicals at his company for quite some years," she said. "He hired other people to do the chemical work. But there is a twist."

"Oh?"

"He was also an expert gardener," she said. "Apparently that was his great passion, and according to his wife, he liked to concoct mixtures for his gardening."

"Ah," said Lang. "So maybe he made his own fertilizers...or pesticides."

"A definite possibility," she said," but the family all say they have no information about that. Dr. Dittrich ordered a full toxicology screen specifically including organophosphates, organo-chlorines and carbamates. The specimens also had to be sent to an outside lab. We're still waiting for the results. At any rate, I think we can assume that anything toxic enough to cause the kind of illness this man had would have to be extremely powerful. Powerful enough to be lethal. Don't think it would be anything he might have picked up at a garden center."

"I would agree," he said, "but I think we should see what the autopsy shows before we go too far with speculation about either toxins or infection."

"Yes, of course," she said deferentially. "Any idea yet when you'll be looking at the microscopic slides?"

"I'll submit the tissue blocks tomorrow. We should have preliminary slides out by Friday. When I see those, I'll be able to decide how to proceed. I expect we'll need some immunohistochemical stains next and perhaps some molecular studies."

"Shall I check with you Friday?" she said.

"Sure. Or I'll call you once I've had a chance to see the slides."

CHAPTER NINETEEN

Neither Allen's curiosity nor his determination had abated since he'd spoken to the man at the Census Office in South Carolina. He waited until the morning after the memorial service to broach the subject again with Ellen. He was able to convince her that he would not take chances and would go at least to the place called James Island and the town called Anson Point to see if he could find out anything about Wansaw. She recognized his resolve and reluctantly acquiesced.

He couldn't leave until the end of the following week because of his work and the time he missed there during the previous week. But on Friday afternoon, almost two weeks after Richard's death, Allen was on his way. He had inquired specifically at AAA about directions to James Island. He was told the most direct route was through the town of Summerville to Route 61 along the west side of the Ashley River. That way, he could avoid Charleston traffic.

After close to 5 hours of driving, the Summerville exits on Interstate 26 came up on the right. He took the second exit and drove west through a commercial area and shortly into the center of town. The intersection at the fourth stoplight was cornered by several aged but impressive red-brick buildings. They contrasted strikingly with the dark green of the canopy spread overhead by branches of the trees bordering the streets.

The sign on the corner indicated Charleston straight ahead. When the light changed, he drove past a stretch of small shops then another red-brick building, this one with a white-columned façade and the words **Town Hall** hailing prominently from a sign above the portico. Continuing along slowly, he began to pass a few elegant old houses set back from the street on either side, graceful monuments to a time-mellowed past. The afternoon sunlight dappled the street and sidewalks, and for a few moments, everything seemed to shift into slow-motion in this quietly cloistered place.

But that feeling changed when he approached a five-point intersection where the traffic pattern became confusing. Driving through it, he realized he'd missed the turn to Charleston. He pulled into a gas station and stopped beside a car where a man was pumping gas. "Excuse me. Could you tell me how to get to Highway 61?"

"Yes, sir," the man replied. "That's ol' Chahlston highway. Go back awn this street two blocks," he waved a hand in the direction, "and you'll see a sign pointin' lef'. That'll take you right oat to 61." The man spoke with an unusual accent and a rhythmic cadence as he pointed. "Chahlston's about 30 miles awn down."

He followed the directions turning at the sign, **Charleston 35 miles**. Beyond that, another sign read **Historic Gardens & Plantations**. In less than a half mile, he crossed railroad tracks, another intersection and soon after, the highway led through dense woodlands. Branches of the trees on either side spread above the highway forming a kind of tunnel. As he drove along, bursts of the afternoon sunlight to the west flashed between the thick tree trunks producing a strobe-like effect.

There were occasional small houses set close to the road on either side. Presently the trees disappeared, and the highway coursed for a few miles over a causeway with wide marshes on either side. When the marshes ended, the canopy of branches resumed.

After some 20 minutes or so, a sign came up on the left **Middleton Place, 1706**. He slowed slightly as he passed a broad driveway leading to a tall latticed gate between two brick pillars. He wondered what might be behind such a striking structure of a gate, but he moved on. Farther along, he passed another sign: **Magnolia**

Gardens, 1704, One Mile, and after a few more minutes, he approached a sign reading **Saint Andrew's Parish Church, Next Left**. Beyond that, he caught the words **St. Andrew's Parish Church, 1706** on a metal historic marker. At that point he could see, on the left some hundred yards off the highway, a small white building with green roof and shutters set in a thick grove of trees. Giving way to his curiosity, he turned just beyond the metal marker onto a sandy driveway through the grove. As he got closer, he could see that near the side of the building there were rows of weathered gravestones surrounded by a simple wrought-iron fence.

He pulled to a stop some 50 yards from the church and got out, glancing in all directions. There was no one else around. He walked slowly toward the church but turned toward the graveyard. He stopped at the iron fence. The silence, the stillness, the starkness of the grave stones, the mellowed elegance of the old church, the festoons of Spanish moss hanging from the trees, swaying and floating ghost-like in the twilight…the whole atmosphere suspended him in a few moments of unexpected contemplation as he began to imagine what life might have been like so many years ago in this mysteriously beautiful part of the world. But it was indeed an uneasy reverie when he thought of what had brought him here.

A high-pitched horn blared on the highway and shattered his thoughts. He returned to his car and drove away toward Charleston. The waning sun to the west gave the marshes, now on his right, a purplish cast. The sky was crimson behind the black silhouettes of trees beyond. At one point, the marsh was replaced by a wide expanse of water reflecting the color of the sky so brilliantly, it was as if it were flaming. Again, he felt suspended, but now in such a stunning vortex of nature, he had to force himself to look away and focus on his driving. As he fixed his gaze straight ahead, the flash of a traffic light a half mile or so in front of him brought him back. Getting closer, he could see the glaring neon light of an EXXON sign above a Tiger Mart, and almost instantly, the serenity of the last half hour gave way to the reality of storefronts and parking strips and stores on both sides of the road: **Burger King, Jiffy Lube, KFC, Barton's Used Cars, Horton's Insurance, Thrifty Dry Cleaners** and so on. A jarring transition.

At a **Charleston City Limits** sign, the highway widened into double lanes. After another mile or so, he turned into a convenience store and stopped at a gas pump. He fed a credit card into the slot, pushed the nozzle into the tank, squeezed the handle and cocked it. While the pump droned, he leaned back against the car, looking up at the graying sky as he reflected on what he'd just seen but also what he might find in Anson Point. Or Wansaw.

The nozzle handle gave a loud pop. He hooked it back on the pump and walked into the store. "Good evening," he approached the clerk. "Could you tell me if 61 gets me to Anson Point?"

"Oh, yeah. Tha's over awn James Island," he said. "Stay awn 61 about another fo' miles and you'll come to a big intersection, Holiday Inn awn yo' lef'." He spoke with the same unique accent and cadence he'd heard in Summerville. "You'll see the sign to James Island off to yo' right. That'll be Highway 171. Take that awn out till you see the sign to Anson Point."

"You know about how far it is?"

"Oh, it's 'boat 15 o' 16 miles."

"Any places to stay there?"

"Naw, I don't reckon there's any place to stay in Anson Point. You lookin' for a place to stay, you better stay up here. That Holiday Inn's nice."

A few minutes later, the woman at the registration desk of the Holiday Inn greeted him with the same accent. He registered and got a room on the 2nd floor. He switched on the lights and dropped his bag on the table beside the door as he hurried into the bathroom. Relief after the long drive. He washed hands and face and checked his watch: 7:30. He drove back two blocks for a quick dinner at a Denny's Restaurant he'd spotted coming in, and by 9:15, he was in bed. But anticipation tempered with apprehension made for a restless night. By 5:30 am, he was wide awake. He showered and shaved, and at 6:15, he was checking out. He asked the man behind the desk for a local map as he signed the credit card bill.

"Yes, sir," said the man. "You need directions?" He did not speak with the rhythmic accent.

"Yes," said Allen nodding, "to Anson Point?"

"Oh, sure," the man replied. "Here. I'll show you." He lifted a small folder from behind the counter, unfolded it to lay out a local map. "It's over on James Island. We're here." He pointed with a pen and drew an X. "Turn left out of our parking lot and at the first light, there's a sign to James Island, Route 171. You'll pass several intersections, but stay on 171 'til you see the sign to Anson Point. Turn there and it'll take you right out."

"Okay. Thanks," said Allen as he studied the map.

"They'll be having the big regatta out there the end of May," said the man. "It's great fun if you like sailing. I do some out there myself when I can. We like to go through the channel and out to the islands out there."

Allen perked: The islands out there.

The man continued pointing to the map. "There's Stono Inlet. And the channel between Kiawah and Folly. Then you've got Marsh Island and Bird Key and on out, Jakaw and Wansaw. You've probably never heard of any of those."

"I have heard of Wansaw," said Allen. "Have you ever been there?"

"Oh, yes sir. How'd you hear about Wansaw?"

"My dad used to know a man who was born there," said Allen. "He lived there 'til he was about 18. Eventually he moved to Atlanta. He died some years ago, but I've wondered what happened to his family because I understand there's no one living there now."

"That's right. It's completely deserted. 12 miles out. It's the farthest one. People lived there for many years. Gullah people. But eventually they either left or died out. I've been there several times with some of my sailing buddies just to look around. It's interesting to see, but nothing's there now except some dilapidated old cabins or huts…and an old cemetery."

"And you say Gullah people lived there?" said Allen. "I thought Gullah was a language?"

"Yes. It is. But it's also a whole culture. Language is only part of it" said the man. "Gullah people are descendants of people from West Africa. I think Angola and Sierra Leone. I've heard that's where the word Gullah came from. Angola."

"My dad's friend told him quite a bit about what it was like there when he was growing up. Hearing Dad talk about it always made me curious. I happened to have some work that took me to Columbia this week, so I thought the weekend might be a good time to come down to check it out. In Columbia, they told me that Anson Point is the nearest access point to Wansaw from the mainland. Is that right?"

"I suppose," said the man. "Are you thinking of going there?"

"Well..yes. I'd like to if I can find a way….like a marina with a boat and a guide that would take me out," said Allen. "Anything like that in Anson Point?"

"There're two marinas. I know the owner of one of 'em. He's got couple of guys working for him as guides. They take people out fishin' or just cruisin', and sometimes he takes people out himself. Would you like me to give him a call?"

"That would be great. Might save me a lot of time," said Allen.

"I was thinking of going out there myself this afternoon. I've got a little time off."

"So you work here all week?" said Allen.

"No, actually I'm in med school. I just work the night desk here Fridays and Saturdays to make a little extra money."

"Med school, huh?" said Allen. "I'm impressed. How long before we can call you doc?"

"*Four more weeks*," the young man replied with a heaving breath and broad grin.

Aha, Allen thought to himself: If he knows the owner, maybe he could get a good deal. "So if your friend has a boat available and you've got the time, why don't you come along? Be my guest. Bet you could use a little R & R, and sounds like you know something about that island."

"That's tempting, but I couldn't get out there before noon. Got some things to take care of over at school as soon as I get off here."

"Let me introduce myself. I'm Allen Kanaby." He held out his hand across the counter.

"Yes, sir, Mr. Kanaby. I saw your name on the registry. I'm Dale Hawkins." They shook hands.

"Maybe you could find out if your friend's got something," said Allen.

"Okay, sure. Give me a few minutes. I'll try to call him," said Dale. "I know he's got some nice little inboards. Powerful enough to get out to the islands in plenty of time this afternoon, especially if the water's calm. Have you had breakfast?"

"No. I was going to grab a bite here," said Allen glancing at his watch. "You call, and I'll check back with you shortly." At 7:20, Allen returned.

"Yes, sir," said Dale. "He says he has a nice little Mercury sixteen footer. $75 plus gas for the afternoon. Says he's not real busy today so he'll be glad to take you out himself. His help comes in at noon, so that should work out fine. $125 for a half-day to guide plus the boat and gas so it'd be around $225 total. He's one of the best. Knows all the islands, and he's been out there many times."

"Sounds good. How 'bout you? Think you can join us?"

"Well yes, sir, if noon's not too late, I think I can make it by then."

"Okay, great," said Allen. "Call him back and book it. And by the way, please call me Allen. Drop the sir." They both laughed. "Does he need a credit card number?"

"If I tell him we'll be there, that's all he'll need," said Dale. "He's a real laid-back guy. Tom Guthrie. I'll let him know. You go on ahead, and I'll meet you there at noon. It's called Guthrie's Marina." Allen jotted the name on the edge of the map.

*****

By 8:00, Allen had coursed along highway 171 onto James Island and was just turning at **Anson Point** sign onto a much narrower road. The marshes on both sides were laced with meandering creeks and patches of water reflecting glints of sunlight through the gold-and-green hued grasses. There was very little traffic, and, like yesterday, he felt suspended in a surreal environment but now with bright sky and moist, salt-scented air blowing against his face through the open windows.

In another 15 minutes, he approached another smaller sign to Anson Point. As he rounded a curve, the road led across a short bridge and onto a street between two rows of weathered buildings. Those on the left stood braced on pilings along the edges of the marsh. The few on the right sat in front of sturdy docks. Farther along was a broad wharf where three commercial fishing boats were moored, their angled trawler-arms standing above their decks. Several men on the wharf were washing the boats or piling nets.

A few cars and pickups were parked irregularly on either side of the street. Allen pulled to a stop on the right. He got out and stepped onto the board walkway. He walked slowly along and stopped at a storefront with a weathered sign above the double screen doors reading **Marine Supply**. He pulled one of the doors open and walked in.

A musty smell hung in the rectangular, high-ceilinged room. The floor was bare, traffic-worn wood. In the center, piles of neatly coiled rope and folded nets lay beside two long wooden racks holding dozens of fishing rods. Behind a long counter at the back of the room were shelves of bins holding a metal fittings, rolls of chain and wire and an assortment of tools. Against the wall to the left, there was a small pot-bellied stove set on a metal floor pad. Its chimney pipe veered crookedly upward then bent at a right-angle, there suspended from the ceiling by a sturdy looking wire as it passed through the wall. The room was silent and apparently empty so Allen was startled by the sound of a man's voice, "Mawnin', sir."

Allen turned to see a white-haired man holding a newspaper and sitting behind the far end of the counter. "Good morning," Allen replied.

"He'p you find somethin' this mawnin'?" The man stood and put down the newspaper.

"No thanks. Just looking around if I may," said Allen as he fingered one of the fishing rods.

"Don't cost nuthin' to look." The man sat again and picked up the paper.

Allen walked toward the counter. "Would you know where Guthrie's Marina is?" he said.

"Quarter mile awn down awn yo' right." The accent again. "Goin' oat t'day?"

"Yes," said Allen. "Suppose to meet a friend there at noon."

"Good day for it."

"Sure looks like it," said Allen. He moved closer to the end of the counter. "You been here a long time?"

"Awl my life," the man replied proudly.

"Guess you have a lot of people coming here for fishing, huh?" said Allen.

"Oh, yeah, most of the time 'cept in the fall when hurricane season starts kickin' up. Can get rough then sometimes. 'Course winter's not so good either, but rest o' the time's pretty good."

"How's fishing out toward some of the little islands…like Jakaw or Wansaw? Pretty good?"

"Oh yeah, but you gotta know where you're goin'," said the man. "An' 'course you need to watch the weather. If one o' them squalls comes up, that can get a little rough." The man's eyes narrowed thoughtfully. "You plannin' to do some fishin'?"

"No. Just like to get out on the water," said Allen. "Look around a little. My friend knows the area pretty well. He's from Charleston. We're planning to take a boat out for the afternoon."

"Sailin' or motorin'?"

"Oh, motoring," said Allen. "He's got a 16-footer lined up at that marina."

"That oughta be okay t'day," said the man. "How far out you goin'?"

"He's thinking we might get out to Wansaw."

"It's a good ways, but you can make it in less than hour. Ever been oat t'ere?"

"No," said Allen.

The man folded the paper and laid it on the counter. "Pretty little island. Used to be people lived out there, but nobody's there now. Ever'body moved off or died off…or was scared off."

Allen perked. "Scared off?" he said.

"Oh, yeah. Couple bad hurricanes out there. And after the big one around nineteen fawty o' so, some kinda sickness come up on Wansaw."

"Sickness?" said Allen now paying full attention.

"Yeah. Never did know exactly what caused it. Some folks say it was them ol' feral hogs had diseases. Made people sick. But some claim it was evil spirits caused it. Say the hurricane got'em stirred up. 'Parently after that's when people gradu'ly started leavin' or jus' dyin' out. Nobody's been livin' there fo' yeahs."

"You think anyone around now might know something about that sickness?" said Allen.

The man's eyes narrowed again. "You from the health department o' somethin' ? "

"Oh no." said Allen. If he could quickly come up with something plausible, the man might be able to help him get some information. "I'm ah…working for a company in Atlanta. We study changes in populations. Demographics. So I'm interested in….."

"What 'zat? demo what?" The eyes narrowed again. " 'Zat somethin' like democrats?"

Allen laughed. "No, not democrat. Demo - graphics," he said. "Just means the study of populations in different places. No politics. Right now, we're studying the smaller islands along the coast. And Wansaw is one I'm interested in because I've heard my dad talk about it. I'm looking into how the population changed out there. On Wansaw and Jakaw and some of the others."

"Well I'm mighty glad to know you ain't no politician," said the man. "We got too damn many o' them as it is. Know what I mean?" He cocked his head and shrugged as if he expected confirmation. He seemed to believe Allen's explanation. "Yeah, I reckon the islands have changed. 'Specially the little ones. Like I said, *ain't nobody* awn Wansaw no mo'. Maybe ol' Geo'ge Pelzer could tell you somethin' about that. He lives rightchyeah in Anson Point. Ovah across the road." He pointed toward the street. "He was born on Wansaw. He lived there quite awhile when he was young."

"You think I could talk to him?"

"Oh, I 'spec' so if he's around."

"How could I find him?" said Allen.

"Well…if you c'n wait a while 'til my help comes in, I'll walk you ovah to where he lives. What was yo' name, Mistah?"

"Kanaby. Allen Kanaby," said Allen holding out his hand.

"I'm Jasper." The shook hands.

"I'd appreciate it if you'd take me over and introduce me," said Allen.

"I'll be glad to," said Jasper. "Have a seat if you like. My man'll be here pretty soon."

"I'll just check out your fishing rods," said Allen. He wandered back to the racks.

Presently a stocky, balding man with a thin gray combover ambled through the door. "Mawnin', Jasper," he drawled.

"Mawnin', Hiram," said Jasper. "Good fishin' day looks like, aye?"

"Yeah," said Hiram. "Real good. Wouldn't mind goin' oat t'day myself." The same accent.

"I'm fixin' to take this young feller 'cross the street." He came around the end of the counter. "He's got some business to take care of. We'll be back befo' long."

"Aw'right. You take yo' time. I'll be rightchyeah. "

"Okay," said Jasper. "Let's go see if we can find Geo'ge."

Allen and Jasper walked out to the board walk and across the street. A few steps along on the other side, they turned into a narrow lane which trailed down toward the marsh. It was lined three small wooden houses on the left.

"He lives right down hyeah. Second house. He's probably home. He don't get out much." They stopped in front of the house. Three steps led up to a narrow wood-floored porch. Jasper stood beside the steps and rapped on the floor with four hard knocks. "Geo'ge", he called. "Oh, Geo'ge, you home?" He waited for some sign of life. He called again. "Geo'ge, somebody outchyeah wants to talk to you."

A large elderly black woman opened the screen-door. "Mawnin', Mistah Jasper," she said. "Geo'ge eenside. 'E comin'."

The door opened wider, and a slightly bent old man with very black skin and a shock of white hair moved slowly onto the porch. "Mawnin', Mistah Jasper. How you?" He looked intently at Jasper and Allen as he came toward them.

"Mawnin', Geo'ge", said Jasper. "This here's Mr. Allen from Atlanta. He's wantin' to ask you somethin' 'bout Wansaw. You mind talkin' to'im?"

"Good morning, Mr. Pelzer." Allen held out his hand toward George as he stepped up on the first step.

George reached out a gnarled hand and shook with a strength that surprised Allen. "Yes suh, Mr. Allen. Pleased t'meetcha." He smiled slightly. "Whatchu wantin' t' know 'bout Wansaw? Ain't nuttin' but a little piece o' groun' oat 'deh een 'de ocean."

"I used to know a man who grew up there.. Named Mose Funchess. Did you ever hear of Mose Funchess on Wansaw?"

"Le's see, now." George looked thoughtfully toward the ceiling. "I knowed some o' 'dem Funchess people libbin' deh'. I b'lieve I do r'member Mose. 'E older'n me. Lef' Wansaw long time ago. Went obah to Chahleston. Don' know what happen to'im aftah 'e lef' Wansaw. You know?"

"Yes. He lived in Atlanta," said Allen. "He was a friend of my father. He died about 10 years ago, but he used to tell my father about growing up on Wansaw."

"Yeah, I 'memb'im. 'E baun 'deh *(he was born there)*."

"Yes, and his family lived there for a long time. He used to go back to see his mother before she passed away. Do you know anything about his family, now? I think they all left Wansaw."

"Yeah. Ever'body gone now. Ain't nobody lib 'deh no mo',"' George said quietly. "Jes' too ha'd an' all'em young folks wanta leave *(Just too hard and all the young folks wanted to leave)*. Big harricane come. Nelly wash ebbyt'ing 'way *(nearly washed everything away)*. Aftah 'dat, some people sickened and died. Some say was 'cause o' d'em ol' hogs made people sick. But Momma, 'e al'as say 'e was de hags *(Momma, she always said it was the hags)*."

"What are hags?" said Allen, his curiosity piqued.

"Hags is evil people dat c'n slip outta dey skin een de night *(evil people that can slip out of their skin in the night)* an' cain't nobody see'em," said George. He emphasized the word evil. "Dey sneaks aroun' an' steals from ya or make ya sick. Eb'm c'n kill ya. Suck de win' outcha till ya die *(suck the wind out of you till you die)*. Den dey slips back in 'dey skin befo' daylight like nuttin' happen. Momma say it was de hags was killin' people on Wansaw, and 'e mek us all move obah hyeah *(and she made us move over here)*."

"And nobody lives there now?"

"Da's right. Nobody," said George.

"But we can still go there now," Allen said, half question, half statement.

"Oh, I 'spec so, if yunnah wanna *(if you want to)*. I wouldn' go 'deh fo' myse'f. Too wil' fo' go 'deh now *(I wouldn't go there myself. It's too wild to go there now)*."

"Do you mean dangerous?"

"Well," George drew the word out, "might not be too bad. Ain't nobody been libbin' 'deh fo' long time. All growed up wid' jungle, I reckon. An' 'dem ol' hogs al'as been wil' an' mean *(and those old hogs have always been wild and mean.)* Seem like aftah 'de harricanes, 'e jes' got meaner (*they just got meaner*). Time was w'in 'deh was a lot of'em, sometime 'e run right up on ya' screamin' (*when there was a lot of them, sometimes they'd run right up on you screaming*). We'd kill'em w'in we could. Kill'em and cook'em." His face became animated as if he were delighted expressing the vindication.

"Did many people live on Wansaw then?" said Allen.

"Not too many. 'Roun' 'bout a hunnerd-fifty o' so I reckon."

"How did they get food and supplies?"

"Growed all de food 'dey could. Cawn. T'mata an' okra an' cabbage. An' root veg'table. Yam and tu'nup an' 'taters. Had chickens an' pigs...an' goats. An' plenty o' fish from 'de ocean, ya know. But 'dey had to go to Chahleston awn de steamboat to git supplies. Sometimes people go to Chahleston to wu'k awn 'dem fishin' boats. Mek a little money. Buy few t'ing an' go back to Wansaw. Didn' hab much obah 'deh, but 'e was so peaceful (*it was so peaceful*)." He nodded slightly, obviously enjoying his reminiscence.

"There was a steamboat?"

"Da's right. Went back'n fo'th 'tween Chahleston and Beaufort. Stopped to Wansaw oncet a week."

"Do you remember when the big hurricane was?"

"De real bad one was nineteen-fawty. I 'member 'cuz I's 10 yeahs ol'. An' soon aftah 'dat, some people was gittin' sick and dyin'."

Allen glanced at his watch. Almost 11:30. He still had to find the marina, but George's last few words intensified his curiosity. As he looked up at George, he thought: this gentle, soft-spoken old man's memories, even blunted by age, were a chronicle of a small band of people struggling to survive on a tiny island so remote from the rest of the world that it had virtually never held anyone else's attention. But it had given back to those people the joys of their customs and their heritage until the tragedies of unrelenting storms and cruel pestilence wiped it all away. Was there any way to find out what really happened? He said, "I have one more question if you don't mind."

"Okay, Mistah Allen."

"When those people got sick after the hurricane, do you remember anything about that? What happened to them or how they died?"

"I don' 'member much. Jes' what I heard. Said de people would fall out een fits. Couldn' talk. Couldn' breathe. Like 'dey was undah spells (*like they were under spells*). Said it was de hags suckin' de wind out'em. Go to sleep an' nobody couldn' wake'em up. 'Den 'e jes' die (*and then they'd just die*)." His voice trailed off.

"Was that what they called the dyin' time?"

"Da's right. Da's what dey called it. Dyin' time."

Allen nodded slowly and said, "Well, I've got to get on, Mr. Pelzer, but thank you for talking with me."

"You welcome. Now you be ceh'fulyou go obah 'deh to Wansåw. Don't you stay too long," said George as he shook Allen's hand again.

"Thank you, Geo'ge," said Jasper as Allen stepped down onto the sand. "I'll see y'all later."

They started back along the lane toward street. The old couple stood statue-like on the porch until the two men disappeared around the corner. Allen expected some kind of colorful comment or advice from Jasper, but it was not forthcoming. When they reached the sidewalk in front of the Marine Supply, Allen thanked him and commented that he was looking forward to seeing Wansaw. They shook hands and Jasper strolled back into the store. Allen got into his car and drove slowly along the street until he saw the sign for the marina. Dale was standing beside his car in the small parking area. 50 yards or so to the left was a metal shed marked **Office**. Allen pulled in next to Dale. "Sorry to keep you waiting," he called out.

"No problem. I just got here." Dale opened the trunk of his car and lifted out a duffle and a thick notebook. "My chart book." He held it out. "I like to have it when I go out. It's got markings for dump sites, reefs, artificial reefs, depths. Good stuff to know when you're out there." He slammed the trunk shut. "So how was your morning?"

"Actually, pretty interesting." Allen spoke enthusiastically as they started toward the metal shed. "The man at the marine supply store introduced me to an old man who used to live on Wansaw. He described how hard it was living there and how people gradually left or died. Seemed a little spooked when I told him I was thinking of going there. Said to be careful. Not to stay too long. You think it's safe?"

"Oh, sure," said Dale, "he's probably right. You wouldn't want to stay too long, but it's okay for an afternoon. And believe me, Tom knows his way around out there."

"Well what really got my attention was…he said there was some kind of illness that came up on Wansaw shortly after a big hurricane in 1940s. Apparently quite a few people died then, and that's when the population began to decline…eventually to zero."

"Did he know anything about this ah'm…illness?" said Dale.

"He said nobody knew. He said the people had 'fits', his words. I guess he meant seizures. He said they couldn't talk, couldn't breathe. They would fall asleep like they were 'under a spell,' again his words. And then they died."

"Sounds pretty vague to me," said Dale. "Any idea how many people?"

"No. He just said a lot," said Allen. "One possible clue though, he talked about wild hogs out there, and the man in the store said some people thought the hogs carried diseases."

"I don't think that would explain what he told you about big a group of people having seizures and dying so quickly. We'd need to know more to try to figure that out," said Dale, his medical curiosity piqued.

They entered the shed. A man, late 30s, ruddy complexion and sandy-blond hair, was sitting at a desk against a side wall.

"Hi, Tom. This is Allen Kanaby," said Dale.

The man stood and held out his hand. "Hey, Mr. Kanaby, Tom Guthrie. Good to meet you."

"Nice to meet you. Please call me Allen."

"So you wanta go out to Wansaw, aye?" said Tom.

"I sure do." Allen grinned.

"I think we can do that," said Tom. "12 miles out, but it looks pretty calm out through the channel this afternoon. I've got just the thing for you. Pretty little 16-footer inboard. Put in a new starter yesterday. Starts like a scared squirrel…purrs like a kitten." He laughed.

"Sounds good," said Allen. "What cards do you take?"

"Visa or Master," said Tom, "but we can settle up later. Better be sure we get back okay before you pay." He laughed again.

"Whatever you say," said Allen glancing around the small room. "So how long you been here?"

"Just about all my life," Tom replied. "Since I's about 12. Daddy built the marina in 1978. We came down here from Moncks Corner. He had a little store up there, but long as I can remember, all he wanted was to have a marina. Bought a stretch o' those ol' docks out yonder and added the slips. Took him a while, but he loved it. Just didn't live long enough to see it grow like it did." He glanced at the wall clock. "Chris is s'pose to be here at noon. You guys wanta pick up some sandwiches while we're waitin'?"

"Somewhere nearby?" asked Dale.

"Across the street. Miz Jervey's place. We can walk over."

"Let me get'em," said Allen. "Ham sandwiches and Cokes okay?"

"That's fine."

Dale nodded. In less than 15 minutes, he was back with two paper bags. Tom was standing by the desk talking to an athletic-looking man about Dale's age. "Get what you wanted," he said.

"Yep, ham sandwiches. And Cokes," said Allen. He set bags on the floor beside his duffle.

"Dale's out at the slip," said Tom. "This is Chris. He'll be holdin' down the fort."

"Hi, Chris. I'm Allen." He held out a hand.

"Yes, sir." They shook.

Tom sat at the desk, pushed a few papers to one side and made some notes in a ledger.

Chris addressed Allen. "You ever been to Wansaw?"

"No, but I've heard a bit about it from my dad," said Allen. "He knew a man who was born there. He told Dad some fascinating things about it, and I've always wanted to see it."

"It's an interesting place. 'Specially the history of it," said Chris.

"You mean about so many people dying out there?" said Allen.

"Well, yeah. Nobody knows much about it I guess. But I mean before that. Way back in the 1600s and 1700s, it was a pirate island."

"A pirate island?" said Allen, surprised.

"Yeah, back when there were pirates up and down the coast, the cove at the north end of Wansaw was a hideout for'em. Apparently because it was so isolated and remote. When you see it, you'll understand how that could've been possible."

Tom was finishing at the desk as Chris went on. He closed the ledger and shoved it into a side drawer. Then he stood and lifted a duffle from the floor. "Okay, Chris," he said, "you can finish with all that later. We gotta go. Dale's waitin' for us." He picked up a tool box from a side shelf and walked to the door. Allen could tell Tom had heard Chris's spiel at least several times before.

Tom walked out to the parking area. Allen and Chris followed as Chris continued. "So anyway, the cove is called Stede's Cove. A famous pirate called Stede Bonnet used to hide out there. Eventually a sea captain from Charleston, Captain Rhett, tracked him down. They caught him and hanged him in Charleston in the early 1700s. There's a historic marker on Hasell Street in downtown Charleston that tells about it."

Tom glanced back at Allen, "You need to get anything from your car?" he said as if to end Chris's tale.

"I'm all set." He picked up his duffle, the chart book and the two paper bags.

"Okay. Leavin' it with you, Chris. We oughta be back around 5:00 or so. I've got the two-way." He held the door open for Allen.

A minute later, they were on the dock. Allen could see three sturdy piers projecting perpendicularly from it with boat slips between. At the near end of each pier smaller boats were moored. Farther along, larger pleasure boats and sailors bobbed in the water. And at the farthest end of the first two piers were three cabin cruisers. As they approached the second pier, he saw Dale standing in a mahogany inboard idling in its slip.

"Think that'll do?" Tom said above the engine noise.

"Great," said Allen.

"Let's go."

CHAPTER TWENTY

By 12:20, the boat was churning out through the channel between Kiawah and Folly Island. Tom, at the wheel, sat in an authoritative slouch on the swivel chair.

Dale sat beside him holding the chart book on his lap. Allen settled back on the cushioned seat in front of the hold looking forward expectantly. Dale turned toward Allen and pointed ahead left. "Bird Key," he yelled above the engine noise. Allen could see, set against the bright expanse of water, the silhouette of a small flat land mass. Tom throttled down slightly. Dale turned toward Allen opening the chartbook, holding it out and pointing at the page. "And there's Marsh Island. There's Jakaw. And Wansaw's right there."

Allen could now hear him better as he bent forward to look as the page. He saw four tiny beige-colored spots against the field of blue where Dale pointed. Bird Key and Marsh Island were the smallest, Jakaw looked slightly bigger and Wansaw, an elongated spot, was twice as big as Jakaw and looked to be twice as far out.

Tom revved up the engine again making anymore conversation impossible. Allen sat back against the hold. The sun and the breeze and spray felt good on his face, but as he scanned the panorama around him, he pondered what might be ahead. Occasionally, Tom made an inaudible comment to Dale, but Allen was oblivious as they glided over the smooth water.

Momentarily they were passing Jakaw. Dale turned again and pointed left. Allen snapped out of his ruminations and nodded with thumbs-up as he gazed out at the narrow beach, grass-covered dunes and fronting a dense growth of trees. Jakaw slid by and the horizon became clear of land again except for what appeared to be a dark oblong land mass straight ahead. Dale pointed and yelled, "Wansaw." above the noise of the engine. After a another five minutes, the land mass was becoming larger, but it was still dark on the horizon against the sky. After another 10 minutes, they were close enough to see details. The boat made a gradual left turn and headed north parallel to the west side of the island. The beach, now clearly visible, was wider than the one on Jakaw and stretched uninterrupted along the entire length of the island, but much like Jakaw, a heavy growth of trees rose beyond the dunes. As they got close to the north end, the boat made a wide semicircular sweep and headed directly into the narrow mouth of an inlet which looked to be at least a quarter of a mile wide and nearly a mile long. The water was smooth except for the waves the wake made or where the scattered seabirds dived for lunch. The quiet water, the beach and dunes surrounding it and the trees beyond certainly could have served as a harbor in those earlier times thought Allen…Stede's Cove and the pirate harbor. He wondered what that might have been like…if it ever really was.

Tom throttled down again enough to be heard, and for the first time in almost 30 minutes he spoke. "This is where the old steamer from the mainland used to come in." They glided closer to the far end of the inlet, and Allen could see several clusters of thick black poles at the water's edge. He remembered what George Pelzer said about the steamboat.

"Made stops at all the islands back then, but it's been gone a long time," said Tom. "They say there was another one before that. Went down in a storm in the early 1900s. What I always heard was there was a lot of people from Edisto Island on it, and almost everybody drowned. A hundred or more.

Dale held out the chart book again and pointed. "There's Edisto. About 20 miles down the coast."

The boat came to a slow cruise as they approached the cluster of poles. "Steamer used to tie up at those pilin's," said Tom as he guided to the left of the poles and cut the motor. It drifted up to the beach. Tom jumped over the side holding the bow-line as the bow slid out of the water and onto the smooth packed sand. Dale went over the side and held out a hand to help Allen over. Tom lifted a metal stake from the floor of the boat, walked several feet from the water's edge and pushed the stake into the sand. "Need to secure this line in case the tide shifts while we're lookin' around." He came back to the boat, took a hammer out of the hold and went back to the stake. He drove it deeper into the sand and tied the bowline to it. "That oughta do it," he said inspecting his knot. He went back to the boat again, dropped the hammer into the hold and lifted out a duffle. "We're goin' up to where the old settlement was." He pointed to a wide opening in the dunes to the left of the pilings.

As Allen turned to look, he saw Tom take a holstered pistol out of the duffle. The surprised look on his face registered with Tom.

"Just in case," said Tom attaching the holster to his belt. He patted the gun at his side smiling. "357 Magnum. Smith and Wesson," he said. "Like to have it right by my side when I'm wanderin' around these islands....just in case there's sumpin' needs killin'."

"Sounds good to me," said Dale with a nod.

"One more thing," said Tom as he put the duffle back into the hold and took out two canvas-sheathed machetes. "We'll need these to get through the thickets." He handed a machete to Dale then turned and led the way through the opening in the dunes.

They followed up a steep rise and onto a narrow plateau of sand which afforded a broad view back over the cove. In the other direction, directly in front of them, was a view of a more-or-less circular area at least two-hundred yards in diameter covered by a growth of scrubby trees and brambles. As they moved forward,

Tom took out the machete and began to hack through the thick vines and briars covering a hint of a sandy path. He stopped some feet ahead, making a broad sweep with his arm. "This was front part of the settlement," he said. "It used to be clear, but all these trees and thickets have come up in the last 10 years o' so since ever'body left. You can still see some of the ol' cabins, but weather and time's just gradu'lly beat'em down."

Scanning around, Allen could see vine-covered remnants of small wooden cabins sitting in varying stages of deterioration and collapse around the edge of the circle. A wide swath led through the center of the circle. Though it was barely discernible beneath the overgrowth, it looked as though it might have been a sort of roadway. Of the more dilapidated buildings, there remained broken down walls, nearby scattered piles of rubble and rotting boards, skeletal studs and roof supports holding pieces of twisted, rusted tin. On those still partially intact, he could see deteriorated siding boards between gaping window and door openings. It struck him that on the framing that remained around those openings there was a distinct pale blue color that contrasted sharply the weather-worn gray-brown wood of the rest of the structure.

Allen called to Tom, "What's with the blue around the windows?"

Tom stopped and turned toward him and grinned, "That what they call *haint* blue. S'pose to keep the haints out of the house. You know....evil spirits. They say that blue color scares'em away 'cause it reminds'em of heaven."

"Does it scare the hags away too?" said Allen in a slightly joking tone.

"How you know about the hags?"

"I heard about'em this morning from an old man across from that Marine Supply store."

"Oh, yeah. You talkin' about George Pelzer?" asked Tom.

"That's right. You know him?" said Allen.

"Ever'body knows George. And he knows a lot about Wansaw."

"He told me his mother said the hags made some people on the island sick after two big hurricanes," said Allen. "She made the family leave after the second one."

"That's all just superstitious stuff," said Tom, "but a lotta folks believe it. They say hags are women that can slip outta their skin. That makes'em invisible so they can get into your house through a crack in a window or under a door and nobody can see'em. They can steal from you or make you sick. I reckon that haint blue color keeps'em out, too. 'Course I don't believe all that stuff myself," Tom continued, "but I remember one ol' man over on John's Island who claimed he was whatcha call a *conjure* doctor…like a witch doctor. Said he knew all about hags and how they could hurt people. He said there's other ways besides that blue paint to keep'em outa of your house. Accordin' to him, if you sprinkle dry mustard seeds on the window sill and the floor in front of the door, the hag has to stop and count every seed before she'll come in. If you throw down enough seeds, it'll take her too long, so she just moves on 'cause she has to get back in her skin before sun-up." Tom laughed as he continued to embellish. "He said another way is to stand a broom upside-down against your door. The hag'll have to count all the straws in the broom 'fore she'll try to go in, and that takes too long, too." He looked at Allen with a sly don't-you-believe-me? look.

Allen shook his head.

Tom let out bigger laugh. "Okay, so we gotta move on over to the other part. Back through those trees," He pointed ahead as they approached the back of the circle. "It's not as thick through there. And the cemetery's back there."

Allen hung back, moving slowly and taking in the surroundings. The erstwhile roadway became shadowed as it coursed through a stretch of pines and gigantic live-oaks. The brambles were replaced by patches of grass and a carpet of pine straw and leaves which made walking easier. Tom and Dale continued ahead, but Allen stopped to take in the scene. The shifting shadows on the path and the eerily respiratory sounds of the breeze in the trees seemed to create a feeling of inspirited surroundings that sent a chill down his spine. He quickened his pace. After another 100 or so yards, the shadows disappeared, and the path widened into another circular area.

It was bordered by more broken-down huts and vine-covered piles debris. The backdrop of the dense forest around this circle made it more foreboding than the first. The three of them moved silently through the center until the road stopped at a small enclosure, also circular in shape, maybe 75 feet across. It was surrounded by stark, barkless wooden posts waist high and about 8 inches apart. Within the circle, there were as few rows of irregularly spaced thick wooden slabs standing more-or-less straight up a foot or two above the grass.

"This is the cemetery," said Tom. "The most interestin' thing about this island I think."

As Allen looked across the rows, he could make out what appeared to be intricate carvings in the weathered wood of most of the slabs. He slipped between two of the posts and approached the first row bending down for a closer look.

"Those're s'pose to be some kinda African symbols markin' graves," said Tom. "I asked George Pelzer about'em one time. He said tha's all he knew."

"There's quite a few," Allen said as he counted quickly to himself. He studied the carving on one of the slabs, a neat circle about four inches wide, deeply incised with an undulating groove crossing through it. He moved to another, also a carved circle, this one enclosing three X's arranged around its center. "Amazing these things are still here," he said.

"Yep. That ol' oak's pretty durable," said Tom. " 'Course they'll all eventually rot down. Already happened to the ones toward the back. The earliest ones," he pointed, "but some of these've been here for 30 years or more, I reckon." He motioned toward the closer rows then turned forward and said, "Okay, so moving on, over there's where they grew some crops." He pointed to a clear area beyond the cemetery. "And on over there," he pointed to the right, "is where they kept their animals. There's still some pieces of the fence around it."

"Can we get over there?" asked Allen. He wanted to see everything.

"Oh sure. It's not bad," said Tom.

"We better go on over there if we're going," said Dale glancing at his watch. "It's almost 3:00. We've gotta start back before long."

"Okay," said Allen sliding between two posts.

He followed Tom and Dale moving toward the clearing, roughly rectangular in shape of about two acres. At the far end and on both sides, the forest looked impenetrable. "If we go around this way, we can see where they kept their animals," said Tom as he led toward the right side of the clearing along sections of a dilapidated log fence. "This used to be an enclosure for animals, mainly pigs and goats is what I've heard. I guess this is about as far as we need to go," he said. He turned and began to follow the fence in the opposite direction. "We can go around this way to get back to the road." Allen followed.

Dale, caught up in the aura cast by the mid-afternoon sunlight through the trees, fell behind wandering slowly past the end of the fence. The only sound was the swish of his feet through the grass, but in an instant, he heard a loud crackle in the dense brush 20 or so yards behind and to his left. He startled and turned toward the sound. He could see the bushes move as he heard loud, guttural grunts. Tom and

Allen, ahead and out of earshot, continued to move toward the settlement. There was a louder crackle and closer, this one like the sound of a big stick breaking. The bushes were shaking heavily. Dale didn't stop to see what might be there but walked faster then began to run toward the cemetery, yelling at Tom and Allen. They turned to see the bushes part. The mass of a hulking black hog lunged out and head toward Dale. Tom broke into a run toward the animal, waving and yelling to divert its attention as Dale raced away toward the cemetery. Dale reached the enclosure and squeezed in between two posts.

The hog, by now no more than 10 yards behind him, immediately turned its trajectory and full focus toward Tom. "Get back, Allen." Tom yelled.

Allen retreated back toward the road, breathless and terrified at the sight of the monstrous black form lumbering toward Tom . He stopped and planted himself squarely in its path only 20 or so yards away and stood wide-legged with his pistol drawn. In another instant, as it came closer, he fired a direct frontal blast into the huge, hairy head. A bright red geyser spewed straight up several feet. The animal shuddered violently and collapsed on the grass with a savage, ear-splitting scream.

"GOD DAMN!" Tom bellowed. His arm fell by his side. He gripped the pistol and stood shaking his head. He moved slowly toward the hog lying in front of him grunting and gasping in the blood-soaked grass. Its short legs pawed at the earth as it struggled to right itself.

"Y'all stay back," Tom yelled as he stepped closer to the heaving animal. He aimed the pistol again and fired. Another gush of blood flowed down the back of the head. Now the animal was still.

Dale came through posts and walked toward Tom. "Man, oh man," he said in a loud voice. "Let's get the hell outta here."

"Don't you wanta try for another one?" Tom responded in a sporting bravado.

"Hell no!"

"I'll second that," said Allen now walking toward Tom, Dale and the dead animal.

"That is one *helluva hog*," declared Tom. "Must be at least 350 pounds. We'll leave the sonofbitch for the buzzards." He holstered the pistol as he turned toward Allen and Dale. "That's prob'ly enough excitement for one afternoon. You guys go on over to the road, and I'll bring up the rear just in case there's anything more."

Momentarily, all three were back at the road at the front of the cemetery walking single file, Dale leading. They passed through the remains of the back of the settlement, along the forest path, on through the first larger front part and finally through the opening to the beach. Relief settled over Allen when he spotted the boat.

"Anything else you wanta see?" Tom said to Allen with slightly teasing tone.

"Like what?" Allen asked warily.

"We can go around to the south end. It's different than this. Higher dunes. Less trees."

"I'll take your word for it," said Allen. "I think I've seen enough. And I've gotta drive back to Atlanta tonight."

"Okay," said Tom. He started toward the beach. "We should be back at the dock about 4:30. That give you enough time?"

"Oh, sure. It's not a bad drive. Little over four and a half hours." said Allen as he and Dale followed to the boat.

Tom lifted the lid of the hold and pitched the machetes in. The holstered pistol was still on his belt. "How 'bout some lunch?" he said as he lifted the two bags out of the hold and set them on the floor. Dale and Allen pulled themselves into the boat. Tom retrieved the metal stake and pushed the boat out. It bobbed slightly as he jumped in, bow-line and stake in his hand. The boat drifted slowly backward as he started the engine and throttled into a gentle turn away from the beach, out through the inlet and westward toward Anson Point. Allen passed around the ham sandwiches and Cokes.

*****

The drive back to Atlanta seemed longer than the drive over, but Allen's thoughts hardly veered from visions of Wansaw and thoughts of its strange and tragic history. A raft of questions continued to stream through his thoughts. Would anyone ever know why those people died? Could it have been wild hogs…like the one Tom killed? Was it sick? He thought of George Pelzer's description of the hogs. And of the sickness….that sounded exactly like Richard's. That hung in his mind. But how could there be any connection so long ago and so far away? Yet, there it was, roiling in his head, obsessing him. The doctors had squashed the infection idea based on their tests, and as far as he knew, there was no evidence of anything toxic. So what else could it be? But how could there possibly be any link? Mose? But he died years ago. Something in the gardens or the greenhouse? Maybe the special mixtures? Secret formulas from the island? But again, years ago. If he couldn't convince anyone else, he *had* to investigate further on his own. Maybe get some environmental consultant or company to do some testing. That might be the best way. Certainly nothing to lose. At least it might assuage the intensity of his curiosity.

He arrived home a little after 11:00. Ellen was already in bed, but she'd left a couple of sandwiches for him. He poured himself a glass of wine, finished off the sandwiches and went to bed. Restless sleep finally came, but by daylight, he was awake again. He rose quietly and made his way to the computer in the den to launch a search. In a list billed as the TOP 200 Environmental Consulting Companies Nationwide, seven were in Atlanta. He scrolled through reading quickly about each. One listing particularly caught his attention.

EnviroTech Environmental Solutions, Inc.

"More than fifteen years' experience in Phase I & II Environmental Site Assessment for lead, asbestos, molds, bacteria and radon detection and follow-up abatement and remediation; soil and groundwater assessment and remediation; detection, identification and quantification of environmentally toxic chemicals; standardized laboratory testing."

With a phone call early Monday morning to Envirotech, he spoke to a man named Everett McKenzie who identified himself as the founder and owner of the company. Allen explained his concern about "some kind of contamination, maybe chemical" on his property in Dunwoody. In an impressively articulate and professional manner, McKenzie described his credentials: B.S. degree in microbiology and masters degree in environmental science and toxicology from Columbus State; private and governmental contracts, Georgia and North Florida. He assured Allen that EnviroTech could "cover everything. I can fax you a list of references if you like, Mr. Kanaby."

Allen met McKenzie at the house that afternoon. Following a walk through the gardens, the shed and the greenhouse, all was set to start the testing on Wednesday morning. Allen then informed Evelyn and Martha, and they agreed that Evelyn would move to Martha's during the testing. At 8:00 sharp Wednesday morning, the EnviroTech van and a crew of four arrived.

CHAPTER TWENTY-ONE

On Wednesday afternoon, Stephen Lang rang Cassandra Garriman's office. "Division of Infectious Disease. May I help you," came a crisp telephone voice.

"Yes. Dr. Lang here. Hefner-Cantrell Institute. Calling Dr. Garriman."

"One moment, please." Two short buzzes. He tapped impatiently on the desk.

"Hello, Dr. Lang," Cassandra's voice came on the line.

"Yes, hello. Calling to give you an update. Is this a good time?" he said.

"Oh yes, fine," she replied.

"The progress is slow, but there are a few things I think you should know."

"Okay," she said.

"For starters, the PCR on the tissue from the autopsy was completely negative," he said, "so I decided to wait for the microscopic slides before doing anything more. The preliminary slides came through this morning. Additional slides will be out next week, but I can say, even without those, this is quite unusual. I've never seen such a unique and selective pattern of degeneration, especially in the brainstem."

"Oh?" she said.

"It's only in the large nerve cells in the reticular formation. There is none of the inflammation one would expect to see in an infection, but the cells clearly show that something attacked the genetic infrastructure. The evidence for that is condensation of nuclear chromatin and fragmentation of the nucleolus along with cell shrinkage and membrane changes in the involved nerve cells.

It's a characteristic picture," he paused a moment, "of a phenomenon called *apoptosis*. You familiar with that?"

"Oh," she said a hesitantly. "Ah'm…I must say you'll have to coach me. I'm familiar with the word, but it's been awhile since I've heard anything about *apoptosis*." In truth, at the very least it *had* been awhile. Probably medical school was the last time she might have heard the word, and certainly what it meant was a question she couldn't answer.

"Okay," he said, "so in short, that's when the genome, the entire set of the DNA of the cell, is attacked, and the cell literally implodes. Dies from the inside out, so to speak. It simply collapses and disappears." He was delighted to be able to continue with his most erudite version of an explanation. "The word *apoptosis* is Greek. The first part, a-p-o, means from or away, and the last part, p-t-o-s-i-s, means falling. So the word actually means falling away. Apparently the ancient Greeks used the term in poetry to describe how petals fall away from a flower. But in more contemporary use, at least in pathology, the term has come to mean how certain cells or populations of cells disappear or fall away." He paused as if waiting for her to process what he'd just said.

"I'm with you," she said.

"Okay," he continued, "so we know that can be induced by natural biological phenomena like aging. But it can also be induced by certain unnatural, external insults like radiation or toxic chemicals. The pathological changes we see here in the brain are quite characteristic of *apoptosis*. We can of course confirm that with gel electrophoresis and caspase activation studies. But to me, what makes this case so unusual is that the actual, shall I say, apoptotic process is so selective. The changes extend mainly from the lower brainstem up into the thalamus and in the prefrontal cortex and occipital cortex. As I said, only in the large nerve cells."

Cassandra felt somewhat blind-sided by the cascade of pathology talk, but she tried not to let on. "Sounds as though you've made quite a bit of progress," she said.

"Yes, but this is just the beginning. There's lot more to do. We have no clue as to a cause."

"Could what you see in the brainstem explain the breathing difficulties?" she asked.

"Oh yes," he responded, "the changes there correlate entirely with the clinical picture."

"And what you see in the cerebral cortex, could that account for the seizure?"

"We know that seizures can be associated with *apoptosis*," said Lang, "but at this point I'm comfortable saying there may be correlation here but no conclusion yet about the seizures."

"I see," she replied. "How about…is there anything to suggest viral involvement?"

"Nothing so far, but that's an important consideration. I'm keeping that in mind since we know some viruses can cause *apoptosis*. As I said, the PCR is negative which would tend to exclude viruses. Right now, the most I can say is that the peculiar clinical history and the rapid course plus what I see on the slides all add up to something quite strange, quite *unusual*." His voice intensified. "I've seen a lot of brains and a lot of microscopic sections, but I've never seen anything like this."

"Any other studies you're considering?" she said.

"Yes," he said, "but I'm concerned about handling the frozen brain tissue until we know more. Right now, it's all well-contained and secure, and we've taken all the necessary precautions, but we may need to consider transmission studies using the frozen tissue."

"Oh, so you think this could be something transmissible?" she said.

"I'm saying that's a possibility. If, God forbid, this is something transmissible, we certainly need to know it, so I'm proceeding very cautiously. That's why I'm keen to see the results of the additional slides next week.

"Does anyone else know what you've found?" she asked.

"I haven't discussed it with anyone. I wanted you to know first since we talked last week."

"Could I come out and look at the slides with you?" she said.

"Oh sure" he said, "but I expect to have more information next week when I get the slides with several additional microscopic stains. I'll let you know."

"Very well," she said trying not to seem impatient. "I'll wait to hear from you."

She hung up and sat for a moment reviewing the conversation. Boy, Lang sure packed a lot of information into those few minutes, she thought. She could barely remember textbook pictures of the brainstem from first year med school neuroanatomy much less what Lang called the large nerve cells in the reticular formation. And the prefrontal cortex. And the occipital cortex. It didn't matter though as long as he knew what he was talking about, but his phrase "something quite strange" seemed to be at the very least an understatement. Something this lethal, and *so quickly* lethal, could be catastrophic. This not only had to be understood but also kept safely contained until it was resolved. That was both the puzzle and the dilemma for her and Lang and Dittrich, and of course, Joe Holleran. With that last thought, unexpectedly, ironically out of nowhere, her mind flashed back to that night in New York. And the hotel in Snowmass. It was two years ago, but it was still vivid in her mind.

Stop, she told herself, you've got more important things to think about right now. Then she thought of Blaine. That felt more comfortable though there was something about him that made her wonder what might be beneath his façade.

CHAPTER TWENTY-TWO

It was almost 8:30 Thursday evening. Joe had run late with his afternoon appointments, and when he finished, he headed to the hospital to make rounds with the resident. That took longer than he'd expected, so he was just getting back to his office. He pulled off the white coat, hung it on the back of the door and sat in his desk chair to relax for a moment. The room was lit only by the soft light from the desk lamp. His mind went back to the mystery continually pressing on his mind these last two and a half weeks: Richard Kanaby. He closed his eyes and leaned back wondering if Lang had found anything yet.

As he opened his eyes his gaze rested on the two chairs on the other side of the desk where Richard and Evelyn had sat almost three weeks ago. He felt a pang of sadness as he recalled the emptiness in Richard's eyes, his vague, disjointed responses and Evelyn's terror.

He swiveled his chair around facing the window and stared out into the courtyard. All windows of the first floor offices on the other side were dark except one. He could see, framed in that window, a man sitting in a peculiar posture, slightly bent over a desk. He turned off the desk lamp and moved closer to the window for a better look. As he watched, the guy leaned farther over the desk. One hand came up toward the face for a moment then dropped away. The head rose and slowly leaned backward. What was going on? Some kind of ritual? Never mind. He had to go home.

He made his way across the darkened room. He slipped on his jacket, picked up his briefcase and walked out of his office, on into the deserted corridor and through the courtyard exit. He could see the one lighted window. The light cast a muted rectangle across the grass. He moved cautiously around it toward the window careful to stay in the shadows. When he got close enough, he could see it was the guy he'd met at the last staff meeting, the new cardiology fellow. He remembered the name. Purcell.

The head was still back as if the guy was asleep. The surface of the desk was empty except for a few books and a computer keypad on one side and a yellow legal pad in the center. Next to the pad was what looked like a thin, silver rod...like a pen but shorter. In the middle of the yellow pad there was, clearly and unmistakably, a small mound of white powder.

As Joe watched, the head moved forward again and the eyes opened. The man picked up the silver thing with the left hand. With the right hand, he picked up what looked like a credit card on the desk. With that, he began to push the powder into distinct line on the paper. In an instant, he held one end of the silver thing to his nose and leaned forward guiding the other end along edge of the white powder. Obviously, it was a metal tube, not a rod, and obviously the guy was snorting! As the tube moved, the powder disappeared, the hand and tube rested on the desk and the head went back again.

Joe ducked away, stunned by what he had just seen. He moved carefully in the darkness. In a few more steps, he was through the courtyard and walking swiftly toward the garage. His head was spinning in disbelief.

He drove out of the garage and homeward. As he processed it all, his disbelief turned to indignation. Intense indignation. This guy, new to the staff and touting himself as a qualified, responsible physician entrusted with other peoples' lives, had in those moments, blatantly disregarded and *disrespected* it all. Was he that cavalier? Crazy? Or just stupid?

*****

On Friday afternoon around 3:30, Joe entered the cardiology suite and approached the receptionist. "Hi, I'm Dr. Holleran from the Department of Medicine. Is Dr. Purcell around?"

"He's in clinic until 4:30," she said, "but he'll be coming back after that. He meets Dr. Reed for rounds at 5:00."

"Okay. I'll check back. Or maybe you could ask him to page me when he gets back. I need to speak with him for a few minutes. Again, it's Dr. Holleran. The operator has my pager number."

"Yes, sir. I'll tell him."

Joe returned to his office to wait. He sat, fingering through the few pieces of new mail on the desk. Glancing occasionally at the windows across the courtyard, his anger festered. His thoughts focused and his determination heightened. At 4:45, his pager sounded. It displayed a number for cardiology. He clicked it off and walked quickly around the corridor to the cardiology suite. "I think Dr. Purcell just paged me," he said to the receptionist. "Is he in now?"

"Yes, Doctor. I'll let him know you're here."

"Thanks," he said as he walked to the magazine rack.

Momentarily, the door to Blaine's office opened, and he stepped out looking surprised. "Hello, Dr. Holleran," he said. "Nice to see you again. I just paged you."

"I got it, but I was still in the area so I thought I'd just stop by. You have a minute?"

"Sure. Come in," said Blaine. "What can I do for you?" Joe followed him into the office and closed the door. "Please. Have a seat." Blaine spoke in a most congenial tone but clearly appeared puzzled.

"No. I can't stay," said Joe. "Just a quick word."

"Okay. What's up?" said Blaine.

"Look, I know you just got here. I realize you and I have only just met…and I don't know you at all," Joe spoke in quiet, measured tones looking directly at Blaine, "but what you were doing in here last night is absolutely *un—acceptable* at this medical center. Obviously you forgot to close your blinds, but I can assure you, that kind of behavior will get you a quick and permanent trip outa here." Blaine's mouth gaped open realizing what Joe had seen through window. His eyes widened. He stiffened and clenched his fists as he tried to stretch upward facing Joe's 6-foot-2 frame.

"What the hell are you talking about?" he said defiantly.

"You know exactly what I'm talking about, and you'd better take this as a serious warning."

"Hey, I don't know you either," Blaine bristled speaking in hushed but furious tones, "and I don't know what you're talking about. But if you think you can barge in here with some made-up, cockamamie *shit* like that, you'd better be damn sure you think twice before you go shootin' off your mouth. And, by the way, you get too loud, and I'll be damn sure everyone here knows all about you and Cassandra…and your little secrets."

Joe froze as it came to him. Now Cassandra was cozy with this guy, and in her vindictiveness, she had not been silent or discreet after all. He did not move.

"I think you better get the hell outta here, Doctor…Holleran," Blaine's voice was still hushed but now menacing. "And I recommend you stay out unless you're looking for trouble."

Joe, shocked into silence but shaking with anger, got the message. He glared at Blaine for a moment more then turned, opened the door and walked out careful to maintain a calm demeanor as he passed the receptionist. Blaine stood just inside his office to watch Joe leave then stepped back and closed the door.

At just before 5:00, the phone on his desk rang. It was the receptionist. "Dr. Reed's ready for rounds."

"Okay, thanks. I'll be right out."

It wasn't easy to maintain his concentration during rounds, but he managed. When they finished, he went back to his office, locked up and hurried to the garage. He had to get away to think about what to do. Joe's words were a very real threat to his whole future and especially now to his new relationship with Cassie. Obviously what he said to Joe had stopped him, but would that be enough to shut him up?

He drove to his apartment, showered and dressed and headed for Cassie's. They had plans for dinner. He tried to suppress the afternoon's confrontation in his mind, but that did not diminish it. It was still very much there. He spent the night and the rest of the weekend with Cassie.

Joe spent an unsettled and preoccupied weekend at home with his family. On Monday morning, both men returned to Brakefield as usual.

CHAPTER TWENTY-THREE

At about 9:30 the same morning, a technician from EnviroTech called Allen to say they had finished the site work and would be contacting him shortly with a preliminary report. On Tuesday afternoon, the call came from Everett McKenzie himself. He explained that a written report was in process "...but I'd like to go over a few things with you now, Mr. Kanaby, if you have time."

"Of course," said Allen.

"Okay," said McKenzie. "So to begin with, we took samples of soil and ground water from the gardens and soil samples from various containers in the greenhouse as well as the floor in the greenhouse and the storage shed. Those were tested for several organic and inorganic contaminants. We also took air samples in the shed and the greenhouse. All the tests for the soil and water samples were negative, but what we found in the greenhouse," he paused a moment, "made it necessary to seal it until all the lab tests are completed."

"That sounds pretty serious," said Allen. "What was it?"

McKenzie continued, "It was what we found in the air samples. Extremely high levels of toxic particles called mycotoxins." He spoke slowly. "The first part, myco, means fungus. So in plain English, the word mycotoxin means fungus toxin."

"That means there's fungus in the greenhouse?" Allen queried.

"Yes, and the mycotoxin particles are what's left when spores from such a fungus dry out and break into tiny fragments. The fragments are so small they're virtually invisible, but they can easily become airborne. If they're inhaled, they can be quite toxic. They tend to remain airborne as long as there are air currents like what that ceiling fan created, but of course some settle on surfaces, and you can see them as a fine black dust."

"Oh," said Allen looking dismayed.

McKenzie continued. "We did what's called surface collection for samples of the black dust on the shelves and the bench as well as the work table, and we found that the black dust was mycotoxins, too…the same as in the air samples.

"If that stuff is so toxic you had to seal off the greenhouse, isn't it toxic to you when you're doing all that collecting?"

"We're used to it," said McKenzie. "It's all in the job. We have protective gear and equipment and we know how to avoid the toxicity. But let me go on. Our next step was to try to find a fungus… or maybe more than one…which could be the source of the mycotoxins. We did find a heavy accumulation of fungal spores in the soil in some of those large pots at the back of the greenhouse."

"Do you think those particles, those…myco…toxins…could cause some kind of illness?" said Allen.

"Yes. Certainly possible, but right now, we don't know how toxic they might be," said McKenzie. "That's why we sealed the greenhouse…as a precaution to keep everyone out until we know more about the toxicity."

"So if the spores are in there, where's the damn fungus?" said Allen aggressively.

"Oh, it's in the soil in some of those pots where we found the spores. The actual fungus is a fine hair-like network that grows and spreads in soil or in moist, decaying material. That's called the *mycelium*. It's the main part of the fungus, and that's what produces fungal spores. We're trying to identify the fungus in the greenhouse that's producing the spores. That requires culturing the mycelium. We've got that going, but it'll take a few days. The important thing for you to understand though is that it is *not* the fungus or the spores themselves that are toxic. It's the mycotoxins, the actual breakdown products of the spores that are toxic."

"Okay," said Allen. "I think I understand what you're telling me, but let me back up a minute," said Allen. "I should tell you the reason I contacted you in the first place. That's my dad's greenhouse, not mine. He loved it and all the gardens and spent a lot of time out there, but," he paused and took a breath, "...he passed away two weeks ago."

"Oh," said McKenzie, surprised. "I'm sorry to..."

"I appreciate that," said Allen interrupted, "but the point is, he was sick for only a short time. The doctors said it was a very unusual illness. They thought it was something either infectious or toxic. When I heard that, I began to wonder if it could be something related to Dad's business. He was a chemical engineer. He had a business up in Marietta that produces insecticides and such." He paused. "But then I also began to wonder if it could be something in the gardens... or the greenhouse because he spent a lot of time out there. I talked to the doctors about it. They didn't think much of my ideas, from what you're telling me now, sounds like I might be right. And you're proving it."

"So how much time did your dad spend in the greenhouse?" said McKenzie.

"A lot. Especially on weekends in colder weather."

"If I may ask, when he got sick, did he have any breathing problems?" said McKenzie.

"According to my mom, he was a little congested the week-end before he got sick," said Allen, "but it seemed to clear up. Two days later, he got very confused. And the same day, he had a seizure and went unconscious....and never woke up."

At a loss for more sympathetic words, McKenzie said, "That's really amaz..."

"More like *terrifying* is what it is," Allen interjected abruptly. "How long you think the fungus thing, or those spores, have been there?"

"Impossible to say," said McKenzie. "Some spores can survive for months or even years under the right conditions. They can just remain dormant 'til something disturbs them."

"Did you find spores in the garden?" said Allen.

"No, but we weren't looking for fungus in the garden. We were testing for toxic substances like chlordane or malathion and even mercury and lead. We didn't focus on a fungus until we discovered the mycotoxins in the greenhouse."

"I cannot *believe* this," said Allen, clear frustration in his voice.

"Should I call Dr. Holleran and tell him what you found?" said Allen.

"Yes, but if you don't mind, I'd like to complete my report and fax it to you first," said McKenzie. "Then you can tell him. Even send him a copy if you like. I'll have it done tomorrow."

"Sure. That's fine," said Allen.

*****

By Wednesday, there still had been no call from Lang, but Cassie could barely contain her eagerness for more information. She punched in the number for his direct line at Hefner-Cantrell. He answered.

"Hi, Dr. Lang, Cassandra Garriman. I hope I'm not being presumptuous, but I was just wondering if there's any word on the other slides you were expecting."

"I'm glad you called," said Lang. "The last slides will be out tomorrow afternoon. I think those plus what we already have should give us a pretty comprehensive overview of the pathology. I should be able to show you everything Friday."

"Great," said Cassie. "Any particular time?"

"Friday at 11:00 should be good."

"Fine," she said. "I've been reading up on the subject of *apoptosis*."

"Good. I hope I can show you enough to make your studies worthwhile," he said. "See you at 11:00 on Friday. Do you know where we're located?"

"I do," she replied.

"My office is on the first floor. Room 122. When you get to the lobby, just stop at the security desk and show the attendant your Brakefield ID badge. He'll direct you."

"Thanks," she said. "I look forward to it."

*****

Everett McKenzie called Allen Thursday afternoon to say a written report was ready, and he would fax it right away. He gently suggested that Allen might find some parts of it confusing because of the technical details but that it basically confirmed what he had said earlier about the airborne particles and the black dust in the greenhouse. "It's very important for us to determine what fungus the mycotoxins come from and how toxic they are. It's possible it might be a new species. Maybe a genetic mutation," he explained. "It has to be further analyzed and to determine that. It could be quite toxic." He went on to explain that depending on the level of toxicity, the Health Department might have to be notified and a remediation process might have to be undertaken in the greenhouse. In the meantime, Allen should go ahead and contact the doctors about the findings.

Momentarily the report rolled out of the office fax machine. Allen could hardly wait to read it. As he began, he realized, McKenzie might be right. It did look as if it could be a bit daunting, but he wanted to go through it anyway. He slowly scanned the first few lines beginning with **PHASE I ESA** and moved on to **PHASE II ESA**.

EnviroTech Environmental Solutions, Inc.
4219 Pellton Road NW
Atlanta, Georgia 30007
Tel. 678-328-5500
Fax 678-328-5501

PHASE I & II ENVIRONMENTAL SITE ASSESSMENT (ESA) REPORT

Date: April 29
Client: Kanaby, Allen E.; Client ID # 4329
306 Stone Bridge Road
Dunwoody, Georgia 30338

Environmental Site Assessment (ESA) of grounds, storage shed and greenhouse.

PHASE I ESA: Grounds comprising approximately three acres including cultivated garden areas and surrounding wooded areas as well as a small wooden storage shed, 8' X 10' and a permanent glass greenhouse, 17' X 25' are assessed preliminarily for evidence of potential environmental hazards or contamination. None observed.

PHASE II ESA: The following specimens were collected at random from grounds (approximately three acres of cultivated areas) plus storage shed and greenhouse.

1. Core soil samples, multiple
2. Ground water samples, multiple
3. Ambient-air samples, multiple, collected by Spirospin 465, 1.0 micron filter.

Results: Soil and ground water samples from throughout the site were assessed for inorganic environmental contaminants including mercury and lead and organic contaminants including a variety of organophosphate and organochlorine compounds; a complete list of is available. No evidence of these environmental contaminants was found, and no evidence of hazardous waste in any form was found.

So far, it seemed pretty straightforward to Allen.. He read on.

Ambient-air samples taken outside around the grounds and inside the shed demonstrated no evidence of significant air-borne contaminants. However, ambient-air samples taken in the greenhouse demonstrated mycotoxin contamination prompting the mycologic investigations described below.

Aha, mycotoxin contamination. Just what McKenzie had told him. He read on.

The following specimens were collected in the greenhouse:

1. **Ambient-air samples collected by Spirospin 456 bioaerosol sampler, 1.0 micron filter**
2. **Surface dust samples picked up on collecting swabs; collected on site**
3. **Wet spore samples, multiple; collected on site**

Enzyme-linked Immunosorption Assay (ELISA) of ambient-air samples and surface dust samples demonstrated high levels of trichothecene mycotoxins, types to be identified. Trichothecene mycotoxins are potent protein synthesis inhibitors produced by several genera of fungi including *Fusarium, Claviceps, Myrothecium, Trichoderma, Trichothecium* and *Stachybotrys*.

Quantitative Polymerase Chain-Reaction (QPCR) carried out on spore samples identified a fungus of the genus *Stachybotrys*. Species identification will require DNA analysis.

Genome Identification: Cloning of ribosomal DNA sequences from QPRC samples showed that the nucleotide sequence found in these specimens is **not** compatible with any recognized species of *Stachybotrys* and may represent a mutation in the genus.

Now it was confusing:. Enzyme-linked Immunosorption? Trichothecene mycotoxins? Protein synthesis inhibitors? Quantative Polymerase Chain-Reaction? Five different kinds of fungus? *Very* confusing. He paused for a moment staring at the words but then continued reading to the end..

Commentary & Conclusion: ELISA demonstration of trichothecene mycotoxins in air and dust samples from the greenhouse indicated fungal infestation. A search for fungal organisms in soil samples from the greenhouse uncovered abundant fungal spore colonies classifiable in the fungal genus *Stachybotrys*. Nucleotide sequence, though consistent with the genus *Stachybotrys,* may represent a new and previously unrecognized mutant species of *Stacyhbotrys*. The trichothecene mycotoxin component of this mycotoxin indicates that it must be considered potent and highly toxic. Further evaluation and characterization are necessary. Mass spectral analysis is recommended.

Signed: Everett R. McKenzie, B.S., M.S.

More unfamiliar terms and confusing sentences, but there, in the next-to-last sentence, was all he needed to know: "…must be considered potent and highly toxic." Dr. Holleran had to know about this right away.

CHAPTER TWENTY-FOUR

Joe Holleran was incredulous as he read the report Allen faxed to him. He remembered his skepticism when Allen told him of his idea of something toxic or maybe infectious…in the gardens or the greenhouse. Joe had tried to be sympathetic, but he'd virtually dismissed Allen's suspicions as implausible because he was convinced that the laboratory tests had ruled out toxic substances and infections. Now this report could hold the answer, and they'd missed it. He'd never thought of it or even suspected it. He must let Dave Dittrich know and, of course, Cassie as well.

He dialed her first. A secretary answered. "Yes, Dr. Holleran, one moment please."

Then came a crisp voice, "This is Dr. Garriman."

"Hi, Cassie. Joe Holleran."

"How are you?" The tone was ice cold.

"Fine thanks," he said. "I have a question for you if you've got a minute."

"Sure."

"Are you familiar with something called trichothecene mycotoxins?"

"What?" she said, first a surprised tone then a slightly disdainful one. "Why do you ask?"

"I think we may be onto something relating to my patient, Mr. Kanaby," he said. "Remember the man who died so mysteriously a couple of weeks ago? You were consulting with Dave Dittrich about him, and you came in during the autopsy to see the brain."

"Yes. I remember. Is there something about trichothecenes?" The voice reflected more interest.

"Yes. Possibly. That's why I'm calling. To try to get some information."

"Well," she said condescendingly, "trichothecenes are a class of toxins produced by certain types of fungus. What's that got to do with your patient?"

"Maybe quite a bit," said Joe. "Apparently the son, Allen, has been bird-dogging this thing since before the man died. He had the idea that there was something going on either in the gardens or the greenhouse out where the man lived. He talked to me about it a couple of days before Mr. Kanaby died. I didn't see how there could be anything there that might relate to the illness. As you know, we tried hard to find of evidence of infection or some kind of toxin. Everything came up negative."

"So go on," she said, cool again.

"After Mr. Kanaby died, I didn't think much more about it. I was just waiting on the autopsy results. But apparently Allen did think more about it. In fact, he hired a local environmental consulting agency, and believe it or not, they've found high levels of trichothecene mycotoxins in the greenhouse."

"Oh my," she said, still distantly, but her interest was now momentarily piqued.

"Their report describes how they've traced it back to a probable fungal infestation. Allen called to tell me then faxed me a copy of the report, and I've just read it. It looks legit to me, but I'd like to know what you think. If you have a minute, I'll read you a little bit."

"Okay. Go ahead," she said, her voice reserved again.

"First it says 'ELISA of ambient-air samples and surface dust samples demonstrated high levels of trichothecene mycotoxins.' Then further down, 'QPCR carried out on spore samples identified a fungus of the genus *Stachybotrys*.' Then it goes on to say that amplification of ribosomal DNA from the QPCR showed that the nucleotide sequence is *not* compatible with any recognized species of *Stachybotry* therefore it may represent a mutation. How about that?"

"That is incredible," she said, now with clear enthusiasm.

"The report gives a lot more detail, but I'm not sure what to do with it. I thought you could advise me or maybe take it from here. Can I fax it to you?"

"Yes. Please. I want to see it." Now she was in. "I can do some computer searches based on what it says. And I'd also like to know more about this environmental consultant, whoever he is. From what you just told me, the report sounds pretty solid so I would assume it's reliable…at least until I look into it further."

"It's a company called EnviroTech Environmental Solutions. Here in Atlanta," said Joe. "I can find out more from Allen. He wants to come in to talk to me about it, and I think it would really be important for him to talk to you, too. *You're* the expert on this.*"

"Don't patronize me, Joe," she said sharply. "Just send me the damn report. I want to see that before I talk to Allen or anyone else."

"Okay. Sure. I'll fax it to you in the next five minutes." Now his words were as clipped as hers. "Let me know when you're ready to talk about it."

"I'll get back to you."

The conversation ended. It was clear she had no extra words for him. She was all business. He wondered if she knew anything about his confrontation with Blaine. If so, she gave no hint. He walked out to the secretarial area and faxed the report.

*****

She had been increasingly perplexed and challenged by this case after seeing the brain at the autopsy, so much so that she had gone back to the records in a diligent search for clues. She reviewed all the available clinical lab data, the MRIs, the EEG reports and of course the hospital records: admission notes, doctors' notes, nurses' notes, medications, running records of vital signs and daily orders: everything. The lab reports didn't seem to offer help. Routine blood tests, initial and follow-up, were okay. White cell counts…mild lymphocytosis which did not change, hemoglobin, electrolytes, enzymes: all normal. Lumbar puncture, normal. Cultures of blood, spinal fluid and urine, negative. The first and only routine immunoglobulin assay was reported shortly after admission as borderline elevation of IgG. She did, however, remember being particularly puzzled by the elevation of the IgE. She couldn't relate that to anything, but she'd mentioned it to Lang.

In short, she found nothing to indicate an infection even though that had been a working diagnosis. The idea of a chemical toxin likewise had no support from any of the clinical lab tests or toxicology screens. But now, as she read and re-read the report, it made sense. The words at the end glared up at her:

"….a new and previously unrecognized mutant species of *Stachybotrys*".

It was almost 5:00. She called Lang's office; it was closed. She'd have to wait 'til tomorrow when she would go to look at the slides with him. This would blow him away. In the meantime, there was work to do. Mycotoxins, trichothecenes, nucleotide sequences, mutant species, *apoptosis*, the words fairly tumbled over themselves in her head as she booted up and navigated to the online database, MedIQ.

The last time she had given serious thought to the word mycotoxin was in her fellowship days. From somewhere in her memory of those days, she vaguely recalled an intriguing talk she'd heard about the witches of Salem. A visiting speaker presented some evidence offering support and controversy for the theory that some of the women involved in the Salem Witch Trials in the late 1600s may have been suffering from effects of mycotoxins which caused erratic behavior, hallucinations and seizures. Esoteric as it seemed at the time, the idea now took on new significance.

She went to the search window and typed in the word mycotoxin looking for a clear definition. She found several, but the one that was most succinct and informative was:

Mycotoxins: Toxic secondary metabolites which are produced by certain types of fungi and are capable of causing disease and death in both humans and animals. Found on surfaces of fungal spores and their breakdown fragments resulting in fine dust-like particles. They are neither infectious nor contagious but, if inhaled, may cause symptoms including pulmonary edema, areflexia, blindness, seizures and stupor which, in severe cases, can combine to become fatal.

Searching the database with the key word mycotoxins yielded 1,843 articles published since 1996. The key word neurotoxicity for the same period indicated 7,246 citations, but cross-referencing mycotoxins and neurotoxicity brought up only 35 articles. Her conclusion: neurotoxicity from mycotoxins is rare. Her next search for articles on *Stachybotrys* yielded more than 300 citations, but cross-referencing *Stachybotrys* and neurotoxicity yielded only 6.

She printed out the abstracts. One in particular described "four major classes of fungus which produce mycotoxins capable of causing severe lung problems as well as a spectrum of neurological symptoms." Another pointed that mycotoxins from a particular species, *Stachybotrys chartarum*, can, though rarely, produce neurological involvement which can be highly fatal. What about the others?

She searched on. Information was random, but in another 20 minutes or so, she learned that there were at least 6 recognized species of *Stachybotrys*. The most widely studied was *chartarum*. One description said spores are produced in slimy greenish masses with high moisture content and that the mycotoxins themselves result when the spores dry and disintegrate into microscopic particles which can become airborne. Another said: "Mycotoxins are hard to detect and identification as well as determination of the source is often difficult". In other articles, caveats and contradictions came through like "Caution should be taken to relate health effects of *S. chartarum* and poor indoor air quality"; "Health risks from environmental exposure to *Stachybotrys* remain poorly defined". Then there were more specific phrases such as "...trichothecene mycotoxins can become airborne with important implications for indoor air quality..." and "...trichothecene mycotoxins can be demonstrated in tissues of individuals exposed to *Stachybotrys chartarum* in contaminated buildings".

Now she was even more challenged. Could this really be a new species of *Stachybotrys* in this greenhouse? And could it be the culprit that killed Richard Kanaby?

It was almost 7:00, but her fingers continued to fly over the keyboard as she put in new search words, found more information. The total number of known, naturally occurring, identified trichothecenes was more than 160. The most efficient technique for characterizing them was mass spectrometry. Possible but complicated, she thought.

Her desk phone rang. It was Blaine. "Hi", she said, almost automatically lowering her voice in response to his. In the short time they'd been together, he'd managed to bring her to such a point of abandon when she was with him that even now, just hearing his voice obliterated everything else. She could feel excitement building inside her as he spoke, but she restrained herself. "Oh, just finishing up in my office. Been tied down for awhile with computer searches." She paused. "Oh?" She paused again. "Oh, you would, huh?" She gave a quick one-syllable laugh. "And how would you do that?" Another pause. "Oh, really?" She laughed again. "Uhummm. Okay. About another hour." Pause. "Me too."

She hung up and leaned back in the chair still hearing his voice. She smiled, but the moment passed, and her thoughts clicked back to the urgency of her searches. She couldn't stop yet. She had to find out as much as possible before meeting with Lang tomorrow. She wondered if he'd been able to confirm *apoptosis*. What about *apoptosis* and mycotoxins?

She moved on. Mycotoxins cross-referenced with *apoptosis* yielded 439 articles, but for mycotoxins crossed with *apoptosis* and neurotoxicity, only 7, and trichothecene mycotoxins with *apoptosis* and neurotoxicity, only 3. She printed the abstracts of the 7 and the 3. Her mind was spinning and hungry for more, but glancing at her watch, 8:35, she decided it was too late. She closed her eyes for a moment trying to clear her thoughts, but as she did, Blaine's voice on the phone call came back, pulling at her. She stuffed the printouts into a folder, pushed it into her briefcase and turned off the computer.

*****

His car was in the driveway. She drove into the carport and hurried through the back door. The kitchen was dark, but light from her bedroom cast out into the hall. She dropped her keys on the counter, slid off her jacket and walked toward the light. She stopped at the doorway then moved quietly to the side of the bed. He was asleep. The sheet was pulled up just above his waist. His chest was bare. She stepped out of her shoes and unbuttoned her blouse. He didn't stir. She watched him for a few seconds as she released the waist band of her skirt and slowly unzipped the side. It slid to the floor. She touched his cheek and gently stroked the side of his head. His eyelids flickered. He moved slightly then opened his eyes and, without a word, lurched forward, grabbed both her forearms and pulled her on top of him. His arms wrapped around her neck as he pulled her head forward and forced his mouth onto hers. His hands slid beneath the open blouse, and without breaking the kiss, lifted it away. She raised her head absorbing the full intensity of his expression as he unhooked her bra and rolled her onto her back with a deep guttural sound. The weight of his naked body came down on her. He kissed her again, a deep, intense kiss. His hands moved over her shoulders and breasts. She was breathing short pants with little sounds of pleasure catching in her throat. He leaned slightly to one side. His right hand slid down past her waist, and his fingers began to explore. She threw her head against the pillow and arched her back uttering an intense moan. She felt the heat of his breath against her shoulder as he finished undressing her and fell onto her again, this time with such intensity, she surrendered unconditionally as he claimed her. Mycotoxins were the farthest thing from her mind.

CHAPTER TWENTY-FIVE

At 11:05 Friday morning, she was sitting across the microscope table from Stephen Lang holding the folder of printouts while he read the EnviroTech report. After several silent moments, he looked up with his eyebrows raised. "This is quite a surprise," he said quietly. "What I've seen with our studies confirms my suspicion of *apoptosis*, but I have no idea how mycotoxins can be related."

"I certainly didn't either until I went online last evening" she said, "but I found quite a number of papers."

"About *apoptosis* and mycotoxins?" he asked.

"Yes," she said." She laid the folder on the table. "If you don't mind, could we go over some of the slides first to give me an idea what *apoptosis* looks like, then I'll show you what I found."

"Of course," he said as he placed a glass slide on the stage of the microscope. "This is what made me think about it when these slides came through last week." He leaned toward the binocular viewer on his side of the double-headed microscope as he motioned toward the one on her side. She leaned forward and peered into the eye-pieces adjusting the focus. "This is a cross-section of the medulla," he said. "You can see that most of the large nerve cells show an irregular blebbing of the cell membrane." He moved the pointer around the field of view to demonstrate the features he was describing. "And the nucleus shows dark clumps of condensed chromatin." She stared at the image as he continued. "It's the typical appearance when the genome of the cell is attacked...as I think I mentioned last week."

"Yes, I remember," she said leaning slightly away from the microscope. "It's interesting though that even though I found more than 300 publications relating *apoptosis* to mycotoxins, I found only 7 concerning the nervous system. One describes *apoptosis* in the hypothalamus, another in the hippocampus and another in olfactory neurons. Three talk about specific trichothecenes mycotoxins, but here we're dealing with an unidentified trichothecene mycotoxin, possibly a mutation. And we have no idea about its neurotoxicity."

"That's true," said Lang, "but remember, the information in the report is only preliminary. We've got to delve deeper before we can relate the mycotoxin to what we see here." He put a finger on the microscope stage. "It has to be analyzed and characterized, but let me show you a few more slides, then we'll talk about your information." He put another slide on the microscope stage.

As she viewed successive slides and listened to Lang's theories, her suspicions about the danger of the mycotoxin were getting stronger. What Lang was describing as dramatic changes in the brain was convincing her they should act quickly. His point about analysis and characterization would take too long. She had an idea to try to convince him, but she had to make him listen.

She looked up. Her eyes fixed intently on him as she said, "I know you're right about analyzing and characterizing, but that'll take some time to arrange. It'll require mass spectroscopy. My immediate concern is toxicity, especially neurotoxicity. I think we have to explore that before we get into structural analysis because from a clinical a point of view, this thing could be extremely dangerous."

Lang was surprised at her unexpected assertiveness. "So what to do you suggest?" he said.

"It occurred to me this morning," she said, "that a quick way to test the toxicity might be to check it out in tissue culture." Giving up no territory, she said, "I've had experience using tissue culture models to study various types of infection. I went online to see what I could find relevant to this situation. Fortunately, I found three papers describing *apoptosis* induced by mycotoxins in primary cerebral cortical cell cultures. One study looked at the effects of the mycotoxin produced by a well-known species of *Stachybotrys* known as *Stachybotrys chartarum*. When I saw that, I thought that might be a way to test the toxicity here. You think that's do-able.?"

"Yes, but I'd like to see your references," Lang said with a hint of condescending skepticism.

"Certainly." She opened the folder and began to thumb through the pages.

"We can easily set up primary cortical cell cultures," he said anticipating what she was about to show him, "but we also have continuous cortical cell line cultures in the lab."

"You have those available now?"

"We do," he said nodding slowly.

"Then we should be all set," she said. She was excited.

Her new directness intrigued him. "So how do you propose to get hold of the mycotoxin?" he asked.

"I'll contact McKenzie, the environmental guy directly," she said. "He's the one who wrote the EnviroTech report. I can call and find out if they have samples we can use. Of course we have to be careful how the samples are handled until we know more about the toxicity."

"Exactly, Dr. Garriman," Lang said pointedly. "All the more reason to have it analyzed and characterized even if it does require mass spectrometry." He seemed a bit irritated. "How do you propose to handle it for tissue culture studies?"

"The first thing is to find out if samples are available," she said. "McKenzie's lab must be accustomed to dealing with this kind of thing. I'm sure they have a protocol. If he'll let us have enough for tissue culture studies, we can probably use his protocol. Or we can work out our own. I can do that. And meanwhile," she said thinking a slightly conciliatory note might be appropriate just now, "I'll be happy to check into the mass spectroscopy. I know the guy who runs the mass spectronomy lab at the university. Dr. Solomon Zelinski . In fact, I worked on a virus project with him a few years ago. I'll see if he'd be willing to do an analysis."

"Good," said Lang sounding satisfied. Her concession seemed to have placated his reaction when she resisted his suggestion for mass spec analysis. "Would you like to see any more of the slides?"

"I would," she said. "You're teaching me something."

"I'm learning some things here myself." He laughed and put another slide on the microscope stage.

*****

She left the institute just after noon. Driving back toward Brakefield, she began making plans. She needed to pull up the full texts of the tissue culture papers to see how the cultures were exposed to the mycotoxins, what the end-point was for determining toxicity and how *apoptosis* was confirmed. And, oh yes, she needed to call Zelinski, but that should wait until she knew about the samples from McKenzie.

She was back at her desk a little before 1:00. She tried Joe Holleran's office. He was not available. She left a voicemail message saying she could meet with him and Allen Monday afternoon any time after 2:30. As she read the report again, she decided to call Everett McKenzie right away. Dialing the phone number on the report took her immediately to him. She identified herself and explained her involvement as one of Richard Kanaby's doctors and now in the search for the cause of his illness. Following his cordial response, she proceeded to ask if there might be samples of mycotoxins available for neurotoxicity studies. He confirmed there were at the EnviroTech lab. They had been adequately prepared for study, he said, but he could only release them to her upon clearance from his client, Allen Kanaby.

Okay, she thought, so she would contact Allen, but right now she should call Zelinski. She dialed the number for the University. "Yes, operator," she said, " Dr. Solomon Zelinski, please. Department of Biochemistry."

"Dr. Zelinski's lab, Tracie speaking," came a quick response.

"Hi, this is Dr. Garriman at Brakefield Medical Center calling for Dr. Zelinski," she said.

"He's left for the day, Doctor, but I can have him return your call on Monday."

"That's fine. Please tell him I'm calling about a mass spec analysis. I think he'll remember me. I did some work with him a few years ago." She repeated her name, recited her office number, and upon thanking Tracie, hung up.

She then logged into MedIQ again and printed full-length copies of the tissue culture papers before she left for the day.

*****

She met Blaine for dinner at a quiet little restaurant in Buckhead where they'd been twice before. They took a table toward the back, but in spite of the relaxed, romantic atmosphere, the conversation never strayed from her intense focus. She had not said anything about the EnviroTech report last night because, well...there had been distractions. But tonight was different. After the day she'd had today, she was irrepressibly excited. She began with some details of the report, what she'd found on MedIQ, then her meeting with Lang and her idea of using tissue culture. He listened and watched her, fascinated and hardly believing this was the same woman who woke him up last night.

CHAPTER TWENTY-SIX

Over the weekend, Joe Holleran emailed Cassandra confirming that he and Allen Kanaby could meet her on Monday afternoon at 4:00 in his office. Monday morning, she called Lang to let him know she had contacted McKenzie and hoped to have samples of the mycotoxin on Tuesday. "And," she added, "I've left word with Zelinski's lab about the mass spectroscopy. He should call me back today or tomorrow."

She arrived at Joe's office at 4:00, the EnviroTech report and a notebook in hand. Joe introduced her to Allen.

"Nice to meet you, Mr. Kanaby," she said in a quietly authoritative voice as she held her hand toward him. They all sat.

Joe looked at Cassandra and said, "I've explained to Allen that you and I have discussed the report. I think I can speak for both of us when I say that frankly we find it astounding."

"Indeed," she said, "and I can speak for both of us when I say we need to take some immediate steps to investigate what was found in your greenhouse."

"My dad's greenhouse," Allen said quickly.

"Oh, yes, of course. Sorry," she said nodding toward him deferentially. "You've had a chance to read the report?"

"Yes," Allen replied.

"And you understand that they found airborne toxic substances called mycotoxins?" she continued in the same authoritative tone and manner.

"Yes."

"I must say, mycotoxins are something we rarely encounter," she said. "Until now, I thought there were only a few different mycotoxins. But to my surprise, with the bit of research I did this weekend, I discovered there are many. Most seem to be relatively harmless, but some can cause serious illness. Even death. I found two anecdotal cases of an illness caused by mycotoxins which sound very similar to your father's illness. But what sets the mycotoxin we're dealing with apart is that it is apparently produced by a *new* fungus," she said glancing at Joe. "According to the report it's an unrecognized mutant species, at least as far as we can tell. We don't know how toxic it might be, but it seems very likely it caused your dad's illness."

"May I say something, Doctor?" Allen interrupted.

"Yes, of course," she said. "Just let me finish this one thing. I've been working on this with Dr. Lang, the neuropathologist out at the Hefner-Cantrell Institute. We think we have a way to answer the question of toxicity fairly quickly if we can get samples of the mycotoxin. After I read the report, I contacted EnviroTech and spoke directly to Mr. McKenzie. He said they do have some samples we could use, but since you engaged him for the investigation, he said he'd have to have your permission to the release any samples to us."

"By all means," said Allen. "What do I have to do?"

"I think just a phone call would do it," she said. "I'll find out when we're finished here. Now, you were going to say something?"

"Yes," he said turning to Joe, "Dr. Holleran, you remember I said I talked to the son of the man who used to help Dad in his gardening. Mose Funchess."

"Yes," said Joe.

"I'll have to repeat myself a little to explain it to Dr. Garrison," said Allen.

"Of course, please do," said Joe.

"So after Dad got sick," said Allen, now addressing Cassandra, "I started thinking there might be something in the gardens or the greenhouse causing it. Some kind of toxic chemical, maybe some insecticide or something for the plants. I took a quick look around the storage shed and the greenhouse, but I didn't find anything. Since Mose was the only one who might have known about that and he died more than 10 years ago, I thought that was a dead end. But Dr. Holleran suggested we should try to find Mose's family. See if they might know anything that might be helpful. I figured it would probably be just a shot in the dark, but my mother remembered that Mose had a son and daughter. We didn't know if we could find them, but I decided to give it a try." He paused. "On the off chance that I might find something in telephone listings, I did kind of a search for name and dialing information in all area codes around Altanta. Funchess is an unusual name, so I thought maybe I'd have luck. And believe it or not, after long enough, I was able to locate Mose's son Charles up in Gainesville.

"Long story short, I drove up to see him the weekend before Dad died. He remembered me from years ago when he used to come out to our house with Mose. I explained about Dad's illness. That we were concerned it might have something to do with the garden, and I wondered if he'd ever heard Mose talk about any kinds of insecticides or chemicals my dad used in the gardens. He didn't know anything about that, but he did tell me something that got my attention. He told me about an island off the coast of South Carolina where Mose grew up. It's called Wansaw Island. And he said according to Mose, at several times many years ago, there were episodes of a weird illness among the people on Wansaw. Hearing his description, I was struck with how similar it sounded to Dad's illness."

"How so?" said Cassandra.

"He said what he understood was that when people got sick on the island, the first thing was seizures. Then they went unconscious, couldn't breathe and died like...in just a few days. It seemed impossible to relate that to Dad because it was so long ago. But I couldn't get it out of my mind. So last weekend I made a quick trip over there. To that Island. Actually, it wasn't so quick," he chuckled. "A five hour drive plus a twelve-mile boat trip out in the ocean. Luckily I found a place where I could hire a boat and guide. Went out there only for the afternoon, but I think I got a pretty good idea of what it might have been like when Mose lived there. After I saw it, I began to wonder if that illness on the island, or as Charles called it, the sickness, might have come from something in the environment, something toxic or maybe some kind of infection."

"Did you see anything that made you think that?" Cassandra asked.

"Nothing specific," said Allen. "Old dilapidated and rotting cabins and debris...overgrown and neglected. The whole place was overgrown and completely deserted. Nobody has lived there for years. Seemed like a pretty unhealthy place now. Made me wonder what might be lurking." He paused thoughtfully for a moment. "I talked to a few people around where I hired the boat. They'd all heard about the illness. One described it the same way Charles did. Seizures, unconsciousness, trouble breathing then...death.. In fact, one man told me that when it happened back in the 1940s, so many died, they put a name on it. They called it the *dyin'* time." He paused waiting for a reaction from Cassandra or Joe. There was none.

He continued, "A few people I talked to had superstitious explanations about evil spirits, but the thing that got my attention was the similarity between what they described and Dad's illness. The more I thought about it, the more I began to convince myself there must be some kind of a connection. Of course the distance and the time thing, all the way back to the '40s and '50s, made it seem impossible to relate it to what Dad had."

He paused and looked away for a moment. "But I just couldn't get past the weird parts of the whole thing. Mose growing up there, coming here, working with Dad for so many years and Dad ending up with an illness so similar to those people." He looked back at Cassandra. "It seemed too strange to be coincidence. I kept dwelling on it all driving back last weekend…what I heard and saw and what I was thinking about something lurking. That's when I decided to have Dad's garden and the greenhouse tested somehow. I did a computer search to find EnviroTech, and it seems it was a good choice."

"I agree," said Joe. "Now we have to see how they follow up on what they've got so far. But let me ask you this. Do you know how Mose died? Anything like your dad?"

"According to his son Charles, Mose had a stroke," said Allen. "He was 86, but he lived several months after the stroke so it wasn't anything like Dad."

"Mmm," Joe mused. "Well let's go back to the island for a minute. You say there's no one living there now?"

"Yes," said Allen, "and it's been deserted since the 1990s. What I heard was that in the early '50s, the last time the illness came back as far as anyone could say, there were a lot of deaths. That's when people began leaving. I don't know what the population was in the 1950s, but when I checked with the South Carolina census office, I was told that by 1980, the population was only 68. It dropped to 36 in 1990, and by 2000, there was nobody there."

"So how do we connect the dots?" said Cassandra. "We know we've found something that very likely caused your father's illness. Assuming that *is* the culprit, it seems to work in mysterious ways. Dr. Lang tells me he finds what he calls an unusual pattern of brain damage due to a process that attacks the genetic structure of the brain cells. And even more unusual, he says he finds that the damage particularly involves parts of the brain that control respiration and consciousness."

"Could that be some kind of infection?" asked Allen.

"No," replied Cassandra. "In fact it is specifically *not* an infection."

"I thought funguses cause infections," said Allen.

"But this is different," she replied. "You remember the part of McKenzie's report that describes black dust in the greenhouse? That's what's left when the spores dry out and break apart?"

"Yes," said Allen.

"That dust is what the report calls the mycotoxins. Millions of tiny *toxic particles*. If the dust becomes airborne, even though it's not noticed, the particles can be inhaled. That's the danger."

"McKenzie did explain all that to me. He said he thought the ceiling fan kept the black dust stirred up. Like you say, airborne.",

"*Ceiling fan?*" said Cassandra, astonished. Joe too looked surprised but said nothing.

"Yes. He called me Friday wanting to know if I knew if it worked," said Allen. "I told him it had been working, but after Dad died, I turned it off. He asked me how long the fan had been there." Allen looked away as he said, almost wistfully, "You know it's really ironic. All these years, Dad wanted to put in a ceiling fan. Said it would be good for the plants to keep the air circulating, but he never got around to it. Just before Christmas, he saw one advertised. Supposed to be made especially for greenhouses. He ordered it. Said he was giving himself a Christmas present. It came the end of January, and he had it installed right away."

"So the fan was there only a couple of months?" Cassandra asked.. "That would have been plenty of time…"

"That's got to be it," Joe interrupted loudly, leaning forward, gesturing with both hands. "Just the right conditions, time-frame, everything. It was a set-up. The fan dried out the spores then delivered a double whammy blowing that black dust around. That's all it took for that microbial *sonofabitch* to do its dirty work.

Dammit!" he exploded, slamming a fist down on the arm of his chair. "So what do we do now?" he said looking at Cassandra.

"We find out if it's toxic," she replied with a calm counterpoint of tone. "Specifically, if it's neurotoxic. If we can get those samples I was referring to earlier, we can do some testing. I've found some published reports that describe using tissue culture to test the toxicity of mycotoxins. I think that approach could give us some important information. Lang says he has several types of tissue culture we could use, so we should be able to start almost immediately."

"I'll call McKenzie right away," said Allen.

"Okay." said Joe, "That'll get things started. But we also have to find out where the hell the damn thing came from. If it's a mutation like the report suggests, the question is did it mutate in the greenhouse or somewhere else?"

"Like that island," said Cassandra looking at Allen. "It seems plausible that if a mutation occurred there, it could have been contained there if the island is remote enough. You said 12 miles out, right?"

Allen nodded. "That's right."

"So if it does exist there and nowhere else, how did it get here?" That's what we've got to figure out," said Cassandra. "Maybe some clues in the greenhouse."

"It's been sealed," said Allen. "McKenzie says no one should go in 'til it's cleaned up."

"Has that been started?" she said.

"No. He's just says it has to be done."

"I'm sure if we explain to him, we can get in," she said. "When I call him about the samples I'll see what he says about letting us go in."

The meeting ended a little after 4:30. She took Allen's cell number and assured him him she'd let him know about the permission. When she returned to her office, she dialed Everett McKenzie. She got the answering machine but left a message and her cell number.

CHAPTER TWENTY-SEVEN

The first thing Tuesday morning, McKenzie returned her call. Verbal permission would be all he needed, and she could have samples of the mycotoxin as soon as he heard from Allen Kanaby. She relayed the message to Allen at his office. After another thirty minutes, McKenzie called her again, this time to say he had clearance, and she could pick up the samples at EnviroTech any time after 1:30.

Shortly after the second conversation with McKenzie, Solomon Zelinski returned her call. A professor of biochemistry and molecular biology at the university, he was highly regarded among his peers as an expert in mass spectral analysis of naturally occurring proteins. Since working with him four years earlier on a virus study, she'd maintained a cordial if only occasional contact with him. She hoped that would come in handy now.

Of course he remembered working with her, he said, and happily regaled her with his successes in securing grant funding for his work as well as for the expansion of his laboratory. He told her of his good fortune at finding a full-time technical assistant for the mass spectrometer and also bringing on a talented associate, Dr. Eliina Amorov, whom he'd hired away from a government lab near Washington, D.C. She came from Moscow, was trained in physics and mass spectrometry in Moscow and Boston. In the three years she'd been in his lab, they had co-authored 9 peer-reviewed publications. Obviously, he considered her addition to the lab to be a real *coup*.

"So," he said in a manner signaling the end of his litany of recent accomplishments, "what can I do for you, Dr. Garriman?"

She gave him a short summary explaining that in her medical practice in infectious diseases, she had recently been consulted on a patient suspected of exposure to either a toxic or infectious agent. "Following up on the infectious line of investigation we've found a mycotoxin we think the man was exposed to," she paused for a moment, "...and after some rather detailed studies, we think it may be produced by a mutant, a previously unidentified species of fungus. We're about to start some toxicity studies in tissue culture. But we believe it's important to have a mass spec analysis to try to characterize the mycotoxin structurally and compare that to known mycotoxins."

After a few questions from Zelinski and what must have been adequate responses from Cassandra, he seemed genuinely intrigued at the prospect. He told her he thought it could be an interesting project and that an analysis should not be a problem. He would need a very small sample of the mycotoxin. "We use only nanogram quantities," he said. She said she would call again shortly to let him know when she could deliver the sample.

She arrived at the EnviroTech at 2:00, introduced herself to a man at a desk in the narrow hallway, and McKenzie was summoned immediately. As he came through a side door, he greeted her deferentially. He led the way to a laboratory in the rear of the building. It was a small-to-moderate size rectangular room, but apparently well-equipped and efficiently arranged. There was a glass-fronted sterile hood and a table holding a microscope against one sidewall. There was a long stainless steel work table and sink in the center, and a stainless steel counter holding a pH meter, a centrifuge and a glass-enclosed chemical scale along the other sidewall. Along the back wall stood a refrigerator and an upright freezer. McKenzie, obviously proud to show off the lab, briefly but enthusiastically described the kinds of studies they carried out in this space.

Then he pointed to two small styrofoam boxes sitting at the far end of the work table. "We have packed five vials in each box, 5 mls. in each. They're all labeled and frozen." He pulled one box across the table. "The vials in this box have a concentrated suspension of mycotoxin dust from the greenhouse," he touched one box. "And the vials in this one," he touched the other box, "have the suspension of mycotoxins which we milled from spores. They've been filtered to remove RNAses, and I can assure you, the concentration of mycotoxin is quite heavy in all the vials. We have more of the spores in storage. And we can produce more of the mycotoxin if you think you need it, but I believe you'll have plenty for your purposes."

"Sounds like you've worked with mycotoxins before," she said.

"Oh yes," he said. "It's not unusual for us to find mycotoxins in water-damaged buildings from time to time. It's pretty straight-forward, but I must say this is the first time I've come across one that's never been identified. That's really intriguing."

"That'll have to be confirmed of course," she said, "but whatever it is, our first step is to test it for toxicity. We think it may be strongly neurotoxic."

McKenzie listened fascinated as she began to describe what Lang had found in the brain and how they were planning to use tissue culture to test for toxicity. She answered his questions patiently and in considerable detail, hoping that establishing a bit more rapport would help as she was about to broach the issue of getting into the greenhouse.

"I'd like to go into that greenhouse myself," she said cautiously. "See if there's any indication where the thing might have come from. Would that be possible?"

McKenzie was more than accommodating. Not only would he open the greenhouse, but he could provide the necessary protective gear, and he'd be happy go with her. They agreed to meet at the

Kanabys' house the following morning at 9:00. She thanked him and hurried excitedly to her car."

The afternoon traffic on the beltway was annoying, especially because of her eagerness to deliver the samples to Lang. At about 3:15, she walked into his office holding up the Styrofoam boxes and the Manilla folder triumphantly announcing, "Dr. Lang, I think I've got what we need."

"Oh, do you?" he said looking up with a patronizing smile. "So when do we get started?"

"Whenever you say the cultures are ready. I've put together a protocol...subject to your approval."

"Tell me about it," he said.

"Okay, but I think I should get these samples into a freezer first," she said. "That's how they're stored at McKenzie's lab."

"Okay, let's take them up to the lab," said Lang. "I'll introduce you to our technician. She'll put'em away then we can discuss your protocol with her. She's been with us for 8 years. A real tissue culture expert. She was over at the CDC before she came here." I've told her about our plans." He seemed excited. "Now that we've got the samples, we need to go over specifics."

As they headed to the lab, she said, "I was able to reach the mass spec guy at the University this morning. The one I told you about. Dr. Zelinski. "

"Can he do it?" Lang asked.

"Yes. And he needs a very small sample. Only a couple of milliliters of the suspension. I want to take one of these vials to him."

They entered the lab where Jean Baker, a thin, rather weathered grey-haired woman, mid-50s, was sitting at a desk against the wall. She stood and walked toward them. Lang made introductions and pulled two lab stools up beside the desk. Cassandra laid the boxes and the folder on the desk and took one of the stools. Lang took the other. Jean returned to her chair.

Cassandra spoke. "So…what we have is two different suspensions of mycotoxin. Five vials in each box, milliliters frozen in each vial, each individually labeled. They've been stored frozen so we should keep them that way until we're ready to use them."

"All right," said Jean. "I have a batch of the cortical cell line cultures ready to go. They're set up in three-centimeter dishes, eight per tray, and I've got 10 trays in the incubator." She glanced toward Lang.

"Sounds good," he said with a nod.

"What I suggest here in this procedure plan," said Cassandra as she opened the folder, "is two sets of cultures, one for each type of suspension. Three different dilutions for each type plus negative controls. I've spelled it out here."

"Okay. The measured-drop dilution method is a reliable way to make low, medium and high concentrations," said Jean confidently,

"Good," said Cassandra. "According to the two reports I have, cultures were monitored every 6 to 8 hours. Is that possible?"

"No problem," said Jean.

"I'd say let the assay go for at least 48 hours or unless we see an effect earlier," said Cassandra. "If there's no effect by then, we'll have to re-think."

"We'll start first thing tomorrow morning and see how it goes," said Lang. "But understand now," he directed his words to Cassandra, "if we get an effect on this first run, we'll have to do several more to pin down the timing. We'll need additional runs for histologic stains and caspace activity. And of course I want some for electron microscopy, but I guess the first thing is to see if we get an effect." He picked up one of the styrofoam boxes. "You're satisfied with the way these specimens were prepared?"

"McKenzie says they're high concentrations," said Cassandra.

She reached for the other box as she continued, "For this one, they dried and milled the raw spores and made the suspension from the fragments. The one you're holding has vials with a suspension of the black dust collected from the greenhouse. We really should get them into the freezer."

Lang handed his box to Jean. Cassandra handed her the other one. "I'll put these away right now," she said, "but just to clarify, I'll check the culture trays this afternoon. Tomorrow I'll pick out the best cultures and work out the dilutions. If that goes okay, I should be able to start around 8:00."

"Fantastic," said Cassandra, her anticipation palpable. "I'm supposed to meet McKenzie at the greenhouse tomorrow morning. We're going in to see if we can tell anything about where this might have come from. But after that, I could come in to help if you need…"

"Thanks," said Jean, "but it's pretty much a one person job."

"She'll take care of everything," said Lang with a hint of territorial condescension. "You can come back when there's something to see." He stood. "I've got to get back downstairs now. Check with me tomorrow." He turned and left the room.

Registering Cassandra's surprise at his abruptness, Jean said quietly, "Don't mind him. Let's put these things up." She moved to the front of a stainless steel upright freezer and set the boxes on the counter just to the left. Cassandra watched as she slipped on rubber gloves and lifted the top off of each box. She pressed a security code into the key pad on the door and the lock released. She pulled the door open revealing a bank of metal storage drawers. She lifted out an empty drawer, just at eye-level. "Look how I place these." She took out the frozen vials one by one noting the labels. "I'm putting the mycotoxin dust suspension vials on the left in these slots, and the milled mycotoxin suspensions on the right."

As Jean put the last vial in, Cassandra thought of her conversation with Zelinski. "Oh," she said, "I need to hold out a vial of the black dust suspension for the mass spectroscopy lab at the university. I'll take it there myself."

"Okay," said Jean. She took out a vial from the left side, put it back into the styrofoam box, handed the box to Cassandra and pushed the drawer into the freezer. "Be sure you remember the drawer number. 4-D," she said. Cassandra took out her pocket notebook as Jean closed the freezer door. The lock clicked into place. "And you should also make note of the security code in case you need to bring in more samples and I'm not around. It's simple. Just press the four corner buttons. 1,3,9,7...then 1." Cassandra jotted the numbers in the notebook as they returned to the desk.

"Like I said, I'll be ready to go by about 8:00," said Jean. "You can check with me anytime though. You don't have to wait to be invited." She smiled.

"I understand," said Cassandra. "Nice to meet you."

"Same here," said Jean. "This should be interesting."

Cassandra, sytrofoam box in hand, started back to Brakefield now fully charged about what the tests might show. If the mycotoxin produced *apoptosis*, that could explain what happened to Richard Kanaby. And if in fact the fungus proved to be a new species producing a mycotoxin with such lethality, wow! And all the other questions continued to stream through her mind: Where did it come from? Could it have come from that island? How? Could it be there now? Could it have caused such devastation there? Did that really happen or was it only bizarre, undocumented hearsay?

She had to get back to her office to catch up on a few things, but she was eager to get home. Blaine would be there at 7:00.

*****

It was an impromptu dinner at home. He brought Mexican food, and she had beer and wine in the fridge. Over the weekend just past, she'd showed him the EnviroTech report, and had told him about what she'd found online. But tonight, she was overflowing with information about her day: talking to Zelinski, getting the samples from McKenzie, meeting with Lang and Jean Baker, making plans for the testing, anticipating the results. Her enthusiasm was so intense, she was almost breathless at times describing it all. But as he began to fathom this dimension of her, he realized she was not only a woman so willing to submit to him, to be possessed by him, but also a detective, a *medical* detective in excited pursuit. The aura fascinated and intrigued him. To him it was very sexy. It reassured him to think of how he could control her, but now more than ever, he realized she was his security. He would accommodate anything she might want from him…physically, emotionally, intellectually… because he had to keep her in his corner and make certain she trusted him. And above all, she must not know about his dark side. If Joe Holleran wanted to make trouble, he wouldn't hesitate to use the trump card he had up his sleeve.

CHAPTER TWENTY-EIGHT

Jean Baker was in the lab before 7:00 Wednesday morning. She went immediately to the incubator, removed four trays of culture dishes, brought them to the microscope and began examining each dish. After 30 minutes, she had chosen, marked and numbered 16 cultures and put them back into the incubator. Next, she paced through the ritualistic procedure of arranging glassware and instruments in the tissue culture hood. That done, she went to the freezer and took out one vial of the mycotoxin suspension from either side of the drawer. She checked the protocol, made notes in her <u>Experimental Records</u> notebook and at a little after 8:00, began making dilutions of the mycotoxin suspensions in culture medium. That done, she went back to the incubator and took out the cultures she'd marked. By 8:30 she was underway, meticulously placing each specified dilution of the mycotoxin suspension onto the culture designated for it.

*****

McKenzie was waiting by the door to the greenhouse at 9:15 when Cassandra pulled into the driveway. She hurried toward him dressed in jeans, a long-sleeve sweatshirt and well-worn sneakers. "Sorry to keep you waiting."

"Not at all. Just got here myself," he said as he lifted a bundle of loosely folded white cloth from the large canvas bag beside him. "Here's a jump suit for you. It'll fit over your clothes. Zips up the front. Slip these over your shoes." He held out a pair of shoe covers as she unfolded the bundle. "And here's a hat and gloves. Are you wanting to take some more samples or just look around in the greenhouse?"

"Yes I'd definitely like to take some more samples."

"Okay," he said as he unfolded another suit and stepped into it. Then he reached into the canvas bag again and took out two face masks. He handed one to her. "This is called a HEPA respirator mask. You can see, it's a full-face mask. It filters the air so you can't breathe in any kind of airborne particles."

They entered the greenhouse looking almost like astronauts. It was eerily silent and still. Where barely three weeks before there had been thriving seedlings and larger established plants, now there remained rooting trays and plastic pots on the bench holding only dried brown stems and leaves. Across the back of the space were six large tubs set close together holding thickly branched plants, some as high as 6 feet. These too were pitifully wilted or thick with dead leaves. Sunlight filtering through the white-washed glass ceiling produced splotchy patterns of light on the plants, the benches and the floor. As she stood for a moment glancing about, it seemed a surreal scene considering what secrets it might hold.

McKenzie set the canvas bag on the work table. He took a patch of white cloth from a pocket in his protective suit, rubbed it across the work table and held it up for her inspection. "See. The black dust," he said, his voice muffled by the face mask. "That's the mycotoxins."

"Yes," she said nodding. She fingered some of the dead branches on some smaller plants set around the floor on the sides. Then she moved toward the larger plants at the back. She approached the one farthest to the left and bent down to inspect the soil around the base. It was covered by a dry greenish crust. She shook the thin trunk gently, and a shower of dead leaves fell away revealing a plastic tag dangling from one of the upper branches. The words

Chinaberry/Wansaw/ 5/79 were neatly printed on it. She moved to the next plant, this one taller with thicker foliage. She shook it. Again, leaves fell away, and another tag showed itself deep in the branches. On it were the words Swamp Bay/ Wansaw/Mose, 6/78. She turned toward McKenzie. "Look at this."

He came closer to look. "Any idea what it means?" he said.

"Yes. That word Wansaw is the name of an island in South Carolina. Mose is the name of a man who used to work out here with Mr. Kanaby. According to Allen, Mose grew up on that island. I think this has to be what we're looking for," she said trying to bridle her excitement. "I'm guessing that these plants labeled Wansaw must have been brought in here by Mose. Maybe as small plants years ago." The implication of what she was finding and realizing made her spine tingle as she went on. " They've obviously been here a long time. I think the fungus got in here with those plants. That fits if you know the rest of the story."

"Oh?" McKenzie looked puzzled.

"Allen said Mose's son told him about an illness on that island supposedly many years ago. A lot of people died. He said it sounded so much like his father's illness, he went to Wansaw last week to check it out. He said people he talked to all told the same story."

"So he's thinking there's a connection?" McKenzie asked. "That's why he wanted the testing?"

"Exactly," she said. "When we saw your report, the most obvious question to us was the toxicity of the mycotoxin, but of course we were curious about where it came from. We didn't know Allen had pursued it like he did. Now I think what we've found on these tags tells us his curiosity led him in the right direction."

"Certainly could be if the fungus was in the soil the plants were in when they were brought in," said McKenzie. "Even a small amount of soil around the roots would be enough. This is the perfect environment for the mycelium to thrive. And once the spores are formed, some types can survive for decades under the right conditions. And *Stachybotrys* is notorious for that. I have several papers that say as much…as long as they are moist and undisturbed. They have to dry out and break down to produce mycotoxins.

"That looks pretty dried out." She pointed to the green crust at the base of the Chinaberry.

He knelt beside the pot and touched the crust. "I'll get some samples."

"He told you the ceiling fan was just installed in January, right?" she said.

"He sure did." He gazed up at the fan and shook his head. "Who would've ever thought?" He moved to the third plant. "How about this one? Says M. Grandiflora/Wayside Nurs/Atlanta/ 4/82. Not from Wansaw." He looked down moved to the next plant. Another tag hung deep in its branches. "This one says Yaupon/Wansaw/9/80.

"I wish I'd brought a notebook," she said.

"I've got a pad if that'll do." He went back to the work table and took a small pad and pencil from the canvas bag. "I didn't notice those tags when we were here last week." He handed her the pad and pencil.

"Okay, let's number the pots starting with that first one, the Chinaberry," she said. "You match your new samples with the pot number, and I'll record what's on the labels. Oh, and by the way, I'd like to see those papers you mentioned….about viability of *Stachybotrys*."

"Sure. They're at the office. Just a minute," he said as he reached into the bag again. "I need to grab my trowel and some Ziplocks bags."

At just after 11:00, they finished and exited the greenhouse. McKenzie began to gather the gear as Cassandra took off the mask, hat, jumpsuit, shoe covers and gloves.

"I'll let Allen know what we've found," she said.

"Okay," he said.

She thanked him and walked quickly to her car. She had to get home to shower and change before delivering the mycotoxin vial to Zelinski. She pulled into her driveway. She went into the house and called Zelinski to say she could bring the vial at 1:00.

"That's fine," he said. "You know where the chemistry building is?"

"Yes."

"You can park right in front. There are several visitor spots there. Unfortunately, I'll be in a meeting, but if you can call the lab as you are getting close, I'll have Dr. Amorov meet you in the lobby. She's the associate I told you about. Eliina Amorov. She'll be in a white lab coat. Medium height, long dark hair."

"Sounds good," Cassandra replied.

By 12:30, she was on her way to the university with the precious Styrofoam encased cargo. In another 20 minutes, turning into the circular driveway in front of the building, she parked and entered the lobby. She spotted a woman matching Zelinski's description.

"Helena?" she said.

The woman came forward smiling. ""E—liina," she emphasized the first letter. She held out a hand. "Is unusual name for Americans." She spoke with a distinct accent, "You are Doc-torr Garrri—-man, yes?"

"Yes," said Cassandra as she shook the hand. "And here is the material for Dr. Zelinski. I've explained to him." She held the box forward.

"Yes, he told me. Is...veddy interrresting."

"So you work with Dr. Zelinski?"

"Yes. I am associate of Doctor Zelinski."

"I worked with him a few years ago. It was quite productive," said Cassandra. "How long have you been here?"

"Three yearrs."

"You like Atlanta?"

"Yes. Veddy much. Is…beautiful city."

"Where are you from?" Cassandra explored a bit further.

"I come from Rrrussia," Eliina replied. "Moscow."

"Oh," said Cassandra. "Well. we look forward to what you find with this material."

"Yes. Will be…veddy interrresting," said Eliina.

"It's a pleasure to meet you."

"Yes. Thank you," replied Eliina. "Goodbye."

Cassandra was scheduled in the clinic starting at 2:30 so no time for lunch. She stopped by the snack bar alcove just off the hospital lobby, picked up a sandwich and made her way to her office. When she got to her desk, she punched in Allen Kanaby's office number. "Hello, Allen, it's Cassandra Garriman."

"Oh. Doctor Garriman," he sounded surprised. "Nice to hear from you."

"Just took a chance I could catch you. I'm calling to let you know Mr. McKenzie and I went to the greenhouse this morning."

"Oh," he said. "That was quick."

"Well," she said, "it just worked out that we could both go today," she said, "and I must say, we have some interesting findings. I wanted to see what you think."

"Of course," he said.

"You said you never spent much time in the greenhouse, but I am wondering if you might have any information about any of the plants in there, especially the large ones toward the back," she said.

"No. Not really," said Allen. "As I told you, the only time I've been in there in years was when I went in to turn off the fan."

"Well, as we looked around, it was the big plants against the back wall that got our attention. What we found indicates they came from that island. Wansaw."

"What do you mean?" he said.

"Notes on plastic tags…attached to the plants" she said. "Specifically, the words Wansaw and Mose, and dates like June 1978 or May 1979…or 1982 written on the tags."

"Oh my gosh," he said.

"Did your dad ever say anything about plants from Wansaw?" she said.

"Uhmm…now that you mention it, I remember his talking about how Mose would occasionally bring plants from Wansaw when he came back from visiting his mother. He said they were presents. For the greenhouse."

"Well, it's quite possible they are the source of the fungus," she said.

"After all this time?" said Allen. "That's amazing."

"We're still investigating, but we know the spores McKenzie described in his report were found in the soil those big plants live in. I think what you're saying confirms how they got there."

"So what's next?" said Allen.

"Right now we're focusing on the toxicity of the mycotoxins. We should have more on that in the next few days."

*****

At 7:00 Thursday morning, Jean Baker adjusted the magnification of the microscope and focused on the first culture dish, the one that had received the highest concentration of the mycotoxin dust suspension. Last evening at 8:30 she had checked all 16 cultures. By then, they had been incubating in the mycotoxin solutions for almost 12 hours, but there was no evidence of an effect, so she had decided to leave the lab and come back early in the morning. Now, after almost 24 hours, her experienced eyes were on alert for even the most subtle changes, but she was not prepared for what she saw. She increased the magnification.

It was clear. The cells were severely distorted, and there was a distinctly abnormal appearance of the nucleus in almost every nerve cell. The change had occurred sometime between 12 and 23 hours. She felt a tinge of excitement but reminded herself that this was only the first one. She had to examine all the others before she could conclude anything. She quelled her enthusiasm and began the slow process, inspecting each culture at several magnifications and making notes. After 30 minutes, she was convinced. She set the tray aside and called Lang's office. He was not in yet. She left a message on the machine and began to plan an agenda. She knew exactly how he'd want to proceed.

After another 20 minutes, the phone rang. "Good morning, Dr. Lang. Yes. I think you should come see." She put the first culture dish on the microscope stage again. He appeared in less than 5 minutes and took a seat at the microscope. She sat patiently as he began to look. He moved from one dish to the next without a word until at last, after what seemed a very long time to her, he said, "I think we've got what we're looking for. Let's get some pictures, then the special stains."

"Yes, sir," she said.

"Let me know when you're ready," he said as he walked away.

Two hours later, she called. "All done, Doctor. Can you come up?"

Again, she sat across the microscope table from him as he began to inspect silently. "After the 10th stained culture, he looked up. "I think I'll give Dr. Garrison a call." Jean smiled and nodded.

*****

The news from Dr. Lang was exhilarating. Cassandra could hardly wait to get back to the institute. When she walked into the lab Jean was sitting at the microscope engrossed. She looked up and flashed a delighted smile. "Did he tell you? We've got it. We've *definitely* got it. "

"He told me," she said, "but no details. Just said to come see."

"He says it's a typical pattern. Have a look." Cassandra sat and adjusted the eyepieces on the microscope. "This first one was incubated in the highest concentration of the dust suspension." Jean slid the dish onto the microscope stage. "This is a special histological stain shows how the nuclei of the nerve cells are breaking down. See the dark blue clumps? It's called a Giemsa stain." Cassandra peered into the binoculars as Jean spoke. She removed the dish and slid another one onto the stage. "This is another kind of special stain," she said. "It confirms the breakup, the fragmentation of the DNA. Dr. Lang says it's clear confirmation. We know the changes started somewhere between 12 and 20 hours. He wants to run another assay to try to pinpoint the time of onset of changes. He says the shorter the time of onset, the more intense the toxicity."

"So when will you do another run?" asked Cassandra.

"Tomorrow," said Jean. "He says he thinks we may see the earliest changes by 14 to 16 hours so he wants to start early. 'Course that's gonna run into the weekend, but I'll get everything ready this afternoon and come in around 6:00 in the morning. Start the incubation at 7:00. I'll check several times during the day. Then at 7:00 in the evening...that'll be the 12 hours...I'll start checking every hour and I'll just stay 'til I see some changes."

"That'll be a long day."

"I'll just stay over," said Jean. "I've done it before."

At 3:45, Cassandra was on her way back to Brakefield. The microscopic images she'd just seen percolated through her mind. She could hardly wait to tell Joe Holleran and David Dittrich. And Everett McKenzie, too. She was the messenger with a message they all wanted to hear.

When she got to her office, her first call was to McKenzie. "I just got back from the institute. Dr. Lang says the tissue culture tests definitely show that the samples I got from you are toxic. They're running another assay tomorrow for confirmation."

She next called Joe Holleran's office next. He was not available but would call her back shortly the secretary said. She dialed David Dittrich. He would call back after clinic.

She booted up her computer and opened her email. There were the references from McKenzie. She went back to MedIQ and printed out the full text of each. From the one with the most detail, she jotted telegraphic notes: "Members of the *Stachybotrys* genus found worldwide, from Finland to the South Pacific"; "because of the wide geographic range, considered ubiquitous"; "first identified in U.S., 1930s"; "relatively low prevalence"; "found in soil rich in cellulose such as hay, straw, grain, plant debris, rotting wood, cotton"; "survives in a wide temperature range dying only at temperatures greater than 60 degrees Centigrade": "can survive winter temperatures"; "spores can remain viable for years to decades."

How much better could it fit? *Stachybotrys* may be ubiqitous, she thought to herself, but if this is a new mutation, isolated on an island, no way to tell how long it's been there. At least as of today, evidence seems to explain how it got to the greenhouse.

Joe Holleran called little after 5:00. It gave her considerable satisfaction to tell him in her coolest, most detached voice what she had found in the greenhouse and what the results were from the tissue culture studies which, she pointedly reminded him, she had proposed and designed. He should talk to Dave Dittrich, and she would contact Dr. Lang about getting together. They had to decide how to handle this information. "This is urgent," she said. "Of course you remember what McKenzie said about notifying the health department and the EPA." As her tone became increasingly authoritative, Joe simply listened without comment. When he thought she was through, he quietly said that he would pass the information along to Dittrich and would get back to her about a meeting.

She clicked off the phone. What should come next? The second run tomorrow might deliver more precise information. She wanted to see the autopsy report. They would need the tissue culture information and anything new McKenzie might have along with the Envirotech report. Perhaps McKenzie should be included in the meeting. He'd be the logical one to contact the local health department and the EPA. As for South Carolina, she'd look into that.

Her wheels were turning and there was a lot of work to do. But now at the end of this day, she wanted to get home to relax and think about things. Blaine would be there, and she was eager to tell him the latest. He had become so interested. That pleased her.

The evening was again filled with her preoccupation. Blaine mostly listened, but because he seemed so interested, it occurred to her that he might like to go with her to the Institute in the morning to see the cultures Jean had just showed her.

Of course he'd like to go. Maybe they could go early.

*****

They arrived at the Institute a little after 7:30 Friday morning. Jean was setting up the instruments and glassware in the hood and the three trays of cultures were sitting beside the microscope. She greeted them as they came through the door. Cassandra introduced Blaine.

"This is Dr. Purcell, my colleague from Brakefield. He's been working with me on this case, and I wanted him to see the stains you showed me yesterday. I know you're busy getting the assay going and I don't want to hold you up, but I thought I might be able to show him."

"Oh, sure.," replied Jean. "I was just about to get the vials out of the freezer. Let me do that, and I can get you started while I'm finishing my set-up," she said pulling on rubber gloves and walking toward the freezer. They followed as she continued speaking. "Dr. Lang wants to take some cultures in this assay for caspace staining and electron microscopy. We'll probably be here all day tomorrow. Never let it be said he's not thorough." She reached toward the keypad. "Now remember this?" She glanced at Cassandra. "Four corners. 1-3-9-7, then 1." She pressed the buttons and the door popped open.

"I remember, but it's in my notebook."

"And here we are. 4-D." Jean pulled the drawer open and lifted out two frozen tubes. "This one from the right side is the suspension of the milled spores, and this one from the left is the dust suspension." She closed the drawer and pushed the door shut. The lock snapped. She went back to the hood and placed the two vials in a metal rack. "Now I can get you started looking at the stains."

She sat on one side of the microscope table and Cassandra sat opposite, Blaine standing behind her. Jean lifted a stained culture from the tray and placed it on the microscope stage. Blaine and Cassandra alternated sitting and looking into the microscope with Jean's somewhat hurried commentary guiding them. In less than 10 minutes, they finished the first tray.

"I think you two can go through the rest of these without me. Then you can come watch me get started with the assay if you like"

Jean went back to the hood. Cassandrea and Blaine sat opposite each other at the microscope and viewed each of the remaining cultures carefully. With each, Cassandra proudly pointed out what Jean had showed her yesterday.

When they finished, she went to the hood to say, "Thanks for letting us come in to see them. I wish we could stay, but we both have to get back to the hospital. I'll check with you this afternoon."

On their way back to Brakefield, Blaine seemed so enthusiastic, it surprised her. "Looks like your idea about using the cultures was right on." She beamed at his approbation. They parked in the garage and walked into the hospital together separating in the lobby. He headed to the cardiology lab, and she, to her office.

*****

At 5:00, Cassandra called Lang's lab. Jean reported that there were no changes. "But," she said, "the assay's been running for only 9 hours. Based on the first assay, it's was too early to expect changes yet. I'll stay 'til I see an effect, even if it takes all night." She chuckled. "As I said, I've done this before. Check with me tomorrow… or come in."

CHAPTER TWENTY-NINE

She dampened her curiosity and resisted calling on Saturday, wanting to appear appropriately restrained. But on Monday morning an eager Cassandra called Lang. He told her the second assay had shown changes beginning at 17 hours. In addition to the stains, a caspace activation study, electron microscopy and a gel electrophoresis were underway. He said he expected all the results back by Tuesday afternoon. By Wednesday he should have the reports ready including the autopsy report. They agreed to meet Wednesday at 3:00 in her office. She e-mailed Joe Holleran and David Dittrich to let them know.

Lang arrived at her office Wednesday at 2:30. With his greeting, he handed her a folder, an index of its contents attached to its outside:

A. Autopsy Report and relevant photomicrographs
B. Results of the Tissue Culture Studies:
    1. Timeline and description of changes
        a. in cultures (photomicrographs included)
    2. Description of the special microscopic stains
        a. Giemsa stain
        b. Hoescht stain
    3. Agarose gel electrophoresis results
    4. Caspace activation assay
    5. Preliminary electron microscope studies/photos

"I believe it's all here and in record time if I say so myself," he said in the slightly imperious tone he could sometimes muster, "but in all honesty, it's thanks to you we've come so far so quickly. Turns out, your idea of using the tissue culture approach was rather brilliant."

"Thank you," she said surprised at his compliment. "I appreciate that. Please have a seat." He sat in one of the arm chairs in front of the desk as she laid the folder on the desk and sat in the other.

"I want to go over all this with the group." He said pointing to the folder. "But I came a bit early because there's one thing I want to discuss with you before the meeting. That is, what do we do with this information? This is obviously a potentially very dangerous thing, this mycotoxin. We can't just sit on it, but how do you think we should divulge this information? I think you're best suited to take the lead with your background in infectious disease and your initiative in all this."

"That's very kind," she said resisting the temptation to nod in agreement, "but I think we should talk about that all together."

"Okay, but then the question is with whom do we discuss it next?" he said, "Where do we start?"

"Well, I think we can all agree, it *is* dangerous," she said. "Certainly the autopsy plus the tissue culture information bear that out. I'm eager to get the results of the mass spec, but that may be awhile yet." She paused. "There's another dimension though. Something I learned just last week."

"Oh?"

"I think we may have found the source of the fungus," she said.

"Really?"

"Yes. It looks as though it got into the greenhouse on some plants that were brought in from an island off the coast of South Carolina some years ago."

"An island? In South Carolina?" he said with a tinge of skepticism.

"I know it sounds unlikely, but…" and she proceeded to give him a quick sketch of the story ending with what she'd found on the tags in the greenhouse.

He was silent until she finished, then with the same skeptical tone he said, "That is fascinating, but of course it would have to be confirmed."

At that point, Joe Holleran and David Dittrich arrived. After mutual greetings, Cassandra suggested they move across the hall to the conference room. "It'll be more comfortable," she said as she picked up the folder and led the way.

She sat at one end of the long table motioning to Joe and David to sit to the right and Lang to the left, a maneuver which made it seem perfectly natural for her to take charge. She began by asking Lang to review his findings. He opened the folder, and spread the reports and photographs over the table. The other two men were spellbound as he detailed not only the character and extent of the pathology in the brain, but also results of the tissue culture studies and the similarities to the pathology.

After 10 minutes or so, he concluded saying, "The evidence so far seems to confirm that this is an unknown mycotoxin. Not previously recognized, but nevertheless extremely aggressive and…the cause of the death in this patient." He paused a moment for their reaction.

"I'd say the information you have here is certainly comprehensive," said Joe.

Lang cleared his throat allowing the pause he needed before his next sentence. "I should point out that at my insistence, we've arranged to have the mycotoxin analyzed by mass spectroscopy."

Cassandra, surprised by Lang's somewhat pontifical air at that moment, was determined not to lose control of the discussion.

"That should help characterize it further," she said quickly, "but in the meantime, we're trying to find out more about where it came from. As I explained to you, Dr. Lang, the information in the greenhouse indicates that some plants there came from that island in South Carolina." She quickly diverted to the article from McKenzie about the ubiquity and long-term survival characteristics of *Stachybotrys*. "So it is possible that the spores could have been on that island years ago and came into the greenhouse with the plants. The question is, can the fungus be found there now?" With that, she described a plan to contact the EPA and health officials in South Carolina as well as Atlanta. Obviously impressed, all three men concurred: She should proceed with the plan and she should have the prerogative to use whatever information she needed to convey a message of urgency. The meeting ended with her assurance that she would make the contacts discreetly and would move ahead quickly. Joe and David left together. Lang stayed long enough to put the reports and photographs to the folder.

"You're welcome to keep this," he said as he passed the folder across the table. "You may need it when you make your contacts. I have copies of everything". She thanked him with a firm handshake, and he departed.

The boldly printed outline on the front of the folder seemed to focus her thoughts on what they were dealing with. An unrecognized, possibly new species of fungus capable of producing a lethal trichothecene mycotoxin that selectively targets the brain. She reveled in the prospect of the work ahead. Next step, go online to find the contacts she needed.

She printed each with contact information: Environmental Protection Agency, Region 4 for southeastern U.S.; Division of Public Health, Georgia Department of Human Services, Atlanta and South Carolina Department of Health and Human Services; South Carolina Department of Health and Environmental Control. A subheading under the last one, Environmental Activities and Health

Risks, especially caught her eye. She would make the calls tomorrow. Tonight she would go through Lang's folder to get that information into her notes. And of course she wanted to tell Blaine all about it.

She closed out the last website, turned off the computer and glanced at the screen on the D-Term desk phone. The letters VMM on the screen signaled a message. She dialed in. The prompt said, "You have one new message." She pressed the retrieval key: "Hello, Dr. Garriman. Soloman Zelinski calling. We have some interesting results. Please call me. Very important."

She checked the time. 5:45. Probably too late, but she dialed anyway. After five rings, the answering machine spoke. Right. Too late. Having to wait till tomorrow seemed torturous. But, she thought to herself, she did have a lot to do this evening. And there was Blaine.

CHAPTER THIRTY

She was in her office a little before 8:00 Thursday morning. Glancing at the pages of contact information she'd left on the desk last night, she set them aside, and dialed Zelinski's number. As before, he answered.

"Good morning, Dr. Zelinski. Cassandra Garrison."

"Thanks for calling back," he said. "Sorry I missed you yesterday. You have a few minutes now?"

"Yes, of course," she said, her anticipation brimming.

"Let me start by saying…this is *stunning*," he emphasized the last words.

"Tell me. Please."

"The short message," he said, "is that the mycotoxin seems to be a new, uncharacterized trichothecene most likely produced by a mutant fungal species all of which you suggested," he said, "but more important, we find that it fits structurally into a subclass of trichothecenes called macrocyclic trichothecenes. You know about that?"

"I've never heard of macrocyclic trichothecenes."

"Well," he said, "we know there are quite a number of trichothecene mycotoxins, well over 150 produced by fungi. And a small portion qualify in structure as macrocyclic trichothecene mycotoxins. Several studies have shown that macrocyclic trichothecenes are among the most toxic naturally occurring compounds found anywhere in nature. One reference I have says they are at least ten-fold more toxic than non-macrocyclics, and another says some may be as much as 100 times more toxic. After we got our results I did a…"

"Just a minute," she interrupted sharply. "You're telling me that this particular mycotoxin…found in that greenhouse…could be a hundred times more toxic than…"

"Yes," he cut in, "I'd say somewhere between 10 times and 100 times."

"You're right. That *is* stunning."

"Let me assure you," he said, "the small quantity we needed for our analysis was transported in water so it was not dangerous for us to handle. But in an air-borne state, if this mycotoxin were inhaled in a sufficient quantity, it could be disastrous…to humans or animals." He paused for her response. She was silent. He continued, "so let me go on."

"There's more?" she said.

"Yes, and this is what makes it even more astounding. As I was saying, after we got our results, I went back to the literature. I was amazed to find that trichothecene mycotoxins were used in biological warfare in Southeast Asia and Afghanistan in the 1970s and '80s. That's described in a chapter in a large military publication titled <u>Medical Aspects of Chemical and Biological Warfare</u> published in 1997. The authors of one chapter say there is evidence that between 1975 and 1982, around 7,000 people were killed in Cambodia and Laos and at least 3,000 in Afghanistan with weaponized mycotoxins. Furthermore, they say that depending on dose and route of exposure, death can result within minutes to hours. The effects appear to be cumulative and irreversible."

"Any neurotoxic effects described?" she asked.

"Haven't found anything specific for macrocyclic trichothecenes, but I'm still looking," he continued.

"Well, just so you know," she said, "the neuropathologist out at the Hefner-Cantrell Institute found what he calls a unique neurotoxic effect in this patient's brain. And we've been able to duplicate that effect in tissue culture."

"Really?" said Zelinski, sounding pensive. "You mean with this mycotoxin?"

"Yes. Exactly."

"So," he said, "if that kind of neurotoxicity has not been described in other macrocyclics, that makes this one even more potentially disastrous."

"Yes," she replied almost speechless. "Certainly does."

"Okay," he said, "so another article I found says that macrocyclic trichothecenes have the distinct properties of being highly stable in air, they're not degraded by ultraviolet light and they're able to withstand relatively high heat. And still another says that because they are fairly easy to produce and can be dispersed by different methods such as aerosols or smoke or portable sprays...or even artillery mines...macrocyclic mycotoxins have an excellent potential for weaponization."

"Oh my," she said still processing what he was telling her. "That's overwhelming."

"It is," he said, "and if you extrapolate, it becomes even more so. Think of the devastation it could cause if it were used for terrorism. You know...bioterrorisam. On a small scale, the right concentration airborne in a closed space like an ordinary room could easily accomplish an assassination. But in a large closed space like in an indoor arena full of people, if a large enough quantity of the mycotoxin were released, say through the HVAC system, it would become an invisible, merciless poison for hundreds if not thousands of people. It could produce mass murder. Completely undetectable until too late.

"And for an even worse scenario, can you imagine if the thing were somehow released in large-scale aerosol spray...an aerosol cloud is what one article called it...where there are a lot of people outside? Like in some kind of demonstration or political rally or maybe in a regional population. Taken to that extreme, theoretically it could cause the same kind of tragedy as what happened in Cambodia and Laos…and Afghanistan."

"Yes, I *can* imagine," she said soberly, "but not just theoretically. Something like that may already have happened."

"What do you mean?" he said.

"I mean in a regional population."

"I thought you said it was confined to a greenhouse."

"No. Not confined. Discovered in a greenhouse," she said.

"Where else is it?" he said, alarm in his voice.

"We're not sure," she said drawing a deep breath, "but we think…on an island off the coast of South Carolina."

"South Carolina?" the words burst from him.

"Yes," she tried to sound calm, "possibly the source for what we found in the greenhouse. We found evidence that some of the plants in the greenhouse came from that island. Some more than 20 years ago."

"What about outside, around the greenhouse?" said Zelinski.

"Apparently there was nothing like that found in areas around the greenhouse," she said, "but I think there has to be more testing."

"Yes, indeed," he said. "What about that island? Where is it in South Carolina?"

"Near Charleston," she replied. "I understand it's very small and quite isolated. What is astonishing, in light of what you've just told me, is that over the last 30 years or so, the population has dropped off precipitously. In fact, declined to zero. No one has lived there since sometime between the mid-90s to 2000."

"Any information about why?" he said.

"None that I'm aware of," she said, "but it's possible what you've discovered could be the key if this mutant fungus exists there."

"And if so, think about what a cauldron of a source that would be in the wrong hands," said Zelinski. "As I said, if you extrapolate."

"Yes. Oh my god," she interrupted him again. "It could be horrific! The last reference you quoted …what was it…that the mycotoxins are easy to produce and can be easily dispersed… and so on."

"Yes," he said. "The implication is that if the fungus were propagated to produce relatively large amounts of the spores, they could be reduced to an abundance of the mycotoxin. And delivered in large enough amounts in strategic places, as I just said, it could wreak havoc. It would take only a few cunning but evil people to make it happen. Like 9/11. Just a different way."

"I am reeling," she breathed the words heavily into the phone. "We've *got* to keep this confidential. If it gets out, leaked to the media, the press or TV somewhere, I don't think it's an exaggeration to say it could create a panic."

"It's safe with me," he said. "You're the one who has to decide what to do with it."

"For starters, we keep the lid on," she said emphatically, "until we know if it is on that island. If it's not found there, we might conclude that the mutation occurred in the greenhouse and it's contained. But if it *is* there, it could become a real danger if word gets out."

"Any thoughts about how to find out?" said Zelinski.

"Ironically," she said, "just today, I've been pulling together the contact information for health authorities here and in South Carolina. I was intending to inform them of what we've found and explore how we might determine if it exists on the island as well anywhere else in that area or in this area. I mean outside the greenhouse or the larger vicinity. Now I'm wondering if I should explain the possible magnitude of the toxicity right away or if I should handle it in a more circumspect way. If I tell them up front, that could spur them on to act, but on the other hand, if the information is not handled very discreetly, it could get out of control. What do you think?"

"I think you've got a helluva problem," he said. "I suppose you could start by telling them you have some very important but confidential information. You could even say it might be a matter of regional security but that it has to be kept confidential until it's thoroughly investigated. You know. Try to get a commitment." He paused. "Of course, that might not necessarily be air-tight, but it's probably the best you could do short of getting some kind of legal agreement."

"You're probably right," she said. "In any case we've got to move on it. I just need a little time to think about the best way to deal with it."

"Anyone else have access to the other mycotoxin samples you have?" he asked.

"No. They're safely stored out at the Institute," she said. "The environmental guy has some samples, but I'm sure they're safe with him. I assume no one but you and your staff know about your findings."

"Oh, my technical staff knows the details of our finding but *nothing* about what it means," he said. "I'll prepare a confidential report and keep it to myself 'til you need it. No one else will have access to it."

Assuring him she would get back shortly, she thanked him and hung up. She slid the pages of contact information back to the center of the desk and spread them out as she planned her approach. She would introduce herself as the infectious disease specialist at Brakefield Medical Center credentialing herself sufficiently to get through to the right person.

She dialed the first number. Reaching the Division of Public Health in Atlanta, she was routed to a Dr. Phillip Payne, Director of the Infectious Diseases Laboratory. When she dialed the number for the South Carolina Department of Health and Human Services, she was eventually connected to the director of the Laboratory of Environmental Health and Clinical Pathology, a Dr. Henry Stanfill.

Speaking to each man, she briefly related the story of Richard Kanaby's illness and death "which we believe was caused by a toxin produced by a fungus found in this man's greenhouse. It turns out the fungus is an apparently new, unidentified species and the toxin it produces is lethal, particularly affecting the brain. We have evidence that the source of the fungus may be an island in South Carolina near Charleston." She described the laboratory results in the EnviroTech report but made no mention of the mass spectrometry results.

Payne said he would like to meet with her to go over the evidence. A meeting was set, his office the next morning, Friday at 10:00. Stanfill, on the other hand, responded more skeptically. But as he pressed her for details on the ELISA and PCR in the EnviroTech report, it became clear he was tuning in. She suggested it would be most productive if they could meet to go over the information in detail and consider the possibility of investigating whether the fungus could be found on the island or anywhere in the geographic area. By the end of her spiel, Stanfill seemed eager to set up a meeting.

"There may be a bit of a logistical problem," he said, "because there are several people on our staff who should be informed about this including at least two from Charleston. If you meet with us in Columbia, I believe I can get the group together."

"When might that be?" she asked.

"I'm thinking perhaps this coming Tuesday or Wednesday," he said. "And we can take care of your transportation and lodging." The short notice took her by surprise, but she said she'd try to accommodate whatever he could arrange. Of course she would. It was precisely what she was hoping for. Not only did she want to deliver the information in person, she also wanted to push the idea of launching an effort to track down the fungus. Really, she wanted to go to Wansaw herself with some sort of search, and if the mutation were there, to explore whether it might be unique to that island or might be found on other islands or even the mainland.

At the meeting with Payne, she showed him the EnviroTech Report and all of Lang's information. He seemed impressed but somewhat detached. He said he thought more testing for spores in areas contiguous to the greenhouse should be carried before any conclusions could be drawn about danger of health threats anywhere else. She assured him that could be done and she would discuss it with McKenzie.

An early afternoon call from Stanfill had a different complexion. Apparently attending to what she had told him with a greater sense of urgency, he said he had contacted the people from Columbia and Charleston: 7 people in all, and they could meet with her late morning either Tuesday or Wednesday. They agreed on Tuesday. She would drive over on Monday afternoon.

*****

Blaine anticipated spending the weekend with her, but she made it clear she had to prepare her presentation for the group in Columbia. She took all the information home: articles from the internet, detailed clinical history of Richard's illness, the EnviroTech Report and everything in Lang's folder. Saturday morning, she showed it all to Blaine as she meticulously laid it out on the kitchen counter. It was a good run-through, she thought. He was again fascinated by her intensity.

"There's one thing I can't include yet," she said. "That's the mass spectrometry."

"Mass spectrometry?" he sounded surprised. "Where'd that come from?"

"Lang insisted we should try to characterize the protein structure. Mass spec is the best way to do that, so I contacted the guy at the University. Dr. Zelinski. We worked together a few years ago on a virus project. He was quite willing to analyze our sample."

"Is it done yet?" he said.

"Indeed it is, and it's pretty *astounding*," she said excitedly, "but for now, we've got to keep it completely confidential. I haven't told anyone, not even Dittrich or Holleran."

"Okay. So I can keep a secret," he smiled.

"Well, according to Zelinski, it fits into a subclass of mycotoxins called macrocyclic trichothecenes. He says they're among the most toxic naturally occurring substances in the world. And get this. He says there's evidence this kind of mycotoxin has been used in biological warfare in Southeast Asia."

"Who the hell was using that?" he said.

"He didn't say," she said, "just that thousands of people were killed in Laos and Cambodia...and Afghanistan in the '70s. Apparently if macrocyclic trichothecenes, airborne in a high enough concentration, are inhaled, they can cause death in minutes to hours. He thinks they could be especially lethal in a closed space where the concentration in the air would be more stable. He even speculated that if macrocyclic mycotoxins were to be used for terrorism, he called it *bio*terrorism, it could produce major disaster right here in this country." She paused feeling surprised she'd actually put this terrifying message into words so easily. "But listen Blaine, as I said, this is confidential. It *has* to stay that way until we know if it might be lurking somewhere besides the greenhouse. Maybe on that island in South Carolina? Zelinski and I agreed that if we begin to talk about the level of toxicity, even just the *possible* level, it could get out of hand. Especially if the press were to get hold of it. I said it reminded me of the Anthrax scare a few years ago. Remember how the press jumped all over that?"

"Okay. I get it. You just heard me say I can keep a secret," he said raising his eyebrows and shrugging in a don't-you-believe-me posture. "Anything I can do to help with all this?"

"Well, yes. As a matter of fact if you could make copies of all these reports. I need ten copies of each. Easiest to go to Kinko's?"

"Sure," He said. "I can do that. You want that now or this afternoon?"

"Now would be good while I'm putting my power point together."

*****

On Monday morning, she sent an email message to Joe Holleran, David Dittrich and Stephen Lang summarizing her meeting with Payne and informing them of her plans to go to Columbia for the meeting on Tuesday. She said she expected to get back to Atlanta Wednesday and would keep them informed.

She left for Columbia at 2:30 that afternoon, but just before leaving, she met Blaine for a quick lunch in the hospital cafeteria. In her characteristically self-assured fashion, she continued an excited banter about how she intended to get the people in South Carolina to organize an environmental investigation on Wansaw. "That's what I really want."

He wondered if she could pull it off, but he had learned it was a mistake to underestimate anything about her. After all, he'd been completely schooled on trichothecene mycotoxins before he realized it. Now *macrocyclic* to boot! He knew the people in South Carolina were in for quite a crash course.

CHAPTER THIRTY-ONE

Monday had been another long day for Joe. He didn't finish rounds until 8:30 so he was just leaving his office at 8:45. He turned off the light, closed the door and headed to the garage. When he entered, he became aware of an intense but unintelligible conversation coming from somewhere toward the back. He glanced in that direction to see three men huddled against a large, expensive looking car along the concrete wall. Though they were more than 150 feet away, he could see that one of them was unmistakably Blaine standing in his long white coat between the other two men, both in dark jackets. He moved into a shadowed area and though he could not understand the words of the conversation, he was close enough to see Blaine hand one of the men a white business-size envelope. The man opened it quickly flipping out what appeared to be bills. He nodded, slid the bills back into the envelope and pushed it inside his jacket. There were a few more unintelligible words as the other man handed Blaine a small brown envelope. He held it open for a few seconds as if inspecting it then closed it and dropped it into his coat pocket. The conversation ended. The two men got into the car and drove away. Blaine turned and walked rather nonchalantly toward the Medical Office Building unaware he was moving directly toward Joe. When he came closer, Joe stepped out of the shadows and stood silently in a challenging wide-legged stance, waiting to be discovered.

Blaine spotted him. Apparently stunned for a moment, he stopped and stared then spun around and hurried toward the hospital never looking back. Joe felt the same searing anger he'd felt that afternoon in Blaine's office, but he didn't move until Blaine had disappeared.

He broke his stance and walked to his car. He knew he couldn't ignore what he had just seen, but how could he prove it, he thought remembering Blaine's threat. He unlocked the car door as he scanned around the deserted garage, got in and drove away.

*****

By 9:15, Blaine was back in his office seething with anger and fear. The image of Joe standing motionless in front of him in the garage blazed in his mind. He could feel his stomach grip. He knew what Joe had seen and worse, what he might do. Thoughts of their confrontation in his office washed over him. But more than the angry words, he remembered Joe's expression and retreat when he mentioned Cassandra. Would that stop him now?

He had to think. Get away even if only to his depressing, lifeless apartment. At least there was the scotch, and he had the brown envelope. He took it out of the coat pocket, dropped it into his briefcase, hung the coat on the back of the door and left.

It was nearly 10:30 when he got to the apartment. He went to the kitchen and reached for the Scotch. He poured generously and took a sip as desperation rolled over him. The words *How has my life come to this?* flowed through his mind. He sat on the stool by the counter and took another sip. His cell phone jangled. It was Cassie.

"Hey," he said.

"Hi." Her voice was a welcome sound. "Sorry I didn't call sooner, but when I got here, I had a message from Dr. Stanfill. He wanted me to join him for dinner here in the hotel to talk about the meeting."

"Good," said Blaine, wanting to sound casual as she continued excitedly.

"He really seems to be into this," she said. Originally he said there would be 5 or 6 people, but now he's got 11 coming tomorrow including two from the EPA, and he's even talking about setting an environmental study on the island. I said I thought that was getting a little ahead of the game, at least until they've heard my presentation, but you know that's *exactly* what I said I was hoping…."

"I miss you, Cassie," Blaine broke in.

"Blaine, you're not listening. I said that's exactly what…"

"I heard what you said, but I miss you."

"I miss you, too," she said, "but I'll be back Wednesday night. Right now, I'm up to my neck with stuff for the meeting. I'll call you tomorrow."

"I wish you were here."

"You get some rest," she said. "We'll talk tomorrow, okay?"

It was clear. She was so focused on that damn meeting, she didn't have time for him. And she was rushing him off the phone.

"Okay," he said quietly, "Good luck tomorrow."

"G'night." The phone went silent.

He took a big slug of scotch. He was tired and frustrated.

*****

He finished the Tuesday morning clinic a little after 11:00. He returned to his office and shut the door. One detail he had to check. He slipped off his shoes and stepped up on to the desk from where he could reach the HVAC duct cover in the ceiling. He tugged at it. Just as he had hoped, it came away easily. He pushed it back into place and stepped down to the floor. He slid into his shoes, straightened his shirt and called the operator on the desk phone to say he was signing out until 1:30. Then on his cell phone, he dialed 411 for the number. He jotted it down and left for the garage, briefcase in hand. About 20 minutes later, he pulled into the parking lot. He blocked his phone and pressed in the number.

"Hefner-Cantrell Institute. How may I direct your call?"

"Jean Baker in the neuropathology lab please."

"One moment, please."

After six buzzes, the line went to a predictable "You have reached the neuropathology laboratory at The Hefner-Cantrell Institute. We are either away from the lab or on another line. Please leave your name and number, and we will return your call as soon as possible." He clicked off. The dash clock read 12:13. Just what he was counting on, they'd be out for lunch. He opened the briefcase and took out a square of dark terry cloth he had cut from one of his bath towels before he left his apartment. He pushed it into the left side pocket of the white coat and took out a pair of rubber gloves he had also stashed in the briefcase. He pushed them into the right side-pocket, got out of the car and hurried to the front entrance of the building.

When he reached the security desk, he held up the Brakefield ID badge clipped to the lapel of the coat as Cassandra had done Friday. The attendant absently waved him through. He walked to the stairwell, bounded up to the second floor and stepped into the corridor. It was empty. He moved to the door of the laboratory. If he encountered Jean or anyone else, he would say he wanted to look at the cultures again. He pushed the door open and peered in. No one. He entered, closed the door and stood for a moment looking and listening for anyone. Nothing.

He pulled on the gloves and moved to the freezer. He remembered the code, four corners, 1,3,9,7, then 1. He punched it in. The lock released. He opened the door and pulled out the drawer 4D. There were three vials on the left and two on the right. The labels were frosted over and unreadable. He couldn't remember which was which so he grabbed a vial from either side, slid the drawer back in and shut the door. The lock clicked. He took out the terrycloth, wrapped the vials in it and pushed the bundle into his pocket.

Now if he could get out unnoticed, he'd be home free. He remembered last week he and Cassie left through a side exit at the far end of the corridor. He opened the door just wide enough to scan the corridor. A woman in a lab coat passed but never looked toward the door. He waited a few more seconds then stepped out into the corridor and closed it as he pulled off the gloves and pushed them into the other pocket. He moved along the corridor to the side exit down the stairs and out to the parking lot, head lowered, eyes straight ahead. As he reached the car, he was about to open the door when someone called out behind him.

"Hey."

He froze and drew in a breath anticipating a confrontation, maybe a security guard. He turned.

A young man in scrubs approached. "Hey man. Nice car." He grinned. "Sweet."

Blaine released the breath. "Thanks," he said opening the car door open.

"You new here?"

"No. Just visiting," Blaine replied with a small wave as he turned away. He could rely on the Texas license plate to back him up. He got into the car and drove away.

Back in his office just after 1:30, he closed the door, signed in with the operator and took the terrycloth bundle out of his pocket. He unwrapped the vials and laid them on the desk then looked up at the HVAC duct cover in the center of the ceiling. He slipped off his shoes, stepped up onto the desk again and pulled the duct cover away. Stepping back to the floor, he laid the cover face down on the desk and picked up the piece of terrycloth and spread it over the inside of the cover. With a few tucks it flattened and fit almost perfectly. He lifted the cloth away, stood on the desk again and pushed the cover back into place. If he was right, the duct covers were the same in all the offices, so it should work. Should be easy enough: spread the terry cloth inside the duct cover, soak it with the suspension, snap the cover back over the duct, and the HVAC would do the rest. That simple. The only thing left was to get into the office. But he had a plan for that too.

He wrapped the vials again, laid the bundle in the back of the desk drawer and spent the next couple of hours forcing himself to review more articles online, pulling some up and making notes though it was hard to concentrate. A little before 4:00, he decided to go up to the floor to check labs and make early rounds with Dwayne Kersey. He walked out into the reception area and locked his office door. "Off to rounds," he announced to Mrs. Sanders. "See you in the A.M."

By 5:30, they'd finished rounds and he was back in his office. Everyone had left. The suite was quiet. Now to find the housekeeper. Usually she came in around 4:30 and started at the far end of the corridor in the ophthalmology suite. Predictably, that's where he found her, a rather sluggish, overweight older woman moving in her characteristically zombie-like fashion. He had enough of an acquaintance with her that he thought she'd trust him to borrow her master key.

"Good afternoon," he said in a jovial tone. She glanced up. "I'm locked out of my office. You have a master key I could borrow to let myself in?"

"Sure, Doc. I got a extra," she said as she snapped a key off of the chain on her cart.

"I'll bring it back as soon as I make a few calls."

She nodded and continued her work. He exited the suite, walked fast to the garage and drove out to the hardware store two blocks away. Slipping off his white coat, he walked quickly into the store. They were about to close, but he managed to inveigle the clerk to make a duplicate key. He paid and hurried back to his car, drove back to the garage, pulled on the white coat and walked back into the Medical Office Building, all in the space of 15 minutes. The housekeeper, in the same suite but a few rooms farther along, was apparently unaware how long he'd been gone. He handed her the key and thanked her.

Back in his office at 6:20, he laid the key on the desk. He wanted to be sure it worked, but it was too early. Maybe he should go for something to eat. He'd missed lunch and he was hungry, but he couldn't risk a chance encounter with Joe in the hospital cafeteria. He dropped the key into an envelope and pushed it next to the terrycloth bundle in the drawer, shed the white coat and headed to the garage again. In almost no time, he was at the McDonald's five blocks away. He picked up a couple of burgers and a Coke in the drive-thru and pulled into a parking spot behind the building. He unwrapped the first burger and devoured it absently, preoccupied with the plan he was turning over and over in his mind. He sipped the Coke and started on the second burger. He finished it quickly. The dash clock said 7:15. Still too early, he thought. He should just go back and wait.

By 7:30 he was back in his office. Before he switched on the overhead light, he looked across the courtyard at the row of windows of the internal medicine suite. They were all black. He switched the light on, lifted the envelope out of the drawer and took out the key. Now he could check it. He put on the white coat and walked out into the corridor moving guardedly toward the internal medicine suite. When he reached the entrance he could see through the frosted-glass door that the hallway lights were still on, but the door was secured. He slipped the key into the lock and turned it. It released. He pushed the door open. The hallway was quiet. No sign of anyone, but the lights told him everyone hadn't left yet. He pulled the door shut.

Hearing the relock click, returned to his office.

At 8:15, he took the terrycloth bundle from the drawer and slid it into his pocket. He checked the other pocket for the gloves and the key and moved quickly out of the suite and along the corridor to the Internal Medicine Suite again. He could see that the lights were now off. He unlocked the door and opened it again. There was total silence, the hallway now dim, lit only by a row of three low-intensity nightlights along the ceiling. He walked in and pushed the door shut, again hearing it relock. Holding the key, first in one hand then the other, he pulled the gloves on and approached the door bearing Joe Holleran's name. He stood for a minute listening for any sound from inside. Nothing. But just as he was about to push the key into the lock, he heard a rattling at the suite entrance. He could see through the frosted glass a white-clad figure on the other side. He darted around the reception desk and stuffed himself into the knee-space beneath it as he heard the door open and close. The hallway lights went up. He heard footsteps approaching, a key sliding into a lock and a door opening. He could tell from the direction of the sounds, it was not Joe's office. It was the other side of the hall. He pulled his knees closer to his chest and held his breath.

After a few more seconds he heard, "Yes, operator, this is Dr. Elfing signing out for the evening," then the office door closed and the footsteps receded. The hallway lights went down, the entrance door opened and closed, and the lock clicked. All was silent again. He waited a few more seconds then edged out from under the desk, rising on his knees then standing. He moved to Joe's office door again. He pushed the key into the lock and opened the door. The circle of soft light beneath the lamp on the desk startled him. A pager lay on the desk and a briefcase sat open on the chair in front of the desk.

Damn! he thought. Still too early. He pulled the door shut and turned toward the entrance. As he did, another white-clad figure appeared through the frosted glass. He leaped back under the reception desk as the door opened. Again, the hallway lights came up and footsteps approached. He held his breath. His heart raced. The steps halted just the other side of the desk. Again, he heard a key in a lock and a door opening. This time it was Joe's office. There was the sound of rustling papers, a short silence then Joe's voice. "Hey. I'm just leaving. Kids in bed, yet?" Silence. "Good. Tell'em to wait up for me. I'll be there in a flash." The door closed and steps receded. The lights went down and the entrance door opened and closed with the relock click.

He pulled himself out of the knee-space crouching motionlessly on the floor in the dim light. The words "Kids in bed yet? Tell'em to wait up for me" echoed in his ears. That terrible morning rushed back to him, those excruciating moments, his little girls begging him not to leave.

He felt his eyes moisten. He swallowed hard and squeezed his eyelids tight-shut to fight back tears, but his face contorted with the pain he felt. He took a deep breath and stood staring at Joe's office door. He stood for another full minute as torturing thoughts ripped through his mind. *What was he about to do? Why?* He moved slowly toward the entrance, all his energy drained, and opened the frosted-glass door. The corridor was quiet. He went through. The door closed behind him; the lock clicked.

Back in his office, he settled into his desk chair. His mind simmered. It was so well-planned. He was so sure it would work. But he couldn't do it. Not now. *Not ever.* He stood, peeled off the gloves, dropped them into the side pocket of the coat on top of the terrycloth bundle and grabbed his cell phone from the desk. Cassie should have called by now, but there was no voice mail and no missed calls. He picked up the briefcase and still wearing the coat, switched off the light and left for the garage.

It was 9:45 when he got to his apartment. Yet no word from Cassie. He should call her. But first, the Scotch. He went into the kitchen, laid the phone and the briefcase on the counter and took out the bottle. He could feel his hand shaking as he poured. He took a breath and sipped the scotch, then reached into the coat-pocket and drew out the gloves and terrycloth bundle. He laid them on the counter, set the glass down, pulled off the coat and tossed it aside.

With another sip, he picked up the cell phone and hit the automatic dial for Cassie. After five rings, the recorded voice came on: "Please leave your message".

"Call me, dammit!" he yelled into the phone and hit the send button. At that moment, an image of the travel case beside the lavatory flashed to his mind. He opened the briefcase, pushed the terrycloth bundle and the gloves into it, closed it and left it lying on the counter. Then he made his way upstairs, the glass in one hand, cell phone in the other.

He flicked the bedroom light on, set the glass and phone on the dresser and went into the bathroom. He stared at himself in the mirror. He was exhausted, lonely, terrified, confused, and most of all, defeated. He reached down and touched the travel case for a moment but stopped and pulled his hand back. He turned on the cold water, splashed a handful on his face and went back into the bedroom. He picked up the phone and fell back across the bed drifting into a doze.

Presently, a ringtone woke him. He shook his head and sat up.

"Hello," he answered sleepily.

"Hey, are you okay?" It was Cassie, urgency in her voice.

"Hi, baby," he said hoping the word would warm her. "I'm fine."

"Your message scared me," she said. "I thought something was wrong. You sure you're okay?"

"Yeah. Just needed to talk to you. I miss you like crazy."

"I miss you, too, but I'll be back tomorrow night," she said. There was still a tinge of detachment in her voice.

"Tomorrow *night*?" he said. "I thought you said tomorrow afternoon."

"I know, but it looks like I can't leave until late tomorrow afternoon."

"Oh, okay," he said not wanting to let on the desperation he was feeling. "Did everything go okay today?"

"Yes. Great," she said. "It went so well they want me to meet with them again tomorrow," she said excitedly. "That's why I have to stay. These people from the EPA, especially this environmental biologist from Charleston, they're really into this whole thing now. They're talking about going back to public health records from all the islands. And they want to do this intense investigation on Wansaw Island."

"So what time'll you be home?"

"I don't know yet, Blaine." Now she sounded a bit irritated. "Depends on when the meeting's finished. It's about a three-and-a-half hour drive. I hope I can leave here no later than 5:00, but I don't think it'll be any sooner. Where are you?"

"My place," he said. "Just got in. Had a long day. Reed's away 'til Friday. At a meeting in Boston, so I'm holding down the fort. I miss you, Cassie. I miss you…so much."

"Come on, Blaine. I'll be back tomorrow. I'll call you when I'm leaving, and you can come over when I get home." He wanted to hear more, something dramatic like how desolate she was without him, but instead she said, "You sound depressed."

"Well, maybe, but I'll be better when you're back. So just get back as soon as you can."

"Blaine. It's only been two days," she said.

"And two nights. "

"I know," she said, now more warmly. "All last night, I thought about…how much I wanted to be with you." Now she was saying what he wanted to hear until she followed with, "but you have to understand how involved I am with all this."

"I understand that," he said, "but it'll just be better when you're back."

"It will be," she said, but she didn't sound convinced. "You get some sleep."

"Okay. Drive safe and get home as soon as you can." He clicked off shaking his head. He was the desolate one. He looked at his watch. Almost midnight. Time to feel better, he thought. He went back into the bathroom glancing into the mirror as he reached for the travel case. He unzipped the side pocket and took out the envelope and the silver tube.

✳✳✳✳✳

Amazing how quickly the depression melted away. He felt strong and energized. He didn't need to sleep. Still wide awake and wired at 4:30, he was now resolved. He knew what he had to do. If he got there before 6:00, he could slip in unnoticed. He went down and made coffee then came back upstairs. He showered and shaved, dressed and went back down to the kitchen. 5:15. After a few sips of coffee, he pulled on the white coat, picked up the briefcase and hurried out to his car.

About 25 minutes later, he drove into the parking area at Hefner-Cantrell. He parked close to the side door and watched as a few early arrivals walked toward the building. That would be the ticket, fall in with them. They were used to white-coated people coming in at this hour. He wouldn't stand out, but no one would recognize him anyway. He opened the briefcase and took out the terrycloth bundle, pushing it into his pocket as he got out of the car and started toward the side door. He moved with a casual stride, and just as he'd hoped, he passed into the building without so much as a glance from anyone.

He walked up the stairs behind two chatty women oblivious to him. He stopped at the second level and watched as they continued upward and disappeared. He opened the door to the corridor and walked toward the lab. A housekeeping cart stood by the entrance to the men's restroom. The door was propped open. This would be easier than he thought. He stepped around the cart and into the restroom to find a man in a janitor's uniform mopping the floor, a roller-bucket beside him.

"Good morning," said Blaine. "Ah'm...I need to get into a lab down the hall. I left something..."

"No englaise," the man said looking startled.

"Key....to... lab," Blaine spaced the words slowly.

"No englaise," the man repeated with a shrug.

"Key, por favor," said Blaine. "Key." He made an unlocking motion with his hand.

"Ah, si," the man smiled, "Llave," he said as he pointed to the keys hanging from a leather strap hooked to his belt.

"Si," Blaine nodded and smiled. "I bring back...in minuto. Retorno...in momento," said Blaine trying words he thought sounded Spanish.

"Okay, Doc-tor," the man seemed pleased to accommodate him. He fiddled with the leather strap for a moment and pulled away a ring carrying two keys. He handed it to Blaine

"Gracias. Retorno...una minuto," Blaine muddled through the words as he grasped the ring and went back through the proppedopen door. No one in the corridor. He moved quickly to the lab door, unlocked it, pushed it open and entered. He closed the door, flipped on the ceiling light, rushed to the freezer. He pressed in the code and the freezer door popped open. He plucked the terrycloth bundle from his pocket, pulled open the freezer door wide and sliding the 4-D drawer out, he unwrapped the vials, dropped them in, pushed the drawer back and closed the freezer door. When the lock clicked, he tugged at the door to be sure it was secure, stuffed the terrycloth into the coat pocket and darted back to the entrance.

He opened the door a few inches and peered out. The corridor was still empty. He turned off the light and stepped out shutting the door behind him. He walked back to the men's room where the janitor, now intent on squeezing the mop with the bucket apparatus, barely looked up.

"Gracias, senor," Blaine said as handed the keys to the man.

"Si. Okay, Doc-tor."

Blaine went back to the stairwell, down the steps and out onto the concrete walkway. A few more cars were pulling in. Two people some 20 or 30 feet away were walking toward him, but they ignored him. He lowered his head and kept walking. After a few more steps, he was at his car. He got in, sat for a few seconds collecting himself, then drove away.

He was back at his apartment by 7:00. When he closed the door, it was as if he shut out the rest of the world. All his energy was gone, but at least Cassie's precious goddamn mycotoxins were back in place, and no one would know what he had done or…almost done. But those thoughts were disturbing because now it dawned on him that he was no longer faking just to keep her on his side. Her absence had made him realize how much she meant to him, how much he needed her, how much he wanted her to feel the same. To love him, really love him. It was not that simple though. She was his only hope for stopping Joe, but he could *not* tell her about the threat, the terrible threat, Joe was to him now. She'd surely turn against him, and he'd be lost.

It was too much to think about. He was tired. Dog tired. He wanted to sleep. He couldn't make it in today. Kersey would have to take care of things. He poured another cup of coffee now cold in the pot, warmed it in the microwave, made a couple of pieces of toast and waited 'til 7:45 to call Mrs. Sanders.

"Not feeling so well today," he said. "Just a stomach thing, but I think I better lay out today." She assured him she'd let Kersey know. Now he could sleep.

CHAPTER THIRTY-TWO

At 9:15 Thursday morning, Joe rang Cassandra's office. "Good morning. Dr. Holleran calling for Dr. Garriman."

"Yes, doctor. I'll see if she's available. Please hold." The line went dead for a few seconds then, "I'll transfer you now, doctor."

"Dr. Garriman," came the crisp greeting.

"Hi, Cassie," said Joe. "When'd you get back?"

"Late last night," she said.

"Good trip?"

"Yes. Very good. I'm emailing details to you and Dave and Dr. Lang."

"Okay. That'd be great," he said. "But actually I'm calling about something else. Something I have to talk to you about. If you've got a few minutes later this morning or this afternoon, I can stop by your office."

"Why do you have to come to my office?" she said warily. "Why not just talk on the phone?"

"Because I need to talk to you in person, Cassie. It's a private matter. You'll understand that when we talk."

"If it's something about two years ago, forget it. That is gone. Finished…forever."

"No," he said. "Nothing to do with that."

"Well if it's not that and it's not about the meeting in South Carolina, what could possibly be so urgent that you need to talk to me in person?" she asked defiantly.

"Because it's about…," he interrupted himself. "Really, Cassie, it's important for me talk to you face to face, not on the phone."

"Listen, Joe. If you can't at least give me some idea, I don't want to talk to you. I hate a hidden agenda." Her voice bristled with resistance.

"Okay, but it's confidential. When you hear what I'm about to say, you'll understand."

"Oh for God's sake, Joe, quit playing games," she sounded irritated.

"It's not a game, Cassie," he said, "It's serious."

"Okay. Confidential," she said.

"It's about your friendship with Purcell."

"What business is that of yours?" Her tone turned angry. "I think you'd better leave that alone."

"Believe me, you need to know what I have to tell you. He's in trouble. I mean big trouble."

"And just what do you have to do with it?"

"That's exactly what I have to tell you," Joe's tone was convincing.

Her voice mellowed slightly, "So when can you be here?"

"How about 11:30?" he said.

"Okay."

"And don't say anything to him about this until we talk," he said.

"Okay."

She clicked off impatiently as she puzzled over Joe's words. How did he know about Blaine and her? How did he know Blaine was in trouble? What was that? Blaine had sounded a little strange last night, but it was late. He said he was tired and so was she. Maybe he's sick, she thought. Could that be what Joe had to tell her, that Blaine is sick?

She took her notes from the meeting out of her briefcase. Perusing them diverted her attention. She did have to put the report together. She booted up the computer.

Joe arrived at her office shortly after 11:30. She looked up but remained seated, unsmiling and aloof. "Have a seat if you like," she said in an icy tone motioning vaguely. He took the chair across the desk from her.

"So?" she said flatly.

"Let me say I'm pretty sure you don't know anything about this, Cassie," he said, "so I'm gonna just lay it out because I think you need to know. I think Purcell has a serious problem...as in snorting the white stuff, if you know what I mean."

Her stone-face instantly drew into an angry frown as she demanded, "And how do you know *that*?"

"I know because I've seen it," he said. "A few weeks ago and again Monday night while you were away."

"And just what have you seen?" she said, her tone scornful and disbelieving.

"Okay." He took a breath, "So about 3 weeks ago, I was on my way to the garage going home. Around 9:00 or so. I remember it was a Thursday. I was taking the short-cut through the courtyard of the medical office building. It was dark, but there was one lighted window in the building directly across from my office. As I passed, I noticed a man sitting at a desk near the window. It was pretty easy to see through the window what he was doing because I was less than 10 feet away. I couldn't believe it was the guy I'd met at the staff meeting the week before. Purcell. I remembered Dr. Reed introduced him as the new cardiology fellow. I knew that was one of the windows in the cardiology suite, and there he was...in the fellows' office."

"How do I know you're not making this up?" she said sounding less challenging.

"Because I'm not making it up. I'm telling you exactly what I saw," he said firmly. "I think the guy's in trouble, and it's going to get worse if something isn't done to stop him."

"And you think you can do something to stop him?" she snapped.

"No, but I think you can."

"And just what do you mean by that?" she said, defiant again.

"Let me tell you the rest. Believe me, it was clear what he was doing. I got really pissed. Think about it. Where he was doing it with everything he has at stake. His job, his career, his family. You do know he's got 3 kids and a wife back in Dallas, right?"

"How do you know that?"

"I checked him out," he said.

"Okay, but they're divorced," she countered.

"Well yes, but that doesn't give him a pass to do what he was doing right here…in this medical center even if he was alone in his office."

"So, if he wasn't hurting anybody…," she said.

"Oh come now, Cassie," he said. "If he's making a habit of this, and I'm pretty sure he is, he could hurt somebody not to mention what he's doing to himself. My first thought was to turn him in, but I realized it would be my word against his. That would lead to a lot of nastiness. So I figured I should go directly to him. Confront him. Tell him exactly what I saw hoping he'd be willing to own up to it and straighten himself out."

"And?"

"The next afternoon, I went to see him in his office. When I told him what I'd seen and how it was absolutely unacceptable behavior here and so forth, he got furious. He said I didn't know what I was talking about, and I couldn't prove anything. Then he said…if I started making any trouble, he would be sure, as he put it, 'everyone will know about you and Cassandra and your little secrets'. Those were his words."

"Oh, shit," she muttered under her breath, closing her eyes and shaking her head.

"We were at a standoff so I walked out," said Joe. "Obviously I didn't need that and neither did you."

"Oh, thanks for your consideration," she retorted sarcastically.

"At that point, there was nothing more to say," he continued, "so I decided not to pursue it. Just to wait and see what effect the confrontation might have on him. Of course, I didn't know anything about you and him until he said that about little secrets, but then it was clear how he knew…about us."

"Okay, so move on," she said. "What about Monday night?"

"Again, I was leaving late. Probably around 9:00. When I came into the garage, I heard some guys talking toward the back. Really sort of mumbling but making enough noise to get my attention. I could see there were three guys, and one was Purcell. It looked like he was giving one of the other guys money. He handed him an envelope. The guy opened it, took out some bills then put them back in the envelope, and the other guy handed Purcell an envelope. You know, one of those tan-colored mailing envelopes.

At that point, the two guys got in a car and left. Purcell started walking back toward the medical office building. He was coming right toward me. When he saw me, honestly, he looked like he'd seen a ghost. I just stood and watched him. He froze for a minute then turned and walked…or rather almost ran away toward the hospital. I watched until he disappeared in the direction of the hospital entrance. I'm sure he's now thinking I'm going to make something out of it, like turn him in."

"So what are you going to do?" she asked.

"I've just done it. I've told you," he said.

"And what do you expect me to do?"

"That's what we have to talk about right now, before you see him again. Have you seen him since you got back?"

"No. I called him last night when I got in, but it was late. He said he hadn't been feeling well all day. A stomach thing he told me, but he said he'd check with me today. I haven't heard from him yet this morning. Seems a bit strange, but I guess if he's here, he's busy with rounds and clinic. Maybe he'll call me before long."

"Okay," said Joe. "None of my business about your relationship, but did he seem any different when you talked to him last night?"

"As a matter of fact, he did seem agitated," she said. "I thought it was just because he was under the weather. I didn't dwell on it."

"Well, I'd say after Monday night, he's probably feeling extremely agitated," he said. "If I confront him again, he'll probably go ballistic. A few weeks ago in his office, he got really angry. That's when he came up with the threat about being sure everyone would know about you and me. But it's gone way beyond that now. If he believes I'm going to turn him in, I think he could get violent."

"Where do you think that leaves me?" she said. "I'm sure if I confront him, he'll go ballistic with me, too. That frightens me. He's bound to be feeling pretty unstable right now. I know he's worried about his career and his future and his kids and what he's going to do when he finishes the fellowship. If he finds out that I know what you've just told me, that could send him over the edge."

"If he keeps going like he is now," said Joe, "he'll send himself over the edge. There's got to be a way to get him some help."

"And you've got that figured out, I suppose." Sarcastic tone again.

"No, but I have been giving it some thought. As far as I know, you and I are the only ones who know about this...besides those two creeps with him in the garage. I don't think it's wise for either of us to confront him alone. But if we can do it together and convince him we're serious about trying to help him, that might have an impact. Maybe we could go to his office together. Just show up in the afternoon when things are closing down."

"Look," she said, "I know him well enough to know he can be pretty impulsive. I'm sure by now he despises you so expecting him to control himself if he feels threatened in another confrontation is not smart." She paused and with an intensely curious expression said, "Why are you doing this? I mean telling me all this and talking about getting him help?"

"You probably won't believe it, Cassie, but it's partly for your sake."

"Oh really? Why for my sake?" she said disdainfully.

"Because you're obviously in some kind of relationship with him." he said. "Even though you didn't know about any of this before, now you do, so you can't be innocently blindsided by it. I don"t want to see that happen."

"I can take care of myself, Joe."

"I don't contest that, but that's why I'm telling you," he said. "As for him, if I were to do what I'm pretty sure he thinks I'm going to do, he would very likely be brought before the ethics board of the hospital. He wouldn't know that until he was served with written notice stating the reasons. Then it would be too late for him to do anything foolish like try to do something to me. But the issue would become known, at the very least, to a small but significant group of people on the board. And before a hearing could be conducted or even set up, certain information would have to be sent to that board.

If that were to happen, even though it would be confidential information, his reputation could be severely damaged regardless of the outcome of a hearing." He looked at her intently. "So, why am I doing this? Because I think it's the right thing to do. Not only for your sake but also for the *sake* of his career and his future and his kids…everything in his life. If we could get him to see how he's about to wreck all that, maybe he'd be willing to do something about it. Back off. Try to straighten himself out. Whatever it might take. If we go together and talk to him quietly without any threat, maybe he'll get the message."

"I don't know, Joe," she said. "It seems pretty risky. I have to think about it."

"Okay," he said, "but there's probably not a lot of time to think about it. We don't know how deep he's into this thing. But I think the longer he's in the mental state I suspect he's in right now, the more desperate and irrational he's going to become. I'd say he's pretty spring-loaded right now."

"I get the message, Joe," she said, "but I need a little time."

"Okay. Call me," he said and walked out.

Although it was lunch time, she was anything but hungry. She told the secretary to hold her calls, closed the door and sat mulling over what she'd just heard. Is that why Blaine had become so solicitous, she wondered? So she would protect him? She didn't like to think that, but what should she think?

She wanted to call him, see how he was feeling, get some hint of what might be going on with him. Until now, she had been enjoying the natural flow in their relationship. How she wished this were all a misunderstanding. She closed her eyes wanting it all to go away… but strangely, almost desperately, still wanting Blaine in spite of everything Joe had said.

The buzz of her desk phone rattled her thoughts. She picked up.

"Sorry, Dr. Garriman. It's Dr. Lang. He says it's urgent."

What? Maybe something about the South Carolina meeting? "Okay, put him through." She held the phone and waited. The call clicked in. "Hi, Dr. Lang. How are you?"

"Fine thanks, but there's a problem."

"Oh?"

"Yes," he said. "Jean Baker just came in to tell me she thinks something is going on with the vials in the freezer. You remember she did the second assay last Friday, almost two weeks ago now, for confirmation. She routinely checks the freezer on Thursdays. After that last assay, the next time she checked the freezer was this past Thursday. A week ago. She said she was sure there were 3 vials of the suspension on one side of the drawer and 2 on the other then, but today the vials were scrambled around in the freezer drawer. Not arranged like last week."

"How could that happen?" she said.

"Someone trying to get some of the mycotoxin," he said.

"Are any of the vials missing?" she said.

"No," he said, "but it certainly could be possible to thaw the vials, remove some of the suspension and put them back. That's what I am concerned about. The only way we can tell if any of the suspension has been removed would be to thaw and check each vial assuming each one was completely full when they arrived here. Of course the question would be if someone was trying to get the mycotoxin…who and why?"

"Who else knew anything about the vials?" she said. "Only Dr. Dittrich and Dr. Holleran and the environmental guy, McKenzie, But they don't know anything about how and where those vials are stored in you lab."

"Okay," said Lang, "but Jean said even though only you and she know the combination, there's another person who might know it as well."

"Who's that?" she said.

"Your colleague from the hospital," he replied. "She said he came out with you to see the tissue culture stains last week when she was about to set up the second assay." Cassie was silent as he continued. "She said the two of you were watching when she went into the freezer to get the vials out for the second assay. She thinks he may have noticed the combination."

"Why would he have any reason to do anything to the vials in the freezer?" she asked in a calm, controlled voice though suspicions were beginning to develop in her head. She didn't want to sound defensive, but she thought it was bold of Jean to implicate Blaine without something more to go on. "The only reason he came there with me was because he knew the story about the mycotoxin and its effects in the cultures. He wanted to see the stains Jean showed me when I was out there earlier. He's been working with me on this whole thing here at Brakefield."

"I don't think Jean meant any accusation," said Lang. "Just a thought."

"Well, it could be really serious if any of the mycotoxin is missing," she said. "We need to find that out. Is Jean sure the vials were scrambled?"

"She seems convinced," he said, "that sometime between last Thursday and today, someone got into the freezer and did something to shift the vials in the drawer. The only way that could have happened is if someone pulled out the drawer and took them out and put them back or just moved them around. Really doesn't make sense."

"Was anything else in the freezer disturbed?" she said.

"She says not," he said.

"Have you talked to your security people?" she said.

"Not yet, but I will," he said. "You're the first person I've spoken to since Jean came in. But you're right. We need to know if any of the mycotoxin is missing. Could you contact the environmental guy and see if there's a way to check the concen-trations in the vials we have in the freezer?""

"Yes, of course," she said. "I'll get back to you."

She hung up and pressed McKenzie's number. Yes, he said they could analyze the mycotoxin concentrations if she could get the vials back to the EnviroTech lab. A call to Lang assured her that he would have the vials delivered right away.

She clicked off, laid the phone on the desk and sat replaying Lang's words in her head. If Blaine were trying to get the mycotoxin, why, she wondered? And how could he have gotten into the lab? She picked up her phone and pressed in Joe's number.

"Hey," he answered.

"Where are you?" she said.

"In my office. Starting my afternoon appointments in a few minutes. What's up?"

"I just had a call from Dr. Lang. He says they think someone's been tampering with the vials of mycotoxin in the freezer at the institute. The technician discovered it this morning."

"What does that mean, tampering with the vials?" he said.

"When the she was doing her routine check this morning, she thought they were scrambled in the freezer drawer. Not the way they were on her last check a week ago."

"Any missing?" he asked.

"Apparently not. They're all accounted for," she said. "My first reaction was maybe she made a mistake. Maybe she didn't remember exactly how they were arranged last week, but Lang says she's certain. And based on what you told me two hours ago, my suspicions are growing. Think about it. Blaine and I have practically been living together the last few weeks. I've told him everything about the mycotoxin. How we discovered it, what was in the greenhouse, details about the brain autopsy and what the tissue cultures showed: Everything. He's been so interested. I thought he might like to see the evidence so I asked him to go out to the institute with me to see the microscopic evidence in the cultures last week. When we got there, the tech was setting up the second assay. We were watching when she took the vials out the freezer, how she handled them, the whole procedure. After that, she brought out the cultures from the first assay so we could look at them with the microscope. I didn't give it a thought at the time, but now it's occurs to me that if Blaine is as desperate as we think, he may have thought of some way to do something drastic with the mycotoxin, either to himself or someone else."

"Yeah," said Joe with a short, uneasy laugh. "Guess who that someone else could be."

"No, no. I was just thinking out loud," she said. "Anyway, I don't know how he could have gotten into the lab."

"Right," he said, "so we don't know that he had anything to do with tampering with the vials…if that really happened."

"I know, but it does seem possible," she said. "I mean only seven people know about the vials. That's Lang, the tech, McKenzie, Dittrich, you, me…and Blaine. And only three know exactly where they're stored and how to get to them. That's the tech, me and Blaine. Even Lang doesn't know exactly where they are. But when he suggested that my colleague, meaning Blaine, might have noticed the combination for the freezer, I must say that surprised me. I passed it off as unlikely, but Lang certainly seems to be entertaining the idea."

"We need to get to Blaine," said Joe. "If Lang starts making noise about the vials with even the slightest hint of anything about Blaine, that could really make him more paranoid."

"You're right," she said. "We need to get to him. Together. Try to make him see, as you said, what he's doing to himself… and his future. We've got to convince him somehow that we want to help him."

"Okay," he said, "but we've got to get our act together. When can we do that?"

"Let's talk again tomorrow," she said. "Maybe we go see him in his office tomorrow."

"Okay," he said. "Think about it this evening, and call me in the morning."

"I think he's planning for us to go to dinner this evening," she said. "That's what he said before I left for South Carolina. I must say

I'm a little concerned about that now. I'll call him in a little while and see how he's feeling."

"Maybe you can get a read."

"Maybe, but I have to keep it light," she said. "I'll try to find out his schedule for tomorrow. He usually has clinic on Friday afternoon. It's a short one so he should be back in his office by around 4:00. That would be a good time for us to drop by. I go in first, and you come in right after me."

"Well you can be sure, when he sees me, he'll know something's up," said Joe. "We've got to be so careful."

"Of course," she said, "but hopefully, we can talk him down before he comes unglued. I'll call you in the morning."

*****

At that moment, she was torn. She had to finalize the summary of the South Carolina meeting and send it to Lang and Dittrich....and Joe. But she wanted to talk to Blaine. This was all so disturbing. She needed to hear his voice. She pressed in the number for cardiology.

Mrs. Sanders answered. "Yes, Doctor Garriman. He's in clinic now, but I can have him call you or you can call him on his cell, if you'd like."

"I'd rather not interrupt him in clinic. Just ask him to give me a call when he gets back to his office. How's he feeling today?"

"Oh I think he's okay. Says it was just a stomach thing. He didn't sound so good yesterday, but he seems better today."

"Okay. Just ask him to call me."

"It was almost 2:00. She tried to focus on her report for the next few hours, and by 4:30, she had put together a fairly comprehensive draft. The group she met with had been extremely receptive to her information. The EPA representative and the environmental biologist from Charleston were especially enthusiastic about initiating an environmental survey on the island. The biologist said he was vaguely familiar with Wansaw. He said he had heard that the population there had decreased sharply, but he knew nothing about it. He was quite intrigued by the information about the mycotoxin. She liked hearing that. He also said he did not know about storms or hurricanes there, but one of the EPA representatives volunteered to look into whatever records there might be regarding storms on the barrier islands. For Cassandra, the most exciting things about the meeting had been the interest in the environmental survey and investigating health records on the barrier islands.

She printed out what she had composed, stacked the pages together and slid them into her briefcase. Her cell phone sounded. It was Blaine. Yes, he was a little late coming in this morning, but he was feeling much better. Yes, he would come over around 7:00. They could go to dinner wherever she'd like. She closed the briefcase and left for home.

CHAPTER THIRTY-THREE

The traffic was not as hectic as usual considering the time of day. She got home a little before 6:00. For the entire 30-minute drive, her thoughts moved restlessly from the conversation with Joe in the morning to the call from Lang then her call to Joe in the afternoon and finally, the call from Blaine…just that little while ago. How could she possibly deal with it all? She had to keep it light this evening. Maybe the draft of the report in the briefcase and talk about the meeting could occupy the conversation. Avoid any hint at what she knew now.

There was time for a bath. That might relieve her stress. But oddly, even paradoxically, just the thought of being with Blaine again seemed to relieve some of it. It had been three nights since she'd been with him, and she was feeling the void. He said they could go to dinner anywhere she'd like. Some place romantic could set the tone for the evening, she thought. Keep her mind off of everything *and* steer him in the direction she wanted to go. She thought of a place she had been five or six months ago with her two friends from Baltimore, an Italian restaurant called La Leche di Luna, the milk of the moon. She remembered it was small and intimate and definitely romantic. That would be perfect for tonight.

She pulled into the carport, came into the kitchen, laid the briefcase on the table and headed to the bedroom. Quickly out of her clothes, she pulled on a robe and went into the bathroom. She started the bath water, poured in some bubble bath and went back to the kitchen for the glass of wine she'd been looking forward to. She sipped as she returned to the bathroom. She set the glass on a table next to the tub, slipped out of the robe and lowered herself into the warm water as the bubbles built around her.

She leaned against the back of the tub resting her head on the rim, closing her eyes and letting her mind disengage into a relaxed doze. There she drifted in the luxury of unmeasured time…until a hand on the back of her neck startled her awake. Her eyes tore open to see a face only inches from hers. She shrieked and ripped one arm protectively out of the water as a face came into focus.

"Blaine! Oh, my god. You scared me to death."

He was kneeling beside the tub. He said nothing but guided her head forward and pressed his mouth onto hers. She closed her eyes. Her arm came to rest on his bare shoulder. His right hand, still behind her neck, pulled her forward without breaking the kiss. His left hand slid into the water and onto her breasts. After a few more seconds, he pulled away and whispered, "Hi, Baby."

She opened her eyes. "Hi," she said softly.

Her hand curled over his neck and shoulder then fell away as he stood, naked and aroused. He stepped into the tub and knelt between her bent knees. His body displaced so much water, it brought the level sloshing almost over the rim. He leaned forward, wrapped his arms around her waist, pulled her toward him and stroked her cheek with his right hand. "I missed you, Cassie," he whispered. "I love you."

She smiled and brought wet fingers up to trail lightly over the side of his face, but "I….missed you, too," was all she could let herself say. The conflict she felt between mind and body was agonal. Thoughts of what she was committed to for tomorrow battled against her over-powering carnal urges of the moment. Forget tomorrow, she thought. She wanted him now.

Her hand slid down to his shoulder. She squeezed the flesh and felt the muscles tense as his right arm went around her again.

He pulled her farther forward, and with one overpowering motion, he stood and lifted her out of the water and over the side of the tub. He eased her down to standing then stepped out of the tub and pressed his wet body against hers. He reached for a towel on a shelf behind her, shook out the folds and draped it around her. Then lifting her roughly, he carried her into the bedroom, dropped her across the bed, pushed the towel aside and fell on top of her.

She lay pinned beneath him as his mouth locked onto hers, guttural sounds emanating from deep in his throat. He arched up over her for a moment then fell back onto her. There was no stopping now. He thrust into her, writhing, heaving, panting, bringing them both into unrelenting frenzy. Building, burning, blazing. And at the moment of its peak, he threw his head and shoulders back and uttered impassioned words, "I love you, Cassie. I *love* you" and collapsed heavily onto her. He lay motionless for several minutes, breathing long, deep breaths then rolled onto his side, an arm draped over her breasts.

She lay still, watching him for several seconds then glanced at the bedside clock. Only 8:15, but the idea of going out to dinner had no appeal now. As his breathing eased, she let herself slip into a gentle sleep.

She woke a little after 11:00. They had laid against each other not moving for three hours. When she pulled away, he shifted slightly but did not wake. She went into the bathroom and pulled on her robe then moved to the closet, took out a blanket, and covered him. He stirred and opened his eyes.

She bent down and kissed him lightly on his forehead. As she did, he grasped her wrists and pulled her down onto him. His arms went around her shoulders. "Cassie, I meant what I said. I love you. I need you."

She raised up slightly and propped on her elbows. Staring at him with direct intensity, she said. "Blaine, I...I don't know what I'm feeling right now. There are so many things to consider."

"Like what?" he said almost demanding an answer.

"Like how well do I know you? How well do you know me? Everything going on in your life right now. Your kids, your wife, what you'll do after Brakefield? All that."

"If what you're saying is you don't know what you're feeling about...me," he said with a short deprecating laugh, "seems like you feel pretty good about me in bed."

"Of course. That's no news," she retorted, "but I need to know there's more than that.

"So how'm I suppose to show you?" he said. "I just told you.. I love you and I need you.

"Yes, but I..."

He interrupted, "So you're saying you like the *fuckin'*, but you don't think there's anything more. Is *that it*?" His tone was somewhere between belligerent and bitter.

"No that's not it," she countered. I like being in bed with you, yes, but I like *you*. I like talking to you, going to dinner with you, just being with you. Why do you think I've spent so much time telling you about all this...work stuff I'm so involved in? It means a lot to me that you're so interested in what I'm doing. And I'm trying to be the same for you."

"Okay, so what's the problem?"

"I...," she paused as her face saddened, "I don't know how it feels to say I love you. I don't even know if I *could* say that. I've never gone that far with anyone. I guess I don't trust the idea. It's like something to avoid. My family ended up a disaster. My dad was a jerk, my mom was miserable, and...I've never had a very good impression of love, at least that kind."

"Okay, so I'm not pushing, but I mean it, Cassie. I love you. And I want you to love me. If you don't…or you can't, then maybe we just hang on for the sex." He glanced away dismissively. "I guess we've missed dinner. You hungry?"

She pulled back in reaction to his words: Just hang on for the sex. Is that what she deserved? She stood trying to ignore it. "It's too late to get anything delivered," she said. "but I can put something together."

He pushed the blanket back and looked down at himself. "Guess I'm in no shape to go out now anyway," he said laughing as he got up and crossed to the chair where he'd left his clothes. He slipped on his boxers and a tee-shirt, and followed her into the kitchen.

She opened the fridge surveying its sparse content. "How about bacon and eggs?" she said casually trying to lighten the tension.

"Okay, sure," he said lifelessly.

"Maybe with a little chardonnay?"

"Yep."

Over the next 10 minutes, she did the eggs and bacon, he poured the chardonnay and they began to eat and drink rather indifferently. The conversation became forced and self-conscious, each wanting to get beyond the words in the bedroom and back to where they had been just last weekend, enjoying being together, going with the flow. But for both of them now the frustration of uncertainty lay heavily beneath the veneer. She was feeling not only the gravity of things he had said barely half-hour ago but also of what Joe Holleran had told her less than 12 hours ago. And he was feeling her rejection so painfully. If they went back to bed, would that erase the anxiety?

Each wondered but without speaking the thoughts.

They finished the midnight repast and started silently back along the hallway. When they reached the bedroom, they shed their scanty clothes and slid between the sheets. He pulled her to him and wrapped her in a strong embrace. She did not resist but retreated quickly into sleep. For him, the impact of her rejection made sleep difficult.

About 5:30, she opened her eyes. He was no longer lying close to her. The room was dark as were the bathroom and hallway. She was sure the hall light had been on when she fell asleep. She pushed her hand along the sheet reaching for him, but he was not there. She called out to him as she sat up and switched on the bedside lamp. No answer. She called again and stood. His clothes were gone. She pulled on the robe and walked to the kitchen. The overhead light was on. Her briefcase lay open on the table. Next to it was one of her legal pads, a note scrawled across it:

Cassie, I had to leave——to get away to think about all you said last night——and all you didn't say. I couldn't stand lying there with you, thinking about us. It was driving me crazy. I love you, Cassie. But maybe we need more time——and space. Please don't give up on me. Don't give up on us.

She stared at the page. The words, laced with despair like his voice last night, struck deep as she made coffee and returned to the bedroom to dress. The specter of her dilemma kindled in her mind. Maybe she should back away from what she and Joe Holleran were planning to do today. In those moments, the conflict within her seemed to intensify for now an inexplicable urge to protect Blaine rolled over her. Was it pity or was she realizing, actually feeling a much deeper emotion?

*****

When she drove into the hospital garage at 7:30, she immediately saw that Blaine's car was not where he usually parked. She didn't know what to make of it, but she felt uneasy especially considering what Joe had told her yesterday. Where was he? Could he have left? Just cleared out?

She pulled into a space and pressed Joe's number into her phone. He answered quickly and without so much as a greeting, he said, "I don't know where you are with this or what went on last night," he said, "but the weekend's coming up, and things could get worse. I think we've got to do it....this afternoon." That strengthened her wavering resolve. She listened as Joe laid out the plan.

When she got to her office, she pulled up the draft of the report on the South Carolina meeting. For the next couple of hours, she tried to stay focused on finalizing it, but she couldn't get Blaine out of her mind. She thought of Joe's admonition yesterday, "...the longer he's hung up in the state he's in now, the more desperate and irrational he may become." Why oh *why* had she told Blaine about Zelinski's discovery? What could he do with that ? The thoughts gnawed at her as her anxiety and frustration compounded: Zelinski's discovery, the danger it presaged, the freezer intrusion and...Blaine maybe coming unglued. Too much.

She had to find out if Blaine's car might be in the garage by now. She closed the computer screen and walked out of the office suite, down two flights, through the hospital lobby and into the garage. With a quick survey she saw, to her relief, that his car was parked in its customary spot on the third row. She took a couple of deep breaths and went back to her office.

She brought the computer screen up and continued to work on the draft, but even as she tried to concentrate, she couldn't keep the jumble of thoughts at bay. And what was now most deeply painful to her was the revelation of his dark side, his deceptions and the irony of the hours spent with him since 7:00 last night. She had trusted him. Really trusted him. Had no reason not to. But now as she thought of it, she remembered a quote she'd heard somewhere along the way: "Trust, like the wind, once gone, never returns." Had he blown that trust away? Like the wind? What could a confrontation today bring now?

She forced herself to get on proofing the draft she'd finished yesterday. After another hour, she stopped for lunch. In her office again at 1:30, she checked her email in case he might have sent something. Nothing. For the next hour, she distracted herself by focusing on the references she needed to include. At 2:45, she decided she could wait no longer. She called cardiology.

"Yes, Doctor, he's here today," said Mrs. Sanders. "He's in clinic, but he said he'd be back by 4: 00. Shall I have him call you?"

"Yes, please. On my cell." She clicked off and went back to the computer.

At 3:45, her cell phone sounded. Blaine's number. "Hi," she answered. "Are you okay?"

"Yeah. I'm okay," he replied flatly. "Mrs. Sanders said you wanted me to call."

"I was worried about you," she said.

"Oh?" he said, equally flatly.

"Can I come by for a few minutes?" she said.

"I suppose, if you want to."

"Okay," she said. "I'll be there in a little while." She tried to sound casual.

She clicked off and called Joe to let him know, then started toward the Cardiology suite. He was waiting in the corridor. They had agreed that she would go in first. He was to wait outside Blaine's office for her signal for him to come in: when she pulled the door open slightly. They walked into the suite passing Mrs. Sanders. "He's expecting us," said Cassie. Mrs. Sanders nodded.

She knocked on the door.

"Come in,"

She pushed the door open. He sat at his desk, silent and motionless but with an expectant look as if waiting to hear her recant her words of last night.

She came through the door and closed it. "We need to talk," she said moving up to the desk. Her voice was strong. There was no hint of recantation. "I know what you're doing to yourself, Blaine."

His eyes widened as he sprang up from his chair immediately realizing what she meant and how she knew. "What the hell are you talking about?" he growled.

"You're destroying yourself. You've got to get *help*," she said.

Her eyes locked onto his.

"Who've you been talking to?"

"You know who," she said bracing herself in case he might suddenly come at her, but she continued quietly, "I'm here because we thought you'd listen to me better than him."

"That sonofabitch. That cowardly sonofabitch," he spit out the words, "sending you 'cause he's scared to come by himself. God *damn* him!" he hissed in an intense, menacing whisper.

"No, Blaine," she said trying to remain calm. "We want to help you." she eased backward pulling the door open slightly. "We both want to help you."

"Why would that bastard want to help me?" he said, his voice low but fiercely intense.

"Because he...or we...both think if you get help, you can work through..."

The door opened wider, and Joe stepped in and pushed the door shut.

Blaine's face reddened. "Yeah, sure. I know what you're trying to do." His voice sizzled as he edged around the desk and crouched forward about to lunge at Joe. Cassie stood between them. His mind raced. What had Joe told her? They were trying to *trap* him.

"Hey Blaine, listen," Joe said firmly. "We're trying to keep you from throwing your life away."

"Why do you give a fuck?" Blaine growled.

"Please, Blaine. Listen to us," Cassie pleaded.

"For what you high-and-mighty, two-faced bitch!" He spewed the words out. "You and your damn *secret toxin*! Wait'll everybody finds out what you're hidin'. All it'll take is one little leak. One call… to the press. Newspaper… and TV. It's a big story*!* And I'm gonna blow it *wide open*."

"What the hell are you talking about?" said Joe.

"Why don't you ask your secret lover," Blaine retorted.

"Blaine, you said I could trust you," blurted Cassie.

Joe was suddenly speechless.

"Trust. HA! What do you know about trust?" He snarled. "Wait and see what I can do!" He darted between them, ripped the door open and sprinted past an astonished Mrs. Sanders.

"Blaine. Wait!" Cassie shouted and tore after him. Joe followed. They got to the corridor in time to see Blaine go through the courtyard exit. When they reached it, they saw him run to the far end of the walkway and disappear into the garage. They dashed along the walkway, stopping at the garage entrance to scan the rows of cars. They spotted him on the third row. She pulled off her high heels and broke into a run yelling his name, a shoe in each hand.

Blaine reached his car, unlocked it, jumped in and revved the engine then recklessly backed out of the space. Tires squealing, the car careened around the curve toward the entrance as Cassie came through the second row. She was directly in its path. She tried to dodge as the car nosed away slightly but lost her balance. He could hear a thud as she hit the side of his car, but he did not stop. Joe came through the second row rushing toward her as she lay motionless on the garage floor.

Blaine sped on, through the exit and onto the street heading toward the beltway. He made it through three sequenced traffic lights, but the fourth, at the beltway ramp, flashed to red. The car just in front stopped for the light, but Blaine turned sharply and passed on the right, plowed over the shoulder, down the ramp and into the stream of traffic. His head was exploding. He leaned forward and gripped the steering wheel as if he would rip it from its housing. He released his right hand for a second and pressed the buttons on the console to open the windows as he maneuvered erratically to the middle lane. Wind swirled over his face. For a fleeting moment, he felt the ecstatic rush the speed always gave him.

He shot over to the left lane barely missing the rear of a huge 18-wheeler and sped on, approaching an overpass some 200 yards ahead. The truck swerved as its horn issued a skull-rattling blare. The trucker yelled and gestured at him. He screamed back, now almost beyond the truck, but his car began to fishtail between the truck and the concrete barrier on the left. The side of the car scraped against it, veered away and scraped again. The front end shuddered, contorting out of control and crashed in blinding violence into the concrete abutment of the overpass.

*****

A gurney with a silent but conscious Cassie strapped to it, clattered through the garage guided by two attendants. Joe trotted beside them. In less than another minute, they entered the ER where a doctor was waiting for her; Joe had called ahead.

"Hello, Dr. Garriman," he said lifting her wrist, feeling for a pulse. "Are you in any pain?"

"Yes," she replied weakly, "my head." She touched the back of her head. "I hit pretty hard."

He pressed tentatively where she touched, shined a pen-light beam at each eye then directed the attendants to push the cart into the third room along the corridor. He followed the cart through the door. Joe walked behind him and stood back against the wall. The ER doctor began to question her quietly as he started his examination, checking the pupils again with the pen light, then blood pressure, stethoscope to chest, movement of neck, arms, legs.

"Looks like you were pretty lucky," he said momentarily, "but we need to get a CT scan." She nodded slightly.

The doctor raised a thumbs up and walked into the corridor. The attendant pushed the gurney behind him. Joe followed beside it for a few feet until they reached the scanner room two doors along the corridor. As the passed through the door he said, "I'll be in the waiting area."

He moved past a cluster of people at the reception window and took a seat. It was almost 5:00. Rush hour Friday afternoon, he thought as he surveyed the flurry of activity around him. His mind went back to an hour ago. Where did Blaine go? They thought they could help him. They tried. He shook his head.

Cassie lay on the CT scanner table, a thin pillow under her head. "Please try not to move and keep your head very still on the pillow," said the technician. The next few minutes passed and it was done. "All right. That's it, but you'll have to stay here a few more minutes while the doctor checks the images. Let's get you back on the gurney." The technician helped her transfer then said, "I'll be right back."

In those few quiet moments in the darkened room, thoughts of all that had just happened poured through her mind.. Where was Blaine now? What he might do in his crazed state, she didn't want to even imagine. And would he really go to the press with the treacherous secret?

The doctor's voice brought her back. "CT looks good," he said approaching the gurney. "How's your head?"

"Still hurts. But it helps to know it's okay," she said rather weakly.

"Dr. Holleran insists that he'll follow up with you, so I'm going to release you," he said, "but you need to take it easy."

"Thank you," she said as she pulled herself up to sitting. "Thank you very much."

"Of course," he said. "I hope you'll feel better soon. I'll leave a prescription at the desk for the headache. I know Dr. Holleran'll look out for you." He smiled and left the room.

A nurse pushed a wheelchair toward the gurney. Cassie slid off and stood beside it as Joe entered. "Ready to go?" he said gesturing toward the wheelchair.

"Yes, but I don't need that," she said. "I'm okay."

"You sure?" She nodded. "Okay," he said. They walked out into the bustling corridor.

A nurse pushed a woman in a wheelchair toward the registration window. An elderly couple, arm in arm, made their way in the same direction. Two white-clad doctors standing against the wall conversed and gestured intensely. A screaming child being pushed in a crib by an attendant passed in the other direction followed by obviously distraught parents. And at that point, a gurney guided by two men in EMT uniforms, rushed past as bellowing, agonizing groans and wails rose from it. "Oh GOD!!! My Leg! Please. OHH!"

Cassie stopped in her tracks. It was Blaine. She recognized the voice, even yelling. Crying in pain. She froze for a moment then broke away and ran after the gurney. Joe followed in a fast walk as the gurney turned it into a side room with the ER doctor and nurse behind it. Cassie and Joe went in after them.

Blaine was lying motionless on the gurney, covered in a blanket, moaning but now without the loud outcries. The IV attached to the pole on the gurney dripped steadily. A nurse wrapped a blood pressure cuff around his upper arm.

"Took a while to get him out of the car," one of the EMTs said quietly. "The door was wedged shut. By time we got'im out, he was just about in shock. Diastolic was down to 40 by time we got the IV started. Came back up to 90 over 60, and by time we got here it was up to 115 over 70."

"Got a reading yet?" asked the doctor as he lifted the blanket away from Blaine's legs.

"112 over 65," the nurse replied.

A second nurse trundled a medicine cart into the room.

"OW!!" Blaine yelled as the doctor shifted his left thigh slightly.

"Okay," said the doctor. He took his hand away and lowered the blanket. "Lie still. We'll take care of your pain right away." He turned to the nurse at the medicine cart. "Fifty of fentanyl in the IV," he said. She knew the dose he meant. He turned back to Blaine.

"You're…here on the staff, right?" he said trying to distract him.

"Yeah," Blaine heaved in a whisper. "Cardiology."

"I remember you at the staff meeting last month."

"Umm," Blaine mumbled. The nurse held up a syringe, slipped a needle into the IV line and pressed the plunger.

"That ought to help in a couple of minutes," said the doctor.

"Then we'll get you to CT."

Blaine closed his eyes. The other nurse began to wipe blood from the right side of his head. The doctor lifted the upper part of the blanket and placed his stethoscope on Blaine's chest. Cassie moved closer.

"Oh, Dr. Garriman." The doctor looked surprised. "I didn't see you back there."

"Yes," she said equally quietly. "Dr. Purcell and I work together."

Blaine opened his eyes and blinked. "Cassie? I...I'm...," His voice trailed off as he reached toward her.

"We've gotta move him," the doctor said from the other side of the gurney.

Cassie touched the outstretched hand. "I'm here, Blaine." The cart began to roll away.

Joe stood silently by the door as it exited, and the two of them walked back into the corridor.

"How's your head?" he asked.

"I'm okay," she said.

"We need to pick up that prescription in case you need it."

"I'm going to wait here to get some word on his CT," she said

"No need for you to stay. I can pick up the prescription."

"Remember, the doc said he was releasing you to my care," Joe said slightly sternly but smiling. "Call me if you need anything."

"Thank you, but I think I'll be fine. You should go home." The crisp voice had returned.

After another 20 minutes, she was able to pull up the radiology report on one of the computers at the reception desk. The verdict: "Comminuted fracture, left femur. Now stabilized. To be admitted. Surgery scheduled for 7:00 am." No need for her to stay either.

She drove home exhausted and with a head still full of jumbling thoughts. She finally got to sleep around 10:00. Saturday morning, she woke early. Blaine's surgery should be underway shortly. She'd check later. She went back to sleep.

The surgery, beginning at 7:00, lasted about 6 hours and was finished about 1:30. He was moved to surgical recovery still unconscious from the anesthetic. Cassie had called in periodically, and now at 4:00, she was on her way to check on him in person. She wore her full credentials: white doctor's coat with embroidered name, stethoscope in right pocket and her ID badge, all to make it easy for her to get past the desk to see Blaine.

The staff acknowledged her deferentially as she approached the central desk. She learned that he was not yet awake but stable. The austere space was quiet, ceiling lights dim and conversation among the staff, appropriately muted. She went to one of the computers on the counter behind the desk and pulled up the OP NOTE by referencing Blaine's date of birth and medical records number. With a detailed description of the procedure, the note indicated everything had gone smoothly and in a reasonable time.

She logged out and proceeded to the darkened room where he lay sleeping. She moved to the bed and touched his face. No response. She stood for a moment and lifted his hand, squeezed it and spoke his name. No response. She stood a few more seconds, released the hand, leaned forward and kissed his forehead lightly.

She went back to the desk, jotted her name, cell number and pager number on a pad on the counter. She handed it to the nurse. "Please let me know if there's any problem. And please tell him I came by. I'll come back tomorrow morning."

"Yes, doctor. We'll keep you posted. You have a good night."

CHAPTER THIRTY-FOUR

Ilya was her code name. Her real name was Eliina Amilia Azjan Umarov. She grew up in Chechnya in a town south of Grozny. She studied biology and physics at the Chechen State University in Grosny then moved to Moscow to complete a Ph.D. in physics at Moscow State University. In her post-doctoral years at the university, she became proficient in mass spectroscopy and spectrometric analysis. It was in her last post-doc year that she met Bekhan Varayev, five years older than she, also a physicist and a Chechen. A mutual attraction was quickly evident, in part because of their scientific interests, but perhaps even more because they were both Chechen and increasingly concerned about the looming anti-Chechen sentiments in Moscow.

Within a short time, they developed a romantic relationship, but it was abruptly interrupted with the advent of the first Russian-Chechen War and the Russian invasion of Grosny on New Year's Eve, 1994. During that devastating siege, many Chechens including Eliina's parents and a number of other members of her family were killed. When a truce was declared at the end of February, Eliina went back to Grosny to help the members of her family who survived. About six months later, Varayev returned to Chechnya as well, and it was then that they reconnected. With much of Grosny destroyed, they both became staunchly committed to the anti-Russian Chechen underground. Several years later, two years before the second Russian-Chechen war (1999-2000), she learned of a job opportunity at a mass spectrometry lab in Boston. By then, her romantic relationship with Varayev had cooled then dissolved because of pressures of so many tragedies of the first war.

Varayev encouraged her to seek the Boston job thinking of it as an opportunity to break into American scientific and technical expertise which could be useful in their clandestine anti-Russian efforts. With life still so miserable in Grosny and much of her family gone, she welcomed the prospect to move to the United States and, as he urged, keeping in close communication with him for their cause.

To qualify for the job in Boston, she underwent a lengthy vetting based on recommendations from her records and mentors in Moscow as well as a meticulous background check and a security clearance. But because of the competence she had exhibited according to her records at Moscow University, her security clearance for the U.S. came relatively quickly. She was eligible for a green card within six months after her arrival in Boston. Over the next several years she applied for and eventually received American citizenship, also perhaps somewhat fast-forwarded because of the high quality of her work and the all-important clearance. She remained in Boston for three years before being recruited to a government lab just outside of Washington, DC, in 2001. She remained there until Zelinski hired her away to come to Atlanta to work in his lab at the university.

By now, she had worked with Zelinski for almost three years. They had established a cordial and collegial relationship, but never before had she known him to be so protective of any spectrometric analysis result as he was with that from the sample brought in by Dr. Garriman last week. She'd thought about it a few times but had more-or-less dismissed it.

Saturday afternoon, as she strolled slowly across the university campus in the direction of her apartment, the thought came back. Was Zelinski hiding something? It made her think of Varayev's periodic email pronouncements: "Take note of anything unusual" or "watch for new findings." He persisted sending such messages every few months for the 9 years she'd been in the U.S., and in several instances, her vigilance had paid off.

But at this moment, as she walked, her curiosity and her pace picked up. Suddenly she felt compelled to find out what might be going on. Perhaps something on Zelinski's computer could tell her. Perhaps. But she had to be careful. Too risky to search using her university computer, but on her home computer she could use what Varayev had taught her. He had a way to do it no one could detect. It was his code which he called his "special skill." He used those words to protect his methods, but he had taught her well. Just put in Zelinski's User ID and go from there. A discreet and quite rewarding way of hacking, but she had to remember, it was always risky.

Back in her apartment, she went to the desk in the living room, unlocked the bottom drawer and lifted out a notebook where she kept her most important and confidential information. She flipped to the **V** section. There it was in bold print, Varayev's code: the special skill.

She booted up and typed in *szelinski@univcent.org* then the code in the password bar. Almost instantly, the menu for Zelinski's files appeared. Much easier than she'd expected. She opened the DESKTOP file and scrolled through the list. Nothing impressed her. She went on to DOWNLOADS and scrolled, but again, nothing impressive. She went to DOCUMENTS and at the top of the list, she read: **Garriman, C., Report, Hefner-Cantrell Inst.** Just what she was looking for. The report on Garriman's sample:

Date: May 15

Client: Garriman, Cassandra, M.D., Brakefield Hospital and Hefner-Cantrell Institute

Procedure: Mass Spectrometric analysis of unclassified

mycotoxin (*Stachybotrys* Genus) with and without direct chemical ionization (GC/MS plus/minus DCI).

Amount of sample: 15 nanograms

Amount of internal control: 15 nanograms

Results: Macrocyclic Trichothecene with unique protein structure compared to previously identified macrocyclic trichothecenes including Roridin A, D, E, & H, Baccharinol-4 & 5 and KVA. (See attached structural diagrams.) Because of the characteristically high toxicity of macrocyclic trichothecenes compared to non-macrocyclic trichothecenes, this unique, apparently unidentified macrocyclic trichothecene must be considered as potentially extremely toxic. (See attached references.)

Comment: Although macrocyclic trichothecene mycotoxins are considered among the most toxic naturally occurring mycotoxins, no evidence is reported for selective neurotoxic effects of these mycotoxins. However, because of selective neurotoxic effects thus far exhibited by this structurally unique macrocyclic trichothecene, it must be considered to be the product of a genetically mutant fungus which is apparently naturally occurring.

Solomon D. Zelinski, Ph.D.

She scrolled past the structural diagrams and found what she wanted: the references. She began to read through them noting a number of highlighted sentences. The second reference said that trichothecene mycotoxins were used as biological warfare agents in Southeast Asia and Afghanistan by the former Soviet Union. It said that Chinese analysts had alleged that between 1975 and 1982, roughly 6,000 Laotians, 1,000 Cambodians and 3,000 Afghans died from trichothecene mycotoxin attacks. Another reference said:

"Macrocyclic trichothecenes are polar toxic molecules originating from several species of fungi including *Myrothecium and Stachybotrys.*." Her curiosity about Zelinski's secrecy heightened.

Why didn't he want anyone to know about this but Garriman?

She scrolled back to the diagrams to study what the report called the "unique protein structure." Four diagrams appeared side by side on the screen. Three were labelled as recognized or identified macrocyclic mycotoxins. The fourth diagram was labelled "Sample/Garriman/macrocyclic mycotoxin, *unidentified.*"

Though subtle, the structural differences among the four were clear. Her thoughts swirled as she scrolled back to the highlighted words in the sixth reference: "…macrocyclic trichothecenes have been found to be the most toxic of all known naturally occurring trichothecenes." She needed more information. How do macrocyclic trichothecenes differ from non-macrocyclic tricho-thecenes? Why are the macrocyclics so toxic? What appeared to be a profoundly complex swath of science had just become critically important to her.

The only information she had was from the well-guarded Zelinski report she'd just read. It said this was a new "unidentified" and "extremely toxic" mycotoxin produced by a "genetically mutant fungus….apparently naturally occurring." Furthermore qualifying it as macrocyclic underscored its toxicity, but perhaps most amazing, was what seemed to be its "selective neurotoxic effects."

The fungus could certainly be cloned and propagated, but in order to do that, a source had to be identified, and there was only one small vial of the mycotoxin in the lab. Only micrograms. Could that be used to identify and clone the fungus? Could the cloned fungus actually be propagated enough to produce the mycotoxin on a large scale? Large enough to be used like the mycotoxins used in Southeast Asia and Afghanistan years ago…for mass casualties or perhaps for more focused bioterrorism in just the right places?

She could feel her heart pounding as the thoughts rolled through her head. She had to breathe for a moment, collect herself then contact Varayev. Send him Zalinski's report and the diagrams and references. But wait. First just a simple message. The clock on the desk said 5:15 Saturday afternoon. That meant it was 1:15 Sunday morning in Grozny. If she emailed him now, he'd have it when he woke. She saved everything to her hard drive and composed a cautiously cryptic message to alert him before sending anything else: "New discovery. May be important. Have questions. Need advice. Ilya." She typed in his address and hit SEND. Now she'd wait for his response.

*****

Varayev opened Eliina's email message around 9:30 Sunday morning. He responded immediately: "Send all details. Everything!" When she woke Sunday morning, she rose quickly to find his message. She opened Zelinski's report again and forwarded it to him with the diagrams and the 6 references.

He studied every word. He, like Eliina, grew up with their native Chechen language as well as Russian, but both were fluent in English, so with his scientific background, he had no trouble understanding the report. He was elated. Two hours later, he wrote back: "Can you get sample of fungus?" She replied she had no way to get a sample of the fungus, but there was a sample of the mycotoxin in the lab. Would that be useful if she could get it?

"Of course!" he wrote. "Very useful. Now we have diagram of structure. So is critical if you get mycotoxin. We can confirm structure and clone genes in biosynthetic pathway. Should make possible to reproduce fungus. You must be careful. Remember. We are fighting for same cause. Will be incredible!!" and he closed with "Remember protocol!!"

Now, she felt empowered. But it was up to her to get the mycotoxin. One misstep and she could be arrested, fired and deported...or worse. But the protocol was clear.

*****

When Cassie came in to see Blaine around noon Sunday, she woke him enough to see that now he could talk coherently though sluggishly. The mild level of sedation and the pain medication in the IV drip had allowed him to sleep comfortably through the night, but he was still somewhat blunted. She didn't want to upset him with what she knew would eventually become an inevitable reckoning. And she still had work to do on the South Carolina meeting report. So she left saying she would come again Monday morning.

Back at the hospital by 8:30 Monday morning, she went directly to surgical recovery where she learned that he'd been moved to a private room two floors above. She took the stairs, stopped at the desk to get his room number and headed to the room. He was now awake and alert but complaining of pain. It was probably due to post-op reduction of his meds, she thought. But it could signal withdrawal if he were addicted. Too soon to tell.

Their conversation, though somewhat touched with reserve, seemed easy enough in spite of his complaints. But there was no mention of, nor even allusion to, the Friday afternoon confrontation in his office and his explosive exit. Nor to the car crash. Nor to the hours they had spent together Thursday night before that all happened. He didn't seem to, or pretended not to, remember any of it. Nevertheless, satisfied with his progress, she assured him she'd come again in the afternoon. Now she had to get to her office.

*****

About the same time, activities in the Zelinski lab began with the usual Monday morning 9:00 lab meeting. The whole team was there: Zelinski, Eliina, Alex, the technical assistant for the mass spectrometer, Joline the lab manager, Tracie the lab technician, one post-doctoral fellow and two grad students. After 45 minutes of reporting and discussing results and planning the week's agenda, they dispersed to their respective tasks. Zelinski, Alex and Tracie went into the mass spec room; Eliina, to her small office off the main lab; Joline, to her carrell near the lab entrance and the post-doc and grad students, to their desks at the back of the lab. It was a predictable routine.

Just after 11:00, Eliina came out for coffee from the dispenser on the table beside Joline's carrell. She could see that Zelinski, Alex and Tracie were deep into their analysis, and by now everyone else was thoroughly occupied. She filled her mug and went back into her office. She had work to do, too, but she kept replaying Varayev's words in her head. It made her anxious and a bit fidgety. Maybe a walk to the departmental library would help. She took a few sips of the coffee, came back into the lab and said, "Going to library" as she passed Joline's desk.

Back in her office by noon, she logged in again to pull up a few more articles. She still had work to do. She wished she could see all she'd saved on her laptop Saturday evening, but she knew it was safely tucked away in her apartment.

*****

Cassie made it back to Blaine's room later in the afternoon than she had anticipated. He was dozing, but she decided to wake him at least long enough to let him know she'd come by. He was not quite as talkative as earlier and still a bit addled. She mentioned the report on the South Carolina meeting. He showed no interest, but she knew he must be tired. So again telling him she had more work to do on the report, she said she'd be back tomorrow. He smiled vaguely and nodded.

Tuesday morning, she was in to see him by 7:15. He was more alert, and his pain complaints had subsided. An encouraging sign, she thought. Hopefully a good night's sleep had made him more comfortable.

*****

At almost the same time, Eliina unlocked the door to the Zelinski lab with her own key and walked in. Earlier than usual for her. Routinely no one was expected to arrive until 8:00. But today she was busy in her office by then, sitting at the table behind her desk going through a pile of loose pages and several stacks of folders. As Joline passed her door, she stopped to say "My you're in early today."

Eliina turned and smiled.

"Oh, look at you." Joline mirated, "Nice haircut. Very chic... short like that."

"Was getting too long. I think is better short." Eliina smiled again and went back to her work. At 11:00, she pushed several folders and a thin stack of the loose pages into her shoulder-bag briefcase. With its strap over her shoulder, she came out of her office, pulled the door shut and casually announced to Joline and Tracie that she was off to a lunch meeting.

That didn't seem unusual until almost 3:00 when it became noticeable, especially to Joline, that Eliina had not yet come back from her meeting. Four hours. Not like Eliina. But just as she was thinking that, Tracie came through the center of the lab looking intensely agitated. She said nothing, but went directly to Zelenski's office door and knocked.

"Come in."

She opened the door, went through and closed it.

"What's up?" said Zelinski, surprised at her sudden intrusion and her expression.

"That vial….from Dr. Garriman. It's *missing*." She tried to speak calmly.

"What?" he shouted and jumped up from his desk. "You *sure*?! You checked everything?"

"Yes," she said, "and the last notation in the log was when you took out the vial to get some sample for the analysis. And you returned it immediately according to the time record. That was almost two weeks ago. The last time I did my routine inventory check was last Tuesday. Same as I always do…every Tuesday. Everything was in order. I confirmed it in the log. Today everything else is in order, but that vial is missing."

"My God!" Zelinski heaved. "Nobody but you, me and Eliina have access, right?"

"That's right. Nobody else."

"Where is Eliina?" Zelinski asked in an intense tone.

"Not back from an 11:00 meeting she said she had. Said it was a lunch meeting."

"Have you tried to call her?"

"Yes. Once," she said. "On her cell phone. Just now. No answer. I left a message."

"Okay," he said looking down toward the floor, frowning. "Let's check her office." He was trying to stay calm, but he could feel his face flush. They walked to Eliina's door and tried the knob. It was locked. They glanced at each other. He spoke quietly to Joline. "You have a key for this?" He pointed to the door knob,

"Yes." She plucked a tagged key from a rack on the wall behind her and handed it to him.

He pushed it into the lock and opened the door. Everything looked as usual, but he noticed a few things missing. They were things he remembered because Eliina had pointed them out to him several times…several framed photographs of her parents and other family members usually carefully arranged on the desk. And a small Russian doll she seemed especially fond of. Gone, too.

He pulled open the drawer on the right side of the desk where he knew she kept important lab notes, procedure records, calculations and details on her assigned mass spec analyses. Completely empty. His mouth gaped. Glancing up at the wall behind the desk for a moment, he felt both anger and irony as he caught sight of a framed official-looking document reading UNITED STATES OF AMERICA. Under that, CERTIFICATE OF NATURALIZATION and further down, the line bearing the name *Eliina Amilina Azjan Umarov* . He had not noticed that before. He looked down again at the empty drawer and opened the shallow drawer in the center of the desk. It too was empty. He opened the large drawer on the left of the desk to see it was filled with a row of hanging files. He thumbed through a few. All scientific reprints with file-tag labels. Nothing seemed amiss.

"Looks like she's cleared out," he said as he motioned toward the empty drawers.

"What do we do?" said Tracie.

"We call security. This minute." He picked up the desk phone and dialed the operator. "Yes. This is Dr. Zelinski. Connect me with security." Tracie walked back into the lab and closed the door as he began a conversation with Security.

By now the rest of the staff had gathered in the middle of the room standing silent and perplexed. "Something's up with Eliina," Tracie muttered.

Zelinski gave the chief of security a quick version of what had happened along with details about Eliina's job, her background and what he knew of her ethnicity. Chechen. And Russian. "Looks like she's taken some important documents with her. I have no idea where she might be going. Or why," he said, "but if she has taken the missing vial with her, that could be extremely dangerous. Possibly even a matter of national security. I can't emphasize that enough." His words were paced and strong. "And I think she's is a flight risk."

Things evolved quickly: The university Office of Security contacted the Georgia Bureau of Investigation, and in less than 30 minutes, that office contacted Zelinski. He quickly reiterated what he had told the hospital security officer and tried to fill them in with as much more specific information as he could. Eliina's passport information, country of origin, immigration status, education, cell phone number, home address, work address. Driver's license? Yes. A car? No. Sometimes rents. Credit cards? Don't know. Photo-graph? Yes, passport photo.

No driver's license or credit card information, but he could fax the copy of her passport he'd filed when she first came to the lab. He had considered it a safety precaution for her since she'd designated him as her emergency contact in the U.S. The photograph was a good image of her rather exotic facial features, long dark hair and dark eyes. He thought a copy of her Certificate of Naturalization could be helpful also. Along with the cell number and addresses, he faxed the copies of the passport and certificate.

All the information must have been transmitted efficiently to appropriate agencies because after one more hour, the office of the National Counter Terrorism Center, NCTC, called Zelinski on his direct office line. They said the GBI had notified the FBI who had contacted NCTC. The word was that an all-points bulletin was being released electronically at that moment directed to all travel agencies, airlines and airports throughout the state of Georgia as well as Atlanta taxi services, car rental agencies and commercial bus companies. And it would shortly be arriving at TV and radio stations as well.

Within the two-and-a-half hour time span from the discovery of the missing vial to the NCTC phone call, critical information had blanketed the area. As the situation intensified, it dawned on Zelinski that he had not yet brought Cassandra Garriman in on it. He buzzed Joline, "Please call Dr. Garriman's office right now. Ask them to have her call me. Say it's urgent."

He was amazed when, at 5:30, another call from NCTC informed him that using the passport and naturalization certificate information, they'd discovered that one Eliina Umarov was holding a confirmed reservation on Aeroflot Russian Air, flight 103 from JFK to Moscow leaving tonight at 9:10. There was no indication how she might get there from Atlanta. He was told that there were at least 40 flights from Atlanta to the New York area from noon to 8:00 Eastern time. They'd not yet been able to determine if she had flown out of Atlanta or into any New York area airport. But, they said, if she were going to keep her date with Aeroflot, a stake out would be waiting. And if she didn't make it to JFK?

*****

She had no trouble getting to and through the Atlanta airport. She had bought her ticket online. Luckily, a fast cab ride got her to the terminal where she picked up the boarding pass at one of the Delta kiosks and made it through the TSA line without a hitch. Neither she nor the small rolling suitcase and the shoulder bag briefcase nor the laptop and folders attracted any attention. She went into a rest room some distance along the concourse and entered a stall. She set the small suitcase across the toilet seat, opened it and drew out a blond wig and tinted aviator-style glasses. She pushed her short dark hair back, tugged the wig into place and slipped on the glasses. She closed the suitcase and came out of the stall pausing for a moment to look at herself in the mirror. She liked the look. The shoulder length blond wig, the tinted glasses, fashionable short jacket over dark slacks and flat-heeled shoes along with the crisp shoulder bag and rolling suitcase gave her a glamorous, well-traveled look.

To her surprise, the flight left Atlanta and arrived at LaGuardia on time. The crowd at LaGuardia was heavy. The cab ride to JFK in the 4:30 traffic was tedious and a bit stressful, but at 5:20, the driver pulled up to the curb at Terminal 1. She stepped out, briefcase strap over her shoulder and suitcase in tow. She stood for a moment then walked to a bench near the entrance and sat. Her watch said 5:25. She was relieved. She was sure if they had noticed she was gone, she was now far enough away that they couldn't catch up with her. She fished for the pack of Marlboros in the side pocket of the shoulder bag and lit up. It felt good to take a few deep drags. It relaxed her.

*****

5:45 in Atlanta: "Hello, Dr. Zelinski. Cassandra Garriman. My office said I should call you. Sorry couldn't call sooner."

"Okay. I understand," he said sharply, "but I'm afraid I have some bad news.. Your vial with the mycotoxin we've had stored in my lab…is missing. We think it's been stolen."

"Oh NO," she blurted. "How could that happen? I thought you said it was secure."

"I thought it was. Only two other people had access to it. Tracie my technician, and my associate, Dr. Umorov. She's the one you met in the lobby when you delivered the vial.

"I remember. Yes," said Cassandra. "The Russian woman."

"That's right. Well…so about 3:00, Tracie discovered that the vial was gone, and right after that we discovered that Dr. Umorov was gone too. Seems she just took off. I mean cleared out. I guess she took as much of her papers, important reports, computer file CDs and personal things in her office….as she could carry. Looks like it was well-planned."

"Oh, my god. What can be done? I mean, is there some way to find her. Stop her?" Her tone was desperate.

"Yes," he said trying to calm her. "We've been working on that since we discovered she was gone and probably has the vial. I'll explain in just minute, but first let me say that as I began to process everything, it occurred to me that somehow she must have seen my report on the mycotoxin. It's pretty convincingly worded, I must say. I wrote it that way on purpose to emphasize how dangerous I believe the mycotoxin is. If she did see the report, it's possible she decided she could sell that vial to someone or maybe sell the idea. Theoretically, put it into the hands of someone who might use it for destructive purposes. In any event, I've just learned, on good authority, that she may be on her way to Russia as we speak."

"This is blowing my mind!" Cassandra said, heaving. "How do you know *that*?".

"When Tracie came in to tell me the vial was gone, and we saw that Eliina was gone too, I quick called medical center security and explained the situation and my suspicions. They immediately swung into action. They called the GBI, you know, the Georgia Bureau of Investigation, and only a short time later, I got a call from them. They started with some routine questions, but when I filled them in on how important the contents of the vial could be, they pressed me for details. I sent them all the information I had on her. Within another hour and a half, they issued an all-points bulletin complete with her photograph."

"How'd they get a photograph?"

"Her passport," he said. "I have a copy here in my office. I scanned it and faxed it along with the immigration information and a few other items. Believe me, they took it and *ran* with it! They must have contacted the FBI because within another hour, I got a call from the office of the National Counter-terrorism Center in Virginia. Apparently using her passport number, they were able to find out she's holding a reservation on a flight to Moscow at 9:00 tonight."

"Oh, my god," said Cassandra, still reeling in disbelief.

"Assuming she did see my report, she also saw the references I quoted about the use of mycotoxins in biological warfare in Southeast Asia...and Afghanistan. You remember I told you about the articles I found."

"Yes, of course."

"That might have triggered this whole thing, because the significance and the potential danger of mycotoxins like this one are pretty clear." He paused for a moment then continued. "You're not aware of this, but let me tell you. Eliina is originally from Chechnya. Grew up there. Educated there and in Moscow. She appeared to have iron-clad security clearance when she came to this country 9 years ago. But God only knows who she might have hooked up with along the way."

"This is so unreal...I feel like I'm in a bad dream."

"Well, I'm afraid it is real, and there's nothing we can do now." said Zelinski. "Just hope the professionals at NCTC can handle it. Find her. Stop her in her tracks, damn it!"

*****

Eliina sat a few more minutes before going into the terminal. People scurried back and forth on the sidewalk in front of her; cars screeched and honked beyond the curb. In spite of all the commotion, she was feeling more relaxed. No need to hurry. She lit another cigarette thinking about the next few hours. She would pick up the boarding pass at a kiosk just like in Atlanta. Then maybe have something to eat before going through customs. Ah, but she'd have to get rid of the wig first. She had to look at least something like the passport picture. Especially because of the dark hair. Maybe the haircut would be a bit of a diversion, but she'd keep the wig on as long as possible just in case.

She patted the right side-pocket of her jacket. Still there. She smiled a satisfied smile and finished the cigarette. Then she pushed the briefcase shoulder strap over her shoulder and entered the terminal, suitcase in tow. Not hungry, but a ham-on-rye and coffee would be nice. She could have a drink after she got through customs.

On toward 6:30, she finished the sandwich and coffee and walked unhurriedly to the far end of the terminal away from the concourse designated by her boarding pass. She entered the ladies' room, went into a stall and pulled off the blond wig but kept the glasses on. When she came out, she pushed the wig into the waste receptacle at the end of the lavatory counter and looked at herself in the mirror. She laid the glasses on the counter and rearranged and patted down her short hair. Then she took a small make-up case from the suitcase and began to apply a dark red, almost brown, shade of lipstick. She took out her passport to check and looked at her picture. Maybe she should muss the hair a bit and darken the eye makeup to make her a little less recognizable from the picture. She finished, put the makeup back into the suitcase, put on the glasses again and returned to the terminal. She felt more exposed, now. She still wore the aviator glasses, but the wig had made her feel more secure, somehow more invisible.

Oh, well. It had to be done this way. It was nearly 7:00, and she had to get through customs by at least 7:30. She moved toward the passport control desks at the end of the hallway beyond the Aeroflot counters glancing carefully about as she walked. There was a fairly heavy line, so she'd have a several-minutes wait. A few people were standing near the sidewalls away from the line, but the hallway was quiet.

She watched the passport clerks at the three occupied counters, and tried to judge which might be the most casual maybe disinterested and perhaps the most likely to let her through without a hassle. They all seemed robotic. None stood out as the best choice for her. She'd have to take which ever one signaled her to step forward. After another 10 minutes, she was third in her line. Then second. Then first. She approached the counter with what she considered a pleasant half-smile and handed the clerk her passport and boarding pass. He returned the half-smile, opened the passport to the first pages and glanced up at her. He looked back at the passport, paused a minute then asked, "How long will you be in Russia?"

"Fourteen days."

"Is your trip for business or pleasure?"

"Pleasure. Family visit," she said innocently and smiled.

"One moment please."

The clerk seemed to be inspecting the back pages of the passport, but taking too long for those few pages. He looked at her again, now not smiling. Eliina watched as he looked down at the computer keyboard and screen on the desk below the counter. His hands began to type rapidly. He stopped and he looked up. "Miss, you'll have to wait here a moment." He seemed to be shuffling things on the desk, looking uneasy.

"What is problem?" she asked with an authoritative voice.

"Just a moment, please."

She felt a hand on her shoulder. She turned to see a short, stocky man with a crew-cut standing beside her. She had noticed him standing against the wall a few minutes earlier. The clerk handed him the passport open to first two pages.

"Eliina Amorov," the man said as he looked up from the passport and down again. "Please come with me."

He began to pull at her arm. She jerked away, dropped the suitcase, and before the man could fully react, she sprang forward pushing and zigzagging her way through the line of waiting travelers. He followed, but she was faster, and some of the startled travelers as well as the luggage strewn haphazardly around them slowed him up. She hugged the briefcase tightly, using it to push people aside as she reached the full lobby. She glanced back to see now another man rushing after her slightly behind the first one. But she had a good start on them, and the streams of people, large wheeling suitcases and piled-high luggage carts between her and the men were so thick, they hid her well as she raced on. Now 20 feet ahead of them, she ducked low, weaving through oblivious throngs as she spotted the **Hudson News** magazine/newspaper concession coming up on her left. She looked back again, and losing sight of both the men, she darted in and over to a tall greeting cards stand at the back of the store and slinked behind it, hiding herself from view of passersby in the lobby. Bending low and peeking furtively around the side of the card rack, she could see them. They were about 10 feet apart, still surrounded by the sluggish crush of people and glancing about bewildered. The one closest to her raised a hand signaling the other and pointing behind them toward the Terminal entrance far to the right. She did not move but watched them turn and run back in that direction. Obviously they had not seen her go into the news stand. She waited a few more seconds, then edging slowly to the wide entrance of the news stand, she scanned the crowds. No evidence of the men. Time to make a move.

Still ducking and bending, she rushed back into the thick crowd, across the broad promenade, out through the terminal exit on the left and onto the sidewalk. She faded into the crowd and allowed herself to be swept along toward the entrance to Terminal 2 when she suddenly spotted the taller of the two men running fast along the curb toward her. He held up a waving hand as if signaling to the other man. She felt sure he had now seen her. She made it through the entrance, again ducking, crouching, trying to lose herself in the crowd. She was terrified. Where could she go? The restroom was less than 50 feet ahead on her right. Yes. She gathered herself, and still hugging the briefcase, sprinted toward it and through the entrance. Without slowing, she passed several stunned women standing in front of the lavatories and dashed into the last stall at the far end of the room. She locked the door and sat sideways on the edge of the toilet seat, out of breath, shaking with exhaustion and fear, heaving and gulping air.

Sounds of men's voices at the entrance stirred a quick response from the women in the room. One man spoke loudly: "Ladies, you have to leave now. This is an emergency."

The women had seen her go into the stall. They began to shriek and yell protests, "Don't come in here!!" "What's going on?? "You can't come in!!"

The man spoke louder. "Ladies, we have to come in! This is an *emergency*!! "

The women in the open area scurried toward the entrance while those still in the stalls yelled, "Ok. Just a minute." and "Ok. We're coming."

The two men walked in with almost military precision as two more women hurried past them. All the stall doors were flung open except for the last one. The men approached it and stood silently for a moment then one said: "Eliina Amorov. This is the FBI. Please come out. We want to talk to you." No response. "Eliina Amoraov, *please come out.*" The voice was stronger, but still no response. They walked closer, each now holding a small pistol at his right side. They stood guardedly away from the closed stall door listening for any sound.

After a few more seconds, they heard sounds of quiet breathing which quickly changed to heavier more labored breathing. The looked at each other as the sounds increased to gasping and a choking then the sound of something falling heavily against the stall door and onto the floor. One of the men knelt in front of the stall next to the closed door and peered cautiously under the metal partition. There was the lifeless body slumped against the door.

He stood up. "I think she's unconscious. We gotta get her out."

"The door's locked. We'll have to break it down," said the other man.

At that moment, two uniformed policemen ran in. The man beside the stall said, "We think a woman has passed out in there. We've gotta get her out."

"I'll go over that partition," said one of the policemen, a young athletic-looking man. He instantly jumped through the open door of the next-to-last stall and on top of the toilet seat and deftly vaulted over the metal partition. Avoiding the body on the floor, he released the latch, and the door swung open as the body flopped on the floor head first. The wide eyes stared up emptily, the face was flushed red with blood-tinged froth around the nostrils and partially-open mouth.

One of the men pulled the body slightly forward on the floor and the other knelt and began intense chest compression. Each time, more froth erupted from the nostrils and mouth. He stopped the compression and reached for a limp wrist feeling for a pulse for a few seconds then pressed the right side of the neck.

"She's dead," he said as he dropped the wrist. The two policemen stepped back. "Please guys, one of you stay here with me and one block the door 'til we can get some help in here." He pulled the body farther out of the stall. As he did he heard the sound of something rolling on the floor of the stall. The other man reached down to pick up two small round cylinders the size and shape of Life Saver packs. One was tightly taped with tan plastic tape. The other was open. It contained two white tablets. Three more tablets were on the floor beside the body. The agent held the open cylinder sideways as he read the carefully printed letters on its side. First, a series of what appeared Greek or maybe Russian letters. The letters P R O T O C O L were clearly printed beneath the Russsian letters. And beneath that, PRUSSIC / HCN. He held the cylinder out toward the other agent. "Know what this is?"

The other agent took the cylinder and stared down at the word. "Yes. Do you?"

"Yep. I've seen it before. Cyanide. Hydrogen cyanide."

*****

9:30 pm in Atlanta: "Hello, Dr. Garrison. Sol Zelinski here."

"Oh, Dr. Zelinski, I've been so…"

"It's OVER!" he interrupted in a loud, excited voice. "They got her! The NCTC agent called me 20 minutes ago. The same man I spoke to this afternoon. He said the FBI cornered her at JFK as she was about to go through Customs. Said she ran into a restroom and locked herself in a stall. They cleared the room and tried to talk her into coming out. Said they were in there two or three minutes calling her, talking to her. But she didn't respond. After another minute or so, they heard heavy breathing and gasping. Then they heard her fall against the door. They tried to get into the stall, but the door was locked. An airport policemen jumped over the metal partition and opened the door, and they pulled her out. But by then, she was dead. Said it looked like she had a seizure."

"Oh, horrible."

"Yes," Zelinski continued. "He said they found what they described as a small cylinder on the floor. It was wrapped and sealed with tan plastic tape."

"*That's the mycotoxin!*" said Cassandra

"Probably. But next to that, they found an open medicine vial with white tablets in it. The words printed on it indicated it was cyanide."

"Oh, NO," she said. "She killed herself."

"Yes. They said she probably she took at least three tablets at once. Certainly an instantly lethal amount. Said they've seen that before. Where the culprit can't escape, doesn't want to be captured… and is prepared to die."

"So this must have been some kind of plot," said Cassandra, "not just a random thing."

"It seems that way, but we don't know anything more at this point," said Zelinski. "They said the letters printed on the side of the open medicine vial looked like Russian, but they will have that analyzed."

"What about the sealed cylinder?" she said. "They still have it? We've got to get it back."

"Not possible right now. The agent said they're keeping it and the laptop she had with her for evidence, but he thinks they'll probably return it all after the investigation. I'm sure it's secure."

*****

At just before 6:30 Wednesday morning Cassandra woke from a fitful sleep. Last night's conversation with Solomon Zelinski had invaded her dreams and now, fully occupied her consciousness. The information that the mycotoxin vial had been recovered but could not be returned fretted her. She had to know whether it had been opened and if any of the solution had been taken out. True, that was out of her control, but she was also frenzied to know why was it stolen? Moving on with other things while she waited would be a test of her patience, but she had no choice.

By 7:30, she was back at Brakefield and on her way Blaine's room. She felt an inexplicable urge to see him. Perhaps it was because yesterday's events had so unsettled her. Seeing him, touching him, talking to him now could be reassuring. She needn't say anything about the stolen vial and all that. Just touch him, hold his hand. A short conversation, that's all.

When she entered the room, he was sitting up in bed, propped by the mattress and the bed frame. Now fully alert and waiting for breakfast, he looked at her. She stopped just past the door and looked back at him. She smiled gently, silently. He held out his hand. She came to him, took the hand and squeezed it, still silent.

"Cassie," he said as his eyes welled, "I'm... I'm...*so sorry.*" Please," tears streamed down both cheeks, "...forgive me. Please... help me."

She squeezed his hand again.

REFERENCES

Anderson, P.D.: Bioterrorism: toxins as weapons. J. Pharm. Practice. 25(2), 121-129, 2012.

Arch. Environmental Contamination & Toxicology: 18: 388-395, 1989.

Barnes *et al*: Annals of Asthma, Allergy & Immunology, 89(1) 29-33, 2002.29.

Black *et al*: Microbiological Methods, 66(2) 354-361, 2006.

Brasel *et al*: Applied & Environmental Microbiology, 71(1): 114-122, 2005 and 71(11), 7376-7388, 2005.

Gadsden, S. An Oral History of Edisto Island: Sam Gadsden Tells the Story. Transcription by Nicholas W. Lindsay. Published by Pinchpenny Press, Goshen College, Goshen, Indiana, 1974. Pp. 74.

Jarvis *et al*: Applied & Environmental Microbiology, 64: 3620-3625, 1998.

Johanning, E. *et al*: International Archives of Occupational & Environmental Health, 68(7): 207-218, 1996.

Johanning, E., Editor, Bioaerosols, Fungi, Bacteria, Mycotoxins & Human Health. Publisher, Fungal Research Group Foundation, Inc. Albany, NY, pp.508. 2005.

Kuhn & Gannoum: Clinical Microbiolog. Rev.,16:144-172, 2003.

Li & Yang: Japanese Journal of Medical Mycology: 46:109-117, 2005.

Nordess *et al*: Current Allergy & Immunology Reports, 3(50): 438-446, 2003.

Portnory *et al*: Annals of Asthma, Allergy & Immunology, 94(3), 313-319, 2005.

Sorensen in Fungal Infections and Immune Response, pp 469-491, Plenum Press, 1993.

Sudakin *et al*: Medscape General Medicine, 2(1), E11, 2000.

Vojdani: Med. Sci. Monitor, 11(9), LE 7-8 (Letter) 2005.

Wannemacher, Robert W.,Jr. & Wiener, Stanley L. in <u>Medical Aspects of Chemical and Biological Warfare, Eds. Sidell, F.R.</u> & Takafuji, E.T: Trichothecene Mycotoxins, Chapter 34:655-676, 1997.

Wolf, A.: Witchcraft or Mycotoxins? The Salem Witch Trials. Clin. Toxicol., 38(4). 457-460, 2000.